†o Speak

With Elders

Mike Mollman

First Edition

Beaver Castle Media

Becoming a Druid

The Protectors of Pretanni Book One

ISBN   *978-1-7370524-3-2*   *Hardback*

          978-1-7370524-4-9   *Paperback*

          978-1-7370524-5-6   *Ebook*

As his younger brother, I needled him whenever I could.

Tom found no redeeming value in fantasy and was quick to let you know it.

Gone too soon, he will be forever missed.

I can't help it, so Tom, I bestow upon you the status of a half-elf, split-class Gloom Stalker ranger/Arcane Trickster rogue. May your further adventures be fantastical.

Table of Contents

Pretanni

ORLEWIN — PARITERO

UPOKLIA DEXSO

Strait OF Pretanni

Strait OF Eriu

Griffins
·Griffin Eyrie

Centaurs △Centaur Camp
Din Gaurie

Brigantia

Bili Kapno ✕

Griffins

✕Meavll Dun

Meneton Dywyll Derv ⊙

Ganna's Home

Aido Kaballo

Lombinion

Ardy Bryn Cadwy ⊙

Brenin Cairn ⊙

Gwanwyns of Sulis ⊙

Ogof Cawr

Vectis

Bodmin's Moor
Grahme's Camp
Dinas Gwenenen
Pen-An-Tol ⊙

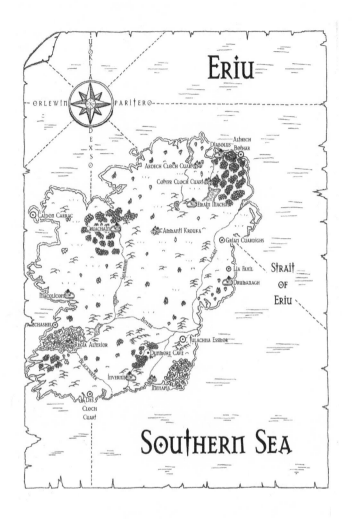

Eriu

Strait of Eriu

Southern Sea

1

Tomb Raider

It has been a month since my master tricked me into dueling him to the death. I faced down the Obsidian Lord of Solent Keep the following day. Each feels like it happened years ago, except for when I sleep. I relive one or both of those horrendous events every night.

I expended all of my animorphing power and I was lucky not to kill myself with too much exertion. It's cruel really, I've had to refrain from using my power, or doing much of anything, in the name of recovery. Everyone urges me to sleep, but that's the last thing I want to do.

At last, the time of sitting alone in my camp or with a group of nagging friends is over. I will meet my fellow Lord Protectors today and we will inter Boswen's ashes in Brenin Cairn, the tomb of the Druid Protectors.

In my master's honor, I take my breakfast of gruel and black bread at the fire before taking the shape of a raven, his favorite animal form, and flying to Black Tor in the far northwest of Dartmoor. Three of Boswen's former students and all fellow members of the Nine, the ruling council of druids, will meet me there.

The moor ponies are in the meadow below the tor. I spy my fellow druids but also my friend, the yearling colt whose affection changed my life. Without him, I never would have attempted to defeat the Obsidian Lord.

I land on an outcrop. The colt and I have a game, where I become a tawny owl and he chases me around the meadow. I'm torn, should I engage in the harmless game, or should I do what is expected of me?

Where's the fun in that?

Hopefully the others don't notice; their nagging would be endless. Launching into the air, I change from a raven to human to tawny owl; all while still airborne. I barely lose a man's height in altitude. It's good to know that my powers are fully renewed.

The colt's nose flips up and he flags his tail while prancing toward me.

I fly right past the colt's nose and the race is on. We circle the meadow twice before I return to more serious duties and disapproving faces awaiting me.

"If you're done with your antics," Caradoc says in his stern voice. "Can you produce Boswen's ashes?"

"Of course," I say as I pull the smooth, glossy urn from within one of my pouches.

The wind picks up and Caradoc's mantle is blown backward into Hedred's face. The short druid punches at the offending cloth.

"I propose we leave before we freeze in place. As most senior, I will lead." Without waiting, Hedred turns into a raven and departs for the north.

Caradoc changes into his preferred avian form, the merlin, and gives chase. Eghan gives me a nod before he too chooses a raven and leaves the tor.

Hedred lands at a cave's mouth in the middle of forested hills. Before I can change back, Caradoc is already complaining.

"Hedred, can you ever go anywhere without stopping at a cave first?"

"I think trouble is likely from Bradan," he says. "But I refuse to fly unnoticed into Brenin Cairn like some common thief. Bradan is a Druid Protector, the same as us, and he deserves our respect."

"Fine," Caradoc says in resigned tones. How far away is Brenin Cairn?"

"It's not far. We will pass Lythyn's burial chamber first." Hedred turns to me, "Lythyn's is where the druids of Brenin Cairn are interred. I think it bad form to not pay our respects to those proud souls as well."

"And are we going to stop and thank every deer we see as well?" Caradoc asks.

A cold, steady rain blows in our faces. Eghan hurries inside the cave and wrings out his mantle. "With as loud as you are, I scarcely think we will encounter any."

We trudge to Lythyn cavern and step inside to get a break from the weather. Caradoc manages to remain quiet for three breaths before his sighing begins. He takes one disgusted look at the rest of us and animorphs back into a merlin, heading northwest.

"The wind makes flying tricky," Eghan says.

"You can walk if you want. I'll wait for you at Brenin Cairn." I choose my favorite bird this time, the tawny owl, and follow Caradoc's lead. It doesn't take long before the other two join us in raven form for the short flight. The rain pelts down on our heads as we retake our human forms.

Caradoc is busy tapping his foot as he waits for us to arrive. "If we're done with the silliness now, let's deposit Boswen's remains where they belong."

"But Bradan . . ." Hedred starts.

"We'll tell him after we're finished. I don't relish standing in the rain listening to that fool bloviate."

Hedred sighs and shakes his head.

"Come along, Grahme," Caradoc commands. "I'd prefer to get this over with before uncontrollable shivers take hold of me.

The long barrow has but a single round chamber. There are no side alcoves like other long barrows I've seen. The smooth walls curve upward to form a round, symmetrical roof. There are three long, horizontal alcoves that encircle the central chamber. Urns of every shape and size are placed randomly throughout.

"How do we decide where to place Boswen's remains?" I ask.

"Listen to what the space is telling you," Hedred says.

Caradoc snorts and rolls his eyes.

"Settle yourself," Hedred reassures me. "This place will lead you to a proper home for Boswen."

Taking a deep breath, I feel the hallowed place pulling me towards the back of the cairn. On the second level, left of center, I place Boswen's remains. It feels right in my gut. "Are there any words to be spoken?" I ask.

"Boswen spoke more than enough for two lives," Caradoc says. "Leave him be and let's get the chat with Bradan over with."

"Is there anything that you left unsaid to Boswen?" Hedred asks.

"No."

"Then loathe as I am to agree with Caradoc, let's let Boswen settle into his new home."

Bradan's mead hall is much bigger than the one from my family's home at Dinas Gwenenen. The warm smoky air from the hall hits my cold, wet skin. There is hope that I'll feel my toes again before spring. Goosebumps form along my arms.

"It's still light outside," Eghan says, as he tries to fan the thick smoke from his face. A half-consumed boar is spitted over the central fire. Dogs fight for scraps whenever the careless let meat fall. Along the walls are the trophy heads of deer and boars. It seems an obscene way to display nature's creatures.

"It doesn't matter what time of day it is, this should never take place amongst druids," Hedred replies, also frowning.

"Bradan! Where is the fat, drunken fool in charge of this place?" Caradoc calls over the inebriated crowd.

"Who dares!" Bradan cries from the corner. He splashes his flagon into a cauldron before tromping over to us, kicking dogs and overturned benches out of his way. His men stumble toward the walls, as if anticipating trouble.

"What are you doing?" Caradoc demands. "You're drunk and it's barely past midday."

"Caradoc," he belches. "You're supposed to be confined to your camp. When Loris finds out about this . . ." He smiles like a clod.

"Bradan," Caradoc says with exaggerated patience, "Loris's absurd attempt at getting a ghost orchid is over. May I present to you your new peer, Lord Grahme Fairweather."

"Grahme?" Bradan shouts. "Grab him!" His men continue size up our group and decide it best to feign deafness.

"Bradan!" Eghan calls. "The search for Grahme is over."

"It's over? Who won and what did Loris give them for capturing the traitor?" He calls out loudly, "to the winner!" He raises his flagon to toast to the nonexistent person's success.

I take two steps forward and knock Bradan on his ass with an uppercut to his jaw. His flagon clatters across the floor. Shaking his head, he focuses his attention on me from his new position on the floor.

"I am Grahme Fairweather, the Protector of Men-an-Tol and the Land's End peninsula. The next time you dare call me a traitor, I will claim insult and insist upon a duel." Standing over him, it's all I can do not to kick him.

Bradan roars something incoherent while his men help him up.

"Seize him!"

"Which one?" His retainer asks.

"All of them. And get me another drink."

Hedred steps in front of Braden's men. "I am Lord Hedred, and these three Lord Protectors are Caradoc, Eghan and Grahme." Despite his diminutive size, he conveys a commanding authority. "Take Bradan somewhere and sober him up."

The man looks to his Lord's bloodshot eyes, then back at Hedred. One of Bradan's men tries to pass his lord another flagon of ale. Hedred slaps it out of his hand and it makes a satisfying thud as it hits the floor.

Caradoc quietly hands me a staff. "There will be trouble," he says under his breath.

"How dare you, you little dwarf!" Bradan roars. With a quick thrust of his left arm, he sends Hedred to the ground.

In one fluid motion, I land a blow to the ribs of Bradan's man before reversing my momentum and stopping my staff as it makes contact with Bradan's neck.

"You are a terrible host."

He tries to grab my staff, but I'm too quick. I slide my hands down the shaft and level it against the other side of Bradan's neck.

"You level your weapon against me? In my hall?" His face is as red as a rooster's comb.

"I do, and I'll rap your head if you dare attack a guest again."

"Leave now or I will challenge you to a duel to the death." He looks around the hall to his cheering men.

"Challenge and I will accept," I say once the noise dies down.

"Grahme . . ." Hedred says as he slowly rises to his feet. "I'm unharmed."

"I challenge this brigand!" a deep, booming voice rings out from behind Bradan.

"Bradan, get a hold of your men," Caradoc hisses.

"I will not stand by and let these intruders lessen the men in this hall." The barrel-chested man, a full head taller than anyone else, pushes his way through the crowd to stand next to his lord. He points his staff at me in anticipation of the duel.

Bradan smirks. "What will it be? Will you grovel for forgiveness or will one of you be demolished for your impertinence?"

7

Hedred stands in front of me. "We have deposited Boswen's ashes with the revered ones. Our entry into your hall is merely a courtesy extended to you."

"Boswen? Where are his ashes? I'll dump them into the swine pens."

"You do that and I'll be the one challenging you," I reply.

"Grahme, you're not helping the—"

"I challenge you, Grahme, the Imposter, to a duel to the death, right now." Bradan's giant calls out over the crowd.

I size up the bruiser. He's much stronger than I, but also much slower. "Then I accept."

"No, Grahme . . ." Hedred starts to say something before throwing his arms up, aware that it's too late.

Caradoc gives me a wink and a smile.

"Clear some space," Bradan orders. Benches and tables are quickly pushed back from us. Only the two of us and the central fire remain.

The giant roars as he rushes toward me, staff leveled at my head.

I sidestep his advance and strike him on his ass. I twirl my staff as I smile to the crowd. Enraged, he snarls and advances with his staff flying wildly back and forth. I step in and knock the top of his staff with mine, halting the momentum. I twirl the bottom of my staff behind his and raise it suddenly. He loses his grip and his weapon drops to the floor. He freezes and looks me in the eyes. I watch him impassively.

He lunges for the ground, grabs his staff and rolls back up. He smiles after this uncontested triumph, and the crowd cheers him on.

Do they not realize I could have killed him had I wished to do so?

He holds his staff in the middle third now, taking a defensive posture. It's the first thing he's done right. I fake an overhead swing and he falls for it. Raising his staff above his head, his entire body is open. I land a blow to his gut. He doubles over, giving me my choice of targets. I spin and rather than take an open head shot, I sweep his legs out from under him, watching him tumble backwards. I kick his staff from his weakened grip and thump the butt of my staff into his chest. It's hard enough that he'll feel it for the next few days.

"Yield, for I do not wish to kill you."

Anger flashes in his eyes. I lift my staff. At last, the lethality of the situation dawns on him.

"I yield," he says in a small voice, so that no one but me can hear it.

"Louder."

"I yield!" he says, with anger in his eyes.

I frown and turn my back on him. "Is there anybody else?"

Blinding pain gives way to my right knee buckling beneath me. I roll with the fall and instinctively raise my staff above me. Bradan's next strike hits the center of my staff and it's all that I can do to maintain my grip with both hands. I swing my leg as if I'm trying to catch his. He jumps back from my feint, allowing me to get to my feet.

All of my anger comes boiling up to the surface. Boswen's death, killing the Obsidian Lord in cold blood, losing friends, now is the time to avenge all of it. "Bradan, as master here, you and your men have violated my guest rights." My hands begin to tremble. "I challenge you to a death duel."

"Die!" Bradan shouts before charging me.

His staff, hovering over his left shoulder slashes diagonally toward me. I sidestep the attack and swing for his ribs. I hear a satisfying crack and he drops his staff to gingerly cradle his chest. I swing for the back of his knees and he drops to the floor.

"Grahme!" Eghan shouts. I turn to see a large object in my peripheral vision, then all goes black.

My temple is too tender to touch and the cacophony of sounds makes the pain worse. Before me are two cave bears standing and roaring at a pack of five wolves. Birds of all types fly in circles through the smoke. Hedred steps in front of me, blocking the surreal scene. He lobs a stone between the bears.

"*Sigel*!" he shouts.

A light brighter than the full glory of Belenos burns inside the hall for but an instant, blinding everyone. Cries of challenge give way to confusion.

"Get up Grahme," Hedred says. "Eghan, Caradoc, change back to your human forms, it will help with the blindness."

Thanks to the great bears in front of me, only part of my vision is ruined. Hedred and I take the others by the hand and stumble out of the hall.

Smoke ripples out of the door and into the afternoon air. My right eye is tender and the swelling is beginning to affect my sight. I look back in the hall and the spitted boar has been knocked over. Embers begin to fly even as Bradan and his men continue to stumble about. A cry of alarm fills the air as smoke billows out of the hall. The flames have spread throughout the hall.

Just like at Dinas Gwenenen, I'm going to get blamed for burning down this hall too.

"I'll retrieve Boswen's ashes," Eghan says. "I don't think we can leave them here after this."

"Where did you learn to fight like that?" Caradoc asks. "I've never thought you particularly good with the staff."

"Fighting alongside Eosiah will do that," I say. Caradoc looks away.

Nice, remind Caradoc that his second died in battle so that I could escape.

A figure runs toward us. "Grahme!" he calls.

I ready my staff, but with a weakened knee and a swollen right eye, I don't like my chances.

It's a boy and he skids to a stop out of staff range.

"Lord Grahme," he begins. "I wish to leave the service of Bradan and join you, sir." He straightens up and waits nervously for my reply.

I glare at him with my good left eye. He nearly melts under my scrutiny. "I've seen you before."

"Yes, Lord Grahme, I was the one who stopped you and the trader, Blachstenius, in the wagon. Though I still don't remember you being there. Later you returned my staff at Boswen's camp, sorry, I mean, your camp the day after Samhain."

I release the tension within me. "What is your name?"

"I am Brehmne."

A large portion of the roof collapses, allowing the chilling rain to fall on the blaze. Men run out, covering their mouths with their robes.

"We can't just stand here," Caradoc demands.

"Can you animorph?" I ask Brehmne.

"Yes, Lord Grahme."

"Do you know how to get to my camp in Dartmoor?"

"Yes, Lord."

"Then go there and await my return."

"I'll go right now!" He says, smiling. He changes into a screech owl and flies off to the south.

"Great," Caradoc says, "Another owl person."

I chuckle at the absurdity of this day. "How can I train anyone to be a druid?"

"You will never make as many mistakes as you do with your first pupil," Hedred says. "But the two of you will be good for each other."

"May I remind everyone," Caradoc begins, "that we are no closer to completing our duty now than we were at dawn?"

"I will bury the ashes next to Uffa Horselord," I say.

"An excellent idea," Eghan says.

"Yes, it will do," Hedred agrees.

2

The Symbols of Our Time

Hedred leads us to the entrance of Ogof Cawr. The others gawk at the steep-sided gorge. Though extraordinary, it only holds anguished memories for me. I glance up at the ledge, where Ysella died. I lower my gaze and head into the cave to await the others.

It has only been a month since Ysella sacrificed herself for Katel and me.

"Grahme?" Eghan calls. "Grahme . . . Grahme," my name echoes through the tunnels.

"I will wait for you in here," I cup my hands and reply.

Hedred frowns and slaps himself on the forehead as he approaches. "Of course, this was thoughtless of me," Hedred says. He joins me and puts a comforting hand on my back. I have to smile at the gesture. His head barely tops my elbow. I'm sure he would have put his arm around my shoulder, if he could reach it. The imp in me wants to rest my arm on his head, but now that I'm a Druid Protector, I can't do such things.

"You're here so soon?" Hedred says as Caradoc and Eghan join us. "I would have thought the view would be worth a bit more of your time." He turns to me. "Did Katel show you the great chasm when you were here?"

"I don't believe so. How is she doing, Lord Hedred?"

Hedred frowns. "First, we are the same rank, so you can drop the 'Lord' title. As for Katel, it has been a struggle. Still, she is young, I will give her time to heal." He lights a reed torch and holds it as high as he can.

"Would she like to visit my camp, to visit Sieffre?" Eghan asks.

"She's not ready for that yet, but I think that day needs to come."

Hedred possesses the only source of light, but his shiny bald head acts as a second beacon. Caradoc mimes rubbing the top of Hedred's head, while Eghan and I hold back our laughter. Hedred stops suddenly and tilts the reed torch backwards. "Careful Caradoc, too close and your beard will be singed."

It seems I'm the only one who hasn't witnessed these antics before. The light flickers on the uneven walls of the tunnels, giving the illusion of motion all around us. Our trip isn't long, but my head constantly swivels, looking for potential threats in the gloom. I'm exhausted by the time we stop.

"Now, get those rush lights from behind you and give yourselves some light. Hedred says. He waves us to come forward. Behind him the feeble light of three torches fails to cast away the blackness. "Watch your feet," he says as he grabs my robe.

Looking down, I'm only one step away from a drop of unknown depth.

"Do watch your step," he says belatedly. "Come right up to the edge." He turns to face the chasm. "Now drop your rush lights and count how long it takes until you can no longer see them."

We do as we are bid. I have to grab Caradoc's robe to keep him from leaning too far over. "I can't see any of the torches," Caradoc says.

"Wait," Hedred says. After another couple breaths we hear a faint splash far, far below. "That's how deep the chasm is," Hedred says with a smile. Once again, he's the only one with a torch. "The bridge is unstable, so we will have to walk around this chamber."

"You mean the bottomless hole," Eghan says.

"Hedred," I say with only the slightest of hesitation, "I believe Katel brought me this way. She wanted me to extinguish my torch, because she is afraid of heights. We took the bridge, she told me it was only—"

"—Sixty-one steps," he finishes for me. "Lately Katel has taken to exploring tunnels that we have labeled as unsafe. I thought it because of her mood after the events on your quest. But now it seems that she was not heeding my orders long before." He purses his lips. "This is quite vexing."

"I feel for you Hedred, but rather than standing here waiting for your light to go out, can you take us to whatever it is that you insist on showing us?" Caradoc asks.

"Follow me."

"Caradoc," Eghan whispers. "Must you be so thoughtless? It is not often that he gets visitors. Let him show off some of his realm. It's not as if we all don't listen to you drone on and on when we come to visit you." Eghan hurries forward, whether to stay within the sphere of light or to avoid Caradoc's retort is anyone's guess.

"Easy for him to say," Caradoc mutters to me. "I bet he's never been forced to find his way back in the dark."

15

I urgently point at the steadily withdrawing light source before rushing toward it. It's no wonder the light bearer left Caradoc behind in the past.

"This is why I asked you to come to Ogof Cawr." Hedred invites us to enter his library. He winks up at me as I file in last of all.

"This is where Sieffre and Katel keep their latest findings on the runestones," he says with obvious pride. "These are the runes they have deciphered." He shows us the runes and a crude drawing of what each does.

"I have seen most of these in action before," I say. "Sieffre was able to use a new one at the tor. The whole slope turned to ice." I scan the runes. "It was this one." I point to a simple straight line.

Eghan grabs my arm and fixes me with an intense stare. "What did he call it?"

"I do not know. I was fighting beside Arthmael. Katel was standing at the top with Sieffre. She can tell you."

Eghan's shoulders slump.

"It is called *iss*, I believe," Hedred says. "Though I cannot be sure."

Eghan relaxes. "Then we are still making progress."

"How would you use these?" Caradoc asks, intrigued.

"You throw the stone into the air and yell out its name. The spell is released and the stone disintegrates," I say. "I used the fire rune to burn down a bridge."

"You simply write these symbols on a stone, throw it and shout out its name?" Caradoc asks, amazed.

"Not exactly," Eghan says. "You must perform a ritual to Lugh, the giant's chief god."

"Lugh? How did you come upon this knowledge?" Caradoc asks.

Eghan turns away. Caradoc looks at me, but I have no idea.

"It was fairly traded with Bodmin," Hedred says after a pause.

"Bodmin?" Caradoc's voice echoes within the chamber. "He's supposed to be killed on sight, not bargained with."

"The mainland peoples have this knowledge. What other druids do you know of who have ever left this isle?"

"Loris came from the mainland," I say.

"Is there anyone we would be more likely to keep this information from?" Hedred shakes his head. "Come now, Caradoc, the decision was mine and I don't regret it. With the loss of Sieffre and with Katel being occupied, Eghan and I are the only ones left who possess this knowledge."

"And that is why we need to teach both of you how to perform the ritual." Eghan says. "It is fortunate that Sieffre was adamant in teaching me, otherwise this hard-won knowledge would be lost again."

Eghan starts a small fire. He selects a few river rocks from a pile and traces his fingers over the surface. "You need a good piece of flint to scratch the appropriate symbol onto the rock." He selects the rock he wants and scratches two offset lines. He connects the bottom of the first to the top of the second line. "This symbol is called *sigel*."

"What does it do?" Caradoc asks.

"You'll see," Eghan says. The rest of us trade knowing smiles. We just saw this one in action in Bradan's mead hall.

Eghan traces the scratches with oak bark dye before he rubs the entire stone with flaxseed oil. He inspects it by the fire to ensure every surface is shiny and coated in oil. "If you are sloppy with your symbol or the application of the dye, the ritual will not work. If you leave even a tiny bit of the rock uncoated in oil, it will not work. We know precious little about Lugh, but he must be an exacting god." He tosses the rock into the flames. "Lugh, by your divine and awesome power, accept this offering of oil and imbue this stone with the essence of *sigel*."

"Only one stone can be done at a time," Hedred adds. "You must leave the stone in the fire until all of the oil has been burned away. While we wait for Eghan's stone to be suffused with the god's power, I have another stone already prepared."

Hedred goes to a low alcove and removes a rock. "Are you ready?"

Caradoc waves his hand to speed up the demonstration.

Hedred throws the stone into the air and cries "*sigel*" before it makes contact with the walls or floor.

A searing light engulfs the entire room. I'm able to shield my eyes from the radiance, but still I'm forced to blink multiple times as the intense brightness shines through my hand. For a moment I see my bones surrounded by translucent red flesh.

Caradoc makes some guttural noises and belatedly shields his eyes. He staggers like a drunk for a few steps before he regains his wits. Blinking repeatedly, it's clear he is unable to see any of us. "That's what you used in Bradan's mead hall?"

"It is," Hedred says.

"This is a dangerous path that you've set us upon," Caradoc says while trying to blink away the afterglow.

"It was once known by our order," Hedred says.

"And now, without knowing the limits, you are determined to wield this magic," Caradoc admonishes.

"The only one who possesses that knowledge is Bodmin. You don't seem fond of turning to him for aid either."

"Do we need this knowledge?"

"At some point, someone from the mainland will invade our land and attempt to take what is ours. If we cannot wield their magic, then we may lose everything," Eghan says.

"You don't need to remind me why we all agreed to this plan," Caradoc says. "I just wish there was some other way."

Growing up, Kenal and I, and sometimes even Ferroth, would plan trips to Bodmin's moor to capture the great beast. We had all heard the stories; he was a former druid who left his land. He came back over a hundred years later with his wife, the witch, Ganna. He spent months if not years lurking on the moor in the form of a great black cat. Kenal and Ferroth would always tease me by swearing they would toss me to Bodmin so they could escape. For his part, Boswen never divulged what he knew about our aged neighbor.

"Have you spoken with Bodmin recently?" I ask, excited.

"I have," Hedred says. "Boswen and I went to see him before he took you on as his apprentice."

"Boswen too?" I ask. "I asked at least a hundred times about Bodmin and he never gave me an answer."

"It was for your own good," Caradoc says. "Knowing you, you would have staked out the moor night and day searching for him."

Out of the corner of my eye, I see another person has entered the room. "Katel?" I stammer. "How are you?"

She's carelessly leaning against the stone entry. She looks as if she has bathed in dirt. Fine powder clings to her face and her poor hair heads off in in a dozen different directions. She looks at me. "Did you come back to kill me? I won't be as easy as my sister." Her voice lacks any inflection. She turns to Hedred. "Everyone who went with Grahme is dead. I think he planned the whole thing with the Dark One."

"Katel," Hedred says gently, "don't speak such ugly lies. Arthmael is not dead, he made his way back to Cynbel's camp. He is studying to become a healer with Lord Eghan. Perhaps we should go see him, so you can put this foolishness behind you."

Katel's eyes flick from Hedred to me and back again. "You can't trust him. He lies to his friends, even if it means your sister will be killed. He's a thief and a liar. He's a killer too. If he sees Arthmael again, he'll try to kill him."

Hedred gives me an apologetic look. "Katel, you mustn't say such things. Grahme is my guest and you are behaving poorly." His voice becomes disapproving, as if he's scolding a little girl.

"I don't trust him," she says in a whisper.

Hedred approaches her and starts to wipe the dust from her face. "Dear little one, I need you to listen. You can't be going off alone in the quaking caverns and you can't spread such lies about my guests."

"But…"

"No. There are no exceptions," he says firmly. "If you can't comply, I will be forced to turn you out."

"To the land above?" Her voice rises. "With the ugly yellow sun and the crunching leaves? What would I do with my rock collection?" She licks her lips over and over. "It's a pretty collection, a nice collection. They are so nice and flat."

"Katel, I need you to join the others in the Great Room. I will be along shortly after I bid my guests a good night."

"They're not coming with you?" She asks, alarmed. She points at me. "He's not coming to the Great Room."

"No Katel, they will all sleep here, away from the rest of us."

"Be careful! He knows the fire rune. He knows to say *cweorth* when the stone is in the air."

"That's why I need you to come back here and work with me. You are the master of the runes now."

She casts a vacant smile. "The master of the runes." She turns and walks out of the library without a care.

Hedred turns to us. "I apologize, but I must ask you three to stay in the library for the night."

"It doesn't matter to me. Everywhere is cold and dank down here," Caradoc says.

"Hedred, go see to Katel," Eghan says. "I will be going over these runes for the next few hours anyway."

"How will we know when it's daylight with all this earth between us and the divine glow of Belenos?" Caradoc asks.

"We have our ways," Hedred says. "And Grahme, I am leaving you in charge. Don't let Eghan stay up all night and don't let Caradoc go wandering off by himself again. It took us ages to find the fool while he huddled alone in the dark."

3

The Heart of the Matter

Caradoc chooses the merlin, of course. There is nothing natural about four merlins flying in formation in the rain in late autumn. Boswen would have had much to say on the subject. I'll have to remind Caradoc of this fact when we land.

Uffa's White Horse is a series of trenches in a steep hillside that exposes the bright white chalk soil underneath. Together, they display a glorious white horse in mid gallop. Even on this overcast day, the chalk is visible from leagues away. Boswen would always tell me that the hill figure exists because of one man's uncontrolled vanity. In his next breath, he would praise Uffa as the greatest of mentors.

"Ducks would have been a much better choice," Hedred says as soon as he's human again.

"Don't start with picking the proper form argument. I've heard it for the last thirty years from Boswen," Caradoc responds.

Eghan looks at me, "slow learner."

"Before we start another verbal joust," Hedred says. "Can we do what we came here to do? I for one don't like standing in the cold rain."

Caradoc takes a deep breath. "As you wish, but we still must obey the proper customs."

"Customs?" Hedred asks. "I was here when Uffa first started this outlandish outline of a horse, and I was here when he finished it. There were never any customs, just a fool's desire that the people took seriously. This poor drawing of a horse is the result of that folly."

"Hedred," Eghan says. "I've never seen this side of you. You are normally the voice of reason and decorum."

"I am always the voice of reason," he snaps. "I left my warm, dry caves for this." He holds out his hands as he looks to the sky. "Let's get on with it."

"A fine thing, first you want to pay your respects as a duck. Then you want to hurry on through the ritual," Caradoc says.

"A duck is the fastest straight-line flyer on this isle and it is made for wet weather. Ducks also fly in formation, so no one would have paid attention to us when we flew here."

"Noble men," Eghan interjects, "Let's begin."

Caradoc tugs at his soaked white cloak. "We start at the head and bow to the memory of Uffa Horselord." We follow him and do as we're instructed. Caradoc holds his bow for quite a while. Water runs down his nose and onto the ground, yet he still holds his bow. I act as if I'm going to kick him in the ass and Eghan has to cover his laugh with a cough. Even Hedred gives me a quick smile.

"Now we must circle the great beast before we stand within it." Caradoc starts down the steep hill and we have to step carefully on the dormant tall grass. Hedred is grunting and wheezing, but Caradoc pays him no attention. We don't reach the feet of the horse until we're halfway down the steep hill. I grab Hedred's arm to save him from tumbling down as we continue walking below the figure toward the horse's tail.

"This is where Caradoc belongs," Eghan says in a low voice.

"Here?" I ask.

"Yes. Specifically, the horse's ass; we must make sure some of his ashes are placed here when his time comes."

Caradoc leads us up the hill and onto level ground. "What do you think?" He asks me. "It's too bad your first time here wasn't on a sunny day. The white chalk of the horse gleams so bright under the rays of Belenos."

Hedred gives Caradoc a murderous look. Caradoc responds with a grin. "Come Grahme, we have completed our circuit around the horse. Now you must pick out the location of the heart and dig down an elbow's length in the soil."

"Just me?"

"It was your idea," Caradoc says.

"And some of us are too old to play in the mud," Hedred adds.

They're testing me.

They want to see if I can properly locate where the heart would be on this figure. It's ridiculous; anyone who has studied with Boswen would be able to do this with their eyes shut. I nod to them with great solemnity. I enter the drawing at the withers. Walking straight down the hill, I don't stop until I'm nearly even with the front legs. I turn to the other three and they stare back impassively. I dig with my hands until I hit a ceramic vase. I wipe away the chalky soil and raise the vase so everyone can see the ornate enameling.

"Excellent job," Caradoc says. "I buried Uffa exactly where the heart would be. Please set his ashes back and place Boswen's next to his."

I make quick work of the burial and I return to my friends atop the hill.

"It is done," Hedred says. Wasting no time, he turns into a duck and heads for home.

"I think that was a touch rude," Eghan says.

Caradoc gives him a lopsided smile. "If someone doesn't push him on occasion, he'll never leave that underground tomb of his."

"You made up the ritual, didn't you?" I ask.

"I just wish he would have slid all the way down the hill. It's good for him to look the fool on occasion."

"How do you manage to have friends?" I ask.

"And look," he says with his hand upturned. "The rain stops the moment Hedred leaves." Caradoc beams at us. "Come, there is shelter on the other side of the hill fort."

To our surprise, the hut is well supplied with wood. Caradoc starts a fire in no time. Besides the fire pit, the hut boasts only a few standing tables and one small bed. There are no looms for cloth nor quern stones for flour.

"Clearly this isn't made for someone to live here," I say. "What's its purpose?"

Caradoc rubs his hands over the fire. "The fourteen light days of Ogronios are reserved for the local tribes to bring their extra horses here and barter with one another. It tends to rain quite a bit, so this hut and the tables you see are where the buyers and sellers meet. As the only true descendant of Uffa Horselord, and a member of the Nine, I preside over the meetings every year. That," he points to the bed, "is where I sleep once the haggling is complete."

"Does Hedred know about this house?" Eghan asks.

"No, and I brought us in low so that he wouldn't see it."

25

This whole trip I've been waiting for the right time. Now Hedred has left before I could broach the subject. My hands feel clammy. I have to ask before they others leave too.

"I want to know if either of you is familiar with my nephew Figol," I say in one long breath. *There, I've asked.*

"I know of him," Caradoc says. "Boswen and I spoke of him while we waited for you to complete your quest."

"I know nothing of him," Eghan says.

"He wishes to become a druid."

Caradoc exhales slowly. "That's going to be difficult." He turns to Eghan, "Figol's mother is a Sorim."

Eghan whistles. "And does Figol have the ability to control minds?"

"He does, but he is earnest in his desire to become a druid."

"I see." Eghan says noncommittally as he and Caradoc exchange a look.

Despite the damp chill being replaced with a warm, dry heat, I've never felt more uncomfortable.

"We will have to take this up with the Nine, and I can guarantee that Meraud and Cynbel will be dead set against it," Eghan says. "Loris, Bradan and Drustan will all vote together, but would it be to spite Meraud and Cynbel, or you?" He looks over, but Caradoc refuses to return his gaze. "After today's activities, you will obviously have to remain silent. Hedred and I would have to be the ones pushing the deliberations."

"I am the preeminent bard of the isle," Caradoc says, daring us to disagree.

"And your mouth is what first turned Bradan against us today," Eghan says. He turns to me. "I have never met your nephew, and I couldn't in good conscience allow him to join without taking his measure first."

"We will meet in just over a month for the winter solstice. I will bring him to you at the Gwanwyns of Sulis before going to the meeting."

"An excellent idea," Eghan inclines his head.

"And if all goes well, you'll join with us and allow him into the order?"

"It will all depend on your nephew."

"I should be the one to present our case," Caradoc says.

"To Meraud?" Eghan counters.

"Bah!" Caradoc says. "I need quiet to think this through." He walks out of the hut and paces back and forth.

"What happened between Meraud and Caradoc?" I ask in a low voice.

"I never get to tell the good stories." Eghan peeks out the door before smiling at me. "Caradoc and Meraud were a dynamic couple twenty years ago. Both were crazy talented and crazy in love with one another. No one knew of the growing tension between them. Each was making a name for themselves and it was only a matter of time before they became members of the Nine. Caradoc rarely mentions anything about their breakup other than to allude to her jealousy leading to the split. He became a member of the council and they were never able to look at each other again. For her part, Meraud has never said a word of any kind about it. She's as tight-lipped as they come."

"Is there any chance of her being on our side?"

"If Caradoc tries to win her over? Not a chance, she can see straight through him and it drives him crazy."

"I don't see a way," Caradoc announces to us. "Not until we can get another sympathetic member on the council."

"Do we normally have to ask to take on an apprentice?"

"Whoa Grahme," Eghan says. "Even if Figol is allowed to become an apprentice, he would not study under you. We never train our own family. In fact, the less contact the two of you have during the training period, the better it will be for all involved."

"But who understands him better than me?"

"Grahme, no matter what, you will not be your nephew's mentor."

4

Can't Go Home Again

Blachstenius had sent a messenger informing me that Figol is staying with Kenal and his family. My nephew was instrumental in my collecting the ghost orchid from Solent Keep. He told me that his desire to become a druid wasn't just a childish want. I aim to reward Figol with a shot to become a member of my order.

The wind is tame in the lowlands of Land's End, compared to the blustery wind up on the moor. Retaking my human form, I walk the rest of the way to the old family farm. How long ago it seems, that I didn't have a care except completing my chores before supper.

The clopping of hooves grows louder on the beaten earth path. The number of people I've met since becoming the Lord Protector is still very small. Not many venture up on the moor, especially as winter approaches. I claim the middle of the road. It will be good to see how the common people fare.

I do a double take. It can't be, yet my brother Ferroth is driving the cart. *Why is he not home at Mai Dun?* I wave at him and I can tell the very instant when he recognizes me. His eyes grow narrow and he exhorts the ponies on ever faster. It would be nice if Ferroth did not become instantly hostile, but it is too much to hope for. I urge the ponies to slow to a stop in front of me.

"It's no use giving them the lash," I yell. "I've commanded them to stop."

"I have business." Ferroth fixes me with his disapproving gaze. I know it all too well.

"All the way here at Dinas Gwenenen?" I ask mildly.

"What is it to you?"

I shouldn't push. It will only add to the animosity between us, but I can't help it. "I am the Lord Protector of Land's End now, brother. I have many interests." I let that sink in for a bit. "Where are you going?"

"Ask Kenal if you wish to know." He flicks his wrists and shouts at the ponies to move. I release my hold on them and stand to the side of the road. How will Ferroth react when I take his stepson to join the druids?

This family reunion just became awkward.

The old homestead is a welcome sight, though I'm nervous about my reception. Seeing Ferroth has unnerved me a bit. How will Kenal and Eseld react? I take on the tawny owl form and land on a tree branch. Figol and Kenwyn are busy ordering the dogs to herd the sheep. Or at least Kenwyn is trying his best to keep Figol out of the way. There are seventeen cows in the adjoining field now, a truly impressive number. Excess animals are butchered prior to the winter season, so they must have enough land to support the burgeoning herd.

Though I'm here primarily to see Figol, it is my brother and his wife I must speak to first. No sense putting it off any longer. I float down a hundred paces from the house and take my human form.

"Uncle!"

Figol must have been keeping his mental powers reaching out for my presence. I smile at my nephews as they run to me. Kenwyn approaches somewhat hesitantly, but Figol has no reservations. He barely slows enough to hug me without sending us both tumbling.

"It's good that I didn't eat yet today," I say, staring down at him. "You would have made me disgorge my meal." Figol looks up at me, smiling. His eyes grow distant even as the smile remains on his face.

"Figol, are you running loose in my mind?"

"Sorry Uncle, I just had to know if I can become a druid or not."

Kenwyn stands several paces away, kicking dirt. I remove Figol's hands and approach Kenwyn with a sincere smile. "You must be Kenwyn," I hold out my hand in friendship. "As you no doubt know, I am your Uncle Grahme. When I left here, you were barely walking."

Kenwyn stands up straight, just as his mother must have taught him. "It is an honor to meet you Lord Protector and Uncle."

I look at Figol. "Did you not share a single tale with him?"

"I told him," Figol says defensively, "Meeting the wolves, the fight with the limping man, outsmarting the Dark Mage, Blachstenius, everything!"

"Then why is it that Kenwyn is so afraid of me? Kenwyn, you should know that Figol is a terrible liar and I am the most mild-mannered of men."

"Then you didn't call forth all the rats and destroy Drustaus's hall?" he asks.

"Well, that wasn't intentional."

"You really did that?" Figol nearly explodes. "I thought Uncle Kenal was making most of that up."

"Father doesn't lie," Kenwyn says.

31

"Kenal is a good man," I affirm. "And I should pay my respects to the man and woman of the homestead."

"We'll take you," Figol says.

"I hardly need help making it the last few paces to my old home." I return Kenal's wave as he makes his way to us. "Now you two should get back to making the herding dogs work harder than need be. At least, that's what it looks like you were doing."

Kenwyn heeds my advice and heads for the pasture.

"You spied on us, didn't you?" Figol asks.

I wink at him as I make my way to my brother. Figol shakes his fist at me before running to catch up with his cousin.

"You are well?" Kenal asks.

"I am. The farm is more impressive every time I return."

He looks out at his son and nephew and his pasture land. "Tettates has been very kind in his blessings to my family."

"No doubt, but I dare say that most of this is your own work rather than any god."

Kenal's face takes on a guarded look. He never could conceal his feelings. "Are you staying long?"

"We'll see. I saw Ferroth driving the wagon to the north."

Kenal sighs. "So you each know that the other is here."

"I had hoped to stay a couple of days." I can see the stress on my brother's face. "Why's Ferroth here?"

"Not just Ferroth, but Figol, Berga and the twins as well."

"The whole family? Did they come on a visit then?"

"Aye, they arrived with Blachstenius just under a month ago. Once they were settled, Blachstenius left. He came back just seven days later and took Conwenna away."

"She's left Ferroth?" I have precious little love for my brother, but I can't believe she would be the type to leave him.

"Not like that," Kenal says. "They had a couple heated conversations before she agreed to go with Blachstenius."

"Where to?"

"They wouldn't say. It was the strangest thing I ever saw; Eseld was pressing them for details, then Ferroth told her to settle down, it was fine what they were doing."

I grin at my brother. He never will get used to the idea that some people have extra abilities. "It was Conwenna's doing, no doubt," I say.

"I don't know how she managed it, but Ferroth has not complained about the situation since that day. Do you know this Blachstenius? He seems nice enough, but he was always vague about where he came from and what he does."

"He's a vagabond trader. He calls no place home so far as I know. He lives on the road as he traverses the isle. But tell me, how has Ferroth taken to working on the family farm?"

"You know how he is. He says precious little and spends all his time working so he can avoid everyone. Now that he's seen you, my guess is that he will be in no hurry to come back."

"One day at least without him trying to beat me senseless."

"It was always tough for me to tell the difference when you were normal or senseless," Kenal deadpans. "I'm surprised you have not asked of Dalna," he says, changing the subject.

Dalna was my first crush. She was several years older and I had no chance of being with her, but that didn't matter to my teenage heart. Most of our interactions played out in my head, but when we did meet, she always had a smile for me. "How is she?"

"Not sure. She and Malry moved back from Arleth two months ago."

"Why would anyone go to such a strange town in the first place?"

"Still afraid of the Si, are you? Do you really think they exist?"

"It's best not to take chances."

The Si are supposedly a race similar to the elves that still live in the Arden. Stories tell of a slender race that regularly run off with daughters, when they don't kill indiscriminately or sing beautiful songs to old trees. They're in virtually every story used to scare and confuse small children.

"Eseld adores Berga and the twins." Kenal says, changing topics again. "May the gods bless us with a daughter, or I fear she will be sorely disappointed."

"You and Eseld are expecting another child?" I clap him on the back. "Why'd you keep this from me?"

He shrugs. "Your prescription did the trick. Eseld has not had her womanly time for two months now. Let me take you to see her."

I scan the woods for a good place to camp as we head for the hut. "I think I should avoid Drustaus's hall this time around."

"I have been asked to tell that tale a dozen times at least," Kenal says. His smile dies and he gives a furtive glance at me. "Kenwyn will want to go with you and Figol."

We reach the apple trees that serve as Mum and Dad's grave markers. Just like father taught us, he's left a handful of apples on the trees for the gods if they should desire them.

"Kenal, I've only come for Figol."

The tension leaves my brother's shoulders. "That's a relief, though he will take the news hard."

"In a couple years, he will discover women and all thoughts of being alone in the woods will be forgotten. Besides, with your holdings, he should have plenty of choices when the time comes."

The smoke slowly wafts up through the rooftop. For once the wind is calm. I see the hearth fire gently heating the cauldron above it. Eseld rushes out the door. "Finally, Kenal," she says as she dashes out of the house. "Oh, and Grahme too," she says with an open mouth. "Well won't this be a day we talk about for years to come?"

Eseld has never been my biggest supporter; I guess helping them with their fertility problem changed all that.

Another figure emerges behind Eseld. The smile on my face freezes as none other than Meraud, the Lord Protector of Keynvor Daras stands behind my sister-in-law.

"Lord Protector," I say, nodding my head.

"Grahme!" Eseld whispers urgently. "She's a lady druid! And she's the head of your order!"

"It's fine Eseld," Meraud says. "The order has some quaint old customs when it comes to greetings. And I am the Lord of only one holy site, not the head druid."

Kenal stops walking and looks at Meraud and me with obvious confusion.

"You're not going to take Kenwyn, are you?" My brother asks.

"Husband," Eseld says as she tries to smooth everything over, "Meraud has come looking for Conwenna."

"Conwenna?" I ask.

"Grahme, show your manners to this great woman," Eseld scolds. She wipes her hands down her skirt in an attempt to remove wrinkles or stains or some such silliness.

"Eseld," Meraud says, "I don't want to overstep my role as a guest in your wonderful home, but perhaps you should invite the men in?"

"Yes, of course, Lady master druid head," Eseld says, flustered.

Meraud shoots me a 'don't you dare laugh' look as they leave the threshold and allow us to enter.

"I'll leave you three to talk," Eseld says. "I need to look in after Berga and the twins. And we'll be needing more cracked grain from the quern stone, that's for sure."

Meraud tries to tell her to stay, but Eseld is too quick in her escape.

"Lord Meraud," I say, "Besides making my family the talk of the area for a very long while, is there another reason for your visit?"

"Grahme!" Kenal chides in a low voice.

Meraud grins wide. "It is fine, master Kenal," she assures him. "We tend to speak directly with one another and avoid all the frivolous formality."

"I've told you this before," I say.

"You've told us many things," Kenal shoots back. "I'm just never sure which ones are true."

"If I may," Meraud says with a smile, "I've come to talk with your sister-in-law, Conwenna."

She pauses, giving each of us a chance to speak. When neither of us do, she retakes the lead. "Thanks to the removal of the Obsidian Lord," she nods her head at me, "Solent Keep is without a leader. For a while now we at Keynvor Daras have heard whispers of a great Sorim power hiding in our midst. We can't help but hold our breath and see who the new leader will be. Once I learned of your nephew's powers, I thought it necessary to seek out your brother and his wife and see if the rumors were true."

"But Conwenna isn't here," Kenal says.

"Yes, that's what Eseld told me. She and her family arrived unexpectantly, then she and Blachstenius left in a rush for parts unknown. Does that about cover it?"

"Yes, great lady," Kenal says. "I vow to the gods that this be true."

She looks at Kenal with a sober expression. "Kenal, I believe you. You are as honest as a man can be. I only wish your brother followed your lead in this."

Kenal bows low. It's embarrassing, really.

She turns her head so that only I can see her wink. "Would Eseld be willing to find a good woman for Grahme? Good women make good men." She's smiling from ear to ear now.

I stare at her open-mouthed. *Does she know how long it took me to get Eseld to stop looking for matches for me?*

She stands up and straightens her robe, mimicking Eseld. "Please give my regrets to Eseld. There is some urgency to me finding Conwenna and Blachstenius. If time allows, I should very much like to come back and chat with you and your lovely family."

"Lord Meraud," I say, before she can literally fly away. "Our nephew, Figol, would like to join our order. Could you meet with him, since you are here?"

She looks at me, pained. "This mission really is of some urgency. We will speak again at the council meeting. If you remember, I thought dear Figol would make a fine druid, though that was before I knew of his Sorim heritage. For now, I must take my leave."

She nods to Kenal, then turns into a gannet and flies off to the east.

"That's amazing," Kenal says. "Did you see her change into a gannet?"

I stare at him disbelieving. "Really?" I've animorphed many times for his amusement in the past. I turn into a gannet and take off over his lands, just to remind him that fact.

At dinner I'm still rubbing my left shoulder. While in gannet form, my nephew, Kenwyn slung a stone and hit me in the wing.

"I do wish Lady Meraud could have stayed," Eseld says for the third time.

"It's Lord Meraud," Figol prompts. "Did you know that Kenwyn almost downed a gannet today? Why would a sea bird fly so far inland?"

"How's your shoulder?" Kenal asks me, grinning.

"That was you Uncle Grahme?" Figol asks.

I keep my head down and eat my porridge and bread.

"That is what typically happens when you start showing off," Kenal says.

I have an unbelievable urge to smack his pious face. "You didn't seem to think that when Meraud animorphed into one," I say.

"Lord Meraud," Eseld says, correcting me as if she ever got it right when Meraud was here. "And I bet she looked the part of a noble bird when she took flight."

"Does anyone here understand that Meraud and I are both Lord Protectors? She does not rank any higher than me." Scanning the table, everyone has their head down, eating their meal. Not a single one of them will acknowledge my point.

"I can't wait to see Sena tomorrow at the market and tell her a Lord Protector made a call on us," Eseld says. "She'll be sick for a month."

"Again, I am also a Lord Protector."

"Eat your porridge, Grahme. You don't want it to get cold," my brother says.

I give my brother a death glare, not that he notices.

"Meraud said she would take it as a personal favor if you were able to set Grahme up with a good woman," Kenal says.

"Kenal!" I resist the urge to flip the table over on him, but it's a close call.

My brother smirks at me. "What did she say? 'Good women make good men'?"

"Did she say that?" Eseld asks. "Lady Meraud is so wise." She looks me up and down, as if she's seeing me for the first time. "I will see to it at once."

"Lord Meraud," Figol says.

"Figol and I must leave tomorrow at first light," I say.

"We must?" Figol asks.

At least my death glare works on him.

"Berga will be very disappointed. She dotes on her brother so," Eseld says.

"You're not going to wait for Ferroth to return?" Kenal asks.

"Definitely not, although I think I'd prefer his punches to the steady stream of women dear Eseld would have lined up for me if I stay."

"Grahme, you need to find someone before you get too old and too set in your ways and no woman will have you."

"Kenwyn, Figol, you should listen to Eseld," Kenal says. "You don't want to end up being sad and alone, do you?"

Would it be rude to leave right now? Do I care?

Figol is openly smiling at me. I guess I have to get used to him jumping into my head unannounced . . . again.

5

Unexpected Guest

I don't feel entirely good about myself, but asking Figol to lightly alter Kenwyn's mind so he doesn't run off with us has spared my brother's family plenty of anguish.

"Uncle, would you hurry up?" Figol begs.

"I don't recall you being an early riser."

"This is the first day of my new life," he says and he pulls on my arm.

"That could be said every new day."

"Uncle, I know you're excited too, so stop being disagreeable."

"Get out of my head."

"It doesn't hurt anything," Figol says with a confidence only shared by fools and boys when they are on the threshold of being an adult.

"Maybe I'll look for Blachstenius and ask his opinion." Figol had been subtly changing my thoughts the first time we traveled together. Once Blachstenius came along, he put a stop to Figol's tampering.

"Are we really going to Bodmin's Moor, Uncle? I thought that place was haunted by a great black cat."

I sweep Figol's legs out from under him with my staff. "Stay out of my head."

"Sorry, I couldn't help it." He says as he jumps to his feet. "Is Bodmin real? I mean I know he *was* real, but does he still live on the moor in the form of a great black cat? Father always said it was a silly story to frighten children, but Lowen said he believed the stories. Dad said that was because Lowen had the mind of a child. What do you think Uncle? Are the stories true? Uncle? Uncle! You're not listening to me!"

"In cases like this, Boswen used to instruct me to say things worth hearing."

"Did you like Boswen? Was he always so mean? Sorry Uncle, but your mind is giving off a powerful signal, but I can't tell if it is love, hate, frustration or admiration."

"That's because it's a little bit of all of those, along with a dozen more emotions. Nothing about Boswen was ever straightforward."

"What was he like? I only met him the one time when Blachstenius and I stopped at his camp. I wanted to stay, but Blachstenius wouldn't hear of it. He claimed it gets too cold."

"How did you find Boswen to be?"

"I don't know; he was kind and gentle, but there was always something going on in his mind that I wasn't privy to. Despite his age and demeanor, I would never have wanted to cross the man. It's as if terrible power lay just behind his care and concern."

"I have never heard Boswen described better by anyone." I laugh.

"Don't make fun of me."

"I'm not. Boswen was a complicated man and I doubt anyone truly knew him in his entirety."

"So why aren't we going to Dartmoor?"

"We'll go there next, but I have never been to Bodmin's Moor and I would like to see it."

"Are we going to search for Bodmin? What's he like? I was told he kills those who come to the moor uninvited. But if he doesn't leave the moor, how could he invite people? What do you think, Uncle?"

"I think it is time for your first lesson on animorphing."

"Really?"

"Yes. See those jackdaws in the clearing?"

"Yes."

"Good. In order to take the shape of an animal, you have to have an understanding of why it is what it is. Watch those birds and learn their mannerisms. That is the first step toward changing into one of them."

"You're just doing this to keep me quiet," he accuses me.

"No, that's merely an extra benefit," I whisper. "See how the sentinel bird is cocking his head to the side? He's heard us and is ready to call the alarm if we do anything threatening."

We watch as the sentinel flicks his head away from us. "They use their eyes as well as their ears. Stay still and you can learn a great deal in this one sitting."

After a good while of blessed silence, I feel the urge to sneeze. At once the birds scatter, flying to the trees and calling to one another.

"Uncle!"

"That's my fault, but you still have an opportunity to learn. What are they doing now?"

One takes off for greener pastures and the rest follow. Figol turns to me, annoyed. "How am I supposed to learn if you scare them away?"

"What did you observe?"

"They keep several sentinels at any given time. The birds performing the duty were constantly rotating and there was food sharing going on."

"And what happened after I sneezed?"

"The feeding stopped and all of them located us."

"Then what?"

"One of them got spooked and headed for the trees. The rest followed."

"So, you learned that jackdaws are social birds, more so than ravens or crows. You learned that they forage in large groups and share the guard duty. Finally, you learned that they value safety highly, since they left the pasture before we could have gotten anywhere close to them. That's not bad for your first attempt. Now, let's make our way up to the moor."

"Why didn't we take one of the ponies? Do we really have to walk all the way up there?"

No doubt the exertion would be good for him, but I'd probably kill him first with all of his questions. "How good is your mental ability?"

"I haven't been using it on you, honest."

"Then why do you rush to assure me of your innocence when I've not cast any blame?" I raise my hand to forestall his denial. "I only mean, if I animorph, can you follow my thoughts and repeat the process?"

"Yes! I mean, I haven't tried that before but I'm sure I can."

"Then pay attention." I take it excruciatingly slow, but at last I'm a jackdaw. Figol takes a breath, closes his eyes and animorphs into a passably good form. His wings are a bit blocky, but still serviceable.

We soar upward, through the buffeting winds to the top of the moor. There is only a thin layer of snow and it fails to mask the delicate pink flowers of the heather. A group of warblers sit in the wild apple tree, picking over the frozen fruit.

I land in front of a giant's cave and retake my human form. Figol tilts his head sideways and hops from rock to rock. I never thought about how he would change back. I do my best not to let the fear show.

Please Figol, change back.

He lets out a distress call and starts pacing about. I want to scream, but what good would that do? I transform back into a jackdaw and Figol calms down at once. Slowly, I retake my human form.

"You can do this Figol, just concentrate," I say, trying not to betray my sense of dread.

Figol's avian form goes fuzzy and grows larger. I release the breath I didn't realize I was holding. Figol stands before me.

What would Boswen say if he knew I did this?

One crisis averted; only now do I notice the bitter east wind cutting through my meager robe. As much as I want to congratulate Figol, I want to get out of this wind more. I should have brought my heavy mantle.

"I would have brought mine, too," Figol says.

"You did a good job, now let's get out of the cold." The bitter wind keeps me from saying more. I point to a small hole in the snow.

"What is it, a badger hole?"

"Watch and learn." I channel my thoughts and become a cave bear. With several powerful heaves, I've moved more than enough snow and dirt for a human to fit through. I revel for just a moment in the warmth of my new form before changing back to myself. "Behold, a giant's home."

Without waiting, Figol jumps down into the subterranean dwelling. "It's dark down here."

"I'm sure it is. Now come back out from there and help me collect wood for a fire." I shake my head in disbelief. He'll be lucky not to kill himself during his training. Literally, we have a saying to look before you leap.

"I didn't see any trees up here."

"Of course not, it's a moor after all. But there is plenty of gorse."

"Gorse is nothing but thorns."

"And it burns very well. So get started."

"What are you going to do?" He asks accusingly.

"Stop with your instruction if you can't follow simple orders."

To my amazement, he retakes the jackdaw form and flies to the nearest stand of gorse.

I remove more dirt from the mouth of the cave and we're able to wiggle in without impaling ourselves on the gorse. We spread it around the cave entrance, to protect us from intruders. With practiced ease, I start a fire with my spark rocks.

The interior walls are solid stone, easily as thick as my extended thumb to little finger. The ceiling forms a pointed arch with huge rocks leaning against one another. I hand Figol his share of the dried roots, nuts and dried mushrooms for dinner. We watch as the smoke collects high up in the arch and travels out the cave opening. The wind changes directions and blows from the west.

"It's going to be a cold one tonight. Wind from the endless sea will be laden with moisture. It'll suck the heat right out of your body."

"Is Dartmoor warmer?"

"No, Dartmoor is even colder." I can't help but laugh. "And your introduction to being a druid will continue. It's always the apprentice's job to keep the fire going throughout the night."

"But I don't know how to start a fire."

"Don't worry, when the flames die down, the cold will bite quite hard."

"Why don't you tend the fire?"

"Because I'm a Lord Protector and you are not." I've spent more than my fair share of cold nights nursing a fire."

"Uncle, Uncle," Figol shakes me until I'm awake.

"What?" I demand.

"There is someone outside our cave."

"In this weather? Who would be fool enough to travel the moor on a night like this?"

"I think you'd better see this for yourself." There is a trace of fear in Figol's voice. I grab a branch and light the end in the fire. If nothing else, I can whack Figol a good one for waking me.

"Who goes there?" I call.

There is a guttural growl in response. Figol looks like he wants to run for it. There are two black pupils within pools of pale green

47

eyes staring down at us. A slight movement from above allows me to glimpse a shiny black coat reflecting Aine's light. He sits patiently, not making any movements.

With effort, I exhale slowly and will my pounding heart to slow. "Bodmin, I presume. Would you care to share our fire on this cold night?" With great effort, I'm able to keep my voice steady.

I step back and Bodmin slinks down the side of the entrance, keeping his distance from the fire. Once past the blaze, he animorphs into human form.

"Thank you," he says.

I try to speak, but only a low throaty sound escapes my lips.

"Who are you and why are you on my moor?"

"I am, Lord, er . . . Grahme, Lord Protector of Men-an-Tol."

"Then Boswen is dead?" he asks.

"He is." I dare not give details.

"I liked him. It is a shame."

"Forgive me, but how should I address you?"

"Bodmin is fine. It is the only title I can claim without dispute from one quarter or another."

"With respect Bodmin, there are many druids who do not believe you even exist," I tell him.

"Good. It is not often that I find visitors on my moor and I wish it happened even less. Why are you here?"

"I mean no disrespect, but I felt it necessary for me to scout out all of the territory that I am now responsible for protecting."

"And you wanted to know if the legend was true? Do I kill every poor wanderer who gets lost on my moor? Fear not, I did not come here in anger, only curiosity. How long has it been since you replaced my grandson as Protector of Land's End?"

"Boswen was your grandson?"

"Obviously."

"It has been less than two moon cycles." The hairs on my arms stand up.

"I knew all of this before I asked," he tells me. "Boswen sought me out last year to inquire about a cure for the wasting disease. I cannot say I fully approved of his plans, but it was not for me to intervene."

"Boswen regularly spoke with you?"

All those times when I asked about Bodmin, not once did he let on.

"Did you seek out this cave to study its runes?"

"Ah, no Lord—" I cough. "No, I chose it because I know how fast the chill comes in from the coast and I didn't want to spend the night shivering."

His eyes dance in amusement. "A fellow moor man, I see. Are you one of the enlightened few who choose to learn the giant's script?"

"I would like to learn, but I've had little opportunity."

He grabs my branch and leads us to the back of the cave. "Tell me which of these symbols you already know."

"I have seen them a couple times, but I can remember seeing these three symbols in Hedred's library."

"Few enough are willing to seek me out. He is a good man, with an agile mind."

"I have not seen this symbol before." I point at a two parallel lines with a slanted connecting line between.

"That is the rune *hahgel* and it will cause a small hailstorm to form from the air."

"Figol, copy this down as well, we can't lose this knowledge." I grab a pointy stick and dip it into the ashes. I draw the symbol onto the surface of wall next to me.

Bodmin grabs my stick and redraws the glyph. "You must be precise for it to work.

"Now I have aided you, I ask only that you tell me where you are going in return."

"We are going to the Gwanwyns of Sulis to meet Eghan, Caradoc and Hedred. From there we go to Nemeton Dywyll Derw."

"Ah, yes, it is almost the solstice." His eyes grow unfocused. "It has been a long time since I have seen either the hot springs or the sacred grove. It is good to know that they are well tended."

"Would you like to accompany us to the springs of Sulis?" I ask.

He smiles sadly at me. "I am afraid that I will never visit any druidic holy sites again."

"Know that you are welcome to visit Men-an-Tol any time you wish."

He cocks his head to the side as he looks at me. "You are the first interesting person I have met in over a hundred years. You are a contradiction of rashness and thoughtfulness. Know that I may, in the future, seek you out to continue our conversation."

"Thank you Bodmin." I don't know what else to say.

"It is good to speak with humans again." He hands me my branch. "But after so many years as a solitary beast, the urge to be on my own is strong. Before I go, I will leave you with a warning. Beware the silvertongue that walks among the Nine. He will destroy all that you strive for, if you let him."

"What is a silver tongue?"

Too late. He changes into the great cat again and races into the cold night air.

"Farewell Bodmin," I say, much too late for him to hear.

Figol and I look at each other, daring ourselves to believe what just happened.

6

New Responsibilities

For at least the fifth time I check my symbol against Bodmin's and the one on the cave's ceiling. There is precious little difference. Unable to sleep, I try to busy myself until dawn. I've managed to cover one wall in *hahgel* symbols.

"Belenos has risen," Figol calls. "Are we going to your camp now?"

"Yes, but only for the day. I have a new student that I need to settle into camp."

"You have an apprentice?"

"Why do you sound so shocked? I am a Lord Protector."

"But with your quick temper . . ."

"Keep it up and see how quick it can be."

"How long a walk is it to Dartmoor?"

"Too long to put up with you and your questions." Hop into my mind and let me show you how to change into a tawny owl, the most dignified bird on the isles."

At the first sight of trees, I land and retake my human form. There are shouts and the clattering of staves coming from my camp. Had I not just met Bodmin, this would have given me pause. But now, why not have the sound of fighting coming from my camp? Nothing can phase me.

Figol hoots at me from an oak tree.

"That call is used to define territory." I shake my head at his lack of basic knowledge. His apprenticeship will be long and painful. "You will need to learn what each call means."

Figol hoots at me again before landing in front of me. It takes several attempts, but my nephew is able to regain his form. "Why is it so difficult to change back to myself?" he complains.

I signal him to remain quiet. At last, he notices the banging of staffs, a barking dog and laughter coming from my camp. He gestures for me to explain.

If only I could.

In the small clearing next to the fire pit and two huts are Brehmne and Arthmael, performing some sort of cross between sparring and dancing. A dog leaps between the two, trying to grab the ends of the staves. Arthmael sees me and stops whatever it was that they were doing. The dog greedily grabs the meat off one end of his staff.

"Welcome master, we've been waiting for you," Arthmael says.

"Were you? It looked as if you were creating a new dance."

Arthmael flips his staff, giving the dog a chance at the meat tied to the other end. "The idea was Brehmne's. He was tired of being on the receiving end of my attacks, and my constant companion," he reaches down to pet the brindle-coated dog, "kept getting underfoot. We tie meat to the ends, so that blows don't hurt as much and our four-legged friend forces us to keep our staffs moving."

"As strange as that sounds, I'm more confused by your presence here."

Arthmael coughs nervously into his hand. "Well, about that," he begins but then falters.

"Arthmael is joining us. You have two students now," Brehmne says.

I change my gaze back to Arthmael.

"Lord Eghan is a good teacher and it didn't take long for him to realize that I do have a good understanding of the healing herbs of the plains. I just lacked the conviction to follow through and there was no one in camp to reassure me. The only way for me to expand my knowledge is to go to a different environment and learn the properties of those plants. I didn't fancy Drustan's camp, so I chose you and Dartmoor instead."

And what other meddling are Caradoc, Eghan and Hedred going to do?

"Do I get a say in this?"

Arthmael turns serious. "Yes, of course, Lord Grahme. I wish to join your ranks, if, if it is agreeable to you, that is."

"Then I will share with both of you my first rule. Anyone who calls me Lord Grahme will be forced to supply firewood to the camp for an entire month. I have barely completed my second set of ten years. Save the lord title for the elder members of the Nine, like Caradoc and Hedred."

"Very well Grahme," Arthmael says with a smile. "Do we have a third apprentice as well?" He looks past me to Figol.

"No, this is my nephew, Figol, and with luck, he will be a druid apprentice soon."

The brindle dog has devoured the meat on Arthmael's staff and wanders over to me. I bend at the knees and bring myself to its level. He sniffs my offered hand and allows me to pet his chest.

"Are you here to stay?" Arthmael asks.

"No, we must go on to the Gwanwyns of Sulis."

"You will be stopping at Isca?"

"I hadn't planned on it." I give the dog three stiff pats on the ribs and he moves on to Brehmne for affection.

"Grahme, even Brehmne here knows that when a new Lord Protector is named, he should personally visit with the kings in the overlapping territory. It's been over a month. Not showing up would be a grave insult to Cunobel."

How does everyone know this but me?

"I see. Have you been instructing Brehmne in staff fighting?"

"I have. He's already better than you."

"Brehmne, have you been showing Arthmael the local medicinal herbs?"

"I have." He looks down at his feet. At least someone is willing to give me respect.

"Very well, continue with what you are doing." Brehmne is staring at me with sycophantic awe. Since he stopped scratching the dog, it returns to me. "Know that I am well pleased with both of you and Arthmael's shadow." I scratch the dog behind the ears, just to underscore the point.

"Shadow," Arthmael says. "I like it. That'll be his name."

"You hadn't named him?" I ask. "Haven't you been together since the battle at Ynys Wydryn?"

Arthmael shrugs. "Nothing seemed to fit." He claps his hands once and Shadow leaves me to return to his master.

"We'll be leaving soon," I say. "But first, I have a test for Brehmne and Figol. You two are to walk to the old moss-covered stump, then return to camp. Arthmael and I are going to change into exact copies of Shadow here. You will have to decide who is who.

"I've never seen training quite like this before," Arthmael says.

"I'm testing you too," I say. "You've been with him for months, so you have no excuses for not becoming a believable copy."

The two students leave us alone.

"What are you doing Grahme?"

I laugh. "I have no idea, but Brehmne looks overwhelmed standing in front of me, so I wanted to give him a task he could easily accomplish. Hopefully building his confidence will mean that he'll think about what I tell him instead of just accepting it."

"Wait until he gets to know you, then he won't think so highly of you." Arthmael smiles.

"Why did I save your life over and over on the tor?"

"What?" Arthmael barks. He can't help but smile. "If you saved me, it's only because you kept getting in my way. It was all I could do not to brain you."

"They're coming back." We change into copies of the dog. Confused, our furry friend begins sniffing at each of us.

Brehmne and Figol watch us for a while.

"I know which one is Shadow," Brehmne says. He points to the actual dog. "See how he is continuing to sniff the other two? He's confused and trying to piece it together. Arthmael and the Lord Protector know who is who, so they don't bother to sniff."

Figol nods. It's good that he's learning from someone other than me.

"That one is Uncle Grahme." Figol points at me.

"How do you know?" Brehmne asks.

"I can just tell."

I bark once at Arthmael and we retake our human shapes. "Very good, both of you," I say.

"Are you going to teach us more today, Lord Grahme?" Brehmne asks, breathless.

"Sadly, I cannot." I look at Arthmael. "Figol and I are going to pay a visit to Cunobel. While I'm gone, continue instructing each other and we'll figure out the next steps when I return."

7

Dodging Arrows,
Aiming for Trouble

The Haldon is one of the two remaining great forests on Pretanni. The Arden's only rival, it stretches upbroken from the River Teign until it reaches the River Exe and Cunobel's city of Isca. It is teeming with life, even in winter, if one knows where to look. Only the pine trees remain green and the leaves from the remaining trees litter the ground. Yet close inspection will yield hares hiding beneath the cover and owls above staring out from their tree trunk homes. The forest floor is filled with voles and their endless underground runs.

"You must not make Cunobel an enemy, Uncle. You need to work with the King of the Dumnones, not against him."

"You're quite the statesman then?" I ask.

"Mother has taught me this for years. Also," he taps his head, "I have an advantage."

I spot a roe deer hopping away. Our conversation alerted him to our presence. Which bothers me more, entering into another city or admitting that Figol is right? Neither is likely to happen again for a long while.

"Very well, I will meet with Cunobel of the Ferns, but I refuse to stay in that pigsty for more than a night."

"I want to see you call him Cunobel of the Ferns," Figol says. "Especially after he's had a few drinks."

We've reached the River Exe, the last obstacle before we reach Cunobel's hall.

"I could call that fisherman and have him ferry us across the river."

"Leave the man be," I say. "Besides, it's time for you to practice animorphing. I will change quickly this time, so pay attention."

It's unfair really; I can change into a tawny owl without effort. But it's good for him to be pushed.

Figol looks at me, exasperated, and I stare back, dispassionate. Once he realizes that he's on his own, he closes his eyes and makes the transformation. I inspect his new form. He nips at my tail feathers in annoyance. He has the attitude of the bird down.

We take to the air and fly over the fisherman to the fields outside of Isca. Grudgingly, I decide that all the niceties must be performed, so I lead us to the city gate.

A guard excitedly calls to his men. They grab their bows and take aim at us. I dive at once, but Figol is slow to react. The arrow whispers as it passes over me. There's a meaty thunk and Figol lets out a screech.

I land and retake my human form at once. Figol's wing sticks up awkwardly. He's desperately trying to fly with only one wing and his calls are getting more plaintive. I can see that his goal is woods, but he's veering ever closer to the river. The frigid water would be fatal. My legs are pumping as I race after him. I don't have time to see if the archers are readying arrows for me.

The arrow in Figol's wing clips a tree and he lets out another plaintive cry. He drops to the ground and continues with alarm calls at the forest's edge. He won't drown at least. I lift my nephew and he digs his talons into my arm. I pry his talons out from my fresh gashes with a little more force than I intended. I grit my teeth to keep from crying out in pain.

"Easy now," I say from between clenched teeth. Figol's owl is nipping at my hands. The owl's mind has gained ascendency. Reasoning with him is not going to work. I cover his eyes and his assault on my arm ceases. I set him on the ground, keeping his eyes covered. Once I uncover his eyes and step back, the owl becomes fuzzy and begins to grow. Figol grasps his left shoulder and I grab my bleeding right arm. We're quite the pair.

The guard drops his bow before sliding down the earthen rampart. He refuses to make eye contact as he hurries to us. "Forgive me, revered ones," he pleads. He kneels five paces in front of us before looking up at us. "We did not know of your arrival. Please forgive me, noble ones." His anguish is palpable.

"Rise," I say, the anger in my voice on full display. "Is it customary for guards to fear owls?" I demand.

"No revered one. It was on the orders of Master Arthyen that we took aim. He told us there was a sick tawny owl in the area and if we see it, to shoot it so that its disease would not be carried to the other animals in the forest."

"Arthyen ordered this?" I say softly, even as my anger boils within me. He knew that I would have to make an appearance and he surely remembers my favorite animal form.

"Yes, noble one. Please don't take issue with me. I was only doing as I was instructed."

"That you were," I confirm. "I do not blame you or your fellow guards for this. Still, can you take my nephew to a healer?" I lift my gaze away from the guard and toward the city. "I wish to have words with Arthyen."

"Be careful, sir," he warns. "Arthyen is a Master druid and there are none more powerful than him in these parts."

"We'll see about that."

Figol nods and I know that if nothing else, he'll compel the guards to give him what he needs. Now is the time to educate Arthyen about his place once and for all.

No one dares stop me as I stride into the city. The market is wrapping up for the day and the merchants give me plenty of space. I spy around the city until I see two guards lounging in front of the mead hall door. I change my direction and make straight for them.

"Halt," one of the guards cries. He and his fellow rise, crossing their spears in front of the door. "You must give your name before you can enter."

I don't slow my gait. One step away from them, I change into a cave bear and burst through the spears and the door as well. The men in the hall stop their chatter and gape at me. I retake my human form.

"Where's Arthyen?" I yell.

The men clear the space before me and cluster at the walls. I give each man a hard look as I scan the room for the coward. I see only terrified faces as I approach the central fire.

"Guards!" A man shouts from the level above me. I shield the firelight from my eyes and I can see Arthyen cowering behind King Cunobel.

"Arthyen, if you mean to do me harm, face me like a man." My finger stabs at the air between us.

"This is my hall," the outraged king roars. "And I give the orders here. Now present yourself druid, before you taste my anger."

"I am Grahme Fairweather, Lord Protector of Men-an-Tol and the leader of Land's End. I am here to discipline the craven druid who has lied to your men in order to do me harm." I point at the ground directly in front of me. "Present yourself to me at once, coward."

Beneath the king, the man-at-arms has assembled several men. I have no wish to harm anyone but Arthyen. Before the king can give the order, I change into a golden eagle and launch myself into the air. My wings are every bit as wide as my human arms. Screeching a battle cry, I soar up to the dais and reach out with my talons for Arthyen's face. The old fool is still an accomplished animorph, however. He too takes the shape of a golden eagle and ducks under my attack.

Before I can come around, he's taken flight. He circles the hall, but the door is blocked by a mass of humanity. With escape denied, he has only one remaining option. We lock eyes and speed toward one another. Our talons lock together as our momentum cancels out. We spiral toward the floor. He tries to release from me but I refuse. I nip at his unprotected neck as we crash to the floor. I gain my feet and leap on top of him. I secure his wings with my talons and take numerous bites out of his plumage.

His form grows hazy and he changes back to human, then on to a cave bear. We played this game once before. I won then too. He spins to dislodge me from his back. Before he can charge, I too, am in bear form. I launch myself into his chest and knock him into the fire. He twists from beneath me and runs for the door, knocking people out of his way as he goes.

I reach the door in time to see him change into a raven and disappear into the last bit of sunlight. I roll my shoulders and take note of any injuries I might have taken.

I feel good. I wish I could have gotten in a few more attacks on Arthyen, but he's been shown to be the coward he is. I smile and nod at the people, still bunched along the walls as I return to speak to the king.

The hostility radiating from King Cunobel is palpable. White knuckled, he grips the railing of his raised dais.

"I apologize for my entrance and the disagreement between Arthyen and myself." I lower my head slightly and spread out my arms.

"How dare you! I am king here. An attack on one of my servants is an attack on me. I should have you flogged."

Don't overreact.

"You are in error, King Cunobel," I say. There is an audible gasp from the crowd. "Master Arthyen is beholden to me, not you." I look around the hall. "And I do not believe you have enough people here to capture me."

Probably not my best effort at peacemaking.

The king sputters. "The druids serve me and my people!" he says with equal parts surprise and anger. "Guards, bring him to me, in chains if necessary."

I don't wait for the guards. I retake the golden eagle form and fly up to him. He raises his arms defensively as I land on the rail. I change back into myself, smiling inwardly as his people see him recoil in fear. I look down at Cunobel's toothless guards.

"Get out of my hall," he sputters even as he backs away from me.

Only now do I realize the irreparable damage I've wrought. "King Cunobel, as I said, I regret how this evening has unfolded.

Please let us speak to one another as powerful men and reach a common understanding."

"You and your kind are not welcome here."

"You don't mean that." I feel sorry for the man.

"If you ever return, you will taste my vengeance."

"Cunobel," I intentionally leave out his title. "If you force me out of your hall tonight, I will see to it that no druid steps foot in your city again." I turn to the crowd below us. "Who will intercede on your behalf to the gods? Who will bless the flocks at Imbolc and the crops at Beltane?" I turn back to face the king. "Do you wish your people to be subject to the whims of the aggrieved gods?"

"No!" a man cries from below. His anguished cry is repeated by the crowd below. "Please, Lord Protector, don't abandon us."

Cunobel looks down at his people and realizes the danger he's in. "Lord Protector," he shouts over the din, "We have indeed let things spiral out of control." The crowd begins to settle, waiting to see what comes next. "I have acted as a poor host. As you say, let's sit and come to a common understanding." He smiles for the crowd.

I smile too, because I know that I've won. "Fear not, good folks, there were many words said in anger, but your king and I are determined not to let those words define us. Please, enjoy this night. We druids will not turn our backs on the good people of Isca."

The king lifts my hand as if we have just triumphed. He smiles first at me, then the crowd. I go along with the act. He waves to his subjects and beckons me to sit with him, away from the crowd.

His smile falls away. "You have won," he growls. "What do you want?"

I can see that he is fingering a knife at his side, but I don't let on that I've seen it. "Your guards shot arrows at my nephew and me as we approached your gates."

"What?" he stares back at me, surprised.

"It was on the orders of Arthyen, according to your men. My anger got the best of me and that is why I entered your hall the way I did."

"He gave my men orders? Outrageous!"

"Arthyen has been disgraced."

"He will get more than that the next time I see him."

"He is a very proud man," I say. "I should know; I studied under him for a time. To return here is to relive his humiliation. You will never see him again."

"And that brings us back to what recompense you require from me."

"I suggest we both forget this unfortunate encounter and agree to work together for the benefit of our people."

"I can agree to that." His hand slides off his knife's handle.

I don't need Figol to know that though we agreed to forget the incident, he will never forgive it.

8

Into Hot Water

The mist around the hot springs pulses yellow from the bonfire below. How Eghan is able to get a blaze that large in the saturated air is a secret he won't part with. Gwanwyn of Sulis is perpetually one of the most popular druid camps. And why not? In the chill winter air, the druids and apprentices below are warm thanks to the powers of the three sister goddesses. Both mead halls stand empty. As is the custom, on nights when they expect snowfall, they assemble around the Gwanwyn of Sulis, knowing the goddess will keep them warm even on the coldest of nights.

The main spring, named in honor of Sulis, is five men wide and nearly a perfect circle. The smaller springs of Nemetona and Coventina are saved for the Druid Protector and special needs, respectively. But the Spring of Sulis is open to all. We spiral around the hot spring so we're noticed before landing. The mist collects in my feathers, weighing me down.

"It's Grahme!" someone shouts. I do not know this person. I scan the druids, looking for threats, but I see only smiles are in the faces before me.

"You're famous now. This is going to happen everywhere you go," Figol tells me.

I give the crowd an anemic smile.

Easy for him to say.

Fortunately, Eghan spots us before it gets too awkward. "Lord Grahme, it is kind of you to pay me a visit," Eghan says as he walks out to greet us. He's well past his third decade of life, though his face makes him look much younger. Such is the benefit of a carefree life.

"Sing us the Ballad of Grahme Fairweather," a voice from the crowd shouts.

"Lache," Eghan shouts back, "It is hardly appropriate for a guest to sing about himself as soon as he arrives at our camp."

"Does this mean it's fine to ask later?" Lache asks with a huge grin. The crowd laughs at his antics. Eghan waves him off and turns to us.

How strange to have everyone at ease at a holy site. I have been to seven of them now, and none are as jovial as this place.

"The Lord Protector sets the mood," Figol says in a low voice.

Get out of my head.

"Let's go someplace a little quieter," Eghan offers.

"Thank you," I say. As he leads us away from the massed druids, I land an elbow into Figol's ribs. His startled exhalation brings a smile to my face.

Eghan takes us to his hut alongside Nemetona's Gwanwyn. A small group of moss-laden trees, a thick undergrowth of ferns and a perpetual, thick mist give us privacy from the throng of druids.

"Nemetona's is the hottest of the springs," Eghan says. "In fact, I can't bear the heat I'm afraid. I must sneak off early in the morning to Coventina's spring to cleanse myself."

He waves us over to sit on stumps near the spring. The mist is too thick here to start a fire, so we must use whatever meager light makes it here from the main bonfire.

"Thank you, Eghan, for agreeing to meet my nephew."

"You look like you're ready to fight off bandits," Eghan says. "Relax Grahme, you're among friends."

"Sorry, I still can't shake the feeling I'm doing something wrong by standing outside a Lord's private residence."

Eghan smiles. "Boswen knew every trick to keep us in awe of him." He winks at Figol. "I doubt your uncle has told you even half of his stories."

"I was there for some of them, but he's been tight-lipped about what happened after Solent Keep."

Eghan gives Figol a good-natured grin. "You are the nephew with mind bending abilities are you not?" Eghan pulls out his protection amulet from beneath his robe, making sure we both see it.

"I am, Lord Eghan."

"Enough of that, does your uncle make you call him 'Lord Grahme' all the time?"

"Never."

"Then don't go calling me 'Lord Eghan' all night. It makes me feel old, like Hedred or Caradoc."

"Should I take my leave, so that you two can talk in private?"

"Thank you Grahme," Eghan says. "You may wish to check in on Sieffre. He's at Coventina's spring."

I know Eghan is right to suggest it, though I dread seeing my friend. His ultimate fate of being stuck in puffin form can be placed directly at my feet. Even if he can't understand, I need to tell him I'm sorry.

"Your nephew did very well last night," Eghan says at our morning meal. "I am willing to support his bid at becoming a druid apprentice."

"Thank you for telling me. I was too tired to wait up for him last night and he's sleeping like the dead this morning."

"After our meal, we should go see Sieffre," Eghan says.

"Do you have any hope?"

"It's been over a month. If the healing springs were the answer, the change would have occurred by now."

We return to our porridge and silent contemplation.

"Eghan! I have some news." How did I forget to mention this?

"Yes?"

"We learned a new rune."

"You have?" Eghan rises, tries to set his bowl on the table, but misses. He ignores his overturned breakfast. "What is it?"

"*Hahgel*, and it brings forth a hailstorm."

"And you have the symbol too?"

"I do." I grab a stick and draw the symbol in the dirt, but in my haste, I'm sloppy. I kick the dirt and try again.

"Outstanding! But how were you able to determine this symbol?" His voice is filled with wonder.

"Figol and I were visited by Bodmin."

His face turns cautious. "I don't always agree with Caradoc, but you'd do better to avoid that one altogether."

"But you backed Hedred when he went to Bodmin." I furrow my brow, confused by his change in demeanor. "And Boswen spoke to him."

"And both of them were thrice as old as you. They had the experience to know what they were doing. How did you even find him? That's what I'd like to know."

"It was an accidental meeting."

"Oh, you just happened to be on his moor by mistake?"

Enough of speaking to me as if he's my disappointed mentor.

"Bodmin's moor is within the area I am sworn to protect." I challenge him by looking straight into his eyes. "I will not go forsaking vast swaths of my area because of pixie tales told to me in my youth."

Eghan pauses. "Forgive my tone. We are equals and I should treat you as such. But Bodmin is not just a pixie tale. He betrayed our kind over a hundred years ago. Do you not wonder how it is that he still alive? He uses dark magic, that's how."

"And he's Boswen's grandfather."

"What?"

"He told me as much in our meeting. On our way here, Figol and I found shelter in a giant's cave on Bodmin's Moor. He came that night to see who was there. In the course of talking to him, he told us the rune's meaning and his relationship with Boswen. Then he told us to get off his moor by morning."

"And you trust him?"

"I do, and there's more," I say.

He snorts. "It won't be good news."

"Bodmin told me before he left, that I should beware of the silvertongue who stands among us in the council."

"I dare say that it is due to Bodmin's charisma that you believe his warning. What makes you think he is an ally?"

I ignore his attempt to scold me. "You do not know of whom he is speaking?"

Eghan scoffs and waves me away with his hands.

"Good morning," Figol says as he emerges from the mist. He looks at Eghan's annoyed face, then to me. "Uncle, you have a unique talent for putting off everyone you speak with."

And you know just when to make your entrance.

Eghan chuckles, despite his mood. "Your porridge is near Nemetona's spring. The goddess is so kind to heal us and keep our food warm too. After you finish breaking your nightly fast, I would like you to join us as we go to see Sieffre.

Unlike the hot spring of Sulis, this spring lacks the head sized rocks ringing the water. Being on a slight incline, the water runs down the hill until it reaches the River Avon. Birch and alder surround the springs on three sides. Sedges and ferns fight for the space underneath while mosses coat the branches. The mist is not so heavy here, making the space feel more open.

"Why don't you animorph into a puffin and show him how to change back?" Figol asks.

"We've tried any number of times. He seems content to swim in the spring and ignore those of us who visit," Eghan says.

"Then what of the runes? If Sieffre and Katel are not continuing their work, who is?"

"As of now we are waiting for Katel to return to her old self. Your find, no matter how it was obtained, is the only advance we've had in months. This is why it's imperative you not jeopardize our efforts to gain the council's support."

"I will vote for it, of course," I assure him.

"It is not your vote we worry about. You have made enemies of Drustan and Bradan. Loris is none too pleased with you either. There are only nine of us, so we must pull either Meraud or Cynbel over to our side."

"They both faced the brunt of the Sorim's thrusts. Why wouldn't they want new weapons to use against the mind benders?"

"They are both very conservative and they believe in keeping to the old ways. Hedred will have the best shot at convincing Meraud. Arthmael's insight into Cynbel has been an absolute boon to me. If I frame my argument right, Cynbel will vote with us."

"I never knew such planning went into preparing for a council meeting."

"That's why Caradoc, Hedred and I are scared to death that you will interject yourself in the deliberations and ruin our chances."

"Why do you think I would do that?" I'm hurt to have so little trust placed in me.

"What did you do when Bradan challenged your placement of Boswen's ashes?"

"You can't hold that against me! Boswen has more than earned the right to be there."

"You'll get no argument from me on that score. But when you were told no, you immediately threatened a duel."

"He was disrespecting Boswen." *What is so hard to understand?*

"You make more friends with honey than with vinegar. Did you ever think of keeping your cool and discussing it like respected colleagues?"

"I'm not sorry that he was embarrassed in front of his followers."

"And this is why I must urge you in the strongest possible terms to be seen but not heard at the council meeting. Are you going to duel Cynbel or Meraud if they choose not to side with us?"

"Of course not!"

"Good. Then leave us to our tasks and don't attempt to kill anybody."

9

Duel Purposes

I don't know what makes me more nervous, my first council meeting or seeing Nemeton Dywyll Derw. The sacred grove was left for the druids by the elves when they departed for shores beyond the west. Most druids go their entire lives and never see the grove. It is only the Nine and those few who are summoned who know the location. Hedred explained that there is always an honor guard formed for the newly installed members of the Nine. It's nice that the other three students of Boswen have agreed to escort me to the sacred grove.

"That's Caradoc," I say, pointing at the lazily flying merlin.

"How do you know?" Eghan asks.

"Watch the upstroke. See how the wings aren't fully raised. You can always tell when Caradoc is coming."

"That's very observant of you," Hedred says. "I'll have to remember that."

I keep a straight face. Not for love or honey will I tell them who taught me that.

Caradoc lands and gives us a high pitched chitter.

"That's rich Caradoc. You're late and you admonish us?" Eghan says. Caradoc chitters again.

"We're going to fly together and Caradoc chooses a solitary bird of prey? Boswen once told me that I had to practice my thinking when I did that."

Eghan and Hedred grin. "He'll do just fine," Hedred says. Both men change into jackdaws and look up expectantly at me. I smile at them and take the shape of the tawny owl. I can't be seen as playing favorites, at least not yet.

The jackdaws give off alarm calls before leaping into the air. Caradoc's chitter sounds almost as if it's a laugh. It is times like this that I wish an owl could smile. I push off as well and our misbegotten group takes wing together.

We cross over the narrow strait of Menai to the island of Ynys Mona. On the horizon there is smoke coming from the middle of the forest. Caradoc, as the fastest flyer among us, increases his rhythm and pulls in front. He circles down to the hamlet below and takes on his human form. Hedred and Eghan also pick up their speed. Left by myself, I arrive to see a hamlet hastily being built from the forest around it. The ringing of hammer on anvil is unmistakable.

There's a blacksmith in a druid camp?

Caradoc is already accosting a druid. His face is red and the poor man is shrinking under Caradoc's verbal attack.

"Who decided to remove a forest and build a town at the most sacred site of the druids?"

"That would be the Head Druid," an officious oaf says as he joins the commotion.

"Where's that lazy, addle-brained fool at?"

"Please Lords," the man says, bowing low as we reach Caradoc's side, "your presence is requested in the great hall." He bows again as if it's some sort of affliction.

"He never should have joined our community," Caradoc says.

Hedred pauses to say something to the druid, but the man has already turned his back on us. Caradoc takes long, quick strides toward the hall. Poor Hedred has to run to catch up with us. For a man of his age and size, running is a most undignified action. I hold the door for the wheezing Hedred. Sweat is forming on his shiny, bald head. There is only a small fire in the central pit and our four fellow lords standing around it.

"I'm glad you went for a subtle entrance this time," Meraud says. "Though there are some in Eriu who have been wakened from their naps because of your exhortations."

"You're as charming as ever," Caradoc responds. There are raised eyes from my fellows. The only one not taken aback is Meraud herself.

"There is some terrible, watered-down wine in the cauldron over there." She points to our right. "And there is precious little wood, save the benches, for the fire."

Hedred bows to the other lords. "Greetings Bradan, Drustan, Cynbel and the ever-lovely Meraud. Can any of you tell us what is going on here?"

Bradan smirks. "Loris is remaking the druidic order for the better."

"Bradan, you amaze me. Just when I think you can't be any more stupid, you open your mouth," Caradoc says.

"They should have kept you confined to your own camp."

"Careful Bradan, Grahme is here and I'm sure he'd be willing to continue your duel."

Bradan ignores Caradoc's taunt, but he does eye my staff from top to bottom before moving away.

"You challenged Bradan to a duel?" Meraud demands of me.

"I believe it was he who challenged me."

"You came to my hall and threatened me with violence!"

Cynbel looks on, incredulous.

Caradoc takes Bradan's old spot by the fire. "Drustan, you're another one of Loris's oafs. What can you tell us?"

Hedred sighs loudly before sinking his head into his hands.

"And to think we worried about you," Eghan says softly to me.

Meraud makes eye contact with me and rolls her eyes.

Drustan, wanting nothing to do with Caradoc, leaves the fire.

"Lord Eghan," Cynbel says, "how is Arthmael faring in your camp?"

"As you know, he is ready for a quest. However, I have sent him to Grahme so he can learn the medicinal herbs of the moorlands."

"You should have sent him to my camp," Drustan says. "Andrilou can teach even you about healing."

"Andrilou is the best healer I've ever encountered," I say. "And Arthmael is beyond ready to take the next step." I ask my colleagues, "Would having Arthmael lead the Imbolc ceremonies at Isca be a suitable quest?"

"You would give up your first chance to lead the festival?" Meraud asks. "Cunobel may be insulted by your absence."

"I doubt it." I can feel my ears growing warm. I might as well have told them of our altercation.

Three long notes of a carnyx, the battle clarion, resounds throughout the forest, saving me from an embarrassing story.

The druids around camp scurry off to the north, though none carry a weapon.

"You can tell us all about it after the meeting," Meraud says, her eyes dancing.

"Are we to go to war?" Hedred asks. "I scarcely know who would dare challenge us here."

Everyone, save Bradan and Drustan, peak out between the wall and the thatch to see what is happening. Poor Hedred is too short to see anything, so he pounds on the door instead. "It's barred!" He says. "Open this door at once or I will break it down."

We look at each other in amusement, but we remain silent.

"Open the doors," a man shouts from just outside our hut. The door swings open and we see the path, lined with the druids from camp.

Hedred peers out, "This is new." His anger gives way to confusion.

"Lord Hedred, Protector of Ogof Cawr and senior member of the Council of Nine, please make your way to the Nemeton Dywyll Derw to pay homage to Head Druid Loris, Druid King of all Pretanni."

A number of eyebrows are raised. "He styles himself the Druid King of all Pretanni does he?"

"Easy Caradoc," Hedred says. "They are nothing but meaningless words unless we consent to them."

"Hurry Lord Hedred," the caller says under his breath. "Head Druid Loris is waiting on you."

Hedred gives us a wry smile. "You must be patient, child. I am in my seventh decade of life, not fresh off my mother's teat like yourself."

The caller bristles but he stands all the straighter as the diminutive Lord passes. Hedred makes a show of leaning on his staff as he slowly shuffles along the path.

Once he clears the bend in the path, the caller prepares for his next big moment. "Lord Caradoc, Protector of Ardri Bryn Cadwy, please make your way to the Nemeton Dywyll Derw to pay homage to Head Druid Loris, Druid King of all Pretanni."

"Oh, I don't know about homage, but I'll give him a piece of my mind."

Meraud says to no one in particular, "Can he afford to lose more?"

Meraud, Drustan and Bradan are next as the caller repeats the same line over and over. Cynbel looks at Eghan. "I hope you deem it no dishonor, but I intend to walk with you and get this farce over with."

"I will join you two, since I don't know my way to the sacred grove."

"As a matter of fact, let's just go now," Eghan says.

We emerge from the hall and surprise the caller. He raises his hands as if to push us back before thinking better of it. He sees Bradan rounding the bend and he calls Eghan's name. As soon as he is done, Cynbel shouts "and don't forget about Lords Cynbel and Grahme, for we are coming to the council as well." The caller hangs his head as the fiasco comes to an end.

"Grahme, please forgive me," Cynbel says once we're past the officious herald. "I completely forgot that this is your first visit to the elven grove. I should have been there as part of your honor guard."

"Think nothing of it. I'm still trying to come to terms with all of this."

With his lazy pace, Bradan is only a few strides in front of us now. He enters the grove and falls to one knee while bowing his head. He rises and moves out of our field of view. Upon entering the circle, Caradoc is in a heated argument with Loris and Drustan. Bradan is headed that way. Cynbel makes a show of pointing out Hedred and Meraud and walking toward them without acknowledging Loris. Eghan and I follow along.

I take my first measure of our Head Druid. He's old, fat, bald and bedecked in white robes with brilliant silver thread shimmering in the afternoon sun. His quarterstaff has a continuous spiral of silver as well, winding its way up from the butt to the top.

He can't perform magic with all that silver," I say.

Eghan shrugs. "It would probably spoil his last meal if he tried druidic magic in any case."

Cynbel belts out a laugh before regaining his composure. Loris shoots us a dirty look as he leaves Caradoc, Drustan and Bradan to argue amongst themselves. He steps upon a boulder which is centered within the ring of trees.

Caradoc splits the two druids and makes a beeline toward Loris. Hedred and Eghan rush to intercept him.

Left to myself, I marvel at the oak trees lining this space. They were all planted by the elves before they departed eight hundred and twenty years ago. The trunks are at least as wide as the outstretched arms of four men. With deep fissures in their silvery bark, the gnarled, hollowed out trunks are short and squat compared to the intertwined branches which form an unbroken canopy over our heads. I can't help but feel small and insignificant standing under such ancient trees.

Loris pounds his staff on the rock and the druids lining the pathway turn and walk out in an orderly fashion. He looks over the eight of us and in a clear staccato voice he begins. "Summoned, you have all arrived."

Caradoc cuts off the rest of Loris's speech. "What happened to the second and third circles?"

Eghan comes over to me and softly explains. "Every two hundred and fifty years, we plant a new ring of oak trees. We can never be sure when one of these trees will die, ending the circle, so new circles have been planted."

"And why have you removed half the forest to create so many huts?" Caradoc demands.

Loris turns from Caradoc and addresses the rest of us. "Behold, I am creating a capital city of druids out of the wilderness."

"A 'city of druids' is the stupidest phrase ever uttered on this island," Caradoc interjects.

Loris ignores him. "For too long you island druids have closed your eyes and ears to what is happening in the wider world. No longer do druid kingdoms hold sway in the mainland, for they were too weak to stand up to the truly powerful men. As we speak, our brothers and sisters have become valuable advisers to the mainland kings. They no longer run naked through the forests calling out the names of animals and trees as they go."

"Is that what he thinks we do?" I ask Eghan. He shushes me.

"Once completed, I will invite emissaries from many powerful kingdoms here so that we may align with the strongest among them."

"You would give away the location of our most sacred holy site?" This time it is Meraud who fails to keep her anger in check.

"Of course," he doesn't hide his disdain. "You are lucky I arrived before some power destroyed your paltry band of tree worshippers. I am here to salvage what I can for this isle."

"For himself," I add. Eghan waves away my comment as he listens intently.

"If you are trying to save this land, then why did you pull out all of the druids from the east of the island?" I ask. "The Wigesta have built temples. No longer do the people look to us to intercede on their behalf to the gods."

"It is the Wigesta who I will parley with first. They are my people."

"These choices are decided by the nine of us. You are but one voice of several," Caradoc yells.

"Continue to be a nuisance Caradoc and I will have you removed as one of my advisers."

Arguments, shouts and accusations erupt everywhere. Bradan and Drustan confront Caradoc. Hedred tries to get between them, but he's ignored by all three. Is this the end of the Pretanni druids? I can see that future unfolding before my eyes. Someone must stop this sundering from happening.

"Quiet!" Loris roars. Slowly the other lords hold their tongues. The Head Druid motions us all to sit? To back down? It is only clear that he believes himself to be higher than the rest of us.

"Head Druid Loris," I shout. Whatever he was going to say would only further tear us apart. I've stolen the moment from him. "I charge you with treason and challenge you to a duel to the death." I have the attention of all the Lords now. "I am not sure how this goes, but I believe you get to choose the weapons, though staffs are traditional."

Stupid me, it sounds like I'm apologizing now.

The other lords are shocked into silence. Are they mad at me? Disappointed?

Why do I suddenly feel like a child?

Loris laughs a loud, belly laugh. "You silly child, I only let you join my retinue because we would need someone to run errands. Your eradication of Boswen was a solid point in your favor, but you need to keep your mouth shut and not interrupt your betters." He looks at Bradan and gets a smile in return. "Otherwise, you will join Caradoc as outcasts of my druid kingdom." He motions Bradan and Drustan to stand beside him.

My jaw goes slack at his pronouncement.

"Leave now, both of you, before I have you removed bodily from this grove."

Cynbel places himself between Loris and I. "Like Grahme, I defeated a Lord to secure my spot on this council. Call all the toadies you have then, for I am the foremost staff fighter on this island. You don't have enough men to do what you promise." Caradoc and Eghan come forward and stand on either side of Cynbel.

"Now that is enough!" Hedred yells. He walks between us. "We are the leaders of this island and we have the responsibility to act the part." He glares at both sides. For once, everyone is willing to listen. "It seems we have two matters we must resolve. First, is Grahme's challenge of trial by mortal combat against Loris. The second is the expulsion of both Caradoc and Grahme from this council. I propose we vote on both matters.

"Who believes Grahme's challenge was fairly given and action is required? Say aye." There are four druids who say aye.

Meraud remains silent, trying to grasp the situation.

"Those opposed, say nay."

Nay" is shouted by Bradan and Drustan.

Loris looks on amused. "Nay."

"Very well, on to the next matter. Who favors that Caradoc and Grahme be removed from this council?" Loris and his cronies say aye. "Those opposed?" Everyone else but me says nay. "Caradoc, since you are one of the people we are voting upon, you and Grahme are unable to vote. Still, it is three votes for expulsion and four votes against. In our time-honored system, Grahme's challenge stands and no one is being expelled from this council." Hedred's voice ends in a flat tone as he turns to Loris. "What is your choice of weapon?"

"He's not a member of this council, so his words don't matter."

"He is and they do. Your weapon?" Hedred says with a firmer tone.

Loris squints at Hedred. "I will assign a champion to represent me."

"Traitors do not get the benefit of champions," Caradoc says. "So will you fight, or do you accept the charge of being a traitor?"

"And what is the punishment for being a traitor?" Loris asks with a wry smile.

"Death and dishonor," Caradoc responds.

"Dishonor hardly matters if one is dead," Loris says, exasperated.

"I believe my honor is more important than my life," Cynbel responds.

"And that is why you are a fool." Loris pivots his gaze to each of the faces before settling on me. He stares down his pointed nose and scoffs. "I look forward to killing you tomorrow at noon."

10

Banishment, of a Sort

The night before I fought Boswen, I couldn't sleep. I remained on my sleeping pelts and stared at the roof all night. I choose not to repeat that again. The other druids are fast asleep in the hall. Earlier I spied an opening between the wall and thatch roof. I change into a tawny owl and silently glide to my exit. I squeeze through into the cold night air and take flight. The owl form has always relaxed me. I circle the newly formed town at a safe distance. Light from the waning half-moon is falling below the horizon. There's no chance of me being seen.

"Hurry it up," drifts upward from the town. I veer over to see who could be out in this bitter cold time of night. "Get the silver and your horses. We don't have much time."

A short man with a thin mustache goes running off between buildings. I land on a thick thatch roof opposite him. The man returns and of all people, Loris steps into the open. He fumbles with his silver adorned staff as the man hands him the reins of a horse. He helps Loris up, into the saddle. Loris stretches out his hand and takes the reins of the second horse.

"Lord, how am I to follow you without a horse?"

"You have done well," Loris says as he inspects a silver drinking cup. This is even better than the work you did on the mainland." Loris says in a flattering tone. "Truly there is no one better at molding silver into beautiful objects."

"Thank you, Lord."

Loris gives a pitiless smile. "Your sacrifice here will not go unnoticed. I will let everyone know that you are every bit as faithful as you are talented in your craft."

"You honor me too much." He bows low to Loris. "Am I to come with you?"

"I will send for you later." Loris says dismissively. He squeezes the horse's side with his legs and starts moving forward. I watch as he leaves Nemeton Dywyll Derw without looking back.

I have an urgent need to tell someone about this. But since I technically should not have left the hall on the night before my duel, I can't say a word. Too excited to sleep, I follow Loris at a safe distance. At the bank of the Menai Strait, Bradan waves him over to a boat. The trees are well away from the shore, but still close enough for an owl to hear what is said.

"I have procured a vessel as you asked," Bradan says.

"Take the horses back and tell no one of this."

Not sure if I should return or stay, I watch Loris as the crew unloads his loot. The crew assembles in front of the ship and bows down before him in a sickening show of deference. The captain gives the word and they make ready to leave.

Relieved I will not have to fight for my life later today, I glide back to the hall and take to my bed before any of the other druids discover my absence.

A constant pounding on the door forces me from my slumber. I grab the door and jerk it inward. The caller from yesterday nearly stumbles into the hall, as he was starting another round of thumps.

"Begging your pardon Lord," he says to the ground. "I was asked by the rest of the council to escort you to the sacred grove."

He's changed his ways since yesterday. No longer does he suffer from a false sense of importance. I take a wild stab at what's been happening. "Did Lord Caradoc give you these orders?"

"Yes Lord, he did," the man says with wonder. A dressing down by Caradoc has this effect on people.

"I will be coming in short order. You can relay that message or remain here, whichever you feel is best." I close the door before he can start a new round of groveling.

I splash my face with water, grab my staff and stride confidently to the ancient oak grove. The man remains a step behind me. The morose pair of Drustan and Bradan stand near the central rock and the rest of my peers stand behind them. Hedred smiles at me as I enter the circle.

"It is good that you managed to make it here before midday," Caradoc says.

I gauge the low-lying Belenos in the sky. "I think I've made it here with plenty of time to spare," I reply confidently.

"It is your opponent whose whereabouts are in question," Hedred says. I raise my eyes as if surprised by the news.

"It seems that Bradan and Drustan managed to lose track of him last night," Caradoc says in a raised voice. Drustan turns his back to us while Bradan's anger is plainly visible.

"It should not be up to Lord Protectors to keep watch," Bradan says.

Bradan makes it hard to hold back, but I decide not to reveal what I saw last night. The act of staying quiet may very well cause me to burst at the seams. "What happens now?" I ask innocently.

"Loris is branded the traitor that he is and all druids have permission to kill him on sight," Caradoc informs me.

"Not yet," Hedred says.

"Right, we must wait until midday has come and gone, then he will officially be branded the traitor we all know him to be."

"If you knew he was a traitor Caradoc, then why did you vote for him last year?" Meraud asks.

Caradoc clenches his jaw and walks to the opposite side of the group from his long-ago lover.

Hedred approaches Bradan and Drustan and speaks quietly with them. With the demeanor of spoiled children, they grudgingly join us.

"Everyone, I think we can agree that it looks unlikely that Loris is going to show. Rather than standing around idly, I propose we debate who should become the next Head Druid. However, if Loris returns, the conversation will be abandoned and we will continue with Loris as our leader," he adds. "Speak freely, for these words have no power until such time that we are officially without a Head Druid."

"Loris will be here," Drustan says.

"In which case our words here mean nothing. If however, he does not show, we need to settle on a new leader quickly," Hedred says.

"I would like to be considered for the lead position," Caradoc says. There is a lack of excitement from the rest of us, though Caradoc is oblivious to it. "Is there no one else who wishes it?" He asks in surprise. "If not, would someone like to second it?"

"Meraud," I say. "I propose that Meraud be the next Head Druid." Caradoc shakes his head as if he'd misheard me. Everyone else is looking to me as if I have more to say.

"It is not customary for a Lord to nominate another member of the council," Meraud says. "The reasoning being that if the nominated is unwilling to speak for themselves, they are not a viable candidate."

"I didn't . . ."

"I'm sure you didn't know that was the custom. This is your first meeting after all. However, I would like to hear your reasoning."

"I think that Hedred would be the best choice, however he is old and I believe he would be reluctant to leave his caves. Cynbel is decisive, however he is the second newest member of the council and I thought he might not be accepted for that fact. Sorry Caradoc, I know that you are decisive, but you also tend to alienate your adversaries. So you're the perfect blend. You have experience on the council, you're decisive in your own way and you try to lead without commanding."

"Did you hear that, Hedred?" Caradoc says. "You're too old and I'm too unlikeable."

Hedred looks up at Caradoc. "I'd say he's right on all counts." He looks at Meraud. "I will second the nomination, assuming you are amenable."

She looks at the rest of us. "Well, I never would have believed this could happen." She wipes her eyes and shakes her head. "If you and Grahme speak truly, then I will nominate myself as the Head Druid."

Hedred looks up at Caradoc. "Will you withdraw your name, or will you fight Meraud to the death for the honor?"

Now it is Caradoc's turn to wipe his eyes. He stares at Meraud, his face reflecting any number of emotions. "I told you once before," he says with a shaky voice, "that I would never stand in your way." In barely more than a whisper he says, "I withdraw my bid."

"Anyone else?" Hedred asks. After a couple heartbeats, he continues. "Then Meraud is our new Head Druid, if it turns out that Loris does not return."

Cynbel and Eghan climb up the oak trees and cut off several sprigs of mistletoe each. Once down, the hand their prizes over to Meraud.

"It doesn't seem right, but you are the only one of us who knows how to weave the crown of mistletoe," Eghan says apologetically.

Meraud good naturedly rolls her eyes. "That can wait. I propose we get our house in order first."

"What do you have in mind?" Eghan asks.

"I propose we abandon the idea of a settlement on any part of Ynys Mona for starters. Does anyone object?"

Bradan and Drustan stand slightly apart from the rest of us, so it is difficult to tell if they are taking part in the conversation. Not that it matters.

"Next, I say we dismantle the village and send these druids back out among the people. Furthermore, I would like for every druid to select an acorn from their home territory and bring it here for planting. It may take two hundred years to undo the damage, but undo it we must."

"A very good idea," Hedred says.

"With Loris's likely departure, we are one person short of a full council." Meraud says. "I would ask that each of us consider who they believe would be a good addition and bring them here eight days before Imbolc. It is imperative that we have the position filled before warring season starts. While I have respect for Cynbel and Grahme, I would rather the council decide on the next member instead of having our best and brightest kill each other for the privilege. Does anyone object?"

"They are all sound ideas," Eghan says.

"I think that is plenty for now. Does anyone else have anything they wish to bring up to the council?"

"I do," I say.

"I dare say patience is not your strength," Meraud says. "But please, speak your mind."

"I speak on behalf of my nephew, Figol. He desires nothing in this world as much as to become a druid. I wish the council's permission for him to begin his training."

Meraud looks uncertain.

"He has already proven to be an asset," I say.

"And how is that?"

"On our way here, we stopped for the night at Bodmin's Moor."

"You should know better than to go there," Drustan interjects. "I warn all of my apprentices on their first day to stay clear of that place."

"Why?" I ask. "Bodmin is willing to talk if you give him the chance."

There are gasps from several of my peers. "You have spoken to Bodmin?" Meraud asks.

"Yes, and he was kind enough to tell us the meaning of another of the giant's runes. It is *hahgel*, and it will cause hail to rain down when the runestone is activated. Neither Hedred nor Eghan knew of it."

"Indeed." Meraud says, letting an intense anger be conveyed in only two syllables. She stares down at Hedred.

"So, the runt consorts with traitors," Bradan says with a malicious grin.

"The same can be said of you Bradan," I reply.

"That's a lie!"

"Where were you last night as Aine was sinking below the horizon? Were you helping Loris get on a boat to leave this island?"

"A good question," Caradoc says. "How do you respond?"

"I refuse to be interrogated by a lying child."

"So, Loris is gone," Meraud's voice rings out louder than anyone else's. "Before someone gets challenged to a duel and our number is reduced further, we have bigger issues to discuss," She faces Hedred. "What is happening with the giant's runes and who is behind it?"

"There are several of us that have begun to decipher the meaning of the giant runes." Hedred says. "We have known for a while now that leaders on the mainland have eyes on our island. Loris was right about one thing, we cannot continue to go about our old ways, oblivious of the world around us. It is a matter of when, not if, a kingdom will invade our island."

"You thought it best to keep this from the council?" Meraud asks.

"In only the last year, Eghan and I have sent our people into long barrows and other giant constructions. We have managed to piece together some of their runic meanings. If the proper ritual is performed, these runestones are imbued with specific powers. This is why the druids on the mainland carry metal. They have forsaken the old ways and use runestones instead."

"Now we know that you and Eghan are conspirators. Are there more?" She scans our faces. "Let me guess, Caradoc is also involved and Boswen was while he was alive. Now Grahme has been pulled into this secret cabal."

"We were waiting to feel out the other lords. In the meantime, we invested our time learning as much as we could," Hedred says in a most reasonable tone.

"By your own words, four members of this council acted in secret to learn the giant runes while the other five were kept in the dark."

The silence stretches uncomfortably long.

"We cannot work this way," Meraud says, "or else we are no better than the clans who fight against their neighbors every warring season. If we don't work as one, all will be lost, be it months or years from now."

"You're right, Meraud," Eghan says.

"I want you to collect all the information you and Hedred have on the giant runes and share it with each one of us before the moon disappears in seven days."

"Yes, Meraud."

"And I want everyone to keep their distance from Bodmin, and Ganna the witch for that matter." She looks directly at me, as if I was planning to do so. "If they are to be approached, it will be with the full knowledge of this council."

"Yes, Meraud," the others intone.

"Yes, Meraud," I say, belatedly.

She looks at me. "I don't know that you did me a favor by nominating me."

I nervously smile back at her.

"If there is no *other* business . . ."

"Meraud," I can hear the groans all around me.

"Yes, Grahme," a weary Meraud answers.

"I have just two more questions." She frowns and waves her hand for me to continue. "Bodmin warned me to beware the silvertongue in our midst. I do not know what that is but I feel I need to share it with the council."

"A silvertongue? That would explain a lot," Hedred says. We all look to him. "A silvertongue possesses a unique kind of magic. With the tone of his voice, he is able to win over all but the most guarded people to his side. It is different from the Obsidian mages, for he doesn't enter into another's head. The subtle magic of persuasion targets the unsuspecting, getting them to agree and obey. It would explain how Loris was chosen to lead us even though none of us knew of him prior to our deliberations. It would also explain how so many solitary druids came running back here and cut down a huge swath of forest to live together in a town."

"Yes, it puts a lot of the past in perspective," Meraud says. She turns to me. "I hesitate to remind you, but you have one more question to ask."

"Yes, you never did answer on whether Figol can become a druid apprentice."

"How does the council feel?"

Bradan and Drustan immediately say no, while Caradoc, Hedred and Eghan say yes. "Cynbel?" Meraud asks.

"I have spent the last five years fighting the dark mages." He looks me in the eye, "I must say no."

"Well, I say yes, so that makes it four to three."

"What do you say, Meraud?" Cynbel asks.

She purses her lips. "I must think upon this. I will give the council my answer in the morning. Grahme, I would like to have a word with you."

The others depart, leaving Meraud and I alone. The still air brings a chill to my bones. Or maybe that's just dread.

"Truly I am sorry, but I don't believe I can support your nephew's bid," she says. "And that makes my next request all the more awkward." She sits on the rock that Loris used as his stage. She pats the spot next to her. "We sat like this once before."

"We did, and neither of us could have guessed what the future would bring." I manage to keep my voice from sounding morose. Still, I lower my head down and stare at the loam beneath us.

"I'm afraid we are at another one of those moments." She scratches my back, just like Mum used to do after I'd lost another fight with Ferroth. "Know that I do this because I respect you and your abilities."

She lowers her head until she can look me in the eyes. "I would like for you to leave this island very soon," she holds up her hand to forestall my objection, "and travel to Eriu. If Boswen's boys, as I call the four of you, are right and our days are numbered, then I would ask you to go to Lia Fahil and renew the bonds of friendship with the Emerald Druids."

"Eriu? The Emerald Druids?"

Has she not seen the trail of animosity I leave behind me?

"How am I supposed to befriend them?"

"I don't know. But I also don't know how I could have possibly evaded the Obsidian Mage as he chased me across this land of ours. You have an earnestness about you that endears you to the people you meet. And you have the skill to defend yourself when your earnestness fails."

"As a Lord, you cannot command me to do this, correct?"

"Correct."

"Then I will do this on two conditions."

"And they are?"

"First, you must tell me your true motivation for sending me."

Meraud gives out a startled laugh. "Clearly you are more perceptive than I was giving you credit. Here is my reasoning: you defeated Boswen to take his spot, you took part in a duel with Bradan," she places a hand on my knee to keep me silent. "And you challenged Loris to yet another duel. Furthermore, you spoke with a declared traitor in Bodmin and you were part of a conspiracy to withhold information about the giant's runes. You have been a Lord Protector for barely over a month."

I have to look away. When she puts it like that . . ..

"We need to select a new member of our order. I doubt you will have any suggestions for us to consider, and an odd number will prevent ties from occurring."

I can't fault her reasoning.

"Now, tell me your second condition."

I want to lean against her as if she were my mother and just be. But I'm too old for coddling. "I will take Figol with me and if we are successful, you will allow Figol to become a druid."

"In my heart I think it is a bad move to accept Figol into our order. His other ability will mark him out as different. Perhaps with luck and perseverance, it can be made into a strength. I fear that it will turn out otherwise." She looks me in the eyes. "What are we to do if a Sorim learns our ways and leaves our order?" She turns away and bites her lower lip. "If you can forge a new alliance for us, I will change my vote and support Figol."

96

"When can we leave?" I ask, excited at getting a second chance.

Meraud lets out a rueful laugh and pats me on the back. "The sooner the better."

11

Gift from the Dead

My trip to Eriu to see the Emerald Druids is a banishment. Meraud can frame it however she wants, but the facts don't change. I'm not upset though; if this is what it takes to make Figol a druid, then this is what I'll do. Eghan has been kind, but distant since we returned to the hot springs of Sulis. Figol spends all his time at Coventina's spring, with Sieffre. It's good that he understands the dangers that comes with a druid's power.

I don't know why Caradoc insisted that we stop to see him at Ardi Bryn Cadwy before crossing the Strait of Eriu, but it's on our path in any case.

"Are you ready Figol?"

He continues to fixate on Sieffre. "I can make out his mind, I think. But only for brief moments."

"That's probably for the best. How would you like to know you are trapped for the rest of your life in the body of a puffin?"

"Uncle, can we fly to Eriu as puffins?"

"If it will get you moving, I'll agree to anything. But we will fly to Caradoc's camp as merlins. You can really get a feel for the land and all its intricate details through the eyes of a predator."

The hills around Caradoc's camp are smooth, treeless, and undulating in their blanket of yellowed grass. We land south of the holy site. The tall stones jut upward from the stone cairn, mimicking a rocky crown.

"Caradoc's camp is over that hill, where the ground isn't so boggy. I wanted to see the holy site before Caradoc gets possession of our ears."

"Can we get closer?"

"We can. Caradoc said to watch the stones making the crown. If they catch the rays of Belenos just right, they can sparkle."

As we approach, there is a massive stone three times as tall as a man and twice as wide lying up against the cairn.

"That is the stone used to close off the tomb. No one has been inside since the stone was laid down hundreds or even thousands of years ago."

"Who's inside?" Figol asks.

I shrug. "The All-King, that's all we know. At no time have the humans had a sole leader on this island and it's hard to imagine one man ruling over the Elder Races. In truth, no one knows who or what has been laid to rest inside."

There is a break in the clouds and the light of Belenos shines upon us. The upright stones have thin veins of glassrock running through them. The brilliance of the reflected light forces us to lower our gazes. Even after all these uncounted years, we bow our heads to the All-King.

The homes in Caradoc's camp are made of stone walls and thatched roofs. The camp is built at the convergence of two small streams. The riparian trees, hugging tightly to the waterways, are the tallest objects in the valley.

"Grahme, Figol, I'm so glad you could make it," Caradoc says as we enter his camp.

"This is impressive," I say. "I'm not used to seeing homes made with rocks."

"That's what happens when rocks are plentiful and trees are not," Caradoc says. Besides, we need the thick walls to keep out the worst of the winter chill. Make yourselves comfortable and see just how much better this place is compared to Boswen's old camp. When you're ready, come find me."

We're left to settle. Caradoc's location may be warmer than Dartmoor, but it also feels cramped. Rocks may be plentiful, but the resolve to bring back enough to make a decent sized hut is not. The tiny huts are cramped and the camp's central bonfire is too small. I reach up into the thatch roof and almost immediately my hand pokes through. "They got lazy with the thatch too," I tell Figol. "It will be a cold night."

Caradoc isn't hard to find. Even with other bards in training, his voice is heard over everyone. He has four druids sitting on the slope of a hill. To my embarrassment, he's reciting my ballad. "Figol, make him stop," I say, desperate.

"But I've never heard your ballad."

"Figol, I will give you just about anything you want, if you make him stop right now."

"Grahme!" Caradoc shouts as he waves us over. He addresses his charges. "This is a rare opportunity, to sing the ballad to the hero himself. Does anyone wish to volunteer?"

Please students, say no.

They look away from me and somehow seem to shrivel before my eyes. Normally I'd take pity on them, but now I pray their discomfort grows several fold.

"Not a bold one amongst you," Caradoc says while shaking his head. "If you're going to be a bard, you can't let people intimidate you." He glances at me and gives me a quick smile. "Be away with you then," he says to his apprentices.

Released, the students waste no time scampering to wherever they will, leaving only the three of us.

"I am truly sorry that I did not support your claim to become head druid. But Meraud is the one person who can unify us."

"Meraud is the best choice; quite possibly the only choice, and for the exact reasons that you gave. I expect her to be a fantastic leader for decades to come." His kind words belie the disappointment in his voice.

"Why do you always choose to animorph into a merlin?" Figol asks.

Before I can reprimand him, Caradoc answers.

"There are many reasons, and all of them are clever." Caradoc answers. "First, the bird is a raptor, so it has fantastic eyesight. Second, it can stay in the air for hours at a time. Finally, it's small, so it's not as conspicuous as larger birds."

Figol has his head down, a dead giveaway that he's reading someone's thoughts. "Can you tell us anything about the Emerald Druids?"

101

"That's why I asked you to visit me before you left," Caradoc smiles. "I have something which will make your task possible, but it will cost you listening to one of my stories."

"He never tells stories," Figol says as he nods my direction.

"Well, let me fix that. That Meraud, she's a clever one, I've always said that, even when I'd rather eat burning wood than speak kindly of her."

He waves us to enter his hut. A much larger fire is roaring inside. With the paltry amount of wood provided for us, we couldn't make a blaze this big unless we used all our kindling at once. Figol gives me a knowing smile.

Get out of my head.

"Now, the task that Meraud has given you is attempted nearly every generation, and each time it yields little success."

"Hedred says it's every other generation," I say.

Caradoc stares at me until I stop talking. "The real reason she gave this to you was to get you out of our deliberations for the new member of the Nine."

"She told me as much."

"And that is how she is so successful. She goes into her motherly act and everyone assumes she's sincere; but I knew her when she was much younger. In fact, I dare say that I know her better than anyone. And I'm not exaggerating when I say she's as shrewd as they come."

"If healing the rift between the orders never succeeds, what am I to do?"

"Sit back and listen. It's time for a secret to be revealed." He stands up and begins to pace. His head is shrouded in smoke, heightening the mood.

"Everyone knows that Branok the Burly founded the druids eight hundred and twenty years ago, but what few know is that he had no skills in the druidic arts," Caradoc begins.

Figol is hanging on Caradoc's every word.

"What he did have was an honorable reputation that impressed the Elder Races. He also had two wives, each being a highly skilled druidess. Their names were Pretanni and Eriu, and yes, they gave their names to the islands on which they lived. They also fostered a passionate hatred for one another. The chasm between our two orders dates back to their founding. Poor Branok had to alternate months on the isles in an effort to satisfy his jealous wives."

I'm not at all happy about finding out the shortcomings of our founder, but knowing that the knowledge exists, I desperately want to hear it.

"There was a desire for nine holy sites on Pretanni, but only eight were obvious. The Tomb of the All-King was not chosen until fifteen years after the Elders left. Pretanni knew Branok was sick, so she had this tomb built and made up a story about a great man in the past who ruled all of the isles.

"As luck would have it, the next year, Branok's illness became common knowledge. He knew that his wives would fight over where his tomb would be, so he struck out into the wilds and never returned; or so it has been told for over eight hundred years.

"Near the end, Pretanni spent every waking hour following Branok in one animal form or another. When he passed, she had his remains brought here."

"Branok is the All-King?" Figol asks.

"No, but that is who is buried here." He smiles triumphantly at us. "And from here, the story gets even better. When Branok married his wives, he presented each with a ring. Pretanni's ring held a

103

sunstone that perfectly matched her eyes. Sunstones can be found on the mainland, and they are usually light yellow, like the rays of Belenos. This was a truly rare gemstone that was brown, yet still sparkled, like Pretanni's eyes. She treasured it more than any other possession.

"For Eriu, the greenest emerald was set in her band and it matched her eyes too. When Branok was buried, Pretanni removed her ring and set it upon Branok's heart. The tomb was sealed and only the keepers of this holy site knew of its true nature."

Figol looks at me in wonder. "Branok is really buried here?"

"But how can you keep this from the people of this isle. Don't they deserve to know the truth?" I ask.

"Let me finish my tale," Caradoc says. "Fifty years later, the second Protector of Ardri Bryn Cadwy entered the tomb to see for himself. What he found was Pretanni's ring, with the gemstone cracked, lying at Branok's feet and what must have been Eriu's emerald ring placed upon his heart."

"She knew about the ruse?" Figol asks.

"She must have, but the question no one can answer is how she entered the tomb without being discovered."

"Easy," I say. "She could have animorphed into a mouse and found a crack to climb through."

"It would be easy for you or me, but Eriu was never able to animorph according to the tales. Pretanni was the expert at that. But Pretanni could not call forth elementals, which was Eriu's strength."

"So how did she get in?" Figol asks.

"No one knows. But when her ring was discovered, the second Protector told his druids that they had failed in their duty. If the other druids knew, they would withdraw this site as one of the holy sites.

Everyone was bound to secrecy. And that secret has stayed in this camp for over seven hundred years."

"How will knowing this help us with the Emerald Druids? Surely telling them this tale will just bring animosity," I say.

"Of course it would, and you are not to reveal this story to anyone." He stares us down. "However, a couple years ago, I decided to take on the shape of a mouse and scrambled inside the tomb. When I returned, I brought this out with me." He opens his hand to reveal a silver ring with a gleaming emerald gemstone.

Figol and I look at each other, there's no telling whose mouth is opened wider.

"If you are able to enter into reasonable negotiations with our brothers on the small island, then this will surely help finish the deal."

"You would part with this ring?" I ask, not believing what I just heard.

"While I was inside, I also found Pretanni's ring. I restored it to its rightful place, over Branok's heart. I also removed the concubine's jewelry." He disdainfully shows us the ring once again.

"I don't know what to say."

"Just make sure that you don't give this away without getting a deal with them." He nearly spits out the last word. "Pretanni was his first and only true love, so I have set things right. If this trinket can bring them to their senses, then I'd be more than glad to be rid of it."

"I will have Figol monitor their minds. Only if they deal in good faith will I tell them of the ring's existence."

"Succeed at this, and regardless of Meraud's title, you will have the most powerful voice at council."

"Thank you, Caradoc. You have given me more than I had any right to hope for."

12

Here Goes Puffin

Thanks to Hedred's instructions, we know that to land in the Emerald Druids' midst in an animal form would be considered a grave insult. I can only imagine what they would say if we showed up as puffins.

The forest clears before us, revealing their capital, Lia Fahil . . . and the city is empty. No one mentioned this possibility.

The houses below are rectangular and made of wood, not the conical waddle and daub structures of home. The roofs are made of turf, and some homes have grass extending down three sides, making them look like a small hill with smoke exiting from the top. We circle the city twice, because I don't know what else to do. The Sun Caves, the Auga Sawels, are supposed to be on the northern edge of the valley. If the druids are not in the city, maybe they're there? We were told that the head druid never leaves this valley. Already the plan is falling apart.

Below us are three massive hills, each with a single entrance. Are they long barrows? It's the only way I can describe them. Each one is more massive than anything on Pretanni. Atop one of the barrows is a collection of a dozen people. Several are richly attired, while the rest wear the white robes of druids. It is unclear whether it is the fish I caught or my nerves making my little puffin stomach feel distended.

We circle the meeting once before landing at the long barrow's base. Well-worn stone steps are laid out along the path up the hill.

We retake our human forms. "Great," I say. "We start out our mission by making ourselves look as ridiculous as possible."

"Maybe they didn't see us," Figol says.

"They're druids. They saw us. Now, do we risk offending them by breaking into their deliberations or do we wait and hope they don't take offence as they wait for us?"

"Uncle, I think she will tell us." Figol points up at a lone druidess descending the stairs.

"I feel awkward standing here waiting. Let's meet her half way."

"Yes Uncle," Figol says. He sighs, in case I hadn't noticed his disappointment by the tone of his voice.

"Hello!" the druidess above us shouts. "I am Crisa, Guardian of the Auga Sawels. May I ask what business you have with us today?" She's friendly and confident, I take an immediate liking to her.

"Greetings Guardian Crisa, I am Grahme, Lord Protector of Men-an-Tol and I have been sent to reestablish the bonds of friendship between our two orders." *There, I said it exactly how I rehearsed.*

"Do my eyes deceive me or are you very young to be one of the Nine?"

Never did the conversation go this way when I played it over and over in my head. "You are very direct. Is that the way of your people?"

"Yes, I am, but no, the rest of the councilors are not like me. They are always 'your majesty' this or 'noble lord' that. I find all the honorifics to be tedious."

I find myself grinning like a silly child. She must be twice my age. "I am new at all of this, so I would like it if you call me simply Grahme."

"Very well Simply Grahme, what else do the Pretanni druids seek, besides our friendship?"

"Just your friendship," I say confused.

"We have a saying here, 'Pretanni only stretches out her hand in friendship when she finds something she wishes to take.'" She beckons us to follow her up the stairs.

"I swear to you, the only objective given to me by Meraud was to bring our orders closer together."

"Meraud, you say? And what does Loris think of this?"

"Loris is no longer a member of the Nine."

"And Meraud is the new Head Druid? And what has happened to Boswen?"

Her rapid questioning throws me off my plan. "You know a lot about our order."

"Always," she smiles.

"Boswen has passed over to the other side. I now fill his old spot on the council."

"Forgive me for having to interrogate you as such, but your news will be of interest to the council, and they are more likely to believe me than you. Please follow me."

Interrogate? I look at Figol, but he's been using his mental powers and he is amused by something. I hurry to catch up with Crisa. "If I may be bold, can you tell me who I am to meet in council above?"

"You really don't know? I have been told that your kind doesn't concern yourselves with the affairs of Eriu, but I didn't believe it. Every druid apprentice here can recite the makeup of your Nine."

"Then can you tell me of your Nine?"

She lets out a startled laugh. "You don't even know that our council is made up of seven druids?" She looks side-eyed at me. "Oh, you're telling the truth." She stops her ascent and faces us.

"Very well, you should at least have that knowledge before you go into battle."

Figol and I share alarmed looks.

"Anach is the Head Druid and he is old and grumpy on his best days. The rest of the Druid Lords have their own areas and holy sites. Mine are the Auga Sawels, of which we are standing on Komsit Lat, one of the three observatories which share the same valley as Lia Fahil. This means that I must maintain both sites, as Anach is too busy with whatever it is that he does."

"It sounds like you are a druid apprentice."

She grins. "Unlike your situation, the newest Druid Lord is always in charge of the Auga Sawels. It is supposed to let the newest member learn their duties by being in proximity to the Head Druid. In reality, it is twice the work and little respect. When one of the other positions comes open, I will move there and a new member will take my place here."

"You're right; we have nothing like this on Pretanni." I glance over and Figol has his head down. I keep from smiling, since I know what this pose means.

"There are five kingdoms on Eriu. Each kingdom has a holy site and a member of our council stationed within it. Anach, is the King of this valley, so he is both a king and a druid."

"Who are the men dressed so gaudily?" I ask. "Are they emissaries from the kings?"

"No," she pauses. "They are the kings themselves. Ours is not a large island, so the kings travel to us."

My guts tighten up. I must speak to both the druids and the kings of Eriu? I've not had much luck with either on Pretanni. I wipe away the sweat forming on my brow.

"You should have very low expectations for this meeting," she cautions. "Even if it were only Anach, he would not embrace your overtures." She stops just before the top of the hill is visible. "There is no need to be nervous. Above us is a group of irascible men. They are only united on one thing; their distrust of our Pretanni brothers and sisters."

"And this is supposed to comfort me?"

She smiles back at me. "You have no chance of success, so there is nothing to be nervous about. Now, I will need your name," she says to Figol, "If I am to introduce you properly." Her brow furrows as Figol's head remains slumped.

"This is Figol, a druid in training," I say.

Crisa nods and walks up the remaining few stairs. Straightening to her full height, she clears her voice. "If it pleases the council, we have two members of the Pretanni Druids who wish to address us."

There is some sort of commotion, but I can't make out what is being said. "The two druids are Grahme, Protector of Men-an-Tol and member of the council of Nine," there are a few startled remarks on hearing my name, "And young Figol, a druid in training. Do I have your blessing Head Druid?"

Crisa returns and escorts us the last few steps. "Whatever you do," she says in a low voice, "Maintain strict formality. Anach thrives on it."

You wait until now to tell me?

"Head Druid Anach, revered members of the Council of Seven and noble Kings, I bid you a warm greeting from Meraud and the Druid Protectors of Pretanni."

"Meraud? What happened to Loris?"

"Quiet Rhalthan!" another king yells.

Anach stands in front of an exquisitely carved wooden chair. Had Loris known of this, he would have been positively envious. There are eleven smaller, less decorated chairs, five to Anach's left and six to his right. The five richly dressed Kings are attired in a riot of colors. Some gold, but mostly silver tassels hang over their shoulders and chests. My guess is that the ones with the most gold are the more powerful kings. To Anach's right, sit five druids. Crisa's empty chair is farthest from the Head Druid.

"Master of Ceremonies!" Anach roars. His hood catches the wind and he struggles to pull it over his mostly bald head.

"Noble kings," Crisa begins. "Let me remind you that you are here as guests of Head Druid Anach and the Emerald Druids. Decorum dictates that you should not speak out of turn." Crisa says in a clipped tone that hints at her need to recite the phrase often.

"Thank you Crisa," Anach says stiffly. "Now tell *me* what has happened to Loris and Boswen."

I stir in my seat away from the fire and ask for another ale. Like their houses, the modest mead hall is built into a hill. It is the smallest of the three halls in the village. There's room for twenty patrons, though it's less than half filled tonight. Like me, the others sit in a morose stupor, drinking away their frustrations.

"Honestly, it is the best you could have possibly expected," Crisa says for the third time.

"I'm not sure who was most hostile, Anach, the kings, or the rest of the druids once they learned that it was Figol and I who flew around their summit as puffins." I take another swig of my ale. "I see no path forward for us."

"Why would anyone get mad at us taking the shape of puffins?" Figol asks. "They are the most ridiculous of birds."

"Ah, it is because you can," Crisa says. "There are very few here who can animorph. Those who try usually end up hurting themselves and giving up."

"It was more than that," Figol says. "They hate the druids of Pretanni, both the kings and the druids. I have never felt such hostility at an introduction."

"Only you have shown us any hospitality and I'm grateful for it," I add. I signal Tiva, the barmaid and she quickly replaces my empty cup.

Crisa plops down several silver coins for the barkeep and places her hand over top my newest ale. "Please, follow me. I have something very important to discuss with you, and I would prefer that you have your wits about you." She signals Tiva and ushers us to the far side of the bar. "This tapestry holds an incredible secret," she whispers.

"Listen up!" Tiva calls. "Anyone who is capable of stumbling over here under their own power, gets a free drink." A cheer goes up and the patrons show remarkable speed at getting to the other end of the bar.

Wordlessly, Crisa draws back the heavy tapestry and waves us into a narrow, stone-lined tunnel leading into darkness. Figol gives me a nod, so I know that Crisa's intent is true.

"Sorry, I would normally have a reedlight, but I wanted us to slip in here without drawing attention."

With a hand on either side of the walls, we go twenty paces until Crisa finds an oil-soaked reed. A couple strikes of her sparking stones and we have light. To our right is a doorway into a room that must butt up to the back of the bar. Crisa sticks her torch into the central fire pit and the kindling ignites at once.

"I apologize for the dramatics, but I need you to meet with me and one other without anyone taking notice."

"Why us?" I ask.

Before she responds, we hear feet shuffling down the tunnel to our room. I look at Figol and he nods at me. There's nothing to fear, yet.

Crisa looks at us. "My apologies. There is a person I wish you to meet and I wanted to avoid us all being seen together." Holding the reed torch, she waits at the entrance for the mystery man to arrive.

"Thank you for coming," we hear her say. Crisa reenters the room with another druid from the council. I'm wracking my brain to remember his name.

"Grahme, Figol, I'm sure you remember Finne, Guardian of Ankenet Starno." Finne nods his head at us tersely.

"Crisa, there may no longer be a need for this."

"If you trust Diardoc then you must have taken a blow to the head," Crisa says. "He is not looking out for you or your holy site. His coffers are all he cares about. Besides, we take no action tonight. We are only here to talk."

Finne takes a seat farthest from me around the fire and crosses his arms. I don't know what game Crisa is playing, but my patience is growing short.

"I grew up in the Darin city of Emain Macha," Crisa says.

Finne snorts in derision.

"Emain Macha is now the capitol of the Ulothins, but before they became a military power, it was the capital of my people, the Darin. For the last three hundred years, we Darin have felt the brunt of the Tusci's advances on our island. And for most of that time we kept the demon summoners from getting a foothold, until five years ago.

"They surprised the inhabitants of Laleah, by sailing into the city's port. Once inside, they loosed their demons. The foul creatures killed indiscriminately. Only after a full day of carnage would they allow the city leaders to swear fealty to them. Laleah is the ancestral home of the Ulothins. In one day, the impregnable, giant-made, stone-walled city fell."

"A giant-made city?" I prompt.

"In a last effort to keep humans at bay, the giants built two cities on Eriu and surrounded them with walls as high as four men. Needing to trade, they opened their gates to humans and were quickly outnumbered."

"It seems like the Elder Races never learned their lesson about humans," I say.

"Indeed," Crisa says. "The giants were the last of the elders to agree to leave the isles. Ever since, Drumanagh and Laleah were thought to be unassailable fortresses."

"The city did not defend itself?" I ask.

"None were ready for those horrors. I have no love for the city of Laleah, but no one deserves to be hunted in their own homes by demons. The Tusci's leader, Tuss Metiana, moved into the city and renamed it Diabolus. Since then, he has eliminated the city's leaders and pushed outward into the countryside."

114

"And their first target was my beloved Ankenet Starno," Finne interjects. "How am I to be a Druid Guardian without access to my holy site?"

Finne fidgets with his hands while keeping watch on the door.

Crisa looks at him. "I am sorry to say this in your presence, friend; after taking the city, they killed every druid they found. It was only because Finne raced here, trying to rally support from the other kingdoms that he was not subjected to those horrors."

Finne is bouncing his leg and beginning to sweat.

How would I react if Men-an-Tol was lost under my watch?

"They were especially interested in our great stone circles of Ardech and Cotypr," Crisa says. "For the stone circles enhance the demon summoner's power, allowing even more ferocious monstrosities to be called."

"Get to the point," Finne says.

"Just last month, we were able to raid Cotypr circle and kill the demon summoners before they could unleash their terrors. This past moonless night, we managed to kill the Tusci at Ardech circle as well. No Tusci dares walk alone in our lands any longer. It is only within the city that they still reside. Our intelligence tells us that there are less than fifty Tusci red robes within the city."

"Then why don't the people rebel?" I ask.

"There is always a summoner, a red robe, on duty in the guard tower. To attack the tower is to invite a demon within the walls. What they do to people . . ." Crisa shudders at the horror.

"And that is the problem for which we have no solution." Finne says. "Demons cannot cross water or solid stone circles. The city boasts two stone walls, one around the city proper and one around the inner city, where the Tusci reside," Crisa says.

"Any summoned demon would be trapped between the two stone walls, feasting on the residents of the city. It is that fear which keeps the people in line. And we have not been able to do anything about it," Finne adds.

"Since the Tusci have no foothold on Pretanni, it was my hope that you could share some wisdom that has so far escaped us," Crisa says.

"And now we don't need to worry about it," Finne interjects. "Diardoc has negotiated with them and Ankenet Starno will be returned to me."

Crisa stares dumbfounded at her peer. "Do you really believe he cares about Ankenet Starno?" She pauses to let the question hang. "Diardoc would happily sell your holy site to the Tusci if it means a favorable trade deal."

Finne points an accusing finger at Crisa. "Anach was right about you. Your Darin blood makes you hot-headed and always searching for a foe, even when there is none."

"Why did you come here tonight if not to court possible allies?" Crisa asks.

"To delay us," Figol says.

"Filthy liar!" Finne yells.

"He hopes to have us caught rebelling against the council," Figol says.

"Treacherous swine!" Crisa shouts. "I have risked my kinsman's blood for you."

Finne smiles triumphantly. "It's too late now, they are coming."

Crisa lets out a primal yell and readies her staff for attack, but Finne is out of the room, screaming like a child. Crisa looks at us. "I am sorry, I asked you here in good faith." She resolutely marches for the door.

"Wait," I say. "Leave us and deny whatever Finne charges."

"It's no use; even if we can make it back to the hall, we will still be seen leaving the building."

"Leave us be and we will not be here when the others come in."

Hope flashes in Crisa's eyes. "If you are still willing to help, meet me atop Komsit Lat, where the council was meeting today. No one will be able to surprise us there."

Wooden cups crash to the ground and surprised shouts inform us that whoever is coming is within the hall. She takes a moment to compose herself, then nods her agreement.

"Ready Figol, watch me closely." I picture a mole in my mind and slowly assume its shape.

"Gods above!" Crisa says in a low voice.

"Go!" Figol says to Crisa before he follows my lead and mimics my transformation.

I should have been standing closer to the wall when I did this.

I can't see well, but I can feel the vibrations from many footsteps. Figol is close behind. Reaching the dirt wall, we burrow into the earth beneath our bench. We continue digging until the cold night air greets us. There is no one about on this side of the hill. Figol and I change into tawny owls and silently flee for the safety of the tree line.

13

Forming an Alliance

The clouds part to give a clear view of the night sky. Ganares the centaur is giving chase in the sky to Cigni the swan while Tasiarn, the elven archer watches. How I miss Boswen in these times. No one was so learned about the night sky.

"Forgive me for my tardiness," Crisa says.

I rouse myself from my contemplations and scan the surroundings.

"Relax Grahme, we are alone."

"What happened with Finne?" I ask.

"After you two left, I kicked the dirt back to cover your escape hole and then sat and stared at the fire. When Diardoc's men came to apprehend us, I told them that I had been sitting there alone for a while, mulling over the news that the Tusci were going to gain a permanent foothold on our isle."

"What did Finne do?" Figol asks.

"He fumed and hollered and made wild accusations that you two had been in that very room only minutes before. I told the men that the strain of having failed at protecting his holy site has obviously worn on him."

"And they believed you?" Figol interjects.

"What choice did they have? You were not present and there is only one way in and out of the hall."

"You lied?" I ask. "A druid should never lie."

Crisa gives me a peculiar look. "I forget, on Pretanni you druids do not take part in statecraft as we do. You practice a more pure form of druidism perhaps, but we must face realities here. We must weigh our words for the political ripples they will cause. Unfortunately, that also means we must lie on occasion, though usually only to the kings." She smiles at me.

"I'm not sure if that makes it worse or better."

"Neither do I," she says. "We have a saying here, 'an honest king is as rare as an elf these days.' But come, I didn't ask you here to share our common wisdom with you. I have a more pressing matter to discuss."

"By all means, tell us what you will," I say. Figol already has his head down, wading into Crisa's thoughts.

"As I told you, we have beaten back the Tusci from our lands, but we lack the ability to take their city. Any approach we make causes demons to be summoned. The town walls prohibit the demons from turning back on the red robes. How have you kept your island free of the Tusci?"

"I know of no incursions upon Pretanni. But for Laleah, what happens if the wall is breached? Can the demons enter the city?"

"Yes, and their first targets would be the ones who summoned them to our world."

"And if the wall were part stone and part dirt, would that stop the demons?"

119

"No," Crisa says, confused. "It is only the stone circles that protect them. But Laleah has robust stone walls. There is no dirt."

"If we were able to replace part of the wall with dirt, the demon summoners would be defeated?"

"Maybe, but we would still have marauding demons within the city. In any case, I doubt you two will be able to undercut enough of the walls with your burrowing to make a difference."

"Leave that to us," I say as I smile smugly at Figol. "My next question is about the demon patrol. Do they attack every living thing or only people?"

"The Tusci have placed a crushed stone circle outside the city walls so that demons can't go wandering off. Somehow, they can sense if a human comes within that area. Otherwise, they remain in front of the city's gate."

"If the gate is breached, you can muster enough men to take the city?"

"We could but how do you suggest we do this?"

"Do you know of the giant's runes?" Figol asks.

Crisa looks from one of us to the other. "I know of them, but it is the firbolgs you should speak to if you want to know more."

"Firbolgs exist?" I ask.

"They do," Crisa says, confused at our questions. "Why do you ask about them?"

It's my turn to be cautious. "We have begun to study the runes and any knowledge I can bring back with me will be a boon to our efforts."

"It seems that we underestimate our Pretanni brothers and sisters. I sense deception, though I believe you tell me only truth."

"What do you mean?"

120

"It's fine Grahme, you do not need to tell me everything. Now, I have arranged a special meeting. It will not be interrupted by guards this time; I promise." She smiles at my apprehension. "If you will accompany me to Lia Fahil and we all receive our dooms from the seer, then I will tell you more of the firbolgs."

Figol nods his head, so I know Crisa can be trusted. "Then it is agreed. Until then, what do you know of the stars," I ask Crisa.

She answers with a relaxed laugh. "You really don't know much about us, do you? Below us is one of the sun caves, which we use to track the movement of the sun and stars. I dare say that few in your order know more about the sky than the newest of our novices."

"Boswen was very learned about the sky. He would tell me stories about Ganares the centaur, Tasiarn the elven archer and others" I say as I point them out above us.

"That's because Boswen was raised on Eriu."

"He was?"

"You didn't know?"

"Boswen kept many secrets, even when he didn't have to do so."

"He was really one of us after all," Crisa says. "Below us is Komsit Lat, equal days, in the old tongue and the oldest of the sun caves built by the firbolgs. This one allows the light of the sun to enter the tunnel and strike the back wall of the deepest room for only five days on either side of the equinoxes. The other two caves are built similarly, but they are aligned to the winter solstice. We are the timekeepers for the world."

"Can someone tell me what a firbolg is?" Figol asks.

"Firbolgs are typically halfway between human and giant in size. If you raise your hand as high as you can, that is about the height of a firbolg. Since the giants tend to pick on their smaller cousins, the firbolgs retreated to Eriu."

"It's a shame we are not closer to one of these dates. I would dearly love to see that phenomenon occur," Figol says.

"We don't have to wait until the equinox," Crisa says. "There are many observatories at Ammanti Krouka, and one of them is always receiving the light of Belenos. It was Eriu herself who convinced Queen Medb of the firbolgs to build them."

I look at Figol and I know exactly what he is thinking. Perhaps we can learn more of the Giant's runes. More than ever, I realize that we need him in our order; with or without his mental gift, he has a sharp mind.

"What does Ammanti Krouka mean?" Figol asks. I'm glad he asked, since my grasp on the old tongue is not great.

"It means the Old Woman's Mound, as the seer, Rhedna of the Sorrows lived there for several lifetimes," Crisa says. "Anach convinced her that her place was at the Lia Fahil, literally the 'stone of destiny'. Once she arrived, he pressed her to tell his fortune," Crisa smirks. "She told him that a person of great ability will follow him as our leader and he will come to nothing. He demanded another fortune, but the seer has remained silent ever since. To keep her is a reminder that he will be forgotten in the future, but to send her away is to admit that he made a mistake."

"It seems weak leaders are motivated by the smallest of desires," I say.

"Be careful, for she will tell your future tomorrow."

14

Chasing Prophecy

We made our camp well back in the woods away from the sun caves. The brisk wind brought with it a light dusting of snow on our lean-to. If not for that and our beds of pine branches we'd likely be frozen. Not liking the cold, Figol is up before midday for once. *Wait until he's a druid apprentice.*

"Why will that make a difference, Uncle?"

"Do you ever spend time in your own head?"

"Crisa is coming."

Crisa approaches us on horseback. "Good, you made it through night unscathed. I would ask you both to turn into birds and follow me. I don't know that anyone is looking for you, but it's best if you're not seen.

I look at my nephew. "What bird should we choose?"

"Ravens are common," Figol says.

"You may make a fine druid after all. Now follow my lead."

Crisa takes us south to the village of Lia Fahil. Figol and I land next to the River Bouwinda.

"Make sure you drink," I say. "Winter has a way of pulling water from you without you knowing." I turn to Crisa. "What if Anach finds us here?"

"I told you, I am the one responsible for running the village. Besides, Anach avoids this place ever since the seer moved here. He hates her, and probably fears her as well." She dismounts and points to a lone standing stone.

It is surrounded by two concentric earthen circles. Almost like a hill fort, but with only the upright stone inside.

"That is the Lia Fahil, the Stone of Destiny," Crisa says.

"Where is the seer?"

"Follow me. She only grants one doom to those who ask it of her. So be thoughtful about what you ask."

As we walk toward the stone, an old crone emerges from the mound adjacent to the circle. Despite her stooped back and frail frame, she gains on us.

"Be kind and slow your walk to that of this poor, old woman," she says. She looks up at me and her milky left eye strays off to the side. Her steps alternate between one long step with her left foot and a short one with her right. Despite this, she carries no walking stick.

"Revered old one, would you like the use of my staff?" I ask.

Thank you," she says while reaching out toward me. She grabs the staff and proceeds to hit us each on our backsides.

"What is that for?" Crisa asks.

The seer laughs. "Rhedna of the Sorrows needs no cane. But be quick, the air is cold and cuts right through me."

"Dear mother, I am Crisa and—"

124

"The former protector of the Auga Sawels . . . ."

"I am the current protector of the sun caves," Crisa corrects the seer. "I ask not where I will end up next," Crisa adds quickly, "But whether we will be successful at liberating Laleah."

"A pity, where you will end up would tell you so much more."

"I have no use for my future to be told," I say. "I wish to know if the Tusci will be driven out of Laleah."

"Too late," the crone cackles. "The question has already been asked by another." She waggles her finger at me. "Make your way to the Lia Fahil stone. One at a time, touch the stone and silently voice your true question. I will pronounce your dooms at the king's seat," Rhedna says.

There are many long, thin rocks embedded in the ground and radiating outward from the Stone of Destiny. The stone itself is no taller than me. It isn't an impressive sight, yet each of us waits for someone to make a move.

"We can't stand around idly all day," Crisa says. She places her hand on the stone and bows her head. That finished, she looks at us. "It doesn't burn. Just place your hand on the stone like such," she touches the stone again, "And let us be off to receive our fortunes."

"You've done this before?" I ask.

"Never, each person receives only a single doom from Rhedna. Otherwise Anach would be back every day until he received a doom that he liked."

Figol approaches the stone. Crisa theatrically lifts her hands as she leaves the stone.

"Hurry Grahme, it is believed that those who make the seer wait receive the worst fortunes."

I hurriedly place my hand on the cold stone. I was expecting there to be some sense of power in the stone. Instead, my hand surrenders heat to the cold, damp surface. The other two are already heading back to Rhedna, leaving me behind. Not wanting to look undignified by running, I become a tawny owl and soar in front of the other two.

"Now you have but to wait a few minutes before Rhedna of the Sorrows can foretell your fates." The old seer says, nodding in a good-natured fashion.

The wind picks up and goosebumps form on my arms and legs. The more naïve would believe it to be the seer's power, but as a man of nature, I know better. Slowly I rub my arms, wishing for the audience to be over.

Rhedna looks up sharply at Figol and hisses. "Can you not wait a few minutes to know my mind?" She says in a dangerously low tone. "I will send you all away if you dare test me again."

"We mean no disrespect," Crisa says, confused. Figol's blush reveals his shame. Poor Crisa, she is the only one who doesn't understand what has transpired.

Before anyone can speak, Rhedna points at Crisa. "You wish to know if taking them to meet Gortor is warranted. You also wish to know if the city can be saved. And you wish to know what post you will obtain on the council of druids."

"Holy one, I wish to know about Laleah."

"We both know that I speak the truth," Rhedna says. She chuckles, but it turns into a fit of coughing. Her tangled gray curls obscure her face. She sweeps the unruly hair back and exposes her milky eye. "Unexpected allies work in your favor."

She stares at each of us and purses her lips before giving us an all-knowing smile. "Muddled are your questions. Two answers are required on this occasion, I think. Of the nearer, yes and no, of the further, success, like beauty is seen differently by all."

"Ah, thank you wise one?" I say.

She chuckles at me. "Rarely do I see as clearly as I do this day. Since you showed this old woman kindness, I will grant an additional boon. For those who did as I bid, one will become outlaw, one will become leader and one will become king before the next blood moon. Now be off and seek your fates." Rhedna pulls her mantle tight around her shoulders as she ambles back to her mound.

Crisa and Figol also look surprised and confused. "When will the next blood moon occur?" I ask at last.

"We will find out at Ammanti Krouka," Crisa says. "There are no more answers to be had here."

Crisa signals us to land and retake our human forms. The road winds its way through the hills, but now we have reached the forest's edge. The hazelnuts were devoured weeks ago by the wild boars, and now only the hoof prints remain.

"She's nervous about something," Figol says.

"Then the barbs of the blackthorn and holly are not the only worries we have."

"I don't like this forest."

"That's because there are no bird calls, no squirrels. Do you know why that is?" I ask.

"The forest is dead?"

I shake my head. "No Figol, we are surrounded." I grab Figol's arm before he can run.

"That you are," a man says as he appears from behind the hemlock bush next to Figol. The man has shaggy black hair, making his head look wider, like a wolf. His ears are unnaturally cupped forward and the tops end in a point. Most ominous are his lips. They are stained black, which only highlight his yellowish teeth. He sniffs at us as the rest of his pack emerges from cover.

"Well met, Mortas," Crisa says.

We're surrounded by a dozen wolf-like men. Their intense eyes never stray from us. They draw back at any unexpected move we make. I have become a wolf on many occasions, but never have I seen men act so similar to a wolf pack. They are strange, yet familiar.

"Is this all of your band?" Crisa asks.

"There are four in front and two each on the sides. I bring you twenty in all, as promised. They are my best."

"I am Grahme, a druid from Pretanni," I say as I stretch out my hand.

Mortas grabs it and pulls me in close. He sniffs my chest before smiling and releasing me. "When did you discover our presence?"

"I felt uneasy as soon as we reached the woods, though I never saw or heard any of your band."

"Grahme, these are the feared manwolves of Ossory. There are no better trackers in all the world."

I turn and nod to those around me, keeping my eyes below their gaze. "To stare at them is to challenge them," I tell Figol.

Each has three throwing daggers on each leg. Above them are two long, curved knives with thick bellies. These men may not be able to run down a deer, but the daggers will weaken their prey and the knives will undeniably end the hunt.

Figol coughs, drawing attention to himself.

"This is my nephew, Figol. He is learning how to become a druid. We are proud to make your acquaintance."

Mortas raises his hands for silence. In a solemn tone he says, "We accept you and call you wolf friends." The men around us mew their acceptance.

"Tonight they will howl at Aine, their goddess, and tell her of this bond," Crisa says. "The firbolgs won't like it, but it can't be helped."

"Osion!" Mortas calls. "Put that away."

The young man pulls back the pouch from Figol's hand. "But they won't be able to keep up," he complains.

"And you have managed to explain wolfsbane to him?"

"I was going to tell him."

"Wolfsbane is a deadly poison," I say.

"Osion, tell our guests of wolfsbane."

> Wolfsbane, Wolf's blessing
> One fatigue is lessening
> Two for pain
> Will keep you sane
> If three are taken
> Madness awakens
> Four or more
> You find death's door.

Mortas nods his head at his charge. "In small doses, it aids the body. What young Osion did not tell your Figol is that you crack the seed with your teeth, and take only a lick of it then spit it out. If you take more than three licks, or worse, swallow it, it is always fatal."

Figol quickly places his hands behind his back. Osion glares at him.

"I've never heard of anyone taking wolfsbane," I say.

"In small doses, it counters fatigue, allowing us to run for hours," Mortas says.

"It is rude to refuse a gift," I say to Figol. "Please, let us have the seeds, we thank you and we will be careful."

Mollified, Osion gives each of us a small pouch.

"Figol and I will run with you, but we won't need your seeds. Crisa, you better start now. Your horse won't like what I have in mind."

"Then keep up," Crisa says. She directs her horse back to the road with her knee before asking for a canter.

The Manwolves watch as first me, then Figol change into wolves. The men cheer wildly and it is only on his third try that Mortas can be heard over his people. "We run!" Mortas shouts before giving chase to Crisa.

15

Illuminating Discoveries

Crisa raises her hand, telling us to stop as we enter the valley. The wolf men ignore her and race up the closest hill. Even after five hours of running, they refuse to walk up the slopes. Once atop, the men cup their hands and start howling at the slender crescent of Aine in the evening sky.

"That was better than I could have hoped for," Crisa says. "The firbolgs are a sedate race, and they can barely abide the manwolves."

"Why did you bring us here?"

"You couldn't very well stay underneath Anach's nose, now could you? Besides, the firbolgs are an ancient race that few have ever met."

She bows to the pale-skinned man coming down the adjacent hill to greet us. "Bow to him," she whispers. What Figol and I lack in timeliness we make up for in the length of our bow.

"I wish to enlist the firbolg's aid," Crisa says before rising.

The firbolg looks in every way human, except for his height. I doubt I could touch the top of his head without jumping. He wears a simple tunic and kilt with a greenish disk attached to a thin leather cord around his neck. His brown hair is pulled neatly back into the shortest of ponytails.

"Crisa," he says, barely bowing his head. "Who do you bring to this place?" He eyes us uneasily.

"Well met Gortor," Crisa says in a measured tone. "I present to you Grahme, Lord Protector of Men-an-Tol of Pretanni and his nephew, Figol."

"Protector of Men-an-Tol?" he says in slow, well annunciated tones. "What of the Si?"

"The Si?"

"Yes, when our peoples last spoke, they lived in the Arden. How do they fare?"

"Noble one, I have walked through the Arden, but I have never met the Si."

A frown flickers across his dispassionate face. "That is a shame, their beech filled homeland is lovely at all times of the year."

"Beech trees?" I ask. "I skirted across a long line with such trees. It seemed foreboding, so I did not enter."

Gortor nods and smiles. "Bless Fagus for watching over our friends. If they had fallen into history, then the beech wall would be broken up with other trees."

"Do you speak often with the Si?" Crisa asks.

"Our peoples have not spoken in four hundred and fifteen years."

"But you still call them friends?" I ask.

"We are both peoples of the forest," Gortor replies.

Crisa takes Gortor's hand in hers. "My dear Gortor, we druids are caretakers of the forests as well. Our people in Laleah have been overrun by the cruel demon summoners. Now is the time to liberate the city. Will you join us?"

Gortor refuses to look at Crisa as he rests his free hand on her shoulder. "As you asked, dear one, I took your arguments to the Galion and spoke as well as I am able. The wisdom of the peers is that this is not our fight. We are few in number and we cannot risk ourselves for others' affairs."

"Was it Arinsal?" Crisa demands. "She is not the Donnan, you are."

Gortor looks up to the sky, his anguish palpable. "I can say nothing other than the council has decided. What is said in private must remain so."

"Then what hope do we have for Laleah?"

"Noble one," Figol begins. "Do you know the runes of the giants?"

Gortor smiles kindly. "Young Figol, we are giantkin."

"My Uncle and several other Lord Protectors are studying the runes. Could you instruct us on their meanings?"

"The runes are inherently powerful." We wait for our host to say more, but he is content to stand in silence.

Figol looks at me and his eyes bulge. He is not subtle, but I know what he wants.

"Noble one, we too are in need of your aid," before he can reply I continue my plea. "It is only a matter of time before the mainland kingdoms invade further into Pretanni. They have mastered the runestones. When the attack comes, we will be outnumbered. If we cannot match them in this magic, what hope do we have? And if Pretanni falls, Eriu will certainly follow."

"You speak well," Gortor says as he stares back at us placidly. And once again silence reins, punctuated only by the renewed calls of the manwolves.

133

"They are only here one night," Crisa says. She lays her head in the crook of the firbolg's elbow. "There are no clouds in the west. Could you show us one of your observatories?"

Gortor practically melts in Crisa's hands. "Of course," he says.

There are several dozen long barrows atop the hills, but Gortor knows the one he wants. Without waiting, he treks up a small rise to the smallest structure. He hands Crisa a reed and claps his hands, uttering something under his breath. Flame springs from the reed head. He retakes the torch and beckons us to follow.

At the end of the tunnel, he hides the reed torch in a small alcove, darkening the cave. The warm rays of Belenos enter into the tunnel and stretch toward us. The walls take on a rosy hue. Figol and I stand on the opposite side of the strike stone. In its center, there is a small, horizontal slit on the otherwise smooth stone.

The red glow reaches our chamber and the direct sunlight hits the stone, illuminating the room we are in. The light dances across the walls, making them look as if the walls are moving.

"Uncle!" Figol shouts. "Put the ring in the stone." Figol shakes me out of my trance. "Uncle," he points at the horizontal hole. "Put the ring in there!"

I feel an overwhelming urge to follow Figol's command. I place the ring in the stone and the giant script appears on the walls around us.

"Garavoge's blessing," Gortor says with a trembling voice. He tries to embrace the wall, but his shadow blocks out the light. Not sure what to do with himself, he falls to his knees.

"Quick, copy whatever symbols you see in the dirt," I say.

Crisa stares wide-eyed at Gortor, then the walls. Before any runes can be copied, the light rises off the stone and retreats along the roof of the tunnel. Everyone is quiet as we try to absorb the experience.

"Gortor, your torch," Crisa says. The firbolg reaches within the alcove and grabs the torch. The rough rock walls are visible, but the glyphs are not. "Follow me," he says in a husky voice.

I grab Figol's arm and we let the others get ahead of us. "Why is he crying?"

"His thoughts were on how this Garavoge left a blessing written upon the walls of these long barrows, but it was lost after Eriu's death. Her ring, the small hole on the stone, it all just made sense."

"Come with me," Gortor calls as he leaves the cave. Once in the open, the night air cools quickly since Belenos has taken his leave. It won't be long before we can see our breath. We follow Gortor as he heads into the forest. He presses on, never adhering to any path as he takes us deeper and deeper. He walks under two majestic oaks and wedges his torch in a rock just past the trees.

"It looks like a smaller version of our Nemeton Dywyll Derw," I say.

"It was we who introduced the elves to the power of the arbor grove."

"Is this the meeting spot of the Galion?" Crisa asks.

"It is," Gortor says. "And I will be justly chastised if any should know that I brought you here."

"We should leave then," Crisa says.

"No, I need Nemetona's aid at a time like this. Grahme, was that Eriu's ring that you placed on the strike stone?"

"It was."

Gortor braces himself on the central rock. "It has been lost for over eight hundred years."

I glance at Crisa, not sure how much to reveal. "It was found on Pretanni and a small band of druids have protected it since her passing."

Crisa looks ready to explode.

Figol has his head down, already influencing the others. "Where has it been all this time?" Crisa demands, not quite accusing me.

"That can wait," Gortor says. "We all have secrets and I doubt Grahme can say much more about the ring."

"It must remain here, on Eriu," she demands.

"That was our plan," I volunteer. "But I refuse to surrender it to Anach." Fearing a falling out with Crisa, I change the subject. "Gortor, are those giant runes written on the walls of the cave?"

"They are," he says.

The three of us share exasperated looks as Gortor has once again gone silent.

"What do they say?" Figol asks.

Gortor ignores Figol's question. "Nemetona, aid your humble servant." The firbolg lowers his head upon the central rock, waiting for a benediction. "In the time of Garavoge," he begins. "Eriu befriended our great leader and begged to learn our ways. She and her druids helped us build this place, Ammanti Krouka. These hills did not exist as you see them today. The Emerald Druids summoned hundreds of earth elementals over the months to build these hills. Upon them are nineteen observatories which mark every day of the year. No longer must we wait for a solstice or equinox to correct our counting of days."

"Everyday?" Crisa asks. "But how can so few observatories count hundreds of days?"

"Some allow Belenos in for more days than others. It is only on the most important days that the long barrows are so shrewdly hewn."

"What do the symbols say?" I ask.

"They are a song that Eriu would sing in our tongue to us. We firbolgs are not a demonstrative race. In her time, no firbolg would agree to sing, for their voices were rough and uncultured compared to hers. She convinced Garavoge to have them written within our observatories. To honor Eriu, Garavoge made the symbols only visible by the reflected light of her ring. What he did not foresee was what would happen when she passed. Within three generations, no firbolg could recite the song."

"No one alive today knows the words to the song?" Crisa asks.

"Not for eight hundred years have we known," Gortor says. "I tell you this so that you may understand what that ring would mean to my people. I must ask you Grahme, will you give up the ring?"

"Thank you for sharing that, Gortor."

How do I possibly tell him no?

"Figol and I were sent here to start a friendship with the Emerald Druids. My plan was to offer the ring as a sign of good faith between druids." Gortor's countenance falls. "But I refuse to surrender the ring to that hateful man. We have agreed to help liberate Laleah in hope that that will bring goodwill. Could you teach us your runes if I give you the ring? This way we all gain something."

Gortor hugs the central stone. "Teaching you our runes cannot be done without a decree from the Galion. As the Donnan, I have sworn to uphold our ways no matter the cost to me. The council will never allow the runes to be taught to men. I tell you this so you know the cost to me. I will teach you a rune that you can use in the battle against the demons."

"For one rune, you wish me to give up the ring?" I ask.

"Grahme, Protector of Men-an-Tol, hear me. If you prove to be honorable, I will instruct you further in our magic, even at tremendous cost to me."

Figol nods his head slightly.

I inhale deeply and pray to the gods that my mind can be calm. I look at Crisa and Gortor. "I am willing to take you at your word." I hand the ring over to Gortor. "What does this rune mean?" I draw *hahgel* in the dirt. I knew nothing of the firbolgs before coming to this island. I need to gauge whether Gortor is as honest as he seems.

16

Onward, to Battle

Crisa roughly shakes me awake. Our fire has gone out and the bone-numbing chill of a clear winter's night has set in.

"Come quick," she says. "Gortor wants to show us something."

Gortor's pale skin is the only thing easily seen in the light of Aine, two days past her full glory. He waves us to follow as he scurries up a different path than before. We are in front of an entrance to different observatory.

"Aine will set very soon," Gortor says in a whisper. "If we hurry, perhaps her light will be bright enough to reflect off the strike stone."

"Won't the other firbolgs see us?" I ask.

"No, though Aine is beautiful, her glow diminishes the light of our ancestors. On nights like this, we sleep knowing that we are bathed in the goddess's light."

Too tired to argue, we follow him to the back chamber. The tunnel brightens, but there is no solid beam of light creeping along the floor. The strike stone brightens and we can see each other's outlines, but nothing on the walls.

Deflated, we march out one after the other. "It was too much to hope for," Gortor says. "I apologize for waking you."

I wave his words away. "It is nothing and the night sky is quite beautiful."

"We have many stories in our history tied to the night sky," Gortor says. "It takes a full year to learn our history."

"Gortor is the Donnan, the head history keeper for his people," Crisa says. "They place tremendous stock in the knowledge of their ancestors."

"'The sky is full' is a common lament among my people." Gortor says. "All the stars in the sky have been accounted for and we can record no new history." He looks up at the stars. "It was in the time of Garavoge and Eriu that continuing our history in song was begun. But it was lost after her passing. Since then, we have no way of being remembered."

"This is why the song is so important to you," Crisa says, patting his back.

"Yes, we cannot go forward as a people without it. I had hoped to collect another line of the song tonight, but it seems Aine's light will not be strong enough."

"How could your people forget a song that important?"

"When Garavoge died, Eriu refused to sing the song. She promised to preserve it in the places most sacred to us."

"Didn't you get the song with the setting of Belenos?" I ask.

"No, we received but a single line. With Aine's light unequal to the task, this too will take an entire year to learn."

"How your people will revere you, now that you have the ring and will soon have the song," Crisa says.

"I will not tell them, not yet."

"Why?" I ask.

"If I tell them, I must mention the ring and the bargain which was struck. Now I do not feel angry in the least for our deal, but others might find fault."

"Could you lose your place as Donnan?" Crisa asks.

"I will most assuredly lose it, unless I can provide the song of Garavoge."

"Is it so terrible to lose your place?" I ask.

Gortor smiles. "We are an old race, filled with stories of heroes past. I do not think I am overly vain, but I wish to be remembered. As I said, 'the sky is full,' so to be remembered means we must learn a new way to keep track of our ancestors."

"Then how will you teach us the runes, if no one else can know?" Crisa asks.

"I fear the teaching will not be easy or quick."

"Can you not scratch each symbol down on tree bark and tell us how to pronounce them?" I ask.

"Each rune has a history. You must know the history to know the rune."

Figol shoots me an exasperated look. I start to smile until I see Crisa looking at me. I cough into my fist, then rub my hands together for warmth.

"Belenos will be rising soon," Crisa points to the false dawn. "We should not be seen together, nor should we be seen up here."

"Can't we get another rune at an observatory facing the rising Belenos?" I ask.

Gortor looks conflicted. "We could, possibly, but we would most definitely be discovered."

"Until Gortor has the whole song, it's too risky," Crisa says.

"I am sorry Grahme, but Crisa is right. If we are spotted by my people, all lessons will be halted."

"Then you go, Gortor, get another line if you can this morning," Crisa says. "Once the song is complete, then you will be free to teach us."

Gortor looks to me and I nod my head. We watch as he disappears down the opposite side of the hill.

"It will take forever to learn about the runes," Figol says.

"Perhaps, but we've sealed an alliance of sorts with Gortor," I say.

"Does that count for our quest?"

I laugh. "I doubt an alliance with one member of the firbolgs is enough, though the knowledge we'll eventually gain will be invaluable."

"To think, Eriu's ring has been returned and none save one of her druids knows of it," Crisa says.

"I could have surrendered it to Anach." I give her a sly smile.

"You could have given it to me."

"And what would you have done with it? Give it to Anach?"

"Hah, no chance of that," she says. "I would have used it to become the new Druid Queen of Eriu."

"I see, and how would you have done that?"

Crisa chuckles, "You Pretanni druids, you really don't know anything about the wider world. With the ring, I could have insisted on a vote for a new head druid, and with the Eriu's ring, no one would have denied my bid."

"You can revote whenever you wish?" I ask, astounded.

"Of course, what would you prefer, duels to the death?"

142

"Can we get somewhere warm?" Figol asks.

"Yes, of course," Crisa says. She opens her mantle and pulls Figol in tight with her. "We can't have you delicate Pretanni druids catching a sickness in our rugged lands."

Figol speaks up before I can refute Crisa's swipe. "You both are missing the point. With or without the ring, the knowledge of the runes will make you both leading figures on your islands."

Crisa and I look at each other, eyes raised.

"I believe young Figol has the best take on this," Crisa says.

"That's good," Figol replies, "Because we have company." He points to Mortas and his pack racing toward us.

"Well met," Crisa says. "How was your hunting last night?"

Mortas nods at us. "It was not good. We found no prey animals worth hunting."

"I'm not surprised, after your baying at Aine last night."

"Are we ready to go north today?"

"You should go without us. We will be delayed here another day."

"Then we will stay," Mortas says. "I see that you do not want us to stay. Must you talk to the longwinded one again?"

"It's not that," I say. "We have been given a new weapon to use against the demons, and we must prepare them."

"What are they?" Mortas and his fianna press tighter, eager to see.

"We must prepare them. That is why we need a day."

"If we go north, we are as likely to be hunted as we are to be embraced as fighters for the cause. We will not leave without druids to vouchsafe for us."

"Then you and your fianna can help us," I say. "We need to leave this area, so we are not seen by the firbolgs, and we need river rocks."

"River Ethlin is a short run north of here," Mortas says.

"Will there be firbolgs there?" I ask Crisa.

"Not if we run around and howl," Mortas says, smirking.

"Then lead the way." Before the manwolves can ask, I transform into a wolf. They break into celebratory howls, even as they begin their run.

It is midday and the manwolves' excitement has waned. Walking in frigid water will do that, even to the most ardent. Figol, having stolen the knowledge from Gortor, teaches us a different ritual than what was known to Hedred. Imparting the magic into the rocks is now a much quicker process. There are about a hundred stones imbued with magic and twice that many left.

"We have scoured the river for an hour's run in both directions. How many more of these rocks do you need?"

"This will be plenty," I say.

"Good, for we are cold and we do not understand what sling stones will do against demons."

"Mortas," Crisa says. "Could you and your men provide a midday meal for us?"

"Yes, and we will demonstrate how to use these rocks after our meal," I add.

Mortas smiles at the thought of the hunt. He organizes his men and they bound off into the forest.

"You have a dedicated following in them," Crisa says once we three are left alone.

"I could teach you to animorph," I offer.

Crisa laughs. "Let's defeat the Tusci's demons and liberate Laleah first."

"Watch and behold what these rocks can do." I hurl a stone into the air and yell "*hahgel.*" It glides along and hits the ground, having done exactly nothing. The manwolves laugh.

I look at Figol. "We can't have another one fail."

He looks over the rocks and selects an orangish colored rock. "This one will work." He hands it over to me and I try not to show fear. I toss it toward the first stone and yell *hahgel* again. This time a hailstorm erupts and peppers the grass with small icy balls.

"Osion," Mortas says, "Bring those back to us."

"And bring back the original stone, if you see it," I call.

Osion dutifully brings back several hailstones and the defective rock. The manwolves marvel at the hail while Crisa, Figol and I inspect the rock.

"This line here should be straight, not wavy," Figol says.

"That's my work," Crisa says. "It's good to know how exacting I need to be."

"How does this help us?" Mortas asks. "Will this hurt a demon?"

"It will be like the midges are to us," Crisa says. "It will not harm, but it will annoy them. Use these to infuriate them and they will be distracted from what they are supposed to be doing."

"We wish to experience your magic first hand," Mortas says. "Throw one at us."

"I can do better than that," I say. "Osion, come here and I will show you what to do."

The manwolf smiles nervously at me.

"Anyone can use the rocks once the ritual is complete."

Osion has to be pushed forward by his pack mates.

"There is nothing to fear," I say. "Simply pick the stone up and toss it in their direction. Once it is in the air, say '*hahgel*' and the hailstorm will begin."

"What if I don't say anything?"

"Then I suspect they will throw the rock back at you." I hand him a rock. "Would you rather I do it?"

"No." Osion throws it high into the air and shouts out the word. The manwolves shield their heads from the falling hail and are equal parts yelping in pain and howling in laughter.

"Now I try," Mortas says. The rest of his men also demand the honor.

"We have made enough for each of you to carry ten stones. You may do with yours as you wish."

"We all get stones?" Mortas says.

"Yes, I think you and your men will need them more so than we will."

The pack surrounds the pile and grabs all they can. Once the stones are gone, they howl until their voices grow hoarse.

"You should get started going north," I tell Crisa. "Your horse will not appreciate having two wolves and a bunch of crazy men running too close behind."

17

Agents of Action

Just after midday on our fourth day of travel, we reach the outskirts of Emain Macha. There are nine druids in their makeshift camp, and each is trying to do less than the others.

"Dasha, are the men ready?" Crisa asks primly as she dismounts. None of the druids rise in way of greeting. There is no fire, nor wood collected. *What do the druids here do with their time?*

"Everyone is here, save Huntas."

"What is he doing?"

"He's about halfway to passing out in the mead hall, I'd wager." Dasha's fellow druids laugh at his weak joke.

"Send someone to get him," Crisa says. "If he's too drunk, then leave him. We will not wait for long before we're off. In the meantime, let me introduce you to the Lord Protector of Men-an-Tol."

"I thought Boswen was an old man?" One of the druids shouts.

"He was. Grahme Fairweather is the newest Lord on Pretanni. With him are his nephew, Figol and these," she walks over to the Mortas and his pack, "are the famed manwolves of Ossory."

"Those feral dogs?" Dasha asks.

Mortas restrains one of his men, Logun I believe, from approaching the druid.

"They will be risking their lives along with us to liberate our brothers and sisters, so show some respect," Crisa says.

Dasha smiles. "See, they need a woman to protect them."

In a blur Logun closes the gap and punches Dasha in the gut.

"Logun—" Crisa shouts.

Both men's heads dip down. Dasha screams out in pain. He rises, holding the bloody left side of his head. Logun, grinning, walks back to Mortas and spits out part of an ear. "Manwolves never retreat from a fight."

The druids rise and form a pack of their own. They grab their staves and spread out so each has room to wield their weapon.

"Now!" Mortas says. He and all of his men toss runestones in the air and as one they shout "*hahgel*." Hail pummels the druids and they quickly break and run for cover in the forest.

Now it's the manwolves' turn to laugh. Figol is quick to hide his smirk.

"Not exactly impressive resolve, is it?" I ask no one in particular.

"I am glad you used the runestones," Crisa says to the manwolves. "Now Dasha and his men will know how to use them in battle."

"Are they going to make their own?" Osion calls.

"No, we made runestones for them as well as for you."

The druids have fanned out at the edge of the forest. None of them is willing to come out in the open.

What good are these feckless louts?

"Mortas, the druids will need a way to protect themselves in battle. Will you and your men retrieve more stones?"

"Let them get their own stones," Mortas glares.

"We don't need childish pranks," Dasha says, while applying powdered clay to his ear to stop the bleeding. "We command real power." He begins shouting out the old tongue and waving his hands.

The ground beneath us begins to rumble. We're all forced to flee from the path. An earth elemental, twice my height rises from the ground from where we stood.

"Long knives!" Mortas shouts and his pack are on the elemental in a heartbeat. Dirt goes flying in large clumps as the manwolves make quick work of the animated earth.

"Got anything better?" Mortas asks.

"You defeated a stationary elemental, true," Crisa says. "But notice that all the druids have their slings out. They could have brained the lot of you if they wished."

"Mortas," I inject. "Will you and your men agree to get more stones for Figol and myself? We have need of different runestones for ourselves."

"You swear that none of these stones will go to them?" He points without looking at the druids.

"I do."

"Then you shall have your stones."

For two days the uneasy truce holds. It's unfair to make the manwolves do all the hunting, but it keeps the peace. Roisair's camp is centered in a clearing. An enormous tent dwarfs all other structures.

A closer inspection reveals that it is covered in wet leaves. The watch is too busy playing dice to note our passage. This is not a promising sight.

That tent has been up since before leaf fall.

Crisa calls us together. "I will go first so as to not rouse the watch."

Mortas' eyes light up with mischief. "Too late for that I'm afraid." He gives three short mewing sounds and his men silently spread out in the forest. He clears the bend in the road and stands in front of the guard.

"Halt!" One man manages to get out before nineteen manwolves simultaneously leave the cover of the forest. As one, they howl into the midday sun. One of the guards falls backward over the dice table, followed by his spear. He's lucky not to have impaled himself. The second man steps clear of his downed comrade and levels a spear at Mortas.

From within the camp, men are racing to the gate. The nervous guard rotates his spear left and right, not knowing where the first threat will come from. Mortas and his manwolves advance slowly, long knives in both hands.

Crisa walks up behind Mortas and places a restraining hand on his shoulder. He mews once and his men relax. "Peace!" She cries. "Throwing dice is a poor way to keep guard. Had we ill intent, you would be dead by now."

"Thank you revered one," the man says. "We were told to be on the lookout for you and a band of druids."

"They are coming," she says. "You'll likely hear them well before you see them."

"They are not with you?"

Crisa's voice flattens. "Even mounted, they couldn't keep up. Is Roisair within?"

"Yes, holy one. He will be in the large tent."

We walk past the chastised guards and enter the camp.

The tent's central post is the height of three men, but the outer posts are no taller than me. The gray wool sags between the posts with leaves and pine needles resting in the dips. As I look closer, I notice moss beginning to grow. I have seen nothing to give me hope of success.

"As we agreed," Crisa says, "Mortas, Grahme and Figol will accompany me to see Roisair. The rest of you, don't start any fights; you and your men will be greatly outnumbered."

"Logun, take the men outside of camp," Mortas says. "To stay is to invite trouble." He nods his head at Crisa.

One more crisis between allies averted.

The four of us make our way to the central tent. The men here are experts at finding ways to waste away the time without taxing themselves. No doubt, they've all experienced war before.

A tall, thin man with a brilliant blue cloak has his back to us. His right arm ends with a smooth bronze cast in place of his hand. He bangs it against the table, giving it a fresh dent. "Without Crisa and her druids, we'll have to count on a direct assault."

"That would be suicide," another man says.

"It would, but you don't have to worry about it now," Crisa says.

The men look up from their table, noticing us at last. The tall man turns and looks at each of us with his piercing green eyes. His cast extends up to his elbow.

"Crisa, it's good that you are back," he says. "Do you have a sufficient number of druids for our attack?"

151

"I believe so, Roisair. I also bring additional allies to you." She places a hand on my shoulder, "This is Grahme Fairweather, Lord Protector of Men-an-Tol and one of the nine ruling druids from Pretanni." She turns to her left. "And this is Mortas, a fianna leader of the Manwolves of Ossory."

"Boswen is dead?" Roisair asks.

"I dueled him and won."

Why does everyone here ask about Boswen?

"I see. The Pretanni druid can stay, but I won't have any man who mutilates himself to be more like an animal around my deliberations."

Glancing at Figol, I see that he already has his eyes cast downward, no doubt calming those within the tent.

Mortas spits at Roisair's feet. "Wolves are far better creatures than men."

"Mortas . . ." Crisa says. "We spoke about this."

They lock eyes with one another. "I will go, because that is what is needed if we are to be successful," he says before raising his voice. "On the field of battle, you will see that one manwolf is worth ten of your warriors." He leaves without waiting for a reply.

"You're late." Roisair says. "Why do you involve him," he nods toward me, "with our affairs?" He turns back to his table. We gather around it and see a detailed map of the city.

"I have come to establish better ties between our islands." I gaze meaningfully at the map of the high walled city. "Can you not attack by the harbor by ship?"

"We could, but they would release their demons within the city and thousands would die," Roisair replies.

"In that case, it seems that you will need all the help you can get to breach these walls. Figol and I should be able to help with that, but if you do not wish our aid, we will go."

"You will stay for as long as I wish it, druid," Roisair sounds bored. "In case you have not noticed, you're surrounded."

I give the fool a slight smile. "Really? I can render you," I circle my hand around the tent "and your men helpless whenever I wish."

"By boring us with useless prattle?" He gives me a forced grin.

Gently, I place my hand on his shoulder and turn him to face me. "I can have my staff across your throat anytime I wish, and neither you, nor anyone in this tent can stop me."

Roisair pauses for a second before letting out an explosive laugh. "You remind me of a badger. A fearsome bluff is all you have."

I open my pouch of runestones. Roisair and his men watch as I search for the one I need. What starts out as grunts of derision have grown to a full laugh at my expense.

There it is, the stone with the lightning symbol.

Looking up at them, I grin wide enough for my teeth to show. It causes even more laughter. Tossing the runestone in the air, I close my eyes and duck before shouting *"sigel."* I cover my eyes with my hands, yet still I see my bones outlined in eerie red flesh.

The men and women around me shout, literally in a blind panic. The commotion is bound to draw men to the tent. I check my pouch, and just for good measure, I toss several *hahgel* runestones in the air and have hail batter the confused men.

While screams warning of an attack ring out around me, I walk over to Roisair, who is still bent over with his good arm gripping the table. I place my staff across the front of his neck and with a slow, constant pressure I encourage him to rise.

In his ear I ask in a low voice, "Do you still mistake me for a badger?"

His men outside the tent arrive with spears, knives and axes. A man calls, "my Lord?" They see me and my staff and the tension builds.

Maybe this wasn't the best idea.

Roisair pats my staff with his brass cast and I release him.

"All is well." He raises his mutilated arm toward the soldier's voice. "Quiet!" he roars and his men obey. After rubbing his eyes, he emits a boisterous laugh. "That was quite a display." Roisair bangs the brass cast against the table and everyone turns their bleary eyes toward him.

"I hereby name Grahme Fairweather, Protector of Men-an-Tol a friend to me and my army." The guards lower their weapons. "Further, I name him the *Brokko kom Gresman*, the badger with bite." The others, still reeling from the blindness, are not amused. Figol smiles at me, his vision also not affected by the runestone.

Is he ever not in my head?

"Let's take this to my private quarters," Roisair says.

Roisair's quarters look no different than any other wool tent in the camp. At least he chooses to live as his men do. He directs us to sit on the stumps by the fire.

"How many men did you bring with you?" Roisair asks me.

"We came here to make friends, not invade. We are the only ones."

"Don't get me wrong, your tricks were impressive, but they will be useless against demons."

"My student can make many more of these runestones for the battle."

"What else can they do?" He asks, excited.

"I can create a fireball, cause a hail storm, call forth light or freeze water instantly."

"The fireball will not affect the demons and the hail will only distract at best."

"But the spell I think most useful," I continue as if he didn't interrupt me, "Is the *ehar* rune, which will turn stone into dirt."

"That would be very useful if we could get close enough to throw them at the walls." He absently removes his bronze cast and sets it on the small table between us. His arm is pink and sweaty, but whatever the injury to his arm, it was suffered long ago. "But if the demons don't get you, their archers along the walls will. Mark my words, they have no honor and they will use their bows against humans."

"I have encountered dishonorable men before."

"We would need some form of subterfuge for your runestones to work."

"That is what I was going to suggest," Crisa says.

I look over at her, bemused. The plan was mine.

"I can only spare twenty men to protect you while you do your work," Roisair says. "I'll need the rest for a frontal assault on the main gate. One way or another, we will enter the city." He lifts his bronze cast with his good hand and pounds the table with it.

"Figol and I will not need any of your men," I say. "We will fly to within a few steps of the walls as birds before changing back to our human forms to throw the runestones at the wall. With any luck, we will go undetected until it is too late."

Roisair smiles broadly. "Nothing is free, so what do you wish of me in return?"

"I was sent here to improve relations between our two peoples. I ask only for your support of this cause when the time arises."

"You will have it," he grabs my hand into his and attempts to crush my bones in his grasp. "Now, how do these runestones work? The wall is made up of many large stone blocks. Do you need to hit each one individually to turn them to earth, or will each strike carry over a large area?"

"In truth, I do not know. If you can supply me with the needed materials and some privacy, I will begin making runestones here as well."

"Crisa, see to it." Roisair says. "You will have whatever you need."

"I have one more request," I say.

Roisair looks at me wearily. "You wait until the end of negotiations to ask for something more. What is it that you want?"

"Allow the manwolves to guard the druids as they summon their elementals. It will keep them away from your army and it will free up some of your men."

"A sound suggestion," he nods at me. "It will be done; now is there any other unspoken request?"

It's my turn to smile. "No, that is all I require."

18

The Battle Begins

The Tusci have not spotted our army. Donned in tough leather armor, the warriors move silently through the forest. No lookouts mean that the Tusci must have supreme confidence in their demon guards. There are two of them standing on either side of the city gate. They have long, serrated claws, each the length of a long knife. Even the translucent wings have claws at each segment.

"Do they have weapons?" I whisper.

"No need," Crisa says. "Their claws are as strong as our iron weapons. And watch out if they take flight. They can gouge you with the talons on their feet."

"How do we hurt them?"

"With iron, a lot of iron."

The vile things have cruel, smoky-yellow horns curving up and back from their faces. These black-as-night demons must have come from man's collective nightmares.

An unbroken ring of rocks marks the midpoint between the forest and the city. This must be the ring laid down by the Tusci to keep the demons from escaping from their posts. It will also serve as our line of safe retreat, when needed. In all, it is about eight hundred paces to the city gate.

I still question how exactly Roisair's men will make it through the city gate. Even more frightening, what will be waiting for us inside?

"The ring of rocks will give us protection from the demons," Crisa says.

"We aim to kill them, not cower in fear," Roisair replies.

He pushes his way between Crisa and me, marching to the front of the makeshift army. He's changed out his bronze cast for an iron morningstar. The newly sharpened spikes gleam, even on this cloudy morning. We join Roisair in the clearing.

At last, the demons take note of our presence. One begins its hideous screeching and the shrill cries are amplified in the cold morning air. Guards atop the wall step into the dank air and are surprised by the force before them. One gestures fiercely and two others leave at once. It would have been better to not give away the size of our force.

Rhythmically, I start my chanting in the old tongue. I will the hazy gray clouds from over the frigid northern sea to come to me. Puffy white snow begins to fall on Laleah, reducing the visibility. Redoubling my effort, I force more clouds to race toward us, blinding the city with a white curtain of snowflakes.

Tiny tendrils of steam form as the snowfall lands on the demons. Deep, guttural cries of frustration rumble across the field. If nothing else, I've managed to annoy the hellspawn.

Roisair motions for half his men to come forward. He raises his carnyx; a bronze clarion horn shaped like a boar's head, mounted on a long, hollow tube, and blows a single pure note of challenge. Traditionally, the sound of a carnyx signals the men to rush the field and meet the enemy in battle. However, Roisair has trained the first and second waves of his men to form into columns twenty men wide and twenty-five deep instead. There is nothing left but the killing.

Packed together tightly, the first column advances with waves of iron-tipped spears bobbing high above their heads. Within the center of the second group is the key to gaining entrance to the city, a three-hundred-year-old oak has been turned into a battering ram. Fifty iron chains have been fixed on its sides. Crisa squeezes my arm as the men disappear into the storm.

With the snowstorm disguising our stratagem, Crisa, Figol and I join the druids on the far-left flank of the battlefield to ready the second prong of our attack. The druids walk to the rubble line and start performing their magic. Crisa is the first to call forth an elemental. Half a dozen more emerge from the ground. One by one, the animated clods of earth march toward the city walls. If the circular wall can be topped with dirt, the demon barrier will be broken. The fiends will turn on their summoners immediately if that happens.

Crisa smiles at us. The first elemental has reached the wall and reverted back into a pile of dirt. I take to the air to scout out the progress. In weather such as this, a green-headed drake is the best option. Three more elementals make it to the wall and build the ramp up to half the height of the wall. The city watch is now aware of our second attack. With luck, they will be too spread out to stop both from succeeding. Archers are readying their weapons above the dirt ramp.

What good will arrows do against mounds of earth?

The first column of warriors approaches the gate. Spears readied in all directions; they take on an appearance of a hedgehog.

At the city gate, a man in red robes appears and the guards give him plenty of space. The wind pushes me around like a child's toy and I lose sight of him. Even the well-oiled feathers of a duck are no match for the biting winds.

The air in front of the city gate erupts, creating a pulsating pressure wave. The snow melts and reforms as tiny ice daggers that are launched in all directions. Several strike me from below.

A rolling, thunderous laugh fills the air. "I am Te'Kuth, annihilator of men."

I turn into the blast and gaze uncomprehending at this new adversary. Three times as tall as a man, its malevolent yellow eyes scan the field before him. Its claws are longer and thinner than the winged demons. He jumps twenty aces forward, shaking the ground as he lands. The men in front of the formation flee in terror. As fast as one blinks, Te'Kuth swipes at two retreating men and slices them into pieces.

"Form up to me," the column's commander shouts. The men hurry to comply but an unfortunate fighter falls to the ground. Te'Kuth steps carefully, so his talons neatly cut the man into quarters. With a flick of its toe, the demon sends the severed head into the column. The winged demons shriek as they fly above the men.

"Circle up and retreat! Spears pointed outward."

The second column, unaware of the new combatant's size, continues to march forward. The columns collide and the men call out in surprise. The winged demons dart in, picking off any unprotected targets. The column commanders shout conflicting orders and the two well-shaped formations become one giant scrum.

Te'Kuth lets out a deep laugh. The booming of each step reverberates off the city walls as he draws closer. He jabs at the warriors, skewering the men in the front of the formation. Roisair's men turn and run, their collective nerve broken. Te'Kuth roars in amusement as the winged demons hunt for easy prey.

Is that all they have?

Te'Kuth raises his arm to reveal a dangling spear. It flicks the spear away. A downed fighter yelps at the near miss to his head.

"Got you," it says, triumphant. A man's scream is cut short, followed by silence. "More," Te'Kuth says, "More blood." As the snowfall wanes, the battlefield is covered in pink slush and mud.

"Look!" Mortas shouts. He points at two winged demons as they take flight toward the elementals. They dive at the one closest to the ramp and cause minimal damage.

Dasha shouts to his men, "Have your elementals fight the demons."

Two of the monoliths break from the line and take up sentry on either side of the convoy. The demons swerve to avoid the sentries and continue their attack on the lead elemental. Shouts come from the city wall. Te'Kuth turns to the red robed man atop the city gate and bellows his defiance. The man points to the elementals and the hulking demon reluctantly complies.

Having moved copious amount of dirt, the druids are forced to move within the rock circle in order to have pliable ground for more elementals. The winged demons take notice. Several druids lose their concentration as the demons fly toward them. Their elementals collapse into mounds, well away from the wall. One of the druids abandons the rest and races for the safety of the rock circle. The fear is contagious.

"Back to safety!" Dasha shouts. Without hesitation, he and his druids allow the rest of the elementals to fall. They run past the rubble circle and continue until they melt into the forest. The ramp is high enough that men could easily enter or leave the city. Only one or two more elementals are needed to complete the task.

Their prey gone, the demons start raking their claws at the ramp, slowly undoing the work of Dasha and his men.

"The ramp," Crisa moans. "All the progress will be lost."

"One for courage!" Mortas cries. The manwolves all place a wolfsbane seed in their mouth. Mortas is the first to spit his out. "Attack!" The manwolves growl as they rush the demons. They run up the elemental ramp and jump off the side as they attempt to grab a demon from the air. Mortas throws his runestone, causing hail to hit the first demon in the face. Logun leaps and latches onto its leg, pulling it downward. Others rush to grab it. The manwolves and demon slide down the ramp's side. The demon is forced onto its back and long knives flash up and down, splashing black ichor everywhere. The demon visibly shrinks as its life force is spilled onto the ground.

The second demon manages to stay out of reach, though it is pelted with hailstones as it circles the manwolves. Mortas is laughing maniacally as he scores hit after largely meaningless hit with his runestones. The demon feints one way before diving low to rake both of Osion's legs.

Flying out of range of Mortas' throws, it licks the blood from its cruel claws. Osion tries to stand, but he falls on his stomach immediately. His hamstrings sliced; all he can do is crawl back to safety.

Te'Kuth slowly advances toward the earthen ramp. With his sword-like claws, the massive demon dislodges huge chunks of dirt with every swipe. Mortas and his manwolves wisely retreat. Watching on in horror, the ramp is destroyed in only a few heartbeats.

The carnyx blares out a defiant note. "Men, form up," Roisair commands. With the two remaining demons at the ramp, the path to the city gate is clear. The men scurry across the field, knowing that this is their last, best chance. The archers on the city wall ready their arrows.

Men grab the chains attached on the sides of the battering ram. Others come to guard the rammers heads with a shield above them

162

with one arm and a spear held high in the other. They lift the tree trunk and attempt to sprint to the city gate. There is no cohesion in their movement and holes in their defenses open up everywhere.

"I told him those shields are too small," Crisa says.

The remaining winged demon begins harassing the sides of the formation. Archers rain down arrows from the wall. Too many shots find their mark and the progress begins to falter. The commander bellows and his men shamble forward. The losses are taking a toll, and the ram veers off to the right. More men fall and the ram drops into the pink, slushy mud. The commander begins calling out orders, until his voice ends abruptly. With no one to lead them, the fighters abandon the ram, twenty paces from the city gate as they flee the field.

Dozens drop in the frozen earth as they present their backs to the archers. Once the men fall, the winged demon gorges on the warriors' life blood. It grows visibly larger as it slakes its bloodlust.

"And just like that, all the damage Mortas and his men did to the second demon is for naught," Crisa says, despondent.

Shouts come from the manwolves. They stand at the rocky barrier, pleading to Osion to retreat faster. He is propped up on his trembling elbows and trying to crawl to safety.

I land in the middle of the manwolves and change back to human. "Quiet! You'll only call attention to him if you keep yelling." I look over meaningfully at the demons.

"We all must go and bring him back," Mortas says.

"A group that size will be spotted immediately," I say. "And you'll never make it back to safety if the demons come for you. You need to select three men to retrieve Osion."

"We should all go," Logun shouts, consumed by his battle rage.

"Logun, you go with Mortas and one other," I say.

"Who else will go with us?" Mortas asks.

The group collapses in on Mortas as everyone volunteers.

"Stop!" I yell. "Stealth is needed." That quiets them down.

"Help," Osion calls before dropping to the ground.

We signal him to be silent, but it's too late. The winged demon follows our gestures to Osion. It doesn't bother to take flight, instead it laughs as it stalks its wounded prey.

"I will not let him die like that," Logun says. "Join me, for I mean to go a-wolfing." He grabs his iron claw gauntlets. Sliding them over his wrists, he flexes each finger to ensure full command of the five blades. Logun smiles at his mates. "And I take two hits of wolfsbane, so that I do not lose my nerve." He places a seed between his teeth and cracks it. He spits out the seed, "For courage and for vengeance." Without waiting, he bolts toward his downed brother in arms.

"Yes!" Mortas screams. "Are we cowards?" Mortas asks even as he too affixes his claw gauntlets. Removing his own stash of wolfsbane, he looks each man in the eye. "For courage and vengeance," he smiles even as he too takes a lethal dose.

The rest follow the examples of Logun and Mortas; dooming themselves. Running on all four limbs, they express their hatred in savage growls. The demon realizes his peril too late. It attempts to take flight but Logun digs his claw gauntlets into the fiend and pulls it back to the ground. Both man and demon rake the other with vicious claws.

We watch as the manwolves race to their suicide mission. Crisa spots Dasha in the forest and calls him forth. Careful not to get too close to the rubble ring, he approaches us.

"Call forth whatever elementals you can!" I shout to Dasha and Crisa.

"It will do little good," Dasha says.

"They will all die!"

He shrugs. "It is their wish." He stares at the manwolves as they make their final charge, unmoved by their bravery. Crisa looks exhausted and confused. There will be no support from that quarter.

"I will not abandon my brothers." I take off into the air, choosing an eagle's form. The demon has managed to get free of the mortally wounded Logun and is circling the manwolves. My talons rip into the back of the demon, right between the wings. The thin, leathery membranes go slack and I ride the demon down until it slams into the frozen earth. The manwolves converge upon the downed demon.

Once more Te'Kuth is called to do battle. I fly in its face to keep the devil from reaching the manwolves, but I know this isn't a battle I can win. One swipe from the demon and I have lost several tail feathers. I screech a warning to Mortas before retreating to Osion's prone form.

The ground shakes as Te'Kuth approaches the manwolves. Mortas turns from the winged demon and yells "We take the bigger one too!"

As one, the manwolves abandon the nearly dead winged demon and advance on Te'Kuth. Madness mixed with bloodlust must be taking over. The first manwolf to reach the demon is sliced cleanly into three pieces. The pack doesn't even take note. They surround the fiend but every swipe of its claws claims another manwolf life.

The winged demon manages to rise and feast on the blood of the slain. Weakened but still lethal, it locates Osion and me. Dropping to the ground, I change into a cave bear and grip Osion's tunic behind his neck. Shielding his unconscious body, I carry him from the field.

The demon recovers enough to fly. He rakes my back several times, trying to weaken me rather than fight. The ground in front of me rumbles and raises up into an elemental. I squeeze through its legs and lay my eyes upon the stone rubble circle. The demon leaves to find easier prey.

Osion moans as I drag him over the rubble circle, letting me know my actions are not for nothing. The healers come at once to take Osion from me. They frown as they look at the red trail of blood left behind us.

"He is too far gone," the eldest healer says.

"I can heal them both," a young woman says. "Leave them with me." She has a patch over her left eye. It's never a good sign when the healer is unable to help themself.

The old healer looks at the woman confused, but there are too many in need for him to ask his questions now. He brusquely leaves us in her care and looks for more promising patients.

"Call me Miss Red," she says with a warm smile as she waves us to a small tent.

19

The Carnage Continues

I carefully lay Osion down on one of the two cots. He's as pale as Aine in the night sky. Miss Red's gentle hand guides me to the opposite cot. "Your robes will have to come off in order for me to heal your wounds."

"I'll be fine," I say. "I need to get back to the battle."

"It's more like a slaughter," she says. "You're no good to anyone dead, Grahme Fairweather, so let me look at your back while my water is coming to a boil. Once I start on this young one, I'll have scant time for anyone else."

"Oh," she gasps before regaining her composure. "These are worse than I thought. I'm going to apply a poultice to numb and heal your skin, though it may burn at first."

"What herbs do you use?" I ask.

"Mint and wlith y mori."

"Dew of the sea? I've never heard of it."

"You know the old tongue," she says. "It comes from far away."

"But how did you get it?"

She slaps the gashes on my back and drags the poultice-soaked rag deep into my skin. I clench my teeth so tight I'm afraid I'll break them. It's all I can do to not scream in pain. She gently rubs her hands over the wounds while chanting something in a foreign tongue. Within only a few breaths, the pain is gone and I feel a cooling sensation from where she fans my wounds.

"That's much better," I say.

She smacks my butt and laughs heartily. "Stop standing around naked and trying to distract me. I have work to do." I rub my hand across my back as best I can. The skin is mostly smooth and dry.

"That wlith y mori is amazing," I say. "Where can I get some?"

The carnyx is blown again and as much as I wish to find out how to make this miracle poultice, I am needed elsewhere. In any case, Miss Red is already kneeling over Osion's prone form and ignoring me. She has removed her eye patch, though I can scarcely guess why. In the shadows, she looks older than when I first saw her. The carnyx blows again and I have no time to waste.

Without me to compel the storm, the worst of it has swept back out to sea. Only a miserable cold rain remains. The battlefield is filled with dead bodies of the fallen. We have only managed to kill one of the smaller demons.

"I'm surprised this many men remain."

"I've been helping," Figol says.

Roisair snorts from behind us. "Yes, I'm sure the boy was instrumental in rallying my hardened warriors."

Figol and I exchange knowing looks. "It's now or else all is lost," I say. "Ravens will go unnoticed on a bloody battlefield such as this. Follow my lead."

We fly away from the elemental debacle and over the reforming army to the far side of the battlefield. The archers have all been drawn to the city gate, leaving this vacant section unguarded. We land less than twenty paces from the wall. "Remember, be forceful, but you don't need to yell for the runestones to work. I'd rather the demons not come our way."

Figol looks over at Te'Kuth as he finishes destroying the battering ram. The combination of reverberating blows and hellfire renders the grand old tree into charred timber impossibly fast.

How can anyone stand up to that?

"I don't know," Figol says with a small tremble in his voice.

Get out of my head.

Each block of the city wall is half as tall as a man's height and twice as wide. There are many of these stones stacked one atop of the other. One by one, we throw our runestones and change blocks of stone into dirt. Even though we score blow after blow, we're more than halfway through our supply and the wall remains stout.

"Aim for the base, it's our only chance."

"But we won't break the continuous line of stone," Figol says.

"Trust me. If enough of the bottom ones become dirt, the wall will collapse."

"Won't it fall on top of us?"

Te'Kuth roars and we freeze in place. Slowly we peer over to the battlefield. He charges Roisair's ramshackle army and they break before they can even cross the rubble line.

"That's it for the army," I say.

From above us, a man begins shouting. He's pointing down at us and gesturing wildly. The remaining winged demon breaks off from routing the army and heads for us.

"Throw all that you have left," I say.

We both shout "*ehar*" as the last of our rocks hit the wall. More stones turn into packed dirt, but the wall doesn't even waver. We have failed.

"Flee!" I shout. Figol turns into a raven and heads for the protection of the forest. I look in my pouch. I have two *cweorths*, fireballs, and one *iss*, which will cause water to freeze.

Is there enough moisture in the blocks of dirt?

The demon is nearly upon me. I throw the runestone at the first spot we targeted and shout "*iss*" as loud as I can. The fiend's shadow is nearly upon me. I settle my mind and become a swift. Small and mobile, I can knife through the air with ease. I fly under the demon and turn to follow it. As a swift, nothing is going to outmaneuver me.

A cracking noise comes from the wall and I see stones beginning to wobble. The demon attempts to spin, but it is ungainly in the air. It must not have recouped all of its powers. Getting in close to the wall, I dodge the stones as they begin to fall. I fly up against the wall and watch as the demon gets hit by a falling stone. They land with a satisfying thud and the demon's head rolls away from the rest of its body.

The rumbling noise increases and I must dodge more and more debris as I make my escape. Something hits my left wing, ruining my rhythm. I ignore the pain as I streak for the forest. Each stroke causes me to lurch farther to the left. The avian brain takes over and I land on the nearest branch, in a holly bush.

Only now do I see that my left wing will not pull in next to my body. Fearing the worst, I retake my human form.

Stupid!

The branch can't support my weight and I tumble into the hard, spiny leaves. Landing on my left shoulder, shards of pain radiate down my arm.

"He's awake now," Osion says, smiling.

"Now you just rest young one; don't go getting everyone's blood pumping for no reason." A hooded healer sits on the stool between Osion and me. "I've never heard of a druid falling from his perch in a tree," she says in her raspy voice.

"Is that how you got hurt?" Osion says, laughing out his words.

"Something hit my wing," I say.

"Aye, and you're lucky it was only one small piece of the wall. You could have been crushed like Alguth was."

"Alguth?"

"The winged demon whose fate you narrowly avoided." She pats my arm with her mottled hand.

"Um, sure," something doesn't make sense, but with my buzzing head, I can't place it.

"Mistress Red is a miracle worker," Osion says. "The other healers can't believe I'm still alive."

"You took a lot out of me," the healer says. "Grahme's injuries were nothing compared to yours. I aged a few decades just tending to you."

Something is familiar about that voice.

"Did we win?" I ask.

"That, like beauty, is in the eye of the beholder," she says.

I've heard that before.

"Mistress Red," I say.

She turns toward me, her milky left eye revealed. Rhedna of the Sorrows winks at me. "Even prophecy needs help from time to time."

"You healed us both?" I ask.

"I healed you twice, actually. Mother showed me a few tricks as you'll see for yourself soon enough."

"You're not making sense."

She pats me affectionately on my good shoulder. "We will speak again, five days hence when you continue your quest." She winks at me and changes into a raven. With a final cah, she takes to the air, nearly hitting Figol as he enters the tent.

"You're finally awake," Figol says.

"Did you know that was Rhedna of the Sorrows?" I ask.

"Yes, she said to leave you and Osion alone in order for both of you to be made whole."

"Did we win?"

Figol blows out a long breath. "That depends," he says.

"If you say that 'like beauty, that's in the eye of the beholder,' I *will* hurt you."

"Easy Uncle, Te'Kuth and the smaller demon entered the city.

"What smaller demon?"

Once the wall fell, Te'Kuth made straight for his summoner. The red robe compelled another demon to appear, but it was much weaker. Te'Kuth swept it away with one blow, sending it inside the walls. Then the brute tore off its summoner's head and threw it at the backs of the retreating guards. It broke open the city gate and there have been screams and smoke trails emerging ever since."

"And the army?"

Figol snorts. "Roisair has been sending men out on horseback to find the cowards and bring them back."

"And the druids?"

"They ran faster than most."

"Crisa?"

"She's with Roisair, plotting what to do next."

I cut my eyes over toward Osion then back at my nephew. The boy is busy pulling loose thread from his tunic. Figol shakes his head, ever so slightly. I didn't expect there to be any other survivors from the manwolves, and I don't envy the one who must inform Osion of that fact.

"I can't lie around here all day. Take me to Roisair."

"There's Grahme," Crisa announces as I enter the meeting tent. Roisair's morningstar cast is stuck in the wooden table. He had been gesticulating wildly, but he stops once I enter. All eyes turn to me.

What am I walking into?

"For the newcomers," Roisair begins, "We have sent a man to ask for a meeting with Tuss Metiana and his ruling council. He has not returned. It is unclear if he made it to the Tusci or if the demons ravaging the outer city got to him first. Regardless, the Tusci have the means to banish the demons back to the hell from which they were summoned, and yet they choose not to do so. If any of our countrymen are to survive, we must be the ones to defeat these fiends." Roisair's words are met with silence.

"What must we do?" I ask.

"The two demons do not cooperate with one another. In fact, Te'Kuth tried to kill the lesser demon before it entered the city. I propose we form up and mount an attack on the smaller demon. After we vanquish him, we will have a much better grasp on what tactics work."

I look around the room. The men are still staring at the ground. Only the manwolves and the falling section of wall have managed to kill a demon, and neither of them are options anymore.

"Lord Roisair," I start. In truth I'm not sure what to say, but the tomb-like atmosphere must be banished. "I would like for Figol and I to use the remaining runestones to start turning the inner wall of the city to earth. If the Tusci believe the demons might get in among their people, they are more likely to banish the demons and talk terms."

"Yes!" Roisair cries. "This is what we need. Now men, are you going to cower here as two Pretanni druids fight our battle? Will you turn your backs on our people inside this once great city? Grahme will breach the inner wall. We just need to give him the time he needs to do so." He sticks his arm back in the morningstar cast and wretches it from the table. The wood splinters and bits of the table fall upon the map, though only Roisair and I seem to notice. He winks at me and slams the table with his good hand.

Figol is poking me in the back, but I show no acknowledgement.

"Uncle," he whispers, desperate to get my attention.

I know, we'll speak later.

"We must rid this land of the foul Tusci," I shout. The men around me cheer. The sense of doom has lifted and the poor fools are contemplating future heroic deeds once more.

"Should we wait for ten or twenty more of our people to be killed by the Tusci's evil creatures?" Roisair asks.

"No!" His men scream back.

"The time is now! Get your men, get your gear. We take back the city now!"

The assembled warriors cheer. The crush to get out of the tent would be comical in a different setting.

"Can you bring down the wall?" Roisair asks soberly.

"In truth, I don't know how many runestones we have left. I only spoke because the men were so deflated that to not speak would have meant defeat."

"You did right. If we fail to take the city, the Kings of Eriu will label us all traitors and see us hanged. If we are doomed to fail, I choose to die on the battlefield."

"What about the rest of the men?" Figol asks. "You're sending them to their deaths."

Roisair shrugs. "They knew what they signed up for. It's what Darins do."

Crisa looks as if she's been slapped. Her mouth moves, but no sound comes out of it. "I called forth my people on your behalf." Her voice begins to rise. "They left their homes to fight for this cause. You can't just throw their lives away."

Roisair shows Crisa the palm of his hand. "You're emotional. The battle is not over." He pivots toward the door. "I must go speak with my men." He nods at me before leaving.

"He can't mean that." Crisa shakes her head. "It must be the battle stress." She looks up at me, her eyes begging for reassurance. "Roisair can't be that disdainful of his men."

What am I supposed to say?

Figol rescues me. "Uncle, what do we do?"

"Good question." My limbs feel heavy, so I know my ability to animorph is limited. It's beyond me to call forth another storm and we're out of almost all of our runestones. "Crisa, go with Roisair, perhaps you can help him to see reason when the time comes. Figol and I have another mission."

Crisa seizes on my words and nods excitedly. Poor woman, she still believes that we can succeed.

I turn to Figol, "Follow me."

I keep my mind focused on the problems at hand. If Figol knows that animorphing will be taxing for me, there's no doubt that he and Crisa will try to stop me. They both have good hearts, but I have faced death multiple times and I have dealt it out to others. I'm prepared to mete out more death if I must. There's no sense in burdening them with crushing guilt as well.

Figol and I fly to the now deserted guard tower of the inner wall. Whatever men were here must have fled when they saw the demons breaching the outer wall.

"What are we going to do?" Figol asks.

"We are going to aid Roisair and his men in taking down the small demon, then we are going to find this Tuss Metiana and you are going to bend him to your will as I pretend to negotiate with him."

"Now you want me to use my power?"

"It's war, and the Tusci have chosen not to banish the demons. We must use whatever advantages we have to protect the innocent lives trapped here."

"Then why aren't we going straight to the Tusci?"

"I saw you with your head down," I give my nephew a penetrating look. "What is Roisair thinking?"

"Roisair doesn't believe victory is possible. He wishes to die in battle."

"I thought as much. Leading his men to slaughter is unforgivable. Therefore, we must kill the demons if we can, in order to save as many people as possible from both sets of callous leaders."

"Roisair and his men are entering the outer gate now," Figol says.

Flying from rooftop to rooftop, we spot the smaller, barrel-chested demon. It is only twice the height of a man. The cruel creature is killing whoever it finds, just for sport.

"Fly to Roisair and lead him to this demon," I say. "I'll keep it occupied if need be."

I'm exquisitely tuned to how much vitality I have left. I'm close, but I'm not at my limit yet.

Once Figol leaves, I climb from one rooftop to another until I settle on a vacant tanner's shop behind the demon. I don't know how well the thing can smell, so I let the overpowering odors of the shop mask my presence. The demon has stopped the general destruction and is focusing upon the building in front of it.

Like many of the streets we've seen, there is a small summoning circle at its end. The loosely stacked rocks are only knee high and covered with soot. It is the only structure the demon avoids.

The hellspawn lets out a fierce battle cry and stomps its foot into the ground. The vases beside me wobble. I grab them before they can fall. If nothing else I'll throw the pottery at the demon's head.

"Come to me and I will make your end painless," it says to the opened doorway. Falling to its knees, it feels inside the building.

A woman shrieks, giving away her location. The demon smiles and grabs the terrified woman by the leg. She kicks and screams as he drags her from the doorway and into the air. With its other hand, it grabs her chest, pinning her arms against herself. Her shrill cries reverberate inside my head. I nearly vomit at the pain.

"Silence," the demon orders.

She fills her chest with air and repeats the earsplitting scream.

The demon laughs. "I need to remove the noisy part." It grabs her head and twists until there is an unmistakable pop. Her legs hang limp. It continues twisting until the head comes off. Dark red blood oozes out and covers the demon's hand. A sticky, reddish cloud of boiling blood forms around him, discoloring everything it comes in contact with. He throws the head into the doorway from whence it came. Startled shrieks betray the children within.

From an adjacent doorway, a red-haired woman dashes outside of her hiding spot, to the circle. She dives head first, barely clearing the circle's wall. She lands in a heap, but keeps from knocking any stones loose. The demon rises from his knees and stares down at the exposed woman. She pushes her wavy red hair back.

"I claim *thuna* over you, Kugorath," she yells as she scrambles to her feet.

"Who is this scrawny girl?" It asks in a mocking tone. "The pickings are too good for me to waste time on the likes of you." He resumes sweeping his arm in the children's doorway.

"Stay in there Nerie," the woman shouts. "I am Glasna, a *trutnuth* and I claim dominion over you."

"A *trutnuth*? You must not be very good, or you'd know what your own fate will be this day." It chuckles at its own sick humor. "I have never drunk the blood of a soothsayer before."

"*Favin cepen!*" She commands.

Kugorath laughs a deep, terrifying laugh. "Easy for you to say behind your *tularu*. Come out so that we may contend fairly."

Glasna's ears turn as red as her hair. "You wish to contend with me, do you?" She pulls out an ornate silver vessel from her tattered robes. "I will do you one better; for I possess an *aska of eleivana*."

"Put that down, silly girl."

"No, you will be my *marish* or we shall fight to oblivion." She carefully begins pouring the oil onto one of the stones in the circle. "*Eis* of the Abyss, accept my *fase* of *eleivana*. By the laws of *tinscvil*, I will oppose Kugorath of the Metus clan."

Kugorath rises to his full height and approaches Glasna's circle. Only one step away, the demon towers over her.

Her pouring hand begins to shake, so she supports it with the other. The demon seems not to have noticed. She continues pouring the oil around the circle, without looking up at the malignant creature. Once she completes coating three quarters of the circle, she sets the ewer down. "Will you yield to me or will you risk oblivion?" She says in a calm voice.

Kugorath bends down low, so that his face is an arms width away from her and he sniffs. Immediately his demeanor changes, "I could just leave this plane," he offers.

"I have already dismissed you. To leave would be to declare yourself my *marish*."

"Then I propose a *vakhr*," he says with an accommodating grin. A shiver goes down my spine. I don't know how this girl can be so calm.

"Demon contracts end with the reaping of the human's soul," she says. "My soul will be lost forever or it will remain with me for my next life."

179

Kugorath screams in fury. He punches the nearest building and collapses the roof. A white cat with a furry black head scurries from the wreckage. He lets out a gleeful yell as he stomps on the poor animal. Facing Glasna again, "You wish to face me?" The demon glares at her.

Blood begins running out of her nose. Squeezing the vessel of oil, she refuses to take her eye from the fiend. "I do." It's a subtle thing, but her knee rests upon the stone circle. Despite her cool demeanor, the test of wills is taking a physical toll on her.

Kugorath glowers at her, but she doesn't flinch. An uncomfortable silence ensues as Kugorath waits for her will to break. If she were to run, she'd be dead before she could make the three steps back inside the building. She shrugs and places her hand upon the stone circle. It's a sly trick, acting unconcerned while supporting her weight. Glasna picks up the ewer and resumes pouring the oil over the stones.

"Stop!" Kugorath demands, with an edge of panic in its voice.

She silently looks up at him.

"I will go below," it says, defeated.

"You acknowledge that you are *marishi* to me?"

Kugorath glowers. "You are getting what you want. Do not push me little *sech*."

Glasna bows to him and resumes pouring. There are only two dry stones left.

"I yield." Kugorath shouts. The street goes quiet except for the mournful crying of a child. "I am *marishi* to you," it says sullenly.

"Then *favin cepen!*" Glasna says, her anger boiling over.

Kugorath howls as its corporeal form dissolves into flames and is sucked inward. It disappears, leaving only thick, black smoke in its wake. Glasna chokes on the acrid fumes and collapses onto the oil-soaked stones.

20

The Destruction Desists

Figol leads Roisair and his men around the corner just as the acrid black smoke clears.

I lower myself into the second-floor window of the tannery and locate the stairs in the dimly lit room. A man and wife watch, confused, as I bound down and go straight for the door.

I lift the impossibly light woman, a girl really, from the stone circle. She's barely Figol's age and she faced down a demon bent on destruction. She raises her head and looks past me. She twists and stretches out behind me. It's all I can do to keep us from tumbling.

"Roisair?"

"Glasna?!" Roisair shouts. He runs to us and takes the girl from me. He drops his morningstar and lifts her into his arms. Affectionately, he slaps her cheek. "Come on sister, you are stronger than a thousand demons," he says as he strokes her tangled hair.

"Roisair? Is it really you?"

"I'm here," he nuzzles her cheek with his own.

"You came for me," she says with a tentative smile.

"Not that you needed any help."

They begin laughing together. The warriors give Roisair, Glasna and I plenty of space.

"What will father say when he finds out it was his two youngest, the crippled bastard and the girl, who retook his most important city?" Roisair asks.

Glasna sets her feet firmly on the ground. "I can stand now," she assures him.

"Is it safe?" A small voice comes from the doorway. A girl, maybe ten years old sticks out her head. She cranes it out, checking for demons.

"Yes Nerie, it's safe," Glasna says. She tries to brush off her robe, but the dirt and vaporized blood stubbornly cling to her. "Get Rasce and Tages and make for the front gate."

"But there are warriors there," Nerie says. She points at Roisair's men.

The warriors all chuckle. Roisair walks to her, goes down on a knee and grasps her filthy hands. "Brave girl, I am Roisair, the leader of these proud men and the liberator of Laleah. I promise you that none of my men will hurt you or your brothers. Quickly now, make your way to safety. Go right at the end of this alley, then go left on that road. When you reach our camp, ask for our herbalist and she will take good care of you."

"Rasce!" She yells, causing Roisair to cover his ear. "Grab Tages. We're leaving, right now!" She stamps her foot. I can't help but smile. She is clearly the eldest child.

A seven-year-old boy runs from the shadows, carrying his brother. The youngest is about four and he's kicking while his older brother tries to keep a hold on to him.

"I can walk on my own," the little one demands.

"Quiet Tages," Nerie says. "Give him to me." The youngest is passed from brother to sister. "Now, we have to be quiet or the other demons may find us." She looks at the panicked faces of her little brothers, "So no talking." They each give quick nods.

The men step back to create a path for the children. Nerie looks both ways along the main road before running off to the left, as directed.

"Right," Roisair says to his men. "A woman has taken care of one demon. Follow me and we'll take care of the last one." His men cheer. Roisair takes Glasna's arm and together they lead his men out of the alley.

With luck, they won't break and run this time.

"Grahme," Crisa whispers, as she puts a hand on my shoulder. "Let's go in here, we need to talk." She steers me into an abandoned shop next to the tannery.

"I am sorry for getting you mixed up in this," Crisa says. "Roisair is not the leader I thought him to be."

"No?" Figol says mockingly.

"He cares not one bit for these brave men who fight for him."

"He believes that his plan has failed," I say. "He would rather die in battle along with every single one of his men than to face his failure."

"But he's found his sister, well, half-sister. Surely this changes his thinking."

"Crisa!" Roisair calls.

"You don't have to go," I say.

"I do," Crisa swallows hard. "I am the one who recruited these men and I will join them in whatever fate is dealt to them." She squeezes my hand, conveying her silent apology better than any

184

words could. I watch her rush to catch up with the man who means to cause her death.

We watch as the warriors make it to the end of the alley. Roisair jumps on top of some barrels of ale. "Men, we have finished most of the job already. We killed two demons outside the walls." He pauses for the cheers to die down. "My sister," he points at Glasna, "has sent one demon back to the abyss from whence it came." More cheers erupt. "And now we have but one more demon to face." He smiles proudly at his sister. "And Glasna will send that one back to Dubnos as well."

The men start to cheer until Roisair motions for them to remain silent.

"Brother," Glasna says. "Te'Kuth is too powerful for me. I can't hope to control him."

"Nonsense, you don't know your own strength." He turns to his men. "Just pour oil around the rocks again and order it to leave us."

His men cheer the new plan.

"The oil must be *eleivana oil*," she says in a small voice. "I have used all that I have for Kugorath."

The closest men once again look apprehensive. Roisair notices the change as well.

"Then we'll find you more oil," he exclaims. "Flax oil must be plentiful in the city."

"It must be *eleivana oil*," she says.

"We'll find you some," he smiles at her before turning to his men. "The city will be ours!" Another cheer goes up, drowning out her comments. "We cannot tarry long, but we can't continue while parched either." With one swing of his spiked gauntlet, he punctures an ale barrel in two places. His men cheer as they come forth to drink liquid courage.

"Come, the longer we tarry the more of our countrymen will fall to this fiend. We'll finish off the rest of these once our work is complete. Jumping from one of the barrels, he grabs Glasna's hand and pulls her along with him. He seems more than willing for her to share in his fate.

Crisa stares at us, beseeching us to do the impossible.

"What now?" Figol asks.

"We stick with the plan and find this Tuss Metiana before Roisair can make everyone a sacrifice to his foolish pride."

Figol runs to Crisa. "Take these," he says and hands her two runestones. "The *hahgel* runes should distract him for a moment, but that's all."

I check for my pouch, but it seems my nephew can add thieving to his skills.

Figol returns one of my two remaining runes. "All we have left are two *cweorth* stones." He shrugs. "I don't know what good fireballs are against a demon."

"None, but it will do plenty against humans." Reaching down, I grab some rubble. I do my best to fake a confident grin. "Just in case I need to bluff."

If I hesitate to animorph, Figol will know why. I'd prefer a tawny owl, but a merlin is faster, they can maneuver in tight spaces and they're much more likely to be seen during the day.

Coasting high above the city, I can see the destruction in the wake of Te'Kuth. Above the gate of the inner wall, there is an open plaza where a handful of Tusci men and women have assembled. Every last one of them has red hair and red robes, as if the fiery color is mandatory to call forth the foul creatures.

Clearly there is dissension in the ranks, as a woman whose hair is equal parts gray and red, is gesticulating wildly. She punches the air in front of her as she makes her points. A tall, heavyset man is the object of her anger. He laughs mirthlessly at her tirade.

The oblong plaza is rather large, thirty paces wide and twenty paces deep, I'd guess. There is a stone summoning circle next to the Tusci. We split up, landing on opposite walls. So engrossed in their argument, no one notices our arrival. To the group's left is a tunnel leading to two stout wooden doors. They are the only exit I can see.

I land behind the leader, with the circle between us, retaking my human form. The woman stops yelling and points at me. All eight of them turn to face me. I give a quick glance behind them and see that Figol is still in avian form.

Is he able to animorph back?

I shake my head; I can't worry about that right now. "I am Grahme, Lord Protector of Men-an-Tol and member of the Nine." I take a quick step forward. "I have come to negotiate the surrender of Laleah and the peaceful withdraw of your people from the city."

They eye me suspiciously, as if I'm about to strike. The woman is the first to recover her wits. "Cai, call your imp and have it kill this one."

"Halt," the fat man says. "There will be no demon summoning by you on this plaza. Do we all still remember the havoc your hellspawn caused the last time?" He snorts as he turns to the rest of the group. "Call the guards to take care of this nuisance." He waves his hand dismissively at me. A short, nervous man takes several quick steps toward the doors.

187

Wrong choice.

I lob my runestone over his head and call forth the fireball. The stone explodes a moment before it hits the doors and fire shoots out of the tunnel. He throws his arms in front of his face and drops to a fetal position. The fire ignites the doors in an instant. I can feel the heat from the blaze from where I stand. The stone walls darken as the magical fire is unwilling to be extinguished so quickly. Thick black smoke collects in the tunnel and rolls into the plaza.

I give them what I hope is a bored expression. I walk to the nervous man and he hurriedly returns to his cohorts. I hold out the rubble that I pocketed. "Let's try this again, and if you remain so obstinate, I can just incinerate you all."

The fat man comes to the fore. "I am Tuss Metiana, leader of *Diabolus*." He emphasizes the name. The tiniest sliver of a smile forms as he places his hands behind his back and gives me a shallow bow. "You are free to contend with Te'Kuth if you wish. If you can best him, we'll be happy to hear your terms." He's good. He's already managed to calm his people. My surprise entrance worked, but the effect is wearing off.

"I was hoping you would recall your demon and we negotiate in good faith. Had I wanted to take you all out, I could have in one blazing moment."

"Ah, yes." With a fluid gesture, Tuss summons a demon into the circle between us. "Another of your fireballs will release this demon from its prison."

"You'll still be dead," I say.

"As will you, soon after," he sneers. "So, tell me why I should dismiss Te'Kuth?" Next to me, it is the most powerful being here."

"But he isn't here, is it?"

He cocks his head to the left. "I don't need Te'Kuth, any demon can kill you where you stand."

I open my left fist and show them my collection of useless rocks. I select one with my right hand. "If I'm to die, I'll take the rest of you with me."

Tuss nods his head approvingly at me. "Well played. I see that you do not scare easily. But consider, if you kill all of us, Te'Kuth would be free to roam the city for as long as he wishes. It seems that we are at an impasse."

"I think we can move past it."

"And why would I talk to you when I'm guaranteed to win? There is nothing you or that laughable army can do to defeat my demon."

"Because you don't want this city, not really," I say. His eyes open in mild surprise. I glance over the group long enough to see that Figol is back to human form and has his head down. We may just live through this.

"You want the trade contracts that Diardoc is offering," I say. "Your people have never been great in number, and ruling over thousands of ill-tempered Darins is not a job any sane man would want." I mimic Tuss and clasp my hands behind my back. It makes him look unconcerned, and I need to project confidence, even if I don't know what I'm doing.

Tuss rolls his eyes. "I think there are only a few hundred left. Your men have done well at depopulating the outer city. But I'm always one to listen. What do you suggest?"

"Recall you demon and the negotiations can start in earnest."

He scoffs at me.

"Could you not resummon the fiend if the talks are not to your liking?" I ask.

He scratches his chin. "Very well, if you can supply us with enough tin, iron and slaves, I could be persuaded."

"If you would dismiss your demon, we may begin."

"Te'Kuth! *Tuthu mini fase*," he calls forth.

A roar sounds in the distance. A slow-moving cloud of debris forms in the demon's wake as it makes its way to us. Te'Kuth is several stories tall, yet its horned head is still below our plaza. There are several iron-tipped spears embedded in its body, not that it seems overly troubled by them.

"Why do you interrupt my death dance?" It demands.

"You have fed enough for now."

The demon growls and the overheated air from its body rises and engulfs us in a sweltering heat. "With Laxu, it was agreed that I may *hintha tezan.*"

"And now Laxu is dead by your own hand and I am changing the terms. You have gorged enough," Tuss says.

Te'Kuth lets loose an earsplitting bellow. He strikes the wooden roofs around him and the thatching begins to smolder.

"*Favin cepen*," Tuss says with a wave of his hand.

Smoke appears at the extremities of Te'Kuth's form before rapidly collapsing inward. With one last baleful look, the demon is gone.

Tuss points to the black smoke where Te'Kuth was. "I have done as you asked. Now, I will need many trading boats loaded down with tin, iron and slaves in order for my pet to remain elsewhere."

My heart is pounding, but I refuse to let my amazement show. I cross my arms to hide the fact that my hands are shaking.

No, that's no good. I'll appear too haughty.

I pace back and forth, swinging my arms to hide my indecision. Finally, I place them behind my back and face Tuss and his council.

"Many seek to remove tin from the ground on Pretanni. Indeed, the lands I protect are covered with these vile mines. The tin you can have, for I have no need of it."

"Where is this land of yours?" The man tries and fails to be disinterested.

"It is the Land's End peninsula." I can see that he is unaware of the Pretanni lands. "It is the tongue of land that sticks out to the south and west of Pretanni, well into the endless sea. There are any number of folks who will trade the metal with you. What do you offer them in return?"

We may survive this after all.

"You do not understand. This isn't a negotiation," Tuss says with a wicked smile. His hands unclasp from behind his back and rise to the level of his shoulders.

"*Cweorth!*" Figol shouts.

A runestone ignites into a fireball over the heads of the Tusci. I can feel the pressure as the flames ignite from within the group. Instinct takes over and I dive away from the worst of the blast. The trapped demon is blown behind me, all the way to the outer wall.

Its body lands in the middle of two demon hounds behind me that I had not noticed. Black as night, the hounds shake their heads and slowly gain their feet.

"Run!" I scream. Willing my legs to move faster than ever before, I sprint for the smoky tunnel. Figol clears the charred remnants of the Tusci ruling council and runs in step with me toward the only exit. The hounds are snarling at one another, giving us

191

precious time to escape. Daring a look back, I see the demon throw one of the hounds in our direction. The second hound chooses a wide path, but it's coming for us as well.

We clear the blackened tunnel and find another balcony. This one looks upon the inner city. Looking back at our pursuers, I spy two double-headed battle axes leaning up against the wall. The guards must have left without their weapons when the tunnel ignited.

"Figol!" I toss him one of the axes. He fumbles the catch. I race to the other side and secure the second weapon for myself. One of the demonic hounds charges out of the smoky tunnel. I swing will all my might. The ax is heavier than I thought. Somehow the weapon lands in the hound's chest. Its momentum pulls the ax from my grip and they both slide toward Figol.

My shoulder screams out in pain and I notice a fresh wound oozing blood. It must have got me as it sailed past. I peer into the tunnel and see two sets of eyes staring back. Their reluctance to enter the tunnel won't last long. "Figol, hurl your ax into the tunnel, then we'll jump off the wall and land in courtyard below."

"What animal should we take?"

I let out a snort, "Whatever you can."

Figol lobs his ax and the handle bounces on the stone floor. A surprised yelp lets us know he hit something. We turn and run for our lives. Figol hops on top of the wall and leaps into the air. He's a puffin before he can sink out of view.

My shoulder screams with every footfall. I don't trust flying, so I make a hard left for the spiraling stairs. My breath is so loud that even the blind could locate me.

Staggering down the stairs, I let out a soft groan with each step. Figol meets me near the bottom and keeps me from falling on my face. A predatory growl from above keeps us focused on our task.

192

"Why didn't you animorph?"

I hold out my left hand and watch it twitch. "I'm nearly drained."

"The gate!" He says.

The plaza is directly above the inner-city gate. If we can make it out of the inner city, the wall will stop the demons in their tracks.

The doors are made from ancient oaks and are thrice my height. A squared off tree trunk is used to secure the closed gate. There's no way that we can lift the drawbar by ourselves.

The horned demon emerges from the spiraling stairs. Not even healthy would I challenge a monstrosity like this. I notice several bite marks are on his arms.

Has it taken care of the second demon hound?

It hardly matters; certain death is only twenty paces away. "Figol, follow my lead." I don't wait for an answer. In my mind I think through the change carefully. My front paws land on the stone with a resounding thump. A second thump behind me and Figol's roar confirms his transformation. Even as a couple of cave bears, this fight is unfair.

I surge upward, hitting the oak support bar with my paws. It moves the width of a couple fingers. My shoulder screams in pain. I hurtle myself at the bar again and again and Figol roars defiantly behind me. With a quick look backward, I spy that the demon hound and the horned devil spreading out to either side of Figol.

The support beam is nearly clear of its holder. Knowing it is our last chance, I expend all my energy. My forelegs, mushy from the exertion, fail me. They slide off the beam, letting my head take the full impact. The heavy timber strikes my back as it falls, causing my limbs to go numb. I fall into the right door and it grudgingly opens enough for my head to be clear.

I hear Figol's roar behind me right before he slams into the door. The ancient oak door groans and stubbornly gives way to Figol's bulk. My back legs begin to tingle. Desperately I drag myself forward, through the city gate. Figol grabs the nape of my neck and pulls me through.

A demon stomps on my foot, but I'm able to get free of its talons. Its shoulder slams against the opened door and begins to disintegrate as is passes the stone circle barrier. The fiend bellows in pain. The demon hound stays back from the open gate and howls in frustration.

I wheeze out a rejoiceful breath. By all rights we should be dead. I cradle my right arm and notice a piece of demon hound's claw implanted in my shoulder. I pull on it without thinking, and the pain overwhelms me, causing my vision to fade.

"Uncle!" Figol shouts. He tears his robe and roughly ties it around my shoulder. My vision is blurry, but I can make out my nephew as he helps me rise.

The demons have retreated from the gate. It is not long before screams can be heard from the inner city. Once again, we have succeeded at making the situation worse for the common folk. I slide down the nearest wall, standing was a mistake. I have failed yet again.

"How did you manage to wield the ax?" Figol asks. "I thought druids couldn't use iron weapons."

"We can, but we can't use our magic while we're touching iron." Even talking is sapping my strength. "Still, I'll pray for forgiveness from the entire pantheon if we live through this debacle. I close my eyes and willingly accept whatever fate has in store for me.

"Uncle," Figol shakes me awake. "Tuss meant to kill you." He taps his head unnecessarily. "Once you gave away the location of the tin mines, all of Land's End was at risk." His eyes hint at the revulsion he feels. "I had no choice."

"You did not." I agree. I'm annoyed with him for waking me. But now that I'm awake, he seems unsure of himself. He must be coming to grips with the enormity of the day.

My eyes stare out into the outer city, focusing on nothing in particular. My mind wrestles with itself and differing waves of emotion attempt to take primacy, but weariness is winning once again.

Why are we risking our lives for the likes of Roisair?

"Figol, I agreed to this quest so that you may become a druid apprentice. I will not abandon it, unless you tell me you no longer want it." It's the best I can do to reassure him.

"Even if we're likely to die?"

I stare off into the distance. "I gave my word."

"Why couldn't Tuss be honorable like you?" Figol asks.

"You were in his head?"

He nods and slides down the wall next to me. He buries his face in his knees.

"You couldn't bring him around to make a compromise?" My eyelids are so very heavy. What is it that Figol needs from me?

Staring at the ground in front of him, he shakes his head.

"I'm sorry Figol, but he gave you no choice." There, I've told him that it's not his fault. Now I can rest. I close my eyes and lean my head back against the wall.

"There's more to it than that," Figol says. "While I was in his head, I searched for any tender moment that I could exploit. He was a very hard man, but there was one person where his concern was

195

greater than his ambition. It was for a woman." He inhales deeply, "my mother."

Did I hear that correctly?

I turn to look at my nephew.

He looks straight ahead. "I killed my father."

21

The Evacuation Ensues

Something is hitting my left arm. I ignore it, hoping it will stop.

"Un-cle," Figol says. He's shaking my arm now and my right shoulder is demanding action.

"What?"

"You need to get up. Roisair and his men are coming."

"Fine, I'm awake."

I hope he's in my mind so he knows what a concession this is.

The sky has cleared. The rain has moved off leaving a brilliant blue sky. If not for the desperate screams within the inner city and the needless loss of life, today would be a beautiful winter day.

"There they are," Figol says pointing at a mob as it approaches us.

"Is it just me, or does Roisair look like the leader of a band of brigands?"

"He does, but please don't tell him that. I don't like our chances against him and all his warriors."

I laugh and immediately regret it.

Crisa rushes out in front. "The demons, they're gone. How'd you do it?"

"They're not quite gone. Before Tuss Metiana and his council were killed, they summoned more demons. They are trapped in the inner city."

"Good," Roisair says. "Their foul creatures will do our work for us."

"Roisair, there are plenty of innocent Tusci inside there," Glasna says.

"There are no innocent Tusci. They are walking on the bones of our people."

I start coughing and regret every spasm. I grab my shoulder and my hand comes away bloody.

"Let me look at that," Crisa says. She pulls off the bandage and inspects the wound before reaching in her bags for the right herbs.

"Do you have mint and dew of the sea?" I ask.

"Dew of the Sea?" She wrinkles her brow and looks to Figol. "Has he taken head damage?"

"Nevermind," I say.

"Drink some of this," she says as she goes to work cleaning my wounds.

I drink her tonic and feel much better. "What's in this?"

"Fairy glove tea," she says. "Before you start critiquing my care, tell me how you managed to defeat the ruling Tusci and their demons all by yourself."

Roisair is trying to act nonchalant as he strains to hear my answer. I'm not willing to tell him of Figol's powers. I ignore the question and struggle to my feet instead. "Greetings Roisair, Tuss

Metiana and his advisors are dead. The inner city is open to you and your men."

He motions for a couple of men to approach the gate. They peer inside before cautiously entering. Several heartbeats go by before one of them returns. "Lord Roisair, it is as he says. The way is clear."

Lord Roisair? Crisa raises an eyebrow at that as well. Since when do king's bastards rate a title?

"Men!" Roisair yells. His men crowd around us. "Our time is at hand. Purge the city of any and all demon summoners and take your just reward."

The men run headlong through the gate. In moments it is only Roisair, Glasna and Crisa joining Figol and I before the gates.

"Roisair," Glasna says forcefully. "There are hundreds of innocent people in there who just happen to have red hair. They could no more summon a demon than you."

"The men have suffered much this day, defeating the hellspawn. They deserve a reward."

Figol places a restraining hand on my wrist. Crisa too is aware of my outrage. Roisair and his men didn't kill a single demon. They were nothing but sacrificial lambs.

"I will not stand by and let good people be killed," Glasna says.

"There's nothing we can do," Roisair answers.

"There are still demons inside?" She looks directly at Figol and me.

"There are," I say.

"Then I will banish the demons and order the men away from the innocents," Glasna says.

"I'll go with you," Figol says, surprising us all.

"Do you think I need a man to protect me?" She challenges.

Figol bows his head. "No, my lady, I do not. I only wish to aid you in whatever way I can."

"Very well, come with me." Glasna throws off her brother's restraining hand and marches for the inner city. Her head is held high, like a true noble. At the gate, she motions Figol to catch up. "How many and what kind of demons are still loose?" she asks as the pair disappear behind the stout oak doors.

"How did you kill the Tusci leaders?" Roisair asks.

"They were all incinerated with a fire runestone," I say.

"And where did this take place?"

"Directly above us."

"Show me."

Whatever Crisa gave me is surprisingly effective. We climb the stairs and I have no need of resting. From the top of the inner-city wall, we can hear the cries of women and children from within. I shoot Crisa and Roisair a hard look. Crisa at least feels ashamed enough to look away.

"How did it happen?" Roisair asks, bringing me out of my thoughts. "How exactly did you manage to kill all of them at once?"

I grow more and more uneasy with every wail of despair. "I was here'" I retake my spot. "This was a complete rock circle with a demon inside of it." I point to the mishmash of stones before me. "With the demon between us, Tuss was willing to banish Te'Kuth."

A woman's piteous scream is cut short. Crisa flinches, but Roisair shows no signs of being aware of the wholesale slaughter.

"I threw the rune and that gooey mess is all that remains of Tuss and his council. The demon was freed, so Figol and I ran for the city gate and safety. You and your men found us there."

"What was Tuss Metiana like?" Roisair says overtop the screams of a woman.

"I can't. I can't ignore this massacre any longer." I choose the tawny owl and leave Crisa and Roisair on the plaza.

Figol is standing atop an oak piling and directing the people to the ships. I land next to him and retake my human form.

"The city has fallen! The ships! They're your only chance!" He's waving frantically at the locals. The crowd is milling around, not sure what to make of the latest news. I land on the piling opposite him on the dock. A slow trickle of people and their possessions pass between us to the ships.

"Take over calling," Figol says. "I'll try to use my other talent."

Few people heed my warning. Mostly they circle about and call on me to transform into different animals. Behind the crowd, where a narrow passage opens up to the docks, three large, frightened women burst around the corner. Their incoherently screams fill the air. Only a few steps behind them are several of Roisair's men. One of the men grab for the slowest and knock her to the ground. Their doom acted out in front of them, the crowd at last understands.

I hold my left arm out in front of me. It's mostly still, so I should be able to animorph at least one more time. I change into a gannet and fly above the confusion. Using the bird's natural instincts, I plunge downward into the midst of the Roisair's men, scattering them.

The downed woman scoops up her baby and flees the warriors. After several more dives, the warriors give up prowling near the docks. Behind me voices rise in fear. The ships are pulling the gangways off the docks. Several dozen Tusci women and children are stranded even as more of Roisair's men emerge from streets.

I land next to Figol. I can't waste effort changing back, so I chirp at him instead.

"The captains, their hearts are set on escaping. I cannot convince any to stay and take on the survivors."

I will fix this.

I select the largest and slowest boat leaving port. I land on the deck and force myself to concentrate. The transition to human is sluggish. Surprised, a sailor pounds on a small cabin door. A large man with black braids dangling to his shoulders emerges onto the deck above me.

"Bring this boat back into port." My voice sounds hollow.

"Shut up or my men will toss you over," he growls. His eyes flicker over the scene dockside.

I push pass the crew and take the stairs up to the captain's level. "You need to take on the women and children or they will be slaughtered," I say, looking him directly in the eyes.

"Why? There's no profit to be made." He asks, sticking out his chin.

"Sell them as slaves if you must, but you can't leave them to die."

"Watch me," he says with a malevolent smile. "The demon summoners are not my people."

The man is armed with only a short sword and a dagger. "Give the order or I will kill you," I say with a quiet voice.

He looks me up and down and sees that I have only my bone knife. He snorts and turns his back on me. I summon my will and change into a bear. I swing my big left paw and slam him against the wall. His eyes nearly burst at a cave bear towering over him. My roar carries and the entire pier goes quiet. I reposition my paw on his chest, just above his heart. One shift in my weigh and his heart will be shredded.

He trembles in fear.

No one notices the amount of time it takes to retake my human form. "Tell your men to turn this ship around and take on the refugees," I glare at him.

"Yes, yes of course," he blabbers.

"And you're not to sell them as slaves." I draw my head in close to his. "That opportunity has passed. You will drop them off at a safe port and you will not ask for any compensation in return, do you understand?" I push off from his chest and grab the rail behind me. I grip it with both hands so no one can see them tremble.

"Back to the docks," he calls to his men.

I don't dare show weakness now. "I'll be taking the form of a seabird to watch you once you're underway. Defy me and you won't get another chance."

"Yes, of course," he says, his voice still quivering.

If he only knew how helpless I currently am.

The refugees have been loaded on the ship and the docks are empty and quiet.

"How did you get the ship to return to port?" Glasna asks.

"I made myself unbearable."

Figol rolls his eyes.

"What needs to be done next?"

I don't know why Figol is so eager to help. I look at him and it dawns on me. I've seen that look before. Gods above, I've had that look before, when I was around Dalna all those years ago. He's smitten with Lady Glasna.

"I'll do a check of the area," I volunteer. With all we've been through, they deserve at least a little time to themselves. Once I'm in the shadows, I peek back at the two to confirm I'm right.

From across the way, I can see that they are staring into each other's eyes. It seems there will be two broken hearts when we leave Eriu. I wander through the streets and before I know it, I'm climbing the stairs to the city gate plaza.

Crisa rushes over to me. "How are things in the city?"

"The last of the Tusci have made it aboard the ships. I don't know where they will end up, but they leave with their lives."

Roisair shrugs. "They'll be sold into slavery."

How I dislike this man.

"I don't believe so. I've persuaded the captain to drop them off at a safe harbor."

"In that case, they'll go to Ynys Manaw, though since the Tusci took it over, most call it the Demon Isle."

"My commanders are back," Roisair says as a way of excusing himself. "We have much to discuss about ruling this city."

Crisa and I look at each other. We both did as much if not more than Roisair to take Laleah. We follow him and join his council. For reasons I can't fathom, he has chosen a spot next to the fallen Tusci. The bodies have cooled and a semisolid puddle of fluids has coalesced around the charred remains. The flies are only now finding their feast.

"Men, we've done it. Each of you will be given the title and duties we agreed upon before we started this campaign."

One of the men makes a show of coughing as he nods in our direction.

"Welcome druids," Roisair says with a broad smile without missing a beat. "The city is ours."

"At a terrible price," Crisa says.

"Aye, that is true, but with my leadership, Laleah will once again become a powerful center of commerce."

"What of the old Laleah regime?" Crisa asks.

"If they swear to uphold my rule they will be welcomed back," Roisair says.

"You will appoint yourself Lord of the city?" I ask. The dead are not yet buried and yet he cares only about titles.

"Everyone, I would be remiss if I did not acknowledge our friends from Pretanni." He gives me a disingenuous smile. "As you recall, I called our friend a badger on the eve of this battle."

The men chuckle, not sure where Roisair is going with this.

"Grahme stood side by side with us today and played his part in our liberation of Laleah. I hereby proclaim that Grahme of Pretanni is officially given the titles Friend to Laleah to go along with 'Brokko kom Gresman,' the badger with bite."

His men grunt their mirth and approval.

Crisa leans in close. "He means to diminish your efforts with meaningless titles," she says.

"What do I need with titles, real or not?" I say in a low voice.

Roisair puts some distance between us as he approaches one of his men. "Inform your men that they fought like wolves today." The men grunt their agreement. "The city guard will forever be known by that moniker." He turns to the gray-haired man with a fresh scar running down the side of his cheek. "And you, Elithan, will be known as the 'Gray Wolf,' the leader of the guards."

The men cheer loudly for Elithan.

"And what of the manwolves of Ossory?" I call loudly.

Anger flashes in Roisair's eyes for just a moment. He clasps his hands together. "They, like all of my men fought bravely today. It is a shame that none of them survived."

"At least they managed to kill a demon. Something that neither you nor your men were capable of doing," I say.

The plaza goes so quiet that the flies can be heard buzzing from place to place.

"Men," Roisair begins, "Grahme is not a hardened fighter such as us. The rigors of today have clearly worn on him. I pray that no one take offence at his unconsidered words." He glares directly at Crisa and his voice takes on an edge. "Perhaps after he has had time to rest, he can rejoin us."

Crisa grabs the back of my forearm in an unrelenting grip. Cynbel's iron manacles never bit into me quite like this. She nods her head at Roisair. "We shall clear our heads with some fresh air." In a low voice that only I can hear, she says, "Come with me Grahme, unless you care to fight Roisair and all his men with nothing but your knife."

Puzzled, I look down at her and over to Roisair. Now I can see the predator lurking within. I'm angry with myself. I had only seen a pompous, self-congratulating fool. It could not have been more plain unless he snarled at me.

I take a deep breath and unclench my fists. I must keep my eye on my objective here in Eriu.

"If you will excuse us," I say while nodding my head.

We find Figol and Glasna right where I left them. The two of them are holding hands. Figol sees us and waves us over.

"What news?" Glasna asks.

"The city is quiet and Roisair has set himself up to be the Lord of the city."

Glasna nods her head. "It is for the best. He will get nothing from Father."

Crisa squeezes my arm again, as if I was going to say something unkind. I raise my hands at the wrists and she grudgingly releases me.

"Grahme, Figol and I will be leaving in the morning," Crisa says to Glasna. "I must call a council meeting and bring news of our success at once."

"Then I will come with you," Glasna says.

"You will?" Figol says with a smile.

"I will," she says as she rests her head on his shoulder. "Someone should be there to argue on behalf of Roisair."

22

Returning to the Start

The path to Lia Fahil is an easy one. Figol and Glasna spend much of their time smiling foolishly at each other. They have been given the horses so they can be together. Crisa and I spend much of our time together as well, but it is spent with me teaching her how to animorph. The past three days of training have ended with her getting headaches.

"Let's try another approach." It's hard to say who's more frustrated. "What animals were you most familiar with growing up?"

"I don't know; sheep, goats, pigs . . .."

"Is there anything else? For instance, I used to be kept awake at night by a couple of tawny owls. When I found the tree where they nested, I built a hiding place so I could watch them without being spotted."

A faraway look comes over her. "There was a marten that would nest in the thatch of our storage hut. I cried every time Father threatened to kill it. As usual, I got my way." She smiles at the memory.

"And did you watch it?" I ask.

"Every chance I got."

"I bet you know more about the lives of martens than just about anyone else."

She chuckles. "That's true."

"Good, then I want you to imagine that marten: think of its claws, its mouth and its tail—"

"—And the slinky spine."

"And the slinky spine, most definitely," I say. "Now will yourself into that shape."

I take a breath and hear a thin, shrill call at my feet. She's done it! A brown-coated marten runs in circles in front of me. She freezes, her muscles taut, before scurrying halfway up the trunk of the nearest tree. She jumps into the bushes, branches rustling until she comes out with a freshly killed rabbit.

"You've caught our dinner," I say.

She gives me a wheezy hiss before returning into the bushes. In only a few breaths, her human form rises from the bushes with another rabbit in her mouth. "You didn't warn me about this," she says after dropping the rabbit into her hand.

"How was it?"

Her smile stretches across her face. "It was amazing. The dexterity of the creature, and the tail to balance every move, I felt more alive somehow." She stares at me in wonder.

"Wait until you're flying . . .."

"I can't imagine," she says. "I have to do it again."

"Yes, but before you do, make sure that you don't let the animal's natural instincts take over."

"Like hunting for a rabbit?" She raises her trophy up.

"Work with the instincts, but don't become a slave to them. Otherwise, you can lose yourself in the creature."

Crisa turns toward the forest, changes into a marten again and runs in circles up the trunk of the tree. At last, she's learned that art of animorphing.

"Crisa, we don't all need our own rabbit for supper."

Crisa in marten form is nearly impossible to see now that it's dusk. At the edge of the clearing, she animorphs back to human holding her third rabbit. "Are you sure?"

"Do you see the long-eared owl in the tree on the opposite side of the clearing?" I nod my head in the direction of the bird of prey. "He's been very interested in you."

"Oh," she says. "Oh! What would happen if . . ."

"—if it came for you?" I finish. She nods. "Then if it didn't kill you outright, you could change back to human form. But if it managed to break your neck first . . .."

"You can't be serious," Glasna says.

"I most certainly am."

She looks to Figol for confirmation. He nods his agreement.

"Then why would you ever take the chance?" Glasna asks.

"That is why we study the ways of animals for a healthy amount of time before being taught to animorph."

Glasna looks to Figol. "You don't animorph, do you?"

"I do," he says with pride.

"Well, I have a surprise of my own," Glasna says. She stares into the fire and says *"Lichiul srenc Elruzon."*

The fire becomes extra smoky for a moment until a small demon appears. The hobbled horses start snorting in fear.

"This is my imp, Elruzon," Glasna says.

Crisa looks ready to throw her rabbit at the demon. "What have you done?"

"No need to fear, he is a weak one," Glasna says. She looks at the owl, "Chase that off."

The imp leaves at once, flying directly for the owl. It gives off a low, breathy squeal before departing its perch.

"Elruzon, return to me," Glasna says. The imp circles immediately and returns to hover over the fire.

"You should not mess with the natural order of things," I say.

"*Favin cepen*," she says with a dismissive wave of her hand. The imp hisses its displeasure as it evaporates before us. "I just didn't want to be seen as the helpless one."

"I saw you stand up to the demon, Kugorath. Helpless is not a word I would use to describe you."

"We are only a few hours from Lia Fahil," Crisa says. "It would be best if none of us animorph or summon demons near the city." Crisa looks at all of us in turn. "I will request a council meeting at once, though it might take several days for all the kings and druids to arrive. During that time, we have to be extra careful. Flaunting our powers, including the use of runestones, would be disastrous."

"I will be off to see Rhedna of the Sorrows," I say. The others look back at me, confused. "She was disguised as a healer during the battle and she told me that we would speak again five days hence. Tomorrow will mark five days."

"She was at Laleah?" Crisa asks. "Why didn't she go to Roisair? She could have foretold how the battle would unfold."

"Crisa," Glasna says. "Will you walk with me to the stream? I need to fill my water bladder." The ladies leave us to the fire. Once they are out of earshot, Glasna leans in to Crisa and whispers a secret.

"While we're alone, I must caution you. You cannot use your powers to take advantage of Glasna."

"Uncle Grahme," he says, indignant. I would never do such a thing to someone like Glasna."

"That's good to hear. I must also remind you that we are leaving this island very soon. Once your training starts, you will not be able to see her for a very long time."

"Not even at the festivals?"

"If you are allowed to attend them, it will be with your master and you will be stuck preparing for the ceremonies."

Disgusted, Figol throws a branch into the fire, causing embers to fly. He gains control of himself almost at once. "I'm sorry, Uncle."

"You've done no harm and the last few days would be trying to even the most patient of men. Remember, we have been trying to draw the Emerald druids into an alliance for hundreds of years. Whatever else happens, you will be part of that success."

The silence allows my fears to grow. Whether right or not, I need to address them. "Figol, can we trust Crisa?"

"Of course," he looks at me confused.

"She is the key to us learning the giant runes. She has the relationship with Gortor and she will be on Eriu, while we will not. Can we trust her to share that knowledge willingly, and openly?"

"Why wouldn't she?"

I stand up to stretch so that I can check on Crisa and Glasna without being obvious. "I have no reason to distrust her, mind you, but great power can tempt even the purest of heart. I hesitate to ask, but if you can, poke around her head and see if her heart is true."

"We're not going to tell them of my powers?"

"Not yet."

"By withholding the nature of my powers, aren't we doing what we fear Crisa will do to us?"

"You've been in my head enough to know that I don't have any answers." I laugh at myself. Now I've filled myself with self-doubt. Maybe Figol's right, we have not been completely honest with Crisa. I stare darkly into the fire.

How did Boswen avoid being consumed by doubts?

The long-eared owl hoots as it returns to its tree. I'm not sure why, but I'm heartened he did not let the imp frighten him away for good.

"Uncle, thank you for agreeing to this quest," Figol blurts. "I mean, there's nothing in it for you, yet you agreed anyway."

"It's what family does for their own."

23

The Meeting of the High Council

Crisa's poultices have done wonders for my shoulder. The use of wild endive to heal my cuts is new to me. I must remember to speak to Eghan about it. I have eaten the leaves many times, but never was I aware of its medicinal properties. By the time we reach Lia Fahil, I can move my shoulder in all directions with only a little pain.

"Is it a holy day here that we don't observe on Pretanni?" The village is strangely quiet.

"No, not that I'm aware," Crisa says. "People usually stay inside, especially women, to avoid the kings during the meetings. Their appetites are legendary."

"Look! Up on the hill," Figol points to the top of Komsit Lal and the score of men seated there.

"A council has been called," Crisa says. "We must hurry." She kicks her horse gently and heads for the meeting site at a canter. Glasna follows not far behind.

"Do we fly?" Figol asks.

"No, the last thing we need is to throw it in their faces that we can animorph and they can't."

"In that case, you'll be the last one there." Figol breaks into a run, leaving me behind.

We catch up with Crisa as she and Glasna are dismounting.

"What news," she asks the guards.

"There's a council meeting, my Lord. They'll be discussing Laleah, I suspect."

"Why are you two stationed down here?"

"I don't rightly know, but I do as I'm told."

"We are coming from Laleah. I will bring these three up with me." She hands the middle-aged warrior her reins.

"As you say, Lord Crisa."

"Do you often have armed guards?" I ask.

"Never," Crisa responds. "I for one would like to know why they have been stationed here today."

Winded as we are, Figol and I are the last to climb the stairs. There are more guards on top of the sun cave. King Diardoc of the Laigin has the rest of the kings standing behind him as he is forcibly making his point to Anach and the Druid Lords. For his part, Anach is seated in his wooden throne and scarcely paying attention.

"Since when do we allow the kings' warriors at our council meetings?" Crisa demands.

Diardoc turns to us. "So, the murderers have the gall to show up after all."

"We have come from Laleah, where we have liberated the city from the Tusci," Crisa says.

"Liberated it from all life, more like," Diardoc says. "Ten thousand dead, that is what they have wrought." He points an accusatory finger at us.

"There aren't ten thousand people in the city," Crisa says. "And most of the killing was by the demons."

"Which you loosed upon the city." Diardoc thrusts his finger at Crisa, "Even though you knew that peace had been secured by me only a handful of days ago."

"Surely an island free of demons is better than a temporary peace."

"She admits her guilt," Diardoc says triumphantly. "If only you had brought that bandit Roisair with you so we could deal with him as well."

"Roisair is an honorable man," Glasna says, striding forward.

"Glasna," a tall, stocky man says with disappointment.

"Sorry father, but since you would do nothing for your son, he had to find his own way."

"He is not an official son," Loelill says.

"If Loelill and the rest of us went around acknowledging every illegitimate offspring, the whole island would be nobility," Diardoc cuts in.

"And they'd have more dignity and decency than you ever will," Glasna shoots back.

"Why is she not married off yet?" Diardoc asks Loelill.

"Because I haven't found a man that's my equal, that's why," Glasna says. "I will be a queen and I will rule better than the lot of you." She stares at each king in turn, ending with Diardoc.

"Anach, you have witnessed yet another grievous threat to the Eriu. She would ruin the noble peace by marrying a prince of our realm. The bloodline alliances nearly tore this isle apart two hundred years ago."

Despite being a full head shorter, Glasna stands toe to toe with Diardoc. "Let's go onto the field below and I'll show you just how dangerous I can be."

"And she threatens kings," he adds. "I demand she be married off this week, to a shepherd if necessary."

"Glasna," Loelill says with sadness in his voice, "Apologize to Diardoc."

"I will not. Diardoc is a fool who farts out of his mouth. All his words carry a foul stench."

"That is enough," Anach says. "You have not been invited to this council and you will not speak unless I request it." He turns to Diardoc and Loelill. "Your request is most fair, Diardoc. Loelill, see that she is married off at once. If no shopkeeper will have her and her foul temper, then a shepherd or fisherman will do."

"Yes, Lord Druid," Loelill says with a heavy sigh.

A crow lands behind the row of six guards. It turns its head toward me and I see a milky left eye. It has been five days since we've last seen each other.

"As for Roisair, he is to appear before this council and explain himself. His grasp for power may well start a war between the Tusci and us."

"You can't make her marry, just because you want her to," Figol says, his face red with anger.

"Ah, the Pretanni instigators, I haven't forgotten about you," Anach says. "You are to leave this island by the end of this day. If any should see you here after that time, they have the right to inflict great bodily harm, up to and including death. Go home, meddlers. We have nothing to learn from the likes of you."

"But Anach, you're wrong," Crisa says.

"I'll get to you in a moment. But first, I must deal with Finne."

"Me, Lord Druid?" Finne asks, startled.

"Yes you. This needless slaughter occurred in your area, yet you were nowhere to be seen."

"The Tusci, they were everywhere."

"Clearly you are not able to lead the people in Loelill's lands. Your cowardly acts are at fault here as well. I hereby release you from the protection of Ankenet Starno and the surrounding lands, a duty in which you were woefully inadequate. Instead, I place you as my Battle Leader and keeper of the Auga Sawels."

Finne looks as if he wants to complain, but he declines to do so.

"May I remind the Lord Druid, that the positions on the council are not for him to change? That is the work of the entire council," Crisa says.

Anach looks through Crisa. "Your thoughts might matter, if you were still a member of this council. No, Crisa, as a leader at the slaughter of Laleah, I name you outlaw. You have been found guilty of high crimes and your punishment will be death." He turns his back on Crisa. "Seize them all."

"Congratulations Anach!" a shrill voice shouts from behind the guards. They part to let a middle-aged Rhedna of the Sorrows enter the circle. "This is the last momentous decision of your disastrous reign. Your penchant for incompetence will be the legacy for which you are remembered."

"Seize her too!" Anach shouts, pointing at the seer.

Rhedna laughs and she parries the halfhearted swipes at her with her staff.

"I told you as you laid in my bed that you were destined to be remembered as the worse Druid Lord in living memory."

"Kill her!" a red faced Anach screams. She cackles as she weaves between blows. Her effortless battle dance is mesmerizing.

"We must get Glasna out of here" is blasted within my head. Crisa too must have received the order. The guards, realizing they cannot out duel Rhedna, charge us instead.

"We will meet up at the place where we met after Tiva's," I shout. "Figol, follow me." I envision a white-tailed eagle and assume its form. A guard's spear flies over my avian head in what would have been a mortal blow were I still human.

I launch up at his face, beak and talons reaching for delicate flesh. He drops to the ground. I check my talons, but neither grips any flesh. It seems deep gashes is all I inflicted.

A third eagle joins us in the brawl. I assume it is Rhedna, but I see her skipping down the side of the hill, laughing as she goes. So Crisa is even a faster study than I thought.

"Get her!" Anach yells as Glasna runs for the steps. Thrilled to contend with one small woman rather than eagles, the five remaining guards all give chase. The three of us dive at the men until they stop their pursuit and form a circle with spears pointing outward.

At the bottom of the stairs, the two guards wait with their spears ready. Glasna stops ten steps from the bottom and chants "Lichiul srenc Elruzon." As her imp coalesces from the ether, she points at the men below her and shouts "Attack."

The men have no stomach for battle with even small demonic foes. They throw down their spears and dive to each side as Elruzon charges. "Keep them down," Glasna says as she runs past them to the horses. She grabs the reins of one horse as she mounts the second. With a flick of her heels, she and the horses make good their escape. "*Favin cepen,*" she yells. Elruzon disappears in a cloud of thick black smoke in midflight.

Crisa flies to where the Kings' horses are kept. Once in human form, she urges them to scatter. She runs for the forest and disappears into brush. Had the guards been observant, they would have seen a marten out during the day, staring at the commotion below.

Just before dusk we meet back on top Komsit Lal. After a day of shouting and fruitless searching, the men have abandoned the effort for now.

"Tiva will do good business tonight," I say.

Crisa chuckles, "That she will."

She selects Anach's chair. "When do we attack?" She asks.

Good luck to any man who tries to control her.

"Hold on there," I say. "More than enough blood has been spilled for the next several years, at least."

"I will not become a wife to a lowly sheepherder," she says with defiance in her eyes.

I raise my hands as if to surrender. She glares at Figol and Crisa before allowing herself to be mollified.

Crisa turns to Glasna. "You and I can't stay in your father's kingdom. Both of us are too well known to remain hidden for long."

"Then where will we go?"

"You can come to Pretanni with us," Figol says.

Before I can correct him, Crisa answers. "My place is on Eriu, as is Glasna's. We will go to the manwolves. They will allow us sanctuary and neither Diardoc's Laigin nor Caohin's Invern dare send men near the caves of Ossory."

Glasna shivers. "I find that the mere presence of Caohin unnerves me."

"He is . . . unusual, as is Fessach, his druid. They both share an unhealthy fascination with the sick and dying."

"And what of the runes?" I ask.

"The firbolgs do not answer to druids or kings. With the knowledge of animorphing," she nods her head at me, "I can visit Gortor regularly."

Can she be trusted to share the knowledge? I look at Figol as I think my question.

He bows his head and goes to work.

Glasna stands and stretches before letting out a huge yawn. I can't let the group break up yet, Figol must have time to find the answer to my question.

"I wish to visit him as well. Can we meet at Alban Heruin, the summer solstice?"

"Since I no longer have duties as a Druid Lord, I am free to meet you there."

It's a start, but how do I keep the conversation going?

"That was a fun morning," Rhedna says from behind me.

I smile at her greeting. Figol will get his time and I'll get information from Rhedna, I hope. "Revered seer," I start. "What do you have to tell us?"

"Always direct, aren't you Grahme Fairweather, Friend to Laleah and Brokko kom Gresman?"

I don't try to hide my annoyance at the meaningless titles. "I've found speaking simply leads to less miscommunication."

"Very well, then you and young master Figol should leave here and continue your quest on Pretanni."

"How can we make an alliance with the Emerald Druids from there?"

"Don't be too quick to claim defeat," Rhedna says. "Meraud simply said you had to make peace with a powerful ally. She did not limit your choices."

"Who else do I try? The Wigesta? The Sorim?"

"The centaurs," Rhedna says.

"They kill any humans they find on their lands, no questions and no reprieves."

"Then you should go with one who is a centaur friend."

"Who would that be?" I ask, exasperated.

"My father."

"Your father still lives?"

"He does and I must warn you, he won't be easy to cajole the second time you see him."

"I must be going," she nods her head.

"Wait!" I call. She turns to face me. "How did you become so young?"

She smiles. "My mother taught me. Ask her when you see her." Before I can ask any more questions, she turns into a crow and flies toward the sunset.

24

Moor Trouble

The moor of Bodmin is blanketed in snow. The light of Belenos can barely penetrate the thick, gray clouds, yet I must squint to reduce the glare from the snow. The giant's home from our previous trip is at the south end of the moor. I had hoped to find a different lodging place, but the frosted ground makes the task that much more difficult. I resign myself to finding our previous spot.

I circle the entrance and land softly in front of it. Figol crashes into the snow as if diving into water. I squawk at his clumsiness before changing back.

"Since you're so excited for excavation duty, I'll get us kindling for a fire."

By nightfall we've secured enough wood and two healthy plovers for our dinner. "If we make a basin at the entrance, we can refill our waterskins with the melted snow." Figol smiles at me, clearly impressed by the simplest of tricks. Now had he lived on a farm and had to hide for hours from an angry older brother . . ..

"It should be easy to find Bodmin tomorrow," Figol says.

I chuckle to myself. "You think so?"

"He's a black cat and the ground is covered in snow. He'd be hard to miss."

"Unless he's holed up somewhere warm, or hiding in the shadows, or in the middle of a gorse thicket, waiting out the storm."

"I hadn't thought of that," Figol says lamely.

"Or he could be right at your door, ready to knock the silly heads together of men who can't follow orders," a booming voice says from above.

We jump to our feet at once. "Bodmin?" I call.

A large black cat nearly the size of a man prowls down the uneven ground. It lets out a guttural growl and gnashes its teeth.

It's impressive, but we've seen this before. "Well met, Bodmin. If you were going to attack us, I doubt you would have announced yourself first, then change to an animal form."

Bodmin takes his human form. "I must practice," he says. "Stupid people are starting to come to my moor without a care for the dangers." He warms his hands by the fire. "I should throw you out of this place tonight," he growls just as menacingly as when he was the cat.

"Forgive us Bodmin, we only returned because we were directed to do so."

"I don't care what the council says, this is my land, not yours."

"You were once a Druid Protector."

"Aye, and my leaving the order was one of the few things your precious council and I agreed upon. They only protect the small-minded agendas of its lords."

I interject before he can give voice to his full anger, "It wasn't the council who ordered us to return. It was your daughter, Rhedna of the Sorrows,"

224

"Rhedna?" He scoffs, "of the sorrows? That girl was pampered more than any princess." He put his hands on his hips. "What did she say? Be exact."

"She told us that to complete our quest we had to abandon Eriu and seek out the centaurs. She said you were their friend and that we should ask you to lead us to them. Then she told me the answers I seek will be answered by her mother."

His eyes narrow and he watches me for a moment. I stare back, wondering what he wants.

"This is not prophecy, this is Rhedna meddling where she doesn't belong. You have been deceived and placed at the center of a family squabble."

At least he's not angry with us anymore. "What is it that she wants us to do?" I ask.

"You're her father?" Figol asks. "She looks much older than you, well, sometimes."

Bodmin's mood only darkens. "I think I know her aims and I will not be bound by them. Let Rhedna's mother take you to see the centaurs."

"I don't mean to pry, but who is Rhedna's mother?" I ask.

"Ganna."

"Ganna? The witch pariah?" I'm astounded. I wasn't sure she was real.

He stares directly into my eyes. "Tell me of a witch outside of your order that isn't considered a pariah."

Raising my hands, I concede his point.

"Can you tell me how old your daughter is?" I ask.

"Which one? Ganna and I have four daughters."

"Four?"

"Aye, Sabel was the eldest. She was born with a full head of deep black hair." His whole face softens as he recalls his first child. "Ganna was initially afraid of my reaction of having a daughter, so she hid her on Eriu until she could gauge my feelings. She was the happiest of children. I would fly to Drumanagh every time I could. Pretty little Sabel even started telling people that I was her pet owl for a time."

"What kind of owl?" Figol asks.

"A tawny owl."

Figol looks triumphantly at me. "You two have a lot in common."

I roll my eyes but remain silent, not wanting to stop Bodmin now that we have him speaking of his past.

"Cuma and Frona left for their mother's homeland shortly after they reached adulthood. They were twins and preferred each other's company to the rest of the world." He scratches the side of his head. "It has been at least a hundred years since I have seen them." He stares up at the ceiling. "But that is the nature of time, always moving too fast or too slow."

"Where did they go?" I ask.

"Vascones, north of Hibernia."

I nod as if these places hold meaning for me. I will have to ask Caradoc once we finish our quest.

"The only daughter of ours to remain on Pretanni, at least for a time, was Rhedna. She was ever the schemer, even in her childhood."

"What does she want from us?" I ask.

"I told you, family business," he says quickly. And with that, the conversation dies again.

"Is it true that Ganna abducts misshapen infants from their mothers?" Figol asks.

Bodmin flashes a mirthless grin. "What other rumors of Ganna have you heard?"

Figol looks at me, urging me to take the lead.

"I don't necessarily believe all the rumors, but it is said she curses harvests in order to prolong her life or else sickens whole villages. She has pulled lightening down on a commoner's home when she has felt slighted. These are just some of the things people say about her."

Bodmin rolls his head back and laughs without humor. "I started many of these stories a hundred years ago or more. Be warned, Ganna is a powerful woman and quick to anger, but she is no monster. Her wrath is far worse than any monster's."

"How can you and she still be alive?" I ask.

"How indeed? If it were well known, then many would try it and the balance of nature would be upended."

"I asked Lord Boswen many times about this and he had no wise words for me."

"Boswen was wise to keep that secret," Bodmin says.

"Will you take us to see Ganna the witch?" Figol asks.

"You should know, since you've been in my head for quite some time now."

Figol flinches but doesn't deny the charge.

"I can't stop you from entering, but I can lead you to dead end after dead end, young mind mage."

"I'm sorry," Figol says. "How did you know?"

"If you want this one to stay out of your head, think of his most embarrassing moments. The better your recall, the more likely he will be to leave," I say.

Bodmin nods his thanks. "When Ganna and I left Pretanni, we traveled far and wide. The Sorim are not nearly as clever as they believe. Ganna was ever afraid of what they would learn from her, but I never needed an amulet."

"Did you miss being a Lord Protector?" I ask. "I guess you're still a druid, at least."

The silence stretches as he ponders my question.

"No, I am no longer a Lord Protector, nor even a druid, technically. When I had to make my choice, I thought I would gain more than I lost. Most days I still believe that to be true." Without another word, he lays down, facing away from us and drifts off to sleep.

Exiting the cave, I see Bodmin, sitting on his haunches, staring over the frozen moor in his feline form. I sit next to him and take in the sunrise. Most of the snow is gone, blown off the moor by the westerly wind. Moor ponies fight with the thorny branches of gorse to get at the nutritious leaves. Even now, at the coldest time of year, the bushes sport sporadic yellow blossoms.

"Since your apprentice is so eager to prove himself, I sent him ahead to my storage cache. We will break our fast there."

"Figol is my nephew, but he is not yet a druid."

"You taught a commoner how to animorph? In my day you would have been flogged for your insolence. Still, he was very eager to show his knowledge."

"The council is loath to allow him among our ranks. Completing this quest is the only way they will give Figol entrance. I'm curious though, what form did he take when he left this morning?"

"A tawny owl, completely out of place on the moor at dawn," he says, irritated.

"You sound just like Boswen."

"He was wise enough to take my council. Come, we should join the child before he ruins my stores. I for one, desire a hearty meal before traveling to the Griffin Cliffs."

"Ganna lives among the griffins?" I can't have heard him right. "No one could survive with griffins perpetually hunting overhead."

"She lives at their southern foothills."

"How do you know she's still alive?"

"A dragon may be able to kill her, but I pity any lesser creature that would dare try."

The sunrise refuses to provide warmth for our walk. Clouds from the west promise to bring more snow, or even worse, ice to the high plain.

"We are here," Bodmin says. "This is one of my larders. See that slab of stone without snow? That is the roof of my cache. I left the fire going when I went to confront intruders on my moor."

The small pond near the stone has nearly melted off its frozen top. "Why is there no sign of smoke or any motion at all?" I ask.

"It seems that your nephew got lost."

"Not likely, if he couldn't find this place, he has enough sense to follow the river back to us."

Bodmin points to one of Figol's feet, lying at an odd angle.

"Figol!" I race to my nephew and find him lying prone on the floor. "No, no, no . . ." I check his neck for a pulse. It's there, but it's weak. Flecks of white froth are at the corners of his mouth. "Figol?" I slap him a couple times. "Figol?"

He stirs a little, so at least he's still alive.

"Wode whistle," Bodmin says.

He's holding a clay pot.

"What?"

"He grabbed the wode whistle instead of the wild carrot. Had he received proper training, he would have known that hairless stems and—"

"—What can we do for him?" I open his mouth and see bits of leaves still present. With my sleeve, I clear them out. I splash a bit of cold water in my nephew's face.

He sputters and his eyes flitter.

I give him another slap. "Figol? Wake up Figol."

"Uncle?" he croaks.

Relief floods through me. "Figol, can you get up?"

"I can't see you," panic starts to enter his voice. "I can't see anything."

"It's alright. Bodmin and I are here now. Let us do our work." I feel his neck again, no improvement.

Bodmin signals me to come away.

"I fear in his hunger he ate most of the leaves before he felt any symptoms."

I stare at him, trying to piece together what he is trying not to say.

"He is beyond my skill."

"Who could help him? Eghan? I can bring him back here."

"Do druids have such knowledge in poisons? It was not the case in my day."

"Then why do you have it?" I want to scream, but I keep my voice low so that Figol doesn't overhear.

"They can be made into medicine, if worked properly. I fear the only one who could help him is Ganna, and there is not the time to get her and return."

"Then we will all go to her." Without wasting any motion, I return to my nephew. "Figol, we need to take you to Ganna to reverse the effect of the poison."

His breath is fast and weak, but he understands enough to nod his head.

"To take you to her, you're going to have to change into a small animal so I can carry you. Can you do that?"

Figol takes in several deep breaths. "I can become a puffin."

All I can think of is Sieffre and his tragic transformation. I don't have time for pity. "Figol, tell me what you feel."

"My whole-body aches, except my feet. I can't feel them at all. They are still there, right? I can't see either."

"Your feet are fine. Now, do I need to change into a puffin first, or can you manage it?"

His body starts to shimmer and then shrink, gradually reforming in the shape of a puffin.

"Bodmin, lead the way." I change into an eagle owl and grab Figol in my talons.

Bodmin is standing still, watching us. I let out three angry screeches. He shakes the fog from his mind and changes into a black-throated white crane. I have never seen such a creature before. He lets out a trumpeting call, then walks stiffly out of the storage room.

I take to the air, with Figol's puffin form secured within my talons. Once above ground, Bodmin launches himself into the air without looking back.

25

Dying to Meet Ganna

We pass over Tochar Bridge, home to Andrilou, and the Gwanwyns of Sulis, where Lord Eghan teaches the isle's future druid healers. Bodmin does not waver in his flight to the north. The southern foothills descend in three uneven steps from the moorland above. Flush with trees, the hills are a stark contrast to the barren plain above. Where Ganna's home might be, I have no idea.

Bodmin flies straight for an exposed cliff face on the moor. A woman seated in a great stone chair surveys the land below her. He trumpets a greeting and circles down to a rock-hewn cottage two levels down, nestled in the trees. I follow him closely and release Figol's motionless form on the stone outside the cottage. I let out an alarm call before retaking my human form.

"He must change back at once, while he still has the strength," Bodmin says.

"Figol," I call. Can you hear me?"

Where does one slap a puffin?

"You need to change back to your old self now."

Figol lies on the ground, his unfocused eyes ponderously moving from me to Bodmin and back again.

"This is why we don't instruct the common folk on our practices," Bodmin says. He grabs Figol's beak and turns the head back and forth. "There is still humanness to be found within, but if he doesn't take human form, there is little that Ganna can do for him."

Figol blasts a loud rumbling noise and Bodmin and I take a step back.

"Finally!" Figol says, having changed into his human form. "Did you two forget that I can't see? How could I change back with you two standing on top of me?"

Bodmin chuckles. "He still has his wits, it seems."

"Can you stand?" I ask.

"I can't feel my knees."

"Bodmin?" A low, gravelly voice calls from above.

"Ganna, your healing room!"

She runs down the steps, with bare feet slapping each stone. "Why have you come? And who did you bring to my home?" She asks, while trying to recover her breath. A gray-cloaked woman with long hair to match leaps the last couple stairs and appears in front of us. The walls, her cloak and her hair are similar in color, as if she was a natural feature of this land.

"It's the druid, the young one," Bodmin says. "He ate a goodly amount of wode whistle this morning from my stores. He's gone blind and can't feel his knees.

Ganna gives me only a cursory look as she inspects Figol.

"Can you feel this?" Ganna's left hand is on Figol's belly button. She presses her right hand against Figol's neck, checking his pulse.

"It feels like you're pushing on my stomach, but I can't be sure."

She places her fingers over top his eyes, acting as if to poke him. Figol gives no response. She rests her hand on Figol's chest.

"That makes it hard to breathe."

She rises and signals us to follow. "He is far along in the poisoning. It will be over well before nightfall."

I'm too numb to speak.

"Is there nothing you can do?" Bodmin asks.

Ganna purses her lips. "Deadly nightshade acts the opposite of wode whistle. Perhaps a dose of that will counteract his weakening heart?"

"You want to give him *another* poison?" I ask.

"I can make him comfortable, but he will die as surely as Belenos will retreat from the sky. Or I can try the nightshade, though I warn you, I have never done this before."

Her tone is firm, but caring. I look to Bodmin but his face is blank. Figol coughs, a pitifully weak effort.

"Do it." I turn away from them and stare into the blackness of her home.

Ganna heads straight to her table filled with pottery. Her voice echoes to us. "Bodmin, please get me some fresh water from the river."

"At once."

"Now child, tell me who you are."

I stand up straight and force my shoulders back. She may be more inclined to help if she knows who I am. "I am Grahme Fairweather, known as the Brokko kom Gresman and Friend of Laleah on Eriu, the Lord Protector of Men-an-Tol and a member of the Nine here on Pretanni."

235

"So many honors for one so young." She says in a kind but disinterested voice. "Tell me plainly, why are you here?" She throws some deadly nightshade in a small pot before me. She stares into my eyes and I realize Figol's life depends on my answer.

"We've been given a quest by my order, and your daughter told us that to be successful, we must seek you out. Rhedna of the Sorrows told us to appeal to Bodmin to lead us to you."

She nods her head. "Grab that salt behind you and give it to me."

She adds the salt and starts rubbing it into the leaves. I have seen this technique used by Gwalather, one of the few useful things he taught me. It's the best way to release the essence of the plant. It's not lost on me that this will free all the poison from the leaves.

Bodmin returns with a small cup of water. "Is my waterskin too corrupted for your potion? Am I somehow unclean?" He challenges.

"I needed to speak to this child without you prompting him. He may be young and foolish, but he has a good heart and a trusting nature."

Thanks?

She pours enough water into the wooden bowl to make a slurry and rushes over to Figol. "I'm going to pull you up to a sitting position. You need to drink the potion I've made. Do you understand me?"

Bodmin and I raise Figol's motionless body up. "Figol?" I smack his cheek a couple times. His pallid face refuses to redden, despite my slaps. Sluggishly, he moves his head to face my direction.

"There's no time for that," Ganna says. She places the bowl to Figol's lips and pours it into his mouth. She hands the bowl to Bodmin and grabs the hair on the back of Figol's head. She slowly pulls his head backward, letting the potion run down his throat. "He's too weak to swallow," she says, concerned.

My hand goes to Figol's neck. I close my eyes and concentrate on my sense of touch. "There is still a pulse, though it is weak."

"Give me your waterskin," she says to Bodmin. She carefully pours a tiny stream down Figol's throat. Her lips recede, giving a toothy countenance as she focuses on the water. "Too much and I'll flood his lungs," she whispers. Throwing the waterskin back at Bodmin, she looks at me. "That is all I can do. It will be enough or it will not."

Figol's head feels heavy. With special care, I rest it on the stone and issue a silent prayer to Sulis, in hopes that she works this far from her Gwanwyn. "His pulse is getting stronger," I announce.

Ganna's eyes betray neither hope nor dread. Figol coughs, spraying water in the crone's face. She wipes the fluid from her cheek and exhales. "We were not too late." She smacks my hand away and checks Figol's pulse for herself. "Watch him. Don't let him lie down or he's likely to vomit up the nightshade. Keep him still and calm. Now that the worst has passed, I need to speak to my husband." The two retreat into the cottage. I watch them go and realize that the cottage is merely the carved entrance to a cave.

I sit on the floor next to Figol and put my arm around his shoulders. "You gave us quite the scare."

Figol stirs. I tighten my hold on his shoulders. He's not falling down on my watch.

"He is very angry at her."

"What?" I ask.

"I can't read her at all, but he has been hurt deeply by her. He still loves her, but he doesn't want to be around her."

"Quiet Figol. Rest and get better." A foolish smile creeps across my face. Before he even attempts to speak, he's already reading the minds of the people around him. "Never change," I say.

"He's thinking about the moor above us and his desire to hunt. Now I've lost him, his thoughts are gone."

"He animorphed back into the great black cat," I say.

Ganna sighs as she exits her home.

"When will I get my sight back?" Figol asks. "I mean, better than the blurry vision I have now."

She chuckles. "He goes from death's door to wanting to be full strength at once. Oh, the vitality of youth." She grabs Bodmin's waterskin and places it in Figol's hands. "You're not out of danger yet. The nightshade will heat you up inside. Drink this. Until you pass clear water, you're still in danger."

Figol finishes the water at once. "I still have a dry mouth."

Ganna takes the skin from Figol and hands it to me. "The stream is to your left, about fifty paces on the valley floor. You'll hear it well before you see it."

Ganna keeps a close eye on Figol as she lays out furs along the ground. Once he falls asleep, she adds wood to the fire. "He'll feel hot and refuse to be near the fire, but the heat will help his body process the poisons faster. I fed him a thin porridge while you were away. I put a sleeping draught in it, so he shouldn't wake until morning."

"Is that why you sent me away?"

"It was. I'll brook no interference when I treat the sick, and the best way to insure that is to be left alone with them."

"Did you send Bodmin away?"

She stares past me. "No, that was his doing." She walks out into the rapidly cooling afternoon air. "I haven't anything for dinner. Would you mind going and bringing back a suitable meal?"

I eye her carefully. "This is not another ploy to get me away from Figol?"

"I have done all that I can for him, but now my stomach rumbles. It is the least you can do." She fixes me with a maternal gaze and I'm instantly agreeing with her.

I frown at her before taking the shape of an eagle owl. I can't tell if she's being earnest or manipulating me.

I return with three brown rats and fly into the cottage. Dropping them on her table, I hop off and regain my human shape before my feet hit the ground.

"You are an excellent animorph," Ganna says, "Perhaps as talented as my Bodmin." She pays my dramatic entrance no mind and immediately begins cleaning the rats.

I had hoped to provoke her a bit, so that she would speak without calculating each word. It takes more than a sudden entrance and dead rodents it seems.

The meal was surprising in every way. Gone was the oily rat taste of which I was familiar. It tasted of young lamb with a smoky sweet flavor. She smiles at me after I devour my portion.

"Have the other one as well," she says, smiling. "Bodmin will find his own supper."

"If I had not brought the meat back myself, I would never believe this is rat. Did you use magic?"

"Oh yes," she says. "But not all magic comes from spells. This could be prepared by anyone patient enough to learn their herbs."

She watches me as I tear into the third rodent. "Flavors such as these allow the healer to add medicines which go unnoticed."

The meat nearly falls from my mouth. Has she drugged me?

She chuckles slightly. "No, I did not poison you. I merely tell you this so that when you administer to the sick and unruly patient, you can use this trick."

The small fire crackles as I stare at her, trying to determine the truth of her statements.

"Boy, you are no threat to me. If I wanted to harm you, I could choose ten different ways to do so and you couldn't stop me."

"I'm not hungry anymore."

"Suit yourself, but if I had drugged you, the effects would be upon you by now." She stands up and wipes her hands on her smock. "After two nights of rest, your nephew will have the strength to walk short distances. By late spring he should be healthy enough for you to continue your quest."

"Our quest needs to be completed by Imbolc."

She frowns at me. "He will live."

"Thank you Ganna," I rush to say, before she can count me as ungrateful. "I must ask though, how did you know the quantity of nightshade to use? I have studied under Gwalather, a man well versed in the healing craft and I doubt he would have known to do what you did."

"I did not know," she shrugs. "I used all that was in the pottery. I filled the first two pots to the top and saved what little remained in the third. It was what I grabbed without thinking."

I laugh silently. "If I knew what god or goddess to thank, I would give proper deference, but it seems likely that many had a hand in this."

26

The Writing on the Wall

Belenos has risen in the morning sky, but the foothills still hide him from view. Figol has not moved at all during his slumber. Feeling his neck, his pulse is strong and his skin feels cool to the touch. My next concern is the fact that Bodmin never returned from his hunt.

How are we to proceed without him?

"When Figol wakes, he must move about, so I will show the two of you my lands." Ganna says. "Tomorrow Bodmin will return and with luck, you can be on your way."

Figol stirs. "Can I have something to eat? Something that won't put me to sleep this time?"

Ganna reappears from her cottage with a bowl for Figol. "Eat your porridge, then we will see how steady you are on your feet," she says.

Ganna leads us back into the cottage. She stoops down and takes a tunnel I hadn't noticed before. She snakes her way up, through a narrow passage until we emerge from the darkness. Her cottage is below us and to the south.

"Do you often have need of this escape tunnel?" I ask.

"Better to have it and not need it than need it and be dead."

The stairs up the cliff have a rock wall which obscures the view of the cottage below. No wonder no one has been able to catch her all these long years. We arrive at Ganna's stone seat at the top of the cliff. It is wide enough for two. She lounges sideways in her throne and lets us silently take in the view. Below us is smoke from nearly a dozen homes scattered on the valley floor. From here, anyone coming up would be easily spotted.

"I am the Queen of the Rocks, and this is my throne," she says. "This chair originally belonged to King Ludd, the greatest of his people and the first and only king of the giants."

"How can you know that?" I ask. "The giants have been gone a long, long time."

"I will show you, but first, come see where Ludd the Giant gave offerings to his gods." She waves us on and continues her brisk pace. I offer my shoulder to Figol.

"No, I can walk."

Despite his assurance, he quickly falls behind. Ganna waits for us at a set of giant stairs. Each step is as high as my waist. She hums to herself as she walks in the drainage path along the side. The drop-off is enough to kill a person in several places if one were unfortunate enough to stumble.

At the bottom, a deep, narrow fissure opens up in the earth. The moss and lichen-lined chasm has a sense of quiet malevolence about it. Cool moisture, which steals the body's warmth, pervades the area. The walls tighten so that I can touch both sides at once. The mist around us slowly builds until the limit of sight is but three strides in any direction. Ganna disappears around a waist-high boulder. Once we reach the boulder, we have to feel rather than see the rock walls around us.

"What was Bodmin's true reason for accompanying you?" Ganna asks from above us.

The question sounds innocent enough, but waiting for us to be blind in the fog and standing above us, this is the real reason why she brought us here. I don't know what she wants to hear, so I settle on the truth.

"It is as Bodmin said, we found Figol poisoned and prone on the ground. It was unlikely that any druid healer could rescue a man so far enthralled by death. Further, he claimed that your daughter, Rhedna, was meddling in family affairs and that we were being manipulated by her."

"Rhedna is not as wise as she believes."

Silence hangs in the air until a firm, bony hand grabs my wrist. I jump and turn to face the threat.

Ganna chuckles. "Follow me."

Behind the stone is a narrow path that is impossible to see in the dense fog. It takes us away from the mist-shrouded pit and opens up to fresh, clear air. Trees become prevalent again as we descend along the mountainside opposite from her cottage.

"That chasm traces Aine's path perfectly across the sky when the days and nights are equal in length. The mist diffuses and augments Aine's blessing, allowing one to inhale her very essence. Alas, it is the wrong time of year for that. But if you follow me, you will gaze upon the face of the long-dead King Ludd."

We continue downward, but on a stone-lined ramp this time. The mosses between the cracks mitigate the overly slick stones. Ganna stops us abruptly.

"We are here."

I look at her in confusion.

"Look up," she points at the escarpment above.

From the overhang above us, an enormous stone slab juts into the air. An undeniable face gazes skyward. Its eye is an open hole, filled with the blueness of a cold winter sky.

"Behold King Ludd. He led his people to victory in a war against the griffins."

I stare, mouth agape at the gargantuan sculpture. From chin to forehead the length is equal to six men. "And I thought the stone-topped ring of Men Meur Kov Keigh was the giant's most impressive feat."

"How do you know that there even was a war between the giants and the griffins?" Figol demands.

Unperturbed, Ganna inclines her head toward the cliff. "Let me show you." She guides us on a path directly below Ludd's stone face. There on the smooth cliff face are carved symbols in three separate squares.

"Do you recognize any of these?" Ganna asks.

"The symbols on the left are elven," I say.

"And the middle ones are the runes of the giants," Figol adds.

"But from where does the third set of marks come?" I ask.

"Those are centaur marks," Ganna answers. "And the message in all three scripts is the same: King Ludd, mightiest of his kind and the first and only king of the giants, drove the griffins far to the north to the wasteland mountains. This he did in Lugh's name."

"You can read these?" I ask, amazed.

"I can."

"We must scratch these onto stone," I say.

"I am the keeper of this place now. When you have something of equal value to offer, I will allow you to produce your copy."

"What would you want?" I ask. "Druids care nothing for wealth."

"I will let you know if or when you have something of value."

"But this is exactly what we need to learn of the ancients."

"And I will not allow your kind to grow in power without some form of surety. There is nothing that the druids can offer me."

Looking up longingly at the scripts, I have no way of securing the knowledge, for now.

"For the last stop, we will have to hurry if we want to make it to Rock Hall before Belenos gives up on this short winter day. It is a long hike."

"I can animorph," Figol says. "At least into something easy, like a puffin."

Ganna give me a confused look before shrugging her shoulders. "Then follow me." She shimmers in the sunlight and changes into a majestic golden eagle. Figol smiles at me before becoming a stupid puffin. They push off to the east, leaving me as I shake my head at Figol. We fly low over the moor. The snow remains only in the shadows.

She lands outside a small circular rampart and retakes her human form. The entrance through the wall leads to a flattened circle.

"Why have all of the stones in the circle been knocked down?" I ask.

"First, pay your respects at Ludd Lowe. It is the burial place of the only great king that Pretanni has ever known."

There is a low earthen circle surrounding the central mound. The mound is unimpressive, except that all the standing stones have be knocked down and radiate away from the center. Combined, they are a symbol of Belenos and they rest on a plain where our beloved god can see them with each daily pass.

"I suspect the giants did this to mimic Ludd's crown and not to honor Belenos, but the site is up to us to interpret how we will," Ganna says.

"Was the tomb of the All-King made to resemble this?" Figol asks.

Ganna laughs derisively. "No, few humans have ever seen this site. Your fake druid site has nothing to do with this. Come, let me show you what true craftsmen can do."

She takes us to the collapsed doorway into the mound. Two curved, brilliant blue mosaic stones frame the entrance. I feel the stones and they are smooth to the touch.

"I have never seen stones this color before," I say.

"That is because they are not stones, they are griffin egg fragments. Like King Ludd, I too forced the griffins to give up this area. That is why I bestowed the title Queen of the Rocks upon myself."

"Are griffins as fearsome as the tales say?" Figol asks.

"Aye, they are," Ganna says. "They are the ultimate predator, at least on this island. Dragons of course, are fiercer. The griffins have the head, front legs and wings of a giant eagle, and the body and tail of a golden skinned cat. Each wing is as long as four men and their favorite prey is the horse. The centaurs have been locked in battle with the griffins for ages. Arrows may bring a griffin from the sky, but no centaur can reach the cliffside eyries to kill the offspring."

"How did you drive the griffins off?"

Ganna surveys the fields. "Can you call that sheep to you?" She points to a young ram off in the distance.

"I can."

"Good, call it to you and I will show you how I was victorious."

The sheep comes running to us as Ganna leads us back within the ring of fallen stones. "Keep hold of the sheep and don't let it out of the circle. First, I will perform a ritual for myself, then I will perform one for you."

Placing her body between us and the bier, she whispers "*cweorth.*" She has knowledge of the runestones as well.

Figol pulls at my robe. "Uncle, she didn't use a runestone to create that fire."

"She must have hidden it from our view when she threw it." I wave him to be quiet.

The fire burns greedily. Her gravelly voice rings out in powerful waves. "Vozzir! Vozzir of the dark realm, I command you to attend me."

She tosses a yellow stone onto the fire. The air fills with the stench of rotten eggs. The sheep is distressed, but I subdue it with a mental command. Figol kneels down and firmly holds the sheep's front legs.

"Vozzir. *Hinthial tuthi Sa*, you are beholden to me. *Cer tuthina sa*, honor your soul-gift to me. *Tuthu mini fase*. Come to me."

The smoke from the fire begins to collect unnaturally outside of the stone circle. The cloud crackles and thunders as it grows denser.

"*Thu, zal, ci.*" Ganna counts.

The smoke parts and a human-sized demon appears. Two spiral horns start at the center of its forehead and curve around to either side of his mouth. A fiery nimbus surrounds him as he takes on a corporeal form.

"I require your essence," Ganna calls.

"Evil witch, I will destroy you one day," he snarls.

"Your talk is always tiresome," Ganna says. "Come forth." She extends her right arm and bending at the elbow, brings her hand back to her face.

The demon fights the pull Ganna is exerting by planting his feet to slow his forward advance. He screams out in the language of demons, but the compulsion to obey is too much. Figol covers the sheep's eyes as well as closing his own. This knowledge is too important to shy away from, so I look on.

"No, noooo!" the demon screams as he advances to the ring. He stretches out his hands as if to push away. Its hands burst into white sparks and thick black smoke when the fiend's hand reaches the border of the circle. It roars in defiance and pain.

"He is losing his vitality to the circle," Ganna calls over top of the demon's wails.

"Vozzir *cel, rasna fase,*" Ganna calls and the demon smoke slowly breaches the circle and collects around her. Brightness permeates her and she grows younger before our eyes.

"Vozzir *cel, rasna fase,*" Figol calls out and a second column of smoke heads toward him.

"No! I claim *teur* on the usurper! *Mini fase tular cel cehen!*"

Ganna looks over, amazed at Figol. "You are stealing the demon essence that was commanded by me. Vozzir is demanding that as a usurper, you must leave this circle and face him in combat."

Figol goes pale as he tries to speak.

"Ultimately, the choice is mine, since you are stealing from me."

249

"*Teur! Macstrna!*" the demon howls.

Ganna frowns at the hellspawn. "*Favin cepen.*"

The demon bursts into flame and thick, black smoke obscures his exit to the dark realm.

Ganna opens her arms wide and the demon smoke streaks to her. Figol mimics the move. When the cloud dissipates, Ganna looks to be no older than Figol's mother. Her hair is now as black as the demon essence she stole, and the edges of her eyes now boast soft, smooth skin.

"I feel wonderful," Figol says, eyes wide. "I'm not tired and my body doesn't ache."

"You, young man, owe me a debt," Ganna says.

Figol looks to me for aid.

"He is to become a druid?" Ganna demands.

"If we are successful in our quest, yes," I reply.

Ganna stares into the distance. Of what she is contemplating, I know not, but it worries me. She snaps out of her trance and her eyes flick over to Figol. "Bring the sheep."

Ganna kneels on the ground, no longer needing the stilted motions of the old to lower herself. The sheep goes to her and it nuzzles Ganna's face. She strokes the sheep's back with her left hand and whispers calming words to the animal. In a flash, metal gleams from her right hand and the dagger plunges into the surprised animal's neck. It tries to run, but Ganna has it trapped in a tight embrace. She closes her eyes and rests her head on the sheep's.

"Hilde, Ellys and Brythiue, accept my offering and speak truly to me." Once more she wields the blade and slices the belly of the dying victim, spilling the entrails onto the ground. She lowers the body and stands over her grisly deed.

Too shocked to speak, we look on in mute disgust.

Ganna looks up and shakes her head. "Oh, the Hooded Ones foresee dangerous times ahead for you." She points to the intestines below before looking into my eyes.

"My daughter was right to insist on you seeing me. Prophecy demands that you seek out the centaurs."

27

Troubled Farewell

Belenos has nearly completed his trip across the sky. Ganna has gone out and left us at her home. My mind swirls with unresolved questions. Will Bodmin return in the morning? How do we get to see the centaurs without being killed? What do we do once we're there?

"Uncle, what are the Hooded Ones exactly?"

"They are not gods that we as druids choose to worship. As you saw, you must take an animal's life to receive a prophecy. Even then, you must interpret how the entrails spill out of the hapless sheep. The price is high and the results are questionable, so we do not favor them."

"What debt do I owe Ganna?"

"You took some of the demon's essence," I respond crossly. "I know not what would be fair in return. It is between you and the witch."

"You're mad at me?"

"You have the mental powers of the Sorim. Now, you are dabbling with the powers of the Tusci. These are our enemies. I must question if you would truly be a druid or if you would serve the tenets of three different beliefs."

"I didn't know what would happen today. All those Tusci words were at the forefront of his, I mean, Tuss Metiana's . . . my father's mind."

"It would be best if you didn't pursue this magic."

"I won't," Figol says, defeated. "Mum saw to that. She not only blocked the knowledge of my father away in her mind, but she also made me incurious about the summoning of demons. Now that I know, I can sense her meddling in my mind."

"She can do that?"

"Yes, and even though I know it was done to me, I still have no desire to learn the magic. Had I not been in *his* mind, I would have never known that Mum did this to me."

"Doesn't that make you angry?" I ask.

"It comes down to whether or not I trust Mum. When your family has the mental powers of the Sorim, everyone is in your head. As long as you trust them, it makes the bond stronger."

"Are you two going to lounge around my home and expect me to do everything for you?" Ganna's voice echoes from behind us.

She's carrying an armload of wood for the fire.

"How did you get behind us?" I ask.

"The question you should be asking is what's for dinner. You are responsible for that. I'm not be your serving wench."

"How do you feel?" I ask Figol.

"I feel well."

"Then follow my lead and you'll get to experience the thrill of the hunt." Caradoc can have his merlin. There is no better woodland hunter than the goshawk. I examine my powerful talons and the blue-gray plumage of my chest. Figol has made the change as well and I launch myself into the hunt.

We're a good team. I distract our prey by flying openly above the moor, causing the red grouse to freeze. Figol swoops in from behind for the kill. In no time we've acquired our dinner. I lead the way back to Ganna's abode, with the three short strokes followed by a glide that comes so naturally to the bird.

Ganna already has water boiling in her pot. "Drop them in here to scald them, then you can remove the feathers."

Figol grumbles over having to kill and then prepare the birds.

He's in for a rough time when he begins his apprenticeship.

"The goshawk was a good choice for this time of year," Ganna says.

I smile at the compliment. I decide to take advantage of her pleasant mood. "Ganna, did the oracle reveal anything else about our new quest?"

"It doesn't tell you everything," she says, exasperated. "You must use your wits if you want to be successful."

"I understand, but the centaurs shoot humans on sight. We cannot complete our quest if we are left riddled with arrows in a ditch. Can you tell us how we can make contact with them without a fatal outcome?"

Ganna wobbles her head from side to side. "Perhaps you should go in bird form and land within one of their camps. They would be less likely to shoot at you if they could possibly hit another centaur."

Figol's eyes grow large and he wordlessly stares at me. I don't like the suggestion either, but it's the only option we have. Perhaps if I get her talking, she'll share more knowledge with us.

"You said that you drove a griffin from this land. How were you able to do it?"

254

"I drove a mated pair of griffins from here. They are savage, ruthless hunters. To beat them, you must exceed them in this."

"But how did you do it?"

"I don't give up knowledge without payment." She smiles at me. "Both the centaurs and the griffins are aggressive, which is why neither can gain the upper hand on the other. Only the giants proved to be too much, and me of course."

I let out a long breath. There will be no help from Ganna.

"You did provide dinner, so I will share a little of my knowledge," she says. "Centaurs can only achieve adulthood by performing a significant feat. The killing of a human is automatically accepted as such, so I would advise you to approach the older, adult centaurs."

"How will we tell them apart?" I ask.

"Only adults are allowed to tie their hair back, mimicking their tails. Adolescents must keep their hair short. The ones with long, untied hair are the ones most likely to kill you without pause."

Figol and I exchange glances again. The more I learn the more defeated I feel.

"I think I have given more than enough to pay for dinner. If you find this not enough, you can always return to your kind as failures. It happens more than you would think."

We eat our meal in silence. The entrance to Ganna's home faces westward, and as Belenos begins to set, his rays adding little warmth to what promises to be a cold night.

"Ganna," Figol says. "Today, you didn't use a rune to start the fire, did you?"

"You're an observant one," she says.

"We are just beginning to understand the runes. How is it that you don't need the stone?"

"The stone is a crutch, like the old need to walk. When you understand the giant's language, the word is all you need."

"What do you require for us to get a sketch of the three languages below King Ludd?" I ask.

"You possess nothing close to that value. No, learn how to make your runestones. Maybe in five or six generations your kind will be wise enough to learn more."

"In five or six generations the return of the ancients will be upon us," I say. "Then we will have no use for your knowledge."

"The wood will not last through the night. I suggest you find more while there is still light," Ganna says. She turns to a stunning white swan and flies away.

I look at the setting sun. "Hurry, we don't have long before darkness takes hold."

Ganna has scavenged the dead branches from near her home. It's dusk before we make it back with our haul. Figol throws a few branches on the fire before joining me to bid farewell to Belenos.

"Will we be able to complete this quest?"

"Unless Ganna or Bodmin are more forthcoming, I don't know that we should try," I say.

"We've had two prophecies say that we go to the centaurs. I have to believe a path will open up to us."

I once blindly believed in Boswen and all the druid leaders. Poor Figol, one day he will have his trust broken. Then he will have to suffer through doubt and distrust like the rest of us.

A forlorn song about loss floats down from the moor. The song washes over us in a tongue I've never heard spoken before, but the message is unmistakable. Figol closes his eyes and cocks his head, giving his full attention to Ganna's heartsick tune.

"It makes me feel like our situation pales in comparison," I say softly.

"It makes me wonder how much suffering has been inflicted upon Ganna through the years," Figol responds.

Ganna's song ends as we watch the pink sky fade to black. I rub my arms. I don't know what the future holds for us, but at least we can stay warm tonight. We retreat to the fire of the rock-hewn home.

"What news of your quest?" Bodmin asks as he emerges from Ganna's sleeping room.

"Bodmin," I say, surprised. "When did you return?"

"Last night, obviously." He throws the last of the wood onto the fire. "That woman's mournful ballad gets me every time. She is a master at manipulating people in order to get her way," Bodmin shakes his head.

"We'll need more wood, and soon." He looks at me, expectant.

"Get up Figol, firewood duty awaits."

"Surely you don't expect him to collect the wood?"

"You're not the only one with a surprise this morning. Figol is healed."

"How can this be?"

"He took some of the essence from Ganna's demon," I say, letting my displeasure show.

"Do you know how dangerous that was?" Bodmin asks.

"But we stayed in the ring the whole time; the demon couldn't touch us," Figol says.

"It's not the demon you fool, it's Ganna. Failure to pay will invite her wrath upon you." Bodmin shakes his head in disbelief. "She would like nothing better than to corrupt another druid."

"What other druid did she corrupt?" Figol asks.

I jab him in the ribs with my elbow.

"Oh," he whispers.

"Curse that woman," Bodmin says under his breath.

"Are you coming with us to meet the centaurs?" Figol asks.

"Centaurs? Why would you want to get yourselves killed?"

"I delivered a prophecy, as they asked," Ganna says. She ambles over to Bodmin and kisses his cheek.

He turns away, refusing to respond in kind. He approaches the fire and warms his hands. "And how do you plan on avoiding the centaurs' arrows?"

"It was suggested we fly directly into their camp and animorph back to our true forms," I say.

Bodmin turns on Ganna. "You told them this?" He says in a harsh voice. "You would cure this one only to have them both killed?"

"I wouldn't have let them leave. I merely wanted them to see the wisdom of leaving the Elder Race alone," Ganna says petulantly.

He spins to face us again. "And were you set to try this suicidal stratagem?"

"In truth, we had our doubts." I look to Figol. "But I think we would have tried it if no other path presented itself."

He returns to face Ganna. "Your soul is so old and withered that you are incapable of caring. This is why you need a rebirth."

"Very well," she agrees. "Grahme, you and your nephew should return to your own lands. The only way the centaurs don't kill you is if the griffins find you first. Happy now? Everyone lives." She waves her hand in dismissal and walks back toward her bedroom. She spins and looks at Bodmin. "Now come, join me again. I'd almost forgotten about the pleasures we have with one another."

Bodmin eyes her coldly. "Grahme, I am known to the Centaurim and I wish to be your guide to their lands."

Ganna looks stunned. Slowly her face turns hard and she glares at me. "All these years and you still choose the silly druids over me," she says with contempt. "Other than trying to kill you, what have they done for you?"

"I do not hold myself as being separate from people." Bodmin says. "You have lost your touch with humanity. Even with all your powers, you choose to remain aloof and alone from your fellow man."

"You entertain on that cold, harsh moor of yours, do you?" she responds.

He grabs his pack. "Get your packs, we leave at once."

Figol and I scramble to collect our possessions even as Ganna begs him to reconsider. As her pleas get more desperate, he assumes the form of a crane and leaps into flight. Lazily he circles until Figol and I are ready.

Ganna turns on us. "Get out! You druids have taken everything from me."

I can think of nothing to console her, so we obey.

28

The New Quest

I s Ganna really so powerful that she should be feared?" Figol asks

Bodmin merely chuckles.

With no further comment forthcoming, a determined Figol squints at the back of Bodmin's head before lowering his own.

"Beware of the painted consort. She with no hair, no soul?" Figol says out loud.

"You know it?" Bodmin asks, surprised.

"Ah, I've only heard snippets," Figol lies. With all his mind control, I'd figure he'd be better at it.

"I know it," I say. Taking a breath, I recite:

> Beware the painted consort
> Scourge from the Wigesta court
> No power so great
> Bows only to Fate
> She of no hair, no soul
> Her words are spoken
> Our men are broken
> Her vengeance takes its toll

Cursed demons she calls
Our mighty army stalls
Metal needed
For demons defeated
No use a druid's pole
Her runes destroy
Our magic, a toy
All Pretanni, her goal

"Very good. Did you know Ganna is the one being described in that verse?" Bodmin asks.

"I thought it's only a child's rhyme told to those who misbehave. Well, that and talk of Bodmin coming to get you."

Our guide laughs at the thought. "Am I now used to scare children?"

"Boswen taught me that this comes from five hundred years ago, during the Wigesta invasion," I say.

"Yes, and Ganna was considered old then."

Figol grimaces even while his head is bowed.

I should probably scold him, but I want to know more as well. "But what does it mean: Painted and no hair? Did she ride into battle naked like a Pretanni warrior? And why no hair?" I ask.

"No, it refers to the tattoos she has on her head. It was she who brought the knowledge of the rowan protection glyphs to Pretanni. She shaved her head and had rowan ash implanted under both sides of her head to protect from the Sorim."

"How does she live for so long?" Figol asks.

"You experienced it for yourself. She calls forth a demon from Dubnos and forces it to become diminished by contacting the stone ring. She then steals the vitality and regains her youth."

"Is that how you have lived so long?" I ask.

Bodmin's eyes grow hard and he redoubles his pace. Figol places his hand on top of mine, telling me to stop with the questions. He gives it a few breaths before he starts his questioning again.

"When did you meet Ganna?"

Bodmin exhales. "It was nearly two hundred years ago. I was a young druid with tremendous talent. I was known as the best at animorphing among the druids."

"You still are," I say.

He smiles at the compliment before his countenance falls again. "I challenged anyone and everyone to animal duels. It didn't matter who they were, apprentices, master animorphs, even a member of the Nine. No one could best me, until one day an impossibly young lady challenged me. I tried to be gallant, to tell her I couldn't, in good faith, embarrass her. She turned into a boar and charged me. I had to dive for cover in the ferns, but I came out as a boar myself. She bested me in no time. I insisted we compete again as bears, then as ravens and finally as squirrels."

"Squirrels?"

He smiles. "It didn't matter what I chose, she won handily every time. I was smitten from the very beginning. Once I regained some semblance of my pride, I asked her who she was."

"But she must have been hundreds of years old, by then," I say.

"Aye, she was a very experienced woman. Our desire was fiery and frequent." His eyes glaze over as he remembers. "But the druids had labeled her a witch and that was when my fall began. I couldn't get her out of my mind. We would meet, couple and rejuvenate ourselves at the expense of animals, usually deer. The order's suspicion of me grew stronger year by year. At the end, both Ganna and I had to flee Pretanni in order to keep our heads."

262

I motion to Figol to end this interrogation. No man should be made to bare his whole soul.

"When did you learn to summon demons?" I ask.

"Originally, it was I who showed Ganna how to capture animals and absorb their essence. Many a buzzard gave their essences to us. It is only when my mentor told me that when I consume an animal in this manner, I am taking its soul from the great wheel of life."

I look at Figol but he shrugs his shoulders. He's not compelling Bodmin to speak.

"I was horrified, and I made Ganna swear never to do it again. It is then that she showed me how to summon demons. If a demon is diminished, it is only to the good. I created my own stone circle at the most uninhabitable spot on the moor and started my own summoning. My best and most cherished student, Uffa Horselord was the one to discover my clandestine activity. It drove a wedge between us that was never repaired."

We approach a river and stop to fill our waterskins.

"Have you ever heard the ballad, 'The Fall of Bodmin?'" He asks.

"Yes," I say.

"It was composed by Uffa and technically speaking, it is the finest ballad ever rendered. My every failure is exquisitely detailed. My ballad should have been one of beauty and hope. Instead, I have become reviled by the society I hold most dear."

"That's horrid," I say.

He shrugs. "After we fill our skins, we'll fly again."

29

Bordering on Trouble

odmin's crane lands on a well-traveled road. To the west is a rocky escarpment that looms ominously over intrepid travelers. He retakes his human form and hurries us to follow him. I've never seen Bodmin so energized.

"Hurry, Briganti is best seen in the midday light, when the shadows don't obscure it," he says.

Figol hurries on along with Bodmin. I'm left standing alone as I try to make sense of the change in my companion.

"What's Briganti?" I call.

"It's a post where soldiers watch the griffins in the mountains. An early warning has saved countless families and livestock over the years. There are steps up the earthen wall."

What kind of wall gives the invaders steps to walk up?

Bodmin waits at the top, impatiently waving me to join him. Figol looks confused. I take the steps two at a time to assuage his impatience.

"Behold the one-time capital of the second most fearsome tribe on Pretanni." He waves his hands expansively. "To your left was the impenetrable stone wall of the inner town."

All I can see is an open circular area with the remnants of a rock wall which has a large section pulled down.

"The Brigantes believed that as long as the wall stood, they would be invincible. It was I who infiltrated the city and learned its secrets. When my father led the raid on this place, I led my warrior band into the center of their lines. With Belenos at our backs, we overtook them like an angry wave washing over the shore. Their fearsome king was killed by a dozen different blows from my men. Our victory complete, the wall was dismantled as a way to celebrate. I doubt more than a few stones have moved since that fateful day."

His chest swells up with pride as he relives old glories. I can't help but feel sorry for him. All of his other accomplishments have been tainted by his expulsion from the druids. I'm forced to look away so as to not betray my thoughts. "What's that?" I ask to distract him.

"That is where my brother rescued my father. The Brigantes used arrows against us. Arrows!" His voice rings with outrage. "Father was hit with several as he stood atop the wall and directed our men. He fell inside the city and would have died if not for my brother coming to his aid."

He looks at both of us, wanting us to see this space as he still sees it. "We captured all of the royals and killed them at this very spot, the place of their great shame. It was said that the king's massive dog was his favorite companion, so we killed that cur here as well."

"They must have been a threat to your kingdom's survival," Figol says, before I can express my indignation at killing a dog.

"Aye, they had conquered the Selgovae and the Carvetes. They could call upon nearly limitless kindred from the mainland. The Botadin have skirmished with the centaurs for hundreds of years, so we value peace with the other human tribes. Had we not struck, it would have been our city that was laid to waste."

265

"Do you mean the Votadin?"

"The proper name is Botadin, after our founder. It is only in the last hundred years that my people's speech has changed. Since I do not relish being called Vodmin, I maintain the proper names."

"Who goes there?" A man's voice calls out from the cover of the trees.

"Pardon us," Bodmin calls. "I am but a poor traveler who lucked upon a revered druid and his student."

The man breaks into a smile when he sees my robes. "Holy druid, are you here to stay?" He has an ugly gash starting at his forehead, skipping over his left eye and ending on his cheek. He sees me stealing a glance at his scar.

"It came from a griffin," he boasts. Despite being my age, he acts much older.

"We are making our way north," I tell him. "It will not be long before there is a permanent druid here. Sadly, I am not that one."

"Have the griffins been active?" Bodmin asks. "Now should be a quiet time."

"You know your griffin lore," the man says, surprised. "It is halfway through the egg laying season."

"I know a little of the beasts' ways."

"I am Vinhe of the Votadin." He nods at me respectfully.

"Vinhe of the Votadin?" Bodmin says. "I once knew a man by that name."

"That would be my grandfather," a pleased Vinhe the younger says.

"Our passage to Din Guarie will be safe?" I ask. I care not for Bodmin's attempt to make friends with his kinsmen.

Bodmin and Vinhe share a laugh. "The female griffin lays one egg every half month," Vinhe says. "The female must stay in the nest and keep the eggs from freezing. Although only half the griffins are active now, you will do best to stay underneath the trees and not travel in the middle of the day."

I exhale. "That will slow us down."

"I've always preferred watching them during the mating season," Bodmin reminisces.

I look questioning at Vinhe.

"When they mate, the male and female both fly high and lock talons. They spiral to the ground with increasing speed. If the male breaks off first, he'll be rejected. If the female waits too long though, she may pull up but not give her suitor enough time to react. It's bad enough they look at us as prey. During mating, you must also worry about being crushed by the beasts."

Bodmin laughs. "He's teasing you." The best time to attack is during the spirals. If you're lucky, you'll kill them both."

"Are you in charge here?" I ask.

Vinhe shakes his head. "No, that would be my grandfather. He is leading troops out to the hunting grounds, hoping to kill one or more of the beasts."

"You actively hunt them now?" Bodmin asks.

Vinhe looks at us confused. "Of course! We have done so for many years. How is it you know of us and the griffins but not of our hunts?"

"Sorry," Bodmin says. "It has been a while since I've come this far north, and even then, it was during the height of summer."

Vinhe looks at Bodmin again, reassessing his age. Some topics are best avoided.

"What of your father?" I ask.

"He died of the liquid lung when I was fourteen," Vinhe says, expressionless.

"Forgive me," I say. "My father died when I was fifteen. At least we were old enough to learn what it means to be a man."

"Your grandfather," Bodmin starts. "When is he due back?"

"He and his men should be back by sundown."

"It is a shame," Bodmin says stiffly. "We must be on our way. I would have liked to have seen him again."

"We are not in that much of a rush," I say. "What can you tell us about the centaurs?"

Vinhe spits onto the ground. "The boundary between our lands has been the River Tweed since time immemorial. But the last few summers they have been crossing it to the west of the mountains, then coming east. Our farmers have been deprived of their lands and sometimes their lives. May the centaurs suffer a plague of griffins upon their lands."

"Revered one," Figol says, "We should go."

"You shouldn't travel now," Vinhe says. "The griffins are most active now. Come, share our midday meal and start fresh once Belenos begins sinking."

Figol and Bodmin look uncomfortable, but there is wisdom in our host's words. Besides, it would be best to foster goodwill for whichever druid is to be sent here.

The venison steak and winter vegetables were worth the delay. I excuse myself to answer the call of nature. Figol too, decides to leave camp.

"Uncle," he says, once we are out of camp. "We should think about leaving very soon."

"Why?"

"I don't know why, but Bodmin is anxious and desperately wants to leave."

"But he was so flush with excitement?"

"Ever since we spoke with Vinhe, he has grown more nervous."

Belenos is still too high in the western sky. "We must set a good example, so that whichever druid is assigned here will be accepted. We can't leave right after a meal."

There is commotion in camp and threatening shouts.

"So much for the good example," Figol says.

"Be ready with your mental gifts, just in case."

We race back to camp. Bodmin is surrounded by six men, all brandishing spears at him.

"What is the meaning of this?" I roar.

A gray-headed man, points at us. "Surround them too!"

Several men run toward us. I ignore them and walk into camp. The men are tense, but no one strikes at us. We stand next to Bodmin.

"What is the meaning of this?" I ask again, without any rancor.

"I'll have your staff," the old man says.

"I am Grahme of the Nine, explain yourself."

"If that be true, then I am sorry. But this man is a devil." His eyes never leave Bodmin.

I approach to within a few steps of the graybeard. "Explain yourself."

He still refuses to take his eyes off of Bodmin. His spear quivers slightly but he keeps it raised in attack position. "It was twenty years ago, maybe more when I laid eyes on this man. The years have passed and eaten away at my body, yet this *thing* has not aged a day. I shan't lose my men to a demon."

I look at Bodmin. He stares back. "I told you so" is written all over his face.

One of the men slams his spear into the side of Figol's knee, buckling it. I swing my staff in a wide arc as I move to cover one side of Figol. It connects with the instigator. He collapses on the ground and lays unmoving. Bodmin guards Figol's other side.

"We need to be fast and fearsome if we wish to survive," Bodmin says.

"Agreed. Pick the time," I say.

"Now!"

A bear is fearsome, but a wolf is faster. The back of my throat vibrates as I let out a growl. It freezes the men in place. I spring for the nearest man's face and knock him to the ground. I bite his spear arm before jumping away. It's not about killing; it's about creating fear. Bodmin's feline growl causes even the men on my side to shudder. Their eyes search for the source of the noise.

That's all the opening I need. I crash into another man, breaking the spell. He drops his spear, so I dig my teeth into his calf before springing away.

"Regroup!" Vinhe the Elder yells.

I race back to Figol, regaining human form.

"Figol?"

He's holding his swollen knee. There's no chance of putting weight on it.

"Leave me," he says.

"Next time maybe," I smile tightly. "Can you use your mind to give us an opening?"

He grimaces in pain. "It will only buy us a few heartbeats of time."

"Do it, then turn into your stupid puffin."

"I'd need a run to get off the ground, and with this knee . . ."

"I'll take care of the rest."

The heads of all the men around us jerk backward, and for an instant, we have the advantage. Figol's form quivers and becomes hazy before his transformation into a wounded puffin.

"My turn." I change into an eagle owl and hop over to Figol and grab him with my talons. With one good leap, we're airborne. I look down and see Bodmin's feline form leaping over the stone wall. A crane emerges from the other side and flies in front of me. The men below look on in amazement. Only later will they realize how easy it would have been to skewer us as we fly away.

We fly toward the mountains for a good while before turning north. Bodmin dives into the forest as if he knows exactly where he's going. He glides through the sparse winter canopy to a series of connected caves.

"The inner rampart is only a twenty-minute walk from here, so it's best we don't show our faces outside."

"How far are we from Din Guarie?" I ask.

"It's a three-hour walk, due east."

"He'll never make it." I nod at Figol, who lies heavily on the ground. He won't be able to walk on it for several seasons, and even then, only with a pronounced limp.

Bodmin's head drops and he stares, unseeing at the ground. "We don't have much time."

"Before what?"

"Did you not notice that Vinhe the Elder and his men were exhausted after a five-day hunt? They won't leave camp until after a night's sleep. It will take them a day at a forced march to reach my family's city."

"I was too busy noticing their weapons leveled against us."

"Why?" Bodmin looks at me perplexed. "Even a crudely sharpened stick will kill you. Don't study the weapon, study the man."

"And you know they will not chase us because you studied the men in the several breaths in which you were surrounded?"

Bodmin rolls his eyes at me. I glance at Figol and see that he's coaxing Bodmin to explain. "The Botadin are the most feared warriors in Pretanni. Other tribes sprint at the first sign of the enemy, even when they're exhausted. We refuse to do battle when we lack the stamina to see it through. The five-day hunt was first installed in my time. They will rest this night before they travel to the capital." He puts up a hand to forestall any questions. "I know because I took part on the initial hunts."

"I don't understand," I say.

"Other tribes will walk day and night to get to the battlefield, then they will charge right into battle. A tired man is an easy kill. We, the Botadin, show more discipline, which is why we are rarely defeated."

He turns his back on me and examines Figol's leg. Any attempt to straighten it causes Figol to yelp in pain. Bodmin releases his grip and looks at me.

"At the time of Vinhe the Elder, the hunts stopped because of the threat from the Coritani from the south. I did not know the hunts had resumed. The first three days are half day marches. The fourth morning is spent readying the trap and with luck, slaying one or more beasts. It's only on the fifth day that a full day's march is enforced."

"What can we do for him?" I ask. "Can we tie his leg to a branch?"

"Can you find some puleium in this forest?" Bodmin asks.

Clicking my tongue, I consider it. "Perhaps if I can find a protected meadow." Try as I may, I can't remember any potion Gwalather made with the stuff. "For men, it will make you sweat, but what use is that here?"

"Caleto Forest is a two hour walk to the south and west, much faster by flight," Bodmin says. "It is an ancient forest and you would likely have more luck there."

"But what good will that do us?"

"I need it in combination with other herbs I have to make a tea. I will start the fire."

"But won't it be seen?"

"It will be a small fire, well within the caves. We'll have no choice but to chance it. Hurry."

I nod and begin my pursuit of the herb. Caleto Forest is mostly evergreens, and they are wonderful at breaking up the winter winds. I find a meadow which is buffeted from the worst of the weather. Reaching down, to secure two handfuls of paleium, I notice hoof prints in the soft ground. It seems Vinhe is right; the centaurs have crossed the river.

With renewed urgency, I fly back to the caves. Bodmin has mauled a sickly deer in the short time I've been gone.

"Uncle," Figol says, emerging from the cave. "We found these hidden inside." He's holding several large bows.

"They're centaur made," Bodmin says.

"The Centaurim have been in this cave?" I ask. We are nearly out of the forest here. They could strike Din Guarie at any time.

"It looks that way," Bodmin says. "It seems they are building a weapons cache. We mustn't tell them when we enter Din Guarie."

"Why?" Figol asks.

Bodmin takes a couple steps out of the cave. "If we tell them, their warriors will scour the hills and warfare with the centaurs is all but guaranteed. Do you want to talk peace when the two sides are shooting at each other? If we can make peace, then we'll encourage the centaurs to remove their weapons. And if we're unsuccessful, but we manage to keep our heads, then we tell the Votadin so they can increase patrols."

"I saw hoof prints in the meadow where I pulled the herb," I say.

"The River Tweed is the border between the two kingdoms, and it is wide enough and patrolled enough that no one would try a crossing. Caleto Forest has always been considered impenetrable for the centaurs. On the hill country between the forest and Din Guarie is a heavily defended earthen rampart. It extends north all the way to the River Tweed. Along the coast, there are mud flats north of the city and, there's no way the Centaurim would attempt to march in quickly shifting sands. And they're afraid of water, so they would never attack by sea."

"How long are these ramparts?" Figol asks.

"It would take a half day to walk the full expanse," Bodmin says. "There is a smaller rampart protecting the city, if the centaurs were ever able to break through."

"I've never heard of ramparts so long," Figol says, awestruck.

"It is amazing, but equally incredible is how Figol is up and walking after having his knee ruined a few hours ago." I look at the lifeless deer carcass again. No attempt has been made to butcher it. It looks like the life has been drained out of it. My heart sinks into my gut. "You didn't." My hands are shaking with rage.

Bodmin won't meet my eyes. "There was no other way for you to continue your quest." He stares at the blooded deer.

"You took the life essence from this deer?" I ask in barely a murmur.

The smile leaves Figol's face.

"Don't you dare enter my mind," I hiss at him.

Bodmin raises his head and meets my gaze.

"You call yourself a druid?" My fists are closed so tight that I can't feel my fingers.

"Uncle," Figol says.

"Don't!" I return my gaze to Bodmin. "How far have you fallen?" I give my contempt full voice.

"We didn't have the time to build a stone circle, so I did what I must."

I switch my disapproving gaze to Figol, then back at Bodmin.

How could a druid take the essence of a creature we're honor bound to protect?

"We must get moving if we wish to make Din Guarie by dusk," he responds.

"Why would we go there?" I challenge.

"Because I wish to check in on my brother's descendants and Vinhe's men won't arrive until the nightfall after this one."

"What does this have to do with meeting centaurs?" I ask.

"It's the price you must pay if you wish my aid." He stares back at me, unmoved by my anger.

I stalk out of the caves and into the forest. Changing into a tawny owl always clears my head. And I need that now more than ever.

30

Capital Offenses

None of us speak, if only to keep the peace. I know what Bodmin did was abhorrent, and yet I can't muster up any anger. Figol must be manipulating me.

According to Bodmin, it is best that we walk up to Din Guarie instead of flying. I don't know that I can trust him, but I know I can't get to the centaurs without him, so my choice is made.

There are two small earthen walls which funnel traffic to the hill where Din Guarie sits. Each has a line of sharpened wooden stakes on top. They have placed all their faith in these simple defenses. It seems underwhelming to me, but it has held since Bodmin's time.

"Stay on the path," Bodmin says. "There are hidden pits to either side of us." He nods his head to both sides of the flat expanse where knolls run toward the city. "Each hill is a blind, where our archers can remain protected and eliminate any attacker." He looks at me. "We learned long ago that an overconfident foe is an easily defeated foe."

The guards wait patiently for us to reach them before they block our path. "What business do you have here?" The leader asks.

"You must take over from here," Bodmin whispers to me. "I dare not give away my identity."

Thanks for warning me now.

I give him a dirty look. "I am an envoy from the druids. Is this normal hospitality for one of my kind?"

"Sorry revered one," the other guard says. "We can't be too cautious in these times." They part and let us enter into the market.

"Do all cities have markets just inside the gates?" Figol asks.

"It is common enough," Bodmin says. "It is easier on the farmers, who come in from the countryside to sell their wares. It's also easier for the city to levy fees."

Bodmin takes us past the busy market and climbs the path to the hill's crest. The salt air is a welcome relief from the city below. The round houses here are made of stacked stones and thatch roofs. The central hall is the largest structure of all. With a double peaked roof, smoke pouring out from each.

"And who might you be?" A well-dressed young woman asks from the doorway.

"I am Grahme Fairweather, the Protector of Men-an-Tol and a member of the Nine."

A look of surprise flashes over her face for just an instant before she resumes her mask of polite indifference. "Your rank tells me that you do not mean to stay and serve our court. May I ask what your intentions are?"

"The druids serve only nature," I correct her. "A member of our order will be on his or her way soon, if not already. I ask only for a night's rest before I continue my journey."

"Where might you go from here?" She asks, puzzled. "Beyond our hall are the savage centaurs. Surely you don't mean to throw your lives away by entering their lands?"

There is no reason to divulge our plans, especially to nosy nobles, so I stare back placidly at her.

"Oh! You do mean to meet with the centaurs," she says. "I am Princess Rholaand you should speak to father immediately." She barely nods her head before inviting us into the hall.

There are two roaring fires, each halfway between the long walls and the center of the building. Several dozen warriors lounge in the hall, eating, throwing dice or competing with each other in some other way.

At the far end of the hall is a great wooden throne with deerskin covering the seat and floor. The top of the throne depicts a roaring bear's head. The arms have been exquisitely carved into two paws, with the claws curving downward.

There is a robust man leaning against one of the arms, speaking to an enormously tall and stout man. Had I not met a firbolg, I would have believed him to be one. The behemoth glances our way and stops speaking in midsentence.

"Father," Rhola says in a loud, clear voice. "This is Lord Grahme Fairweather, the Protector of Men-an-Tol and a member of the Nine," Rhola says. "He and his group mean to entreat with the centaurs."

The king tilts his head and nods thoughtfully as his daughter speaks, as if he's focusing on every word. His eyes light up and with a less than credible smile, he nods at me. "I am Vriga the Valiant, King of the Votadins and Lord of the North."

I ignore Rhola's slight of not using my title. Vriga is a wide-chested, muscular man of about fifty years. Obviously a very strong man, he strikes me as one who believes his own boasting.

The massive man to the king's right scoffs outwardly. "You seek death by the savage's arrow?" He's a full head taller than me and looks strong enough to pick up a moor pony.

Vriga waves his man silent. "Easy Godod, these are not the first to wish to speak with the Centaurim. It is easy enough to tamp down that particular desire." He looks at me, "Though never has one as important as you attempted such an audacious plan. Perhaps you should stay and serve my court for a time, eh? Once you have an understanding of these lands, then you can plan accordingly."

"With great respect King Vriga, I serve none but nature and my plans are not subject to debate."

Godod snorts out his displeasure. He stomps on the wooden floor, causing a board to bow. The chatter in the hall dies down. A handful of men are trying to look inconspicuous as they eavesdrop on our conversation.

Vriga chuckles and places a restraining hand on his warrior's chest. "Godod, we will return to this conversation later. Please find my son so that he can meet my honored guests.

"Very good your highness," Godod says stiffly.

As Godod leaves us, the people near the entrance part as a tiny woman dressed in white enters.

"And here is my dearest love. May I present Queen Seora?"

Bodmin bows his head at the queen. Figol and I quickly mimic his gesture.

"It is good to have a druid in our hall," she gushes. "It has been a long time since we heard a proper ballad."

"My queen is a descendant of Uffa Horselord." Vriga says with obvious pride.

"He authored the finest ballad ever written," the queen says. "Might we hear the Ballad of the Craven Traitor?"

I swallow hard at the request. I lower my head to think up a suitable response.

"Noble Lady," Bodmin says. "May I be so bold as to sing a few lines about Uffa himself instead?"

Seora's eyes light up. "Yes, please. I consider it presumptive to ask," she confides in us with a gentle laugh.

Bodmin hops upon a bench and clears his throat.

"Hark people," he shouts. "I give you, The Ballad of Uffa Horselord, in honor of the queen." She sits opposite of him, her eyes sparkling as she looks up at the night's bard. The conversation dies down. Bodmin starts a proper beat before humming a few notes.

> Uffa the Horselord strong and fair
> Ladies lust after his flaxen hair
> Stalwart and brave
> Courage won't cave
> Able and wise in druidic arts
> An honest friend
> The weak, defend
> Modest, but first in women's hearts
>
> Shoulder to shoulder he stands tall
> With brothers against the Wigesta wall
> Pressed upon hard
> His life, no regard
> He gallops within the enemy line
> Off his horse he soars
> His cave bear roars
> Broken the cowards must resign

Lucky are we, a hero true
Strong, fearless and clever too
Bravery shone
Solid as stone
Peace again his only concern
Reward forsworn
Fallen, he'll mourn
To their farms the people can return

Uffa the Horselord strong and fair
Ladies lust . . .

"Come, let us go behind the throne, now that the curious have been diverted," Vriga says.

He rises from the arm of his throne and motions us to follow, away from the fire pits. Our conversation will be harder to overhear, but we are also backed into a corner. I'm sure both are reasons for wanting us here.

"I remember well when I was your age," the King says to Figol. "My appetite could never be sated for long." He waves for his daughter, who is ensuring no one comes too close. "Rhola, can you find this young man something to eat, no doubt he's hungry."

"Very well father," she says. She hands him a drinking horn, then places her newly free hand on Figol's waist. Her body rubs against his from shoulder to knee. She gives a poor attempt at an embarrassed smile before she and her swaying hips steer him away.

What appetite does she mean to sate?

He has maneuvered me to be alone with him, so I remain silent and let him start the real conversation.

How did we let ourselves get separated?

"Now, tell me how you propose to speak with the centaurs without being killed." Vriga drinks nearly half his ale without stopping to breathe.

The men break into cheers and shout "one more" at Bodmin. His face glows with elation. If only briefly, he's caught in the ecstasy of his previous life as a druid.

Two servants arrive. The first pulls out a small table from the shadows while the second lays out a large plate of delectables. A large cup of ale is handed to me and as fast as they appeared, the servants melt into the crowd. I smell the drink, it is very potent. One of these would reduce me to a drunken stupor.

"Vriga," I say. "I would not know how to approach the centaurs."

"Ah, I see," he says in a patient tone. "Then may I ask what has brought you so far north?" He takes a deep draft of his ale and slaps his lips in delight.

"My business is my own, but for my curiosity, what can you tell me of the centaurs?"

"Bah, they're a savage race. They hunt man with arrows as if we were some sort of beast. I know of no one who has spoken with them and lived to tell the tale since the great drought of six hundred sixteen. Even then, it was agreed that both men and centaurs could hunt in Caleto Forest for the duration of the drought with neither harming the other. That time is long past and yet still the four-footed horrors cross the River Tweed with impunity."

"Do they shoot first even in the forest, or only on their lands?"

"Don't know, we shoot first if they are on our side of the river." He cocks his head sideways. "Is the ale not pleasing to you?"

"No, it is fine," I say.

He ignores me and claps his hands. "Some mead for our guest," he calls out.

A servant arrives with a new cup and a drinking horn for the King. I thrust my cup into the servant's hand and take the two new drinks from him. The servant freezes, not sure what to do.

"Take this," Vriga says as he hands his drink off to the servant.

I accidentally tip the King's horn too far and let some of his mead spill onto my hand. Apologizing, I give him his drink and quickly taste the mead on my fingers. I take a sip from my own cup and just as I thought, the King's drink is watered down.

From his waist, Vriga gestures for someone to approach. I am sure that I was not supposed to have seen it. Godod and another man stand with their backs to the hall. The second man plays with his blond mustache while sizing me up.

"Lord Grahme, this is my son, Prince Vadan." The prince inclines his head at me. "Lord Grahme is, I dare say, the youngest member of the Nine."

"We are blessed to have you in our hall," Vadan says. Both the prince and Godod take deep drafts of their drinks.

I hold the cup to my mouth, but I only take a small drink. The mead is very good. It's a shame I won't be having much more of it.

"Surely you must like the mead, Lord Protector," Vriga says.

"Indeed, I do. I was raised in Dinas Gwenenen, the Bee's Gate in the old tongue. If there is one thing I know, it is quality mead."

The other three exchange glances. "Then why do you only sip it?" Vadan asks. "We have plenty more."

"At home we always say, 'If mead has good flavor, then sip it to savor. If it causes a frown, be quick sending it down.'"

Vriga coughs. "Yes, it must be very good indeed, if one as well acquainted as you appreciates our mead."

I scan the room, looking for my companions. Bodmin is in the midst of a crowd of warriors, holding his own at least. I search for Figol's red hair. He and Rhola disappear out the entrance, the princess dragging him by the hand.

"You must have come through Coritani land. Tell us, is Queen Eibal over her illness? Has she produced an heir for King Brana?" Vriga asks.

"Can he even produce an heir, that's a better question," Vadan says.

"You were late getting back," Bodmin says to me.

"Vriga and his men were very keen on any information that I might possess."

"Now you know why I refuse to announce my presence."

"I had nothing to tell them, though it took all night before they would accept that fact."

"This is why I haven't told you yet how we're going to meet the centaurs. Without being riddled with arrows, that is."

"How kind," I reply in monotone. "We will soon be away from here, so now you can let us know the plan."

"Not yet," Bodmin says. He smiles at my frustration. "Besides, we must find out if young Figol has the strength to depart today."

From beneath his bedroll, Figol says, "I'll be fine once the sun is up."

Bodmin grabs the covers and turns Figol out onto the floor. "Then once you tell us of your time with the princess, we can go."

"Figol," I start. "Please tell me you did not use your mental powers to seduce that woman."

Bodmin chuckles. "Not likely." Figol and I stare at him. "It has been a common tactic since long before I was born for the princesses to sleep with envoys and gain whatever knowledge they can."

"She took me to the family crypt," Figol says. "It's a nasty place."

"Take care, those are my ancestors you're insulting," Bodmin says.

"It's a dank, moldy place that only bats can appreciate," Figol says. "And all the way in the back there are two centaur skeletons covered in cobwebs and placed in kneeling positions in front of the tomb of the founder of the dynasty."

"You have seen the tomb of dear Botadin? It's a hanging offense for someone other than royal blood to enter his crypt."

"I guess that's why there are so many cobwebs," I say. "The royal family is unlikely to clean."

"She's a disturbing woman." Figol shakes his head. "She only became more excited after she told me that. She told me to make the night count, or she could make it my last."

"Do we need to hurry out of town?" Bodmin asks mockingly.

"We do," I say, "And not because of Figol's activities. If we linger, Vriga will try to get me to drink their horrid mead again."

Bodmin smiles. "It's good to know that the old ways are still followed. Still, we should make our exit now, before the royal family wakes."

286

"We've made no friends here, but no enemies either," I say. "It could have been much worse."

He opens the door to our guest house. "You don't know the half of it. Now, stay close to me and fly low. The sentries get bored easily and they'll shoot at any bird in the sky."

He changes into a jackdaw, leaving us to stare at an empty doorway.

"I won't miss this place, that's for sure." I grab my pack and my staff and follow Bodmin's lead. I watch as Figol sluggishly approaches. He doesn't realize that this is the best part of his day. Once he changes back to his true form, his hangover will be much worse.

31

Speaking With Elders

Bodmin veers well south of the Votadin's rampart, then west into the forest. Once safely out of sight, he changes back into his human form.

"The Centaurim know me by my great black cat," Bodmin says. "We know there are Centaurs in the forest, so I dare not go farther in any other form. You two must remain as humans. And whatever you do, you must avoid reacting aggressively."

"How can they be in the forest? Isn't it supposed to be impenetrable?" Figol asks.

"If patrols have become lax, then the centaurs would have time to create their own paths. It's the only way they could manage it."

"So Vriga is to blame," I say. There's no denying the smugness I feel after having met the vainglorious king.

"Maybe, but it is always the son who is the leader of the defenses. Vriga may well have shouldered the blame in his time, but now it falls squarely on Vadan's shoulders."

"What about Godod? Isn't he responsible?" Figol asks.

"No, it is always the royal family who receive the ultimate credit or blame. Godod will be the future husband of Rhola. If Vadan fails to produce an heir, then Rhola will have to continue the line," Bodmin says. "In that case, the blame will fall to Godod."

"But Rhola is barren. She told me so . . ." Figol's face starts to blush. "She said so last night, in the crypt."

"For someone with your mental powers, you miss the obvious lies," Bodmin says. "The daughter's duty is to induce a pre-birth if it should come to it. The necessary herbs are plentiful here."

"Leave him be," I say. "He has much to process from last night."

"What a hard, wretched life," Figol says, shaking his head.

"Neither of you can understand the strain. There are griffins to the west, greedy centaurs to the north and the Coritani who try to push into our lands from the south. Life along the southern coast is a joy compared to what the Votadin must face."

Before we can reply, Bodmin becomes the great black cat. He makes barely audible growls as he leads us into the forest. Weaving between the pines, he finds a game trail. He stops and paws at the ground. There are many hoof marks in the dirt. He freezes in place and listens intently before guiding us deeper into the forest.

Cold rain start to fall, drowning out any noise from the forest other than the patter of drops on the dried leaves and pine needles. The air takes on a strong pine odor. Normally I would be glad for it, but now our guide has limited use of sound and smell.

"I hate rain, especially freezing rain," Figol says.

Through the splattering of droplets, I hear a faint giggling noise from the scrub. Every time I'm able to get a location on the noise, it shifts to somewhere else. Either Figol hears it too or he's in tune with my unease.

Bodmin emits a low guttural growl. Now is the time for silence. There's a small clearing where Bodmin chooses to stop and smell the ground. Meanwhile we have no protection from being pelted with half-frozen rain. I bow my head to keep the worst of it off my face.

Something grabs at my hood as it flies past my neck. I just manage to glimpse the arrow before it disappears into the evergreen tree.

"Run!" I shout as I race for the nearest undergrowth. Figol and I run at neck-breaking speed between the trees. A big centaur appears on the road and roars out orders in an unknown language. Three younger centaurs break from cover and give chase. The laughter is louder now and moving with us into the forest.

It's no good. Even with our short lead the centaurs are bearing down on us in only a couple breaths.

"Split up!" I shout and veer to the left.

Two of them pursue me. I visualize a wolf in my mind, then I stumble on some unseen root and collide with the ground.

Bodmin is patting my cheek and making strange noises at me. I let out a deep breath and see Figol sitting against a tree, his arms and legs bound. Nervously, my two centaur pursuers paw at the ground.

"What happened?" I ask.

The big centaur gives Bodmin a smile even as he idly twirls his double-sided scythe. "You tried to outrun three centaurs, that's what," Bodmin says. He looks up to our captor. "And the korriks thought to make sport of you. They had great fun."

I shake my head. Why doesn't Bodmin make sense? A mass of unruly brown hair half my height comes over. A rough hand comes out and it gently probes my head wound. It clicks to itself. "Thick hair would have protected you." The whole mass of hair shakes back and forth. "It has so little hair. Why?"

I blink and try to banish this dream from my head.

"Does it have an eye disease? It blinks very fast." The hair mass moves closer and I swear I feel the hair crawling across my face.

"Willex, it's my turn. It was my hair that tripped him." Another hair mass, this time black, bounces and stumbles into view. The first hair ball leaps into the second and they spill on to the ground.

"He pulled my hair out!" One yells. "I claim retribution!" The second one rolls? Stumbles? Somehow it moves into the brush. It's hard to determine what is happening underneath all that hair.

"Willex," our captor says, "You should apologize to Frewalt"

"No! It was my turn to look at the hairless thing. She should have waited her turn."

"Willex . . .."

The second hair ball comes back into view carrying shears that are the same height as itself. "Chop chop! Willex will be naked!"

A high-pitched squeal comes from the unarmed hair ball and it bounces into the forest faster than a wolf. The other, armed with shears, gives chase.

"Will this dream never end?" I ask.

"It is not a dream," Bodmin says. "Korriks have been friends of the Centaurim since they arrived on this island. When you ran, you invited the korriks to give chase.

"So, I was running from the centaurs and these, these little fur balls . . .?"

There's a low grumbling sound from the underbrush. Several branches start to shake.

"I apologize! Forgive me, I have taken a blow to the head and I'm still not sure that I am conscious." The noise dies down around us.

I should have stayed with the Votadin and drank their mead.

A panicked cry of "noooo!" rings out from the forest.

"Driffolk, tell Frewalt to end her feud with Willex and have them both return to me."

"Yes Ozigan, at once." There's some rustling of branches followed by screams "Willex! Frewalt! The Ozigan says to stop it."

One of those was a female?

A gray hair ball steps to the side of Figol and takes the binding off my nephew. With a flick of the wrist the robes coil up in his hand. This is magic the likes of which I have never heard, much less seen. It stands in front of me and speaks in very solemn tones. "I am Harib, the Ozigan. I trust that you are feeling better?"

"Yes Harib, the Ozigan, I am."

"And what is your name?" It insists.

Oh no, I may have just insulted it by not giving my name in return.

"I am Grahme Fairweather, Protector of Men-an-Tol. I'm sorry for not telling you sooner. My fall must have been worse than I thought."

"All is well, Niskai friend. We will go in peace from this meeting." It bows to me; at least I think that's what it did.

"Thank you honored one," I say.

I glance over to see Bodmin and the older centaur sharing a laugh, most likely at my expense. The centaur looks past me. "Jereas, unstring your bow. Anymore nervous arrows and there's no telling who among us will take injury."

I hear a hoof stamping the ground followed by a dejected, "yes, Halanthus."

"I am glad it is your party that discovered us, Halanthus," Bodmin says. "Otherwise, this meeting could have turned out badly."

"Many moons ago, you saved a young, impetuous centaur from his folly." Halanthus says. "Now I have saved these two lives. It is you who are in my debt now."

Bodmin throws his head back and laughs. "You admit the lives of humans are equal in weight to the lives of the Centaurim?" His eyes sparkle. "Then indeed, I am in your debt." He spreads his arms out wide as he bows slightly.

"You always have a ready answer." Halanthus smiles ruefully. "But now you must explain yourselves. Why do you violate centaur land?"

"Centaur land?" Bodmin asks. "I believe the Votadins would argue that point with you, friend."

Halanthus smiles gravely. "You know that I must take you and your friends to see our leader, Aldetes."

"Aldetes? He managed to survive all this time?" Bodmin says in mock surprise.

"Your impertinence has not left you," Halanthus says. "But I must inquire as to why you brought these two with you."

"It was they who asked this of me."

"Are they apt to think like korriks?" The lead centaur's puzzled gaze rests on me.

"We must fulfill our quest," I say.

"I respect that," Halanthus says. "But whoever gave you this quest is not a friend. It is most likely that you should end up dead if you persist."

"It was Ganna," Bodmin says.

"The holy Ganna?" Halanthus asks, awed.

"Yes, that Ganna," Bodmin says darkly.

"Halanthus," I say. "Why did the Ozigan call me Niskai friend?"

"Do you not know the name of the goddess whose site you protect?"

"I thought Men-an-Tol is a pixie holy site."

"Yes, to their goddess, Niskai. They believe that their goddess was the first upon the island, and being bored, she fell asleep. Many, many years later, the pixies woke her, but the ground had collected over time and only her head and the tips of her wings remained visible. Afraid she might be attacked while vulnerable, she changed herself into stone. When pixies are to become betrothed, they would stare through their goddess's face and into the other's soul."

"How little we know of these islands," Figol says before making a show of stretching his formerly bound limbs.

Halanthus directs two of the youthful centaurs to march in front. He turns to Bodmin, "When your men are ready, we'll begin."

I push off against the nearest tree to get to my feet. I am not about to show weakness. One of the younger centaurs sheepishly hands me my staff.

"May I know your name so I can thank you properly?" I ask.

"That's Tantair, and he's only being nice because he should have brained you, but he missed," the second centaur says.

"Shut your mouth Adako," Tantair says. "Halanthus told us to treat them well."

"For whatever the reason may be, I am glad to have not been brained by you or anyone else." I give the youth a short bow.

Now he refuses to meet my eye. It seems the inexperience of youth causes all races to feel awkward in new situations. Perhaps men and centaurs are more alike than anyone is willing to believe.

"I expect you did what you were told," I say. I extend my hand in friendship to him. "Let there be no hard feelings."

"Thank you, Lord Druid."

"Don't get too close. Jereas says there's still a good chance that we'll have to put arrows into him before it's all done," Adako says as he nods back toward the centaurs behind us.

Halanthus and Jereas walk with Bodmin. As a member of the Nine, it is my duty to walk with the leader. Before I can excuse myself, Figol squeezes my hand and gives me a brief shake of his head.

"How is it that all of your kind can speak the language of men, seeing that before today, you shot everyone on sight?" Figol asks.

"When the humans came to this land, they knew none of the elder languages and none of the Elder Races wanted to instruct the newcomers on their tongue. So, we all learned the human's tongue and in time, it became more convenient for us to speak to the other races in this common tongue as well," Tantair says.

"Elvish is ridiculous. Every word has six different meanings and you can't tell which it is without figuring out what every other word means around it. It's maddening to speak," Adako adds.

I glance back and see Bodmin and the two centaurs walking in silence. Now I understand Figol's logic. The young ones will talk to us.

"And the Centaurim's tongue?" I ask.

"We're not allowed to speak it to outsiders," Tantair says.

"Even ones you're likely to stick full of arrows?" I kid.

"You're very friendly for one most likely to die at the range or the gallows, druid," Adako says.

"What is the name of your tribe? And what is your leader like?" I ask.

32

The Centaur Capital

"Lord Druid, come forward," Halanthus says. "Behold, the chief city of the Damol and the meeting place of the full Centaurim."

At first sight, a forest of pruned fruit trees lies before us. It's only on closer inspection I make out wide dirt streets and a single column of smoke in a clearing. Straining my eyes, I see small, stretched-hide houses set near the stream. On the opposite side of the orchard from the houses is a large circular meadow with a flat rocky outcrop at one end. By the look of it, apple and pear trees ring the area.

"There's no smoke rising from the houses," I say.

"We use the homes only for slumber or shelter from the worst of the weather. Otherwise, we spend our time in nature," Halanthus says.

"Will a former prince of the Votadins be willing to stay in such humble dwellings?" I ask Bodmin, teasing.

Bodmin coughs suddenly. "Any accommodations provided for us will be more than adequate," he assures our host.

Halanthus leads us through the rolling meadow toward the city. The partially buried boulders on our left give way and the whole flourishing valley can be viewed. Our guide points to a waterfall and two towering Centaurs carved in high relief on either side. The pair are made to look as if they are standing on the calm water of the lake below.

"They are Stergedes and Abdeneus, great leaders from the time of the Departure," Halanthus says.

Out, away from the city, is an open field where armored centaurs are practicing their martial skills. A group of five tightly bunched warriors run as one, pole weapons up. They turn in unison and gallop to a mark, where they halt and draw their bows. Multiple arrows are shot in blinding succession before they drop their bows and charge the targets. The exercise ends with the human-shaped targets having their grass stuffing released into the wind.

Figol is staring open mouthed at the city, and I can't be much better. "Your men are the most amazing fighters I've ever seen."

"Yes." Halanthus changes to a trot. "It would not be prudent for the warriors to be the first to engage with us."

We jog to keep our guides between us and the warriors. The grass slowly changes to a pounded dirt path with brambles running down the center. "We grow many different fruits throughout the city so that all will have plenty to eat," he says proudly.

Several centaurs have noticed us, but they conspicuously turn and move away, except the young. The young line the street as we pass. There is an undercurrent of mumbling as we approach each group, but each grows perfectly silent as we approach. Every youth has a strung bow, though none possess arrows. Most make a show of drawing their bowstrings as we pass.

"Uncle," Figol says, nervously.

Even I can feel the roiling discontent. "Just keep walking and be quiet," I reply. In truth, I'm every bit as nervous as he is, but to run signals fear and possibly guilt. A display of either could get us killed.

"This hut is currently unused. You will remain here while the elders of the village are assembled.

"Thank you Halanthus. You honor us," Bodmin says with a bow.

"Jereas, go find Aldetes and tell him that we bring Bodmin and two humans to speak with him."

"Why can't you send one of the youths to do that?" Jereas whines. "I *am* a free adult after all."

Halanthus pauses to gather his thoughts. "Jereas," he says with exaggerated patience, "Aldetes is likely within the Council Circle and neither Tantair nor Adako are allowed to enter without an adult escort. If it will make you feel better, they are going to be sent to fetch water and set up our visitors' home. So, act the part of an adult and do as you're bid."

Jereas stomps off, nonplussed. One look from Halanthus and the other two nod and break off from our group. "Let us follow them for a moment," Halanthus says.

We follow the youths to the river. The water crashes into the submerged rocks, creating holes in the river and plenty of frothy, wild water. The shore is nothing but a collection of slippery, uneven rocks. Adako and Tantair are forced to go further downstream to fill the water bladders.

"Behold, the River High Tweed, there is no water on this earth which tastes better."

"I am sure it is good, but I'd rather have your cider," Bodmin says.

Halanthus breaks into a broad grin. "And cider you will have." Next, he leads us to where the cooking fires are producing aromatic smoke.

"Halanthus, I am considered a youth by my people," Figol says. "Should I join Tantair and Adako as well?"

The centaur looks to me to decide. I glance at my nephew and see his head down, in his mental manipulation stance. "Very well," I say. "If it will not give offense." I return Halanthus's gaze.

"Hurry then," he says to Figol.

"Why has Jereas been elevated to adulthood?" Bodmin asks. "He is still very young and lacks enough hair to pull back behind his head."

Halanthus turns to me to explain their ways. "In our society, adulthood is not achieved at a given age, but rather when an adult deed is completed. Since the other races left, killing a human has meant an immediate promotion to the adult ranks. Not long ago, Jereas shot wildly at a deer. His arrow passed through the brush, and as if guided by magic, it struck a lone human hunter in Caleto Forest. He is not ready to act the part of the adult and the women have no interest in him."

"What can be done?" Bodmin asks.

"We amended our ways so that he can go out scouting as my second. I fear that time is the only cure for this problem."

"And you're saddled with him until then?" I ask.

Both Bodmin and our host roll their eyes.

"Grahme," Bodmin says, "It is disrespectful to mention saddles to the Centaurim."

"My apologies," I say, hanging my head.

"Not needed," Halanthus says. "It is best that you say that now and not when you're summoned to the circle."

A crowd of adults eye us with a mixture of curiosity and hostility. If Halanthus is aware of the uncomfortable attention, he's not letting it show. He removes the lid to a brass vase larger than I, releasing the aroma of apples and herbs. He hands us each a cup and I forget all my fears as I drink the fragrant libation.

"Let's make our way to the council circle. The Archon will wish to speak to you at once," Halanthus says. "Be neither haughty nor submissive before him. Be confident but concise. Do this and you'll most likely live until tomorrow."

"And after tomorrow?" I ask.

Bodmin pats me on the shoulder. "Relax Grahme. What our friend here is not telling you is I knew the Archon when Aldete was still just a boy."

"Isn't it Aldetes?" I ask. It is my constant fear that I will not remember important names.

"When a male obtains adult status, his name changes to the plural form. It reminds us all that we have entered a stage when we are more than just ourselves," Halanthus says. "This is what makes the life for Jereas so hard. He is of the same age as Tantair and Adako and he is not mentally ready for the promotion he received."

Halanthus slows his gait. He may tell us not to be nervous, but he's in no hurry to get to the circle. The residents give us a wide berth, as hundreds stream past us. Most settle for sidelong glances. Others let their feelings be known, even if I know not a word in their language.

Where did they all come from?

The circle is indeed a round patch of grass with apple, pear and even a few cherry trees lining it. From here the stone-hewn ramp to the outcrop is clearly visible. The two carved figures feel ever more imposing as we stand underneath their stony gazes. A dozen warriors holding metal swords and shields, all green with age, keep the crowd from the stage. A lone centaur stands above us, arms crossed and a permanent scowl etched into his features.

"Make way," Halanthus yells, though it is not really necessary. The crowd has already parted wide enough for us to make our way to the front. Halanthus makes a beeline for Jereas.

"You will join us as well," he says.

"Me?" Jereas says in surprise.

"You were on the scouting mission."

"But what about Tantair and Adako?"

His words are spoken to our backs. Halanthus continues on to a stone ramp. We join the Archon, Aldetes on the platform. Jereas looks as uncomfortable as I do, if that's possible. Directly behind us, at the bottom of the ramp, are eight soldiers in full battle gear. The bright sun reflects off the polished helmets and breastplates. Each holds their long bows at their sides, ready to shoot in an instant.

Bodmin nods to Aldetes and I follow suit. The Archon takes in my full measure before addressing the crowd.

"Gentle Centaurim," he begins.

"That means he doesn't wish to kill us," Bodmin whispers. "If he wanted swift action, he would have called them brave or some such."

"Quiet," Halanthus says without moving his lips.

"Bodmin is well known to us, but he challenges our good nature by bringing forth humans into our land." There is an audible groan of disapproval. Aldetes raises his hands, settling the crowd, for now.

"Before we judge, let my honorable kinsman Halanthus recite for us a proper accounting."

Halanthus lowers one knee to the ground and bows to Aldetes. I let out a grunt of surprise that he would bow so low. He shoots an annoyed glance at us and rises back to his feet. "Bodmin and the humans were found by Jereas and I in the Forest Caleto," he begins. "They were in the disputed lands, and not Damol proper."

"Then why did you bring them here?!" is shouted out from the crowd.

Aldetes gestures for calm.

"As for why the druids are here, I will let Grahme, Protector of Niskai's Men-an-Tol and member of the ruling council of the druids explain."

All eyes fall on me. I stare out into the crowd with a nervous smile on my face. I cough to cover my unease. Scanning the area, there are no exits. My heart pounds incessantly against my ribs.

Why doesn't anyone ever warn me?

I attempt to speak but it comes out more like horse noises than words. The crowd is getting impatient.

"Noble Centaurim," I blurt out.

What do I say next?

"Noble Centaurim," I say again, this time without screaming. "It is a new day for the inheritors of Branok the Burley's mantle. Meraud, the former protector of Keynor Daras is now our leader at Nemeton Dywyll Derw and she wishes peace, if not friendship with the only Elder Race left on Pretanni."

No one is calling for my head, yet.

I take a couple steps toward the center of the flat rock and take the measure of the crowd. They are waiting on my next words.

Are they willing to listen or only biding their time before they kill us?

"With the help of the venerable Bodmin, we have come here to discuss what measures are needed to end the hostilities. For too long we have refused to speak with one another."

Off in the distance, there is a griffin circling in the air. I point to it. "There are other forces that assail both our peoples and they can be neither entreated with, nor bought off. Let us discuss a truce so that each of us can protect our families and focus upon our shared, implacable foe."

I turn to the Archon and bow low. "Thank you for giving me the honor to speak." I return to Bodmin's side.

"Fine words," Halanthus says, again without moving his lips.

"A very good job indeed," Bodmin says. Jereas gives me a quick smile.

"The druid speaks simply and truly," Aldetes says. "And I am inclined to at least explore this path. It strikes me that the leader of the druids held the merfolk's holy shrine in honor before moving to the Elven temple within the trees. And this druid, though he be young, upholds the esteem of the pixie's sanctuary. I believe the time may have come when the druids will once again look up to the Elder Races for guidance."

He stands even straighter and faces the crowd. "But it is not for us to decide by ourselves. I will give my hospitality to these men until such time that a Council of Archons can be convened and these men stand trial."

The crowd is willing to be convinced of this course of action.

"Damolian Guard, please ask the other Archons to join us here for deliberation on an urgent matter." The eight soldiers depart, with half moving off to the north and half to the west.

"Do those guards always stand ready?" I ask.

"No," Halanthus says. "Like all good leaders, Aldetes knew what he wanted before the assembly took place."

"See, we have nothing to fear until tomorrow," Bodmin says, with a wink.

Halanthus and Jereas lead us to our hut by the rapids. Figol, Tantair and Adako wait for us to inspect their work of preparing the interior.

"It is quite well furnished," Bodmin says. The youths nearly bounce on their hooves. "You have performed both well and amazingly fast."

"Thank you, Lord Bodmin," Adako says.

The two stand around eagerly, but neither is willing to speak. Bodmin shrugs and enters the hidebound shelter and drops his pack along the wall.

Jereas edges over to the two youths and they start talking in hurried whispers. Halanthus sighs dramatically. "I will take my leave now," he says. "Please note that any attempt to leave the city will be dealt with by force, even deadly force if necessary. Otherwise, you have access to the entire city. Meals will be served communally at midday and an hour before dusk."

"Thank you Halanthus," I say.

"One last thing," he says. "When you tire of the youths, send them away. If they will not go, threatening to summon me should do the trick. And if you should need me for anything, don't hesitate to ask."

I bow to our host. "You have been more than kind." I turn my attention to the conspiratorial whispers of the adolescents.

"Jereas, do you have a moment?" I ask.

The other two push him toward me.

"I thought that we might walk for a bit."

"Of course, Lord Druid."

"You see, we are more similar than either of us might have guessed at first."

"Really?"

"Would you believe that only six months ago I was a druid apprentice?"

"Truly, my Lord?"

"Please, call me Grahme. And yes, it's true. I was a little old to still be an apprentice, but that's another story. After I completed my quest, my master arranged for me to take his spot on the Nine. I know what it is to be suddenly promoted beyond my abilities."

"I shot at one of the Nine?" Jereas asks. "I heard your station on the platform, but I hadn't put the ideas together."

"I'm still upright and healthy, so don't be feeling too guilty," I say before he can start a downward spiral. "I just wanted you to know that for me, the path forward is to do as best I can and to listen to those I deem wise. I believe these two principles will also serve you well. In no time, you will quickly fill the role that has been thrust upon you."

"Thank you Grahme," he says. "But I excel at speed, not waiting."

"Then you need to find some way to benefit the tribe."

"All I do is get in the way and get told off when I gather with my friends."

"Tell me, who were those eight soldiers in full battle dress?"

"They are the Damolian heralds. They are to repel griffin attacks, though that hardly ever happens and like today, they are sent to the other tribes when there is news."

"And how hard is it to become one of them?"

Jereas looks at me like I'm crazy. "Who would want to walk around in armor every day and take messages?"

"And perform a vital role to the community and not be disruptive to the students?"

He stops and considers for a moment. "You may be right."

"I believe I am. And with your speed, you would be a natural for the position. You would be able to meet many rising talents from the other tribes as well."

"Thank you Grahme."

"Bah, all it cost me was a few words and they're free. I have been where you are now. I would take great delight if I can make your transformation a little easier."

Jereas breaks into a sprint, filled with bucking and shouting. He doesn't come back until he's winded. "Sorry for that, but I was so excited I had to do something."

"Not at all," I say. "But can you tell me what the others were whispering about outside our hut?"

"We were all amazed when Bodmin changed from the black cat to a human. We all wanted to see it happen again, but no one would ask him."

"I see. If you can beat me back to the hut, I will indulge you and your friends." I transform into a tawny owl and leap for the sky. Circling him, I hoot once, before the race is on.

33

Abandoned With Cause

The Damol prove to be good hosts to us. We gather a crowd, mostly of children, as Figol and I animorph to their requests. Finally, the time comes when Jereas, Adako and Tantair insist on the great black cat. Despite their loud calls, Bodmin doesn't leave the tent.

"I'll give it a try," I say. Remembering Bodmin's cat, I will my body to fill that vessel. The crowd cheers excitedly. I inspect my sable coat. Crouching low and tensing my muscles, the crowd flows away from me. I change back to myself and the crowd cheers. I take a bow before I realize that they are not looking at me. Behind me, Figol has matched my transformation and is stalking me. Once I see him, he changes back to his human form.

Despite calls for more animorphing, Figol and I end our entertainment. With nothing new to see, the crowd disperses, leaving us with only our three child guardians.

We walk freely about the city, albeit with an escort. There is a lot to learn from the centaurs. A city full of fruit trees for one. At the edge of the city is a pear tree which has seen better days. The center has rotted out and its days remaining are not many.

"I hate that tree," Adako says. "I get stung every time I go by it."

"Bees?" I ask.

"Yes. Thank Epona that it's winter now."

"Tantair, can you get fire from the city center and bring it here?"

"Sure, why?"

"I can show you how to get honey without being stung a hundred times."

Tantair gallops to the center and back, clearly excited by the prospect of honey. He hands me the reed torch.

"The secret is to put the bees to sleep before you grab for the honey. And smoke will do just that." Placing the torch in an opening below the nest, I wait until I see smoke exiting from the top of the tree.

"It's winter, so the honeycomb is filled with this coming summer's workers, so we can't take any now. But in late spring, do as I've shown and you will have your honey. But I warn you, take less than a quarter of the prize, or you'll starve the hive.

"At least that way we won't get stung."

"How do you know this?" Tantair asks.

"I grew up in Dinas Gwenenen, literally Bee's Gate. I learned how to do it when my brothers stopped getting the honey for me." The youths run in circles. How long's it's been since I've had that kind of energy.

"Uncle," Figol whispers. "They are holding back because they are in the presence of an adult. If you leave us, I will be able to find out a lot more about this city."

310

"So, no good deed goes unpunished," I smile ruefully. Waving at the youths, I beg off further exploration so that I can speak with Bodmin.

"I'm exhausted," Figol says.

"The two of you shouldn't have expended all your energy animorphing today," Bodmin says. "You may be sorry come tomorrow."

"You're the one who keeps telling us not to worry," I say. "Besides, creating good will can only help us."

"You know what doesn't help us?" Bodmin asks, lowering his voice, "Telling them that I'm a member of the Votadin royal family." He stares directly at me. "I have been coming here for over a hundred years and cultivating friendships with entire lineages. Then you hint that I'm one of their sworn enemies." He shakes his head in disgust. "Why did I ever consent to bring you here?"

"But as you say, you started coming here before any of the residents in this city were born. Surely that counts for more."

He scowls at us. At last, he lets out a deep breath. "What's done is done. At least you knew better than to bring up the centaur skeletons in the royal crypt."

"Um. . ." Figol says, with his guilty face on full display. "I may have told Tantair and the others about them just a few minutes before coming here."

The color drains from Bodmin's face. He gapes at Figol before turning his unfocused eyes at me. He lets out a nervous laugh. "That's it then. You've killed me." He throws up his arms in frustration.

"You don't mean that," I say.

"Oh, but I do." His voice is barely a whisper. "Did you notice the two centaurs carved into the stone on either side of the waterfall?" He doesn't give me a chance to respond. "Those two are Stergedes and Abdeneus, the Archons of the Kratydos and Damol. They convinced the Centaurim to leave this island with the other Elder Races. But my ancestor, Botadin, killed them both as they returned from that fateful meeting. Their deaths are the reason they all chose to remain. It is also why they shoot humans on sight. Between the two of you, this unforgivable crime has been laid at my feet."

Neither Figol nor I can speak. He ignores us and paces in a tight circle. "Did either of you simpletons realize what Halanthus was doing when he showed us the river behind our hut?" He pauses for an answer before supplying it himself. "It was to let us know that trying to cross the river would be deadly. It was a simple warning that there's no way to escape without their leave."

"But Halanthus is our ally," I protest.

"He is *my* ally, that is true. But he must conform to the dictates of his people and his clan. It was a warning masked as a kindness. Neither of you saw it for what it was." He looks at us with a bitter smile. "I suppose you realize they will demand your deaths as well."

"No . . . why . . . how could they?" I ask.

Bodmin ignores me. He's sitting on the ground cross-legged in the mind-calming pose. He rocks slightly forward and back.

"Bodmin, please speak to us," I say.

"There is only one way," he says. "Good luck to you." He changes into his famous black cat. He lets out a low, warning growl, then like a phantom, he disappears into the evening shadows.

The doors of the hide tents all face east. When the rays of Belenos enter the simple hut, there is no hope for further sleep. Not that Figol or I slept at all. Each of us sat alone with our thoughts, waiting for our doom to be revealed. Bodmin has not returned, not that I suspected he would.

"Wake up you lazy humans," Jereas calls, laughter in his voice.

"Blessings to you Jereas," I say as I exit the home. "Can you please find Halanthus and ask him to come?"

"You are too late. He has already asked me to bring the three of you to him. He wants you to know what to expect at the trial today."

"Very well, come Figol. Let's see what our fates will be."

Figol emerges from the tent and leaves the door open, as is the custom here.

"Bodmin has left during the night," I say.

Jereas isn't sure how to react at my news. First, he smiles as if I'm joking, then his eyes cloud with confusion. He pushes past me and enters the hut. He sweeps his gaze over the room, not believing what he's seeing. "This is bad." He mutters over and over. "Follow me and be quick." He breaks off in a canter and Figol and I must sprint to stay close to him.

We arrive at the flat rock platform in the council circle. Jereas is nervously flicking his tail and talking fast to Halanthus. No one else is present. Halanthus motions us to join them.

"Is it true?" he asks.

I solemnly nod my head to him. "It is. He feared what would happen when the Centaurim learned of the skeletons in the Votadin crypt."

"What?" His frame goes rigid and eyes harden.

"It's true," Jereas says. "Tantair told me this morning. His sire was so angry that he paced all night."

"You druids knew of this outrage to our ancestors?"

"We did not," I raise my hand asking for calm, despite my racing heart. "It was only on our trip to the Votadin capital two days prior to meeting you that it was discovered."

"Then why did Bodmin leave?" Halanthus says as he stomps the ground with his left hoof.

"Because Bodmin was once a member of the Votadin royal family," Jereas blurts out. "Figol told us that yesterday."

Figol's head is cast down. His ability to manipulate minds may be the only thing that can save us.

"It is true," I say.

"He *was* once a member?"

"He is still a member, I suppose, though no one alive today knows him as such," I say. "He is over two hundred years old."

Halanthus strokes his graying hair back to the braid of his ponytail and says, "This is how the trial will unfold, at least as best I can guess. One of the Archons, most likely Aldetes, will propose we put you to death."

"Oh," is all I can manage.

"It is the law of the land, so don't be surprised by it. The Basileia will call for other suggestions and I will request we allow you a chance to speak."

"Then we'll be put to death?" I ask.

"First someone will have to second my request. I have very good standing in my clan and they will be honor-bound to back me."

"What if they don't?"

"Then the request will be denied, but don't worry about that. I am an elder in my clan and it would be unprecedented for no one to back me on this."

"Fine, if we aren't killed immediately, then what?" It's all I can do to keep the nervous laughter out of my voice.

"I assume you have good reason for coming here. I suggest you explain."

"You know our reason. What happens after I make my case?"

"If necessary, the Archons will convene a private council and determine what to do next."

"If they go to private council, can we still be killed?"

"Of course. All options are open to them."

I shake my head and look at Figol. "All of this just to get you accepted into the druids." I laugh at the absurdity of it all.

"Are there any other questions?"

"No," I say between chuckles. "I fear anything you tell us will only make the situation appear more bleak." Try as I might, dark humor has taken hold of me.

"Then Jereas, you are to escort them back to their hut and guard the entrance."

"We are to be prisoners?"

"It is for your protection. Cimilles, Tantair's father will be screaming for blood, not that I can blame him. But Jereas and I are your hosts and sponsors, so we are responsible for your safety until the trial. After that . . .."

"Were you able to influence Halanthus earlier?" I whisper to Figol at the back of our hut.

"A little, but he was very sure of what he wanted to do."

"You couldn't force him?"

"Like the Obsidian Mage would do?" He looks askance at me. "Mother taught me to nudge, not to attack. I'm still learning their minds. In some ways, they are very different from human minds."

The shouts and stamping of hooves rise outside our hut. Jereas's retreats backward until his rump is through the doorway. The loudest voice is yelling out something in their native language. They begin circling the hut, the voices growing louder and bolder.

"Stop," Jereas says, but it sounds more like a plea than an order. His body shifts to the right and left, as if he's trying to keep from being flanked.

"You have to do something," I say to Figol.

"What? There are too many to calm down."

"Focus on Jereas. He's about to lose his nerve."

"You want me to make him braver?"

"No, with one so young, that will make him act stupid. Bolster his sense of duty."

Figol drops his head and places his open hands against his temples.

Before my eyes, I see Jereas stop his dancing from side to side and stand up straight.

Confidence rings out from his voice now. "By order of Aldetes, these humans are *not* to be harmed."

The chanting comes to an end and crowd around him try to shout him down.

"I don't care what you want." Jereas declares. "The Archons are meeting here today to discuss the fate of the humans. Do you want to answer to them?" He pauses and the crowd stamps their hooves in disapproval.

"What is the meaning of this?" a booming voice soars behind the crowd.

I jump to my feet. No one can speak that loudly. Jereas stands rigid as the crowd dies down to murmurs. I peek out the entryway.

"Cimilles! Why are you inciting these people?" Aldetes demands. "Present yourself."

Cimilles's front legs go impossibly stiff. His human shoulders are pulled back, making him stare above the crowd. His front legs stab at the ground, since his head is held so high. There is a sheen of sweat over his human half as he approaches his Archon.

Aldetes walks a circle around the centaur, not giving a hint as to his thoughts. Cimilles lets out a quick snort of anxiety, but is otherwise quiet.

Jereas is nervous as well. Facing down an angry mob would do that to the most experienced leaders. "Easy Jereas, you are not in the wrong." I whisper to him as I pet him on his backside. His posture eases and he quietly shoos me away from the entrance with a small movement of his hand.

Aldetes walks up chest to chest with Cimilles. In a quiet voice he asks, "What are you doing here, Cimilles?"

"I, um, we were just checking to make sure that the humans did not manage to escape, Aldetes Archon."

"I see," Aldetes says in a deceptively innocent voice. "Good Pereas, did you by chance call for such aid?"

"It's Jereas." His eyes fall to the ground. "I did not, Aldetes Archon."

"Interesting, and have the humans been discovered trying to escape as you guard them?"

"No, Aldetes Archon."

"Can you have the humans present themselves to us," he looks directly at Cimilles, "just to make sure?"

Figol and I walk out of the hut to stand at Jereas's side. I bow to Aldetes. "We are here, enjoying your hospitality, noble Aldetes."

The barest of smiles forms on his face. "This is good to hear, Lord Grahme, Niskai friend, Protector of Men-an-Tol and member of the druid council. Have you had chance to break your fast today?"

"We have not."

"I see. Jereas, you have performed your task well." Aldetes says kindly. "And I see no need for a quarter of the town to assist him." Aldetes keeps his voice conversational, but his orders are clear nonetheless. "Please go about your routines, and Cimilles, please fetch food for our guests. Keeping them hungry is a poor reflection on us."

"Yes, Aldetes Archon."

The excitement defused, the crowd slinks away.

Aldetes is smiling widely. "You have done very well indeed young Jereas." He pats the young centaur on the shoulder and Jereas shivers with excitement. "You should be undisturbed the rest of the day," Aldetes says.

"Thank you again, noble one," I say.

His smile evaporates and Aldetes leaves without a word.

"The Archons Yanares of Kratydos and Galitrius of Idoos are in our camp now," Halanthus says. "The Archonesses, Lanthea of Ances and Iphilea of Lakonis will arrive after the midday meal."

"Do they have farther to travel?" Figol asks.

"Hardly," Halanthus chuckles. "Iphilea is the current Basileia of the council, and she will be the last to show up. You are lucky to have shown up during the year she leads the council. Yanares would have had you killed at once. With Iphilea, you will get a chance to speak before the council's sentence."

He looks at Jereas. "You have not had a chance to eat yet, have you?"

"It's alright, Halanthus."

"Nonsense, go feed yourself. It will be a trying day."

Jereas is unhappy, but he does as he is asked.

"The time grows near," I say. "What are the likely outcomes?"

"I am sorry to say, but Yanares and Aldetes will most likely push for death."

"I assumed as much from Aldetes," I say.

"Aye, Stergedes was the Archon of the Damol and Abdeneus was from the Kratydos. If they fail to punish those responsible for their murders . . . they would lose face within their tribes."

"I suppose noting that this happened over eight hundred years ago by a specific tribe of humans unrelated to us will not have much purchase."

"You are correct. I confess, I fear mostly for Jereas."

"Jereas?"

319

"He and I are the ones who brought you three here. Bodmin's departure will be seen as a failure. Unless the council is forgiving, we may share your fates."

"Your people are harsh."

"We are the last of our kind. We face attacks from griffins in the air and men on the ground. We must prove to be reliable at all times, or our whole people are endangered."

"Does Jereas know?"

"It's hard to say. This is why I asked him to guard you both all day. I have two offspring of my own, so I have a legacy. It is my hope that he will be spared."

Jereas comes cantering back to us. "They're here," he says. Lanthea and Iphi have arrived.

Halanthus coughs and gives Jereas a disapproving look.

"I know," Jereas groans as only an adolescent can. "During the council it will be Basileia Iphilea, not Aunt Iphi. I *know*, Halanthus."

"It is good that you do, for we have no more time to wait." He gestures us to follow. The street is empty of centaurs this time. I suppose none wish to be associated with us. When we reach the council circle, I realize why none were in town. It is filled with whole centaur families. It seems everyone has come out to see this historic occasion. In all, the Centaurim number much higher than I thought possible.

"Jereas, I will escort them from here. Leave us now and join the assembly of adults."

There are five centaurs standing on the platform, just as Halanthus said. Four are wearing iron breastplates. Iphilea is wearing the ceremonial bronze breastplate of the Centaurim leader. To the

320

right of the platform is a company of ten archers, bows held ready to rise and fire.

"Aldetes insisted on them," Halanthus says in a low voice. "He can't take the chance that you'll change into birds and escape under his watch."

"We should have left with Bodmin," Figol says.

"No, then the Centaurim would have all they need to prove that humans are untrustworthy. Meetings between our kinds would be impossible for generations to come."

"Great, I'll think about that as I lay dying," Figol says.

34

The Trial

Of the five Archons, three are men in their prime years. The leader, Basileia Iphilea, is in her middle years, with only a hint of wrinkles around the eyes. She wears a finely wrought diadem of iron depicting autumn leaves in all their color and fragility. Each leaf is exactingly thin, bendable with one's hand. Her gray eyes take in all that is in front of her. Her features, no matter how beautiful, do not betray the thoughts within.

The final Archon is an ancient centaur. The hump in her back is so pronounced she needs use of a cane to keep her human torso up. Her hair is equal parts gray and silver and left for the wind to style.

"Isn't it cruel to make one so old wear an iron breastplate?" I whisper to Halanthus.

Halanthus doesn't reply. I glance up at him and his body has gone to rigid attention. He gazes upward, like Cimilles had. The old centaur, Lanthea of the Ances, surveys the assembled before her, then promptly lies down. Iphilea looks at her in confusion, and Lanthea waves away the worried look as she leans on her cane to keep her torso up.

"Honored Centaurim," Iphilea calls. A hush falls over the crowd. "We are brought here today to decide the fate of two humans who have been escorted into our lands and remain in this camp today."

Halanthus grabs us by the back of our robes and eases us forward until we are visible to all.

"The standard for human encroachment on our land is death. Are there any here who wish to take a different course?"

"Death!" is yelled from the crowd and is met with sounds of approval.

"Honored Basileia, honored Archons, I would ask that we hear from the humans first before we mete out justice," Halanthus says, his voice booming.

"To what end?" Aldetes asks. "The law is clear."

"But a valid suggestion," Iphilea says. She addresses the crowd. "Will anyone second Halanthus?"

The crowd grows quiet. I listen carefully, but no one is willing to speak up. The silence stretches on for several of my racing heartbeats.

"If no one will second . . ."

"I will!" A small voice calls out.

The crowd breaks away from the lone voice and Jereas is revealed to the Archons. "I will second Elder Halanthus."

"Children are not allowed here," Yanares yells.

"I am Jereas," the youth manages to say without stuttering. "I am of the Calanus clan. Halanthus is brave and honest and fair. We would be well served to take his advice. Furthermore, I say shame upon the members of the Hecteas clan for not backing their elder. He deserves better than you."

A hush falls over the proceedings. It is only now that Jereas notices he is standing alone. He shrinks under the weight of the Archons' collective gaze.

"Jereas is indeed a member of the Damol," Aldetes says. "In fact, I believe he was with Halanthus when the humans were discovered."

"I was . . ." Jereas's voice falters. "I was, Aldetes Archon."

"Then since your voice stands by Halanthus, I must insist that you physically stand by Halanthus and accept his fate as well, whatever it may be."

"Yes Archon." Jereas bows his head.

"Then move child! You are on trial as much as Halanthus and these humans. Go stand next to them." The exasperated Aldetes points to us.

Jereas finally grasps what is being asked of him. He ducks his head low and moves to the ramp. Each clip of his hooves on stone punctuates the silence. He stands next to me and his confusion is palpable.

The Basileia signals me to speak.

"I bear greetings to you Basileia, noble Archons and to the fine members of the Centaurim assembled here. I am known as Grahme Fairweather, Lord Protector of Men-an-Tol, Niskai friend and member of the Nine. I am the bane to the Obsidian Mages. On Eriu I am known as a friend of Laleah and the Brokko kom Gresman, the badger with bite. I count myself friends to Bodmin—"

The crowd mutters darkly at his name.

I could kick myself for being so dumb.

"— and Ganna the Ancient."

Iphilea subtly nods her head and I know I should get on with my speech.

"Yours is a justly proud people and the mission I was tasked with is to make amends. We, the Protectors of Pretanni wish for a friendship with the Centaurim. If that be too much, then we would like to come to an understanding with you and live separately, but in peace. Let us each build up our own rather than tear down each other. I ask plainly, what is needed from we druids, for this good fortune to come about?"

"How dare you!" Aldetes roars. "You come here bragging that the tortured bones of our ancestors are displayed amongst your people then ask for peace? I suggest we flay these animals alive and hang their bones for a millennium after." Certain elements within the crowd burst with excitement.

"Aldetes!" the Basileia calls several times, "Decorum, please."

"It is not your bloodline that has been so humiliated," he retorts. "I claim blood from both Stergedes and Abdeneus. Why do you think that both stand so proudly behind us? There can be no peace while our ancestors are dishonored."

"Honored Archons," Halanthus says. "I beg your indulgence, but upon their word, neither of these humans knew of such debase treatment before setting out to meet with us. Furthermore, they made it known to us once they arrived. There is justice that needs to be meted out to humans, but these two before us are not the proper recipients."

An Archon places his hand on Aldetes's shoulder before Aldetes can respond. "Halanthus," Yanares says. "How many humans did you bring into this camp yesterday?"

"There were three humans, Yanares Archon."

"Yet now there are only two."

325

"That is correct." Halanthus stares at the ground before him.

"So, you and young Jereas there, we mustn't forget him, failed to keep the prisoners even one night?"

"Yanares Archon, the person—"

"—Yes or no please."

"Yes, Yanares Archon." Halanthus hangs his head.

"Conference," Lanthea says from her seated position.

"I don't know that—" Aldetes starts.

"— There's nothing more to be said." Lanthea says. "We have the facts. It's time for a conference," She shakes her cane at the Archon as if he's a misbehaving child.

Aldetes turns from the old biddy and mutters his comments to Yanares. Iphilea smiles at the altercation before stepping forward. "As usual, honored Lanthea sees most clearly of us all. Thank you for witnessing this council."

It was as polite a dismissal as I have ever heard. "Elder Halanthus, master Jereas, it seems your fates are tied to these humans. Please escort them to their hut and wait there for our decision." She turns to the crowd. "If anyone, human or Centaurim were to enter or leave the hut, they will incur the full wrath of this council."

Not waiting for anyone, old Lanthea rises onto her unsteady legs and leaves the platform.

"She comes," Halanthus announces.

The day is nearly at an end and at last we will learn our fate. Figol and I straighten our robes and face our sentence with dignity.

Basileia Iphilea takes her time as she approaches. She is a head shorter than Halanthus but her aura makes one believe that trivial things like size don't matter. The locals all follow in her wake, not daring to come too close but too entranced to pull away. She stops in front of Halanthus and Jereas.

"May I enter?"

"Of course, Basileia," Halanthus responds.

"Both of you enter with me, as this pertains to you as well."

She signals for Halanthus to close the entrance flap. Once we have our privacy, she hugs Jereas tight and rubs his back. Embarrassed, Jereas tries to push away from his aunt. She releases him, but she messes up his hair just for good measure.

She turns to us and sighs. "First, let me say that you seem like upstanding people. But your presence here puts us, the Archons, in a difficult position."

Figol once again has his head down.

"I have done my best to temper the outcomes suggested by the others, but nothing is ever perfect. Grahme, Lord Protector of Men-an-Tol, you and your apprentice are to leave this town at once. You will be shot on sight if seen again, unless you can manage to complete the quest the council has bestowed upon you.

"Another quest," Figol laments under his breath.

"I will speak more on that later. Halanthus and Jeri, you have been found guilty of allowing humans to enter our lands."

Halanthus buries his head in his hands. "It is death then?"

"It is. But your doom is also tied to the quest of these humans. If they should succeed, then all punishment is forgiven. However, the fool Aldetes insists he still has the right to punish you for Bodmin's escape from your custody, so your future is tenuous even under the best conditions."

"What of Jereas?" Halanthus asks.

"I fear you may think less of me, but for Jereas's sake, I lobbied for him to be forgiven, since you were the leader."

"You were right to do so." Halanthus intones without emotion. He stands tall, even though he is being treated unfairly.

"Jereas, you will be coming with me on business of the tribes. Perform well and this will pass over you without staining your reputation."

"Yes Iphi."

"Halanthus, you are to be confined to this city under pain of death for the next seven days. If the druids do not return within that time, your life is forfeit."

My anger bubbles to the surface. "Centaur justice is cruel."

"Would it surprise you to know that I agree with you?" Iphilea asks. "I have a hard-won concession for you and your kind. Any human who possesses a viable griffin egg will be allowed within Centaurim territory. Once an egg is presented, talks of peace may begin."

"But only if within the next seven days?"

"No, at any time in the future. It is only if you do not return within that time that Halanthus's life will be taken. But you can return at any time, with an egg. From your party, it is only Bodmin we will kill on sight."

Figol looks to me for hope, but I have none.

She turns to Halanthus. "Before I take my leave, I would ask you to consider relocating to the Lakonis tribe. We are peaceful farmers and very likable neighbors, I think."

"I cannot great lady, Aldetes would never allow it."

"Aldetes is a fool. Leave with me and I will apologize to him later for the misunderstanding."

"I cannot," Halanthus says.

"The road is quite an easy one, I assure you. And the number of griffins spotted each year are but a few."

"It is not the journey; it is the vows I made before my tribe that prohibit it."

"You would stay and be killed by that fool Aldetes rather than live a long happy life with your family?"

"My honor demands it."

"Frankly, this is why women make better rulers than men. Men are foolish to cling to personal honor and care not for the others in your charge." Iphilea stomps her hoof into the dirt floor. "Think of your mate and children, Halanthus. If the druids fail to complete their near impossible task, then you will be twice sentenced to death."

"No, he wouldn't!" Halanthus goes ashen.

"What does that mean?" I ask.

"If a member of the tribe is given two death sentences, one is carried out and the second is left for his heirs."

"He would kill your children?" I ask Halanthus, aghast.

"No," Halanthus regains his composure. "The Centaurim do not kill children. But my children would bear my shame. They would be outcasts within the city. None would befriend or mate with them. They will be forced to live out their lives alone, knowing that our once proud line will end with them. If it were I, death, even as a child would be preferable."

Iphilea looks at the noble Halanthus. "Still?"

He hangs his head. "I swore never to break my vows."

Figol places his hand on Halanthus's torso. "We will succeed within seven days or die in the attempt."

"Yes, this we pledge to you," I add.

Halanthus is inconsolable. He turns his back on us and the Basileia. His shoulder starts to bounce and I want nothing more than to leave him with his grief.

"Please reconsider my offer to accept you as one of my people," Iphilea says gently. "As for you two," she looks down upon us, "you are to hunt west or north of here. The southern griffins are off limits to you."

"When are we to begin?" I ask.

Iphilea doesn't try to hide her irritation. "I told you. You are to leave at once, as in now, this very instant."

"But it is nearly dark."

Iphilea makes for the exit. "Would you rather stay in a hostile camp that is screaming for your blood?"

We scramble to collect our belongings and exit the hut. Iphilea and Jereas are walking hand in hand.

Figol runs up to Jereas "Don't let Halanthus lose hope. We will be back within seven days." I fly past the three of them in my favorite form, the tawny owl. For once Figol chooses the same form and not his stupid puffin.

35

The Eyrie

"Make sure the nest has eggs this time," Figol says, unhelpfully.

"Sorry, when I'm desperately trying to avoid griffins from tearing me to shreds, I'm not all that attentive to such details."

It's been a rough couple of days. The insistence of the Archons that we hunt north and west of their city means that we have to hunt on unknown ground. Not to mention that if a centaur spots us, they'll most likely shoot us.

"I really don't think they expect us to succeed," Figol says.

"I don't think they want us to *survive.*"

How much nourishment could a griffin get from killing a bird of prey? It makes no sense for the griffins to attack me while I'm a raptor. The centaurs could have told us that griffins will try to kill other avian predators, but of course they didn't.

Belenos is sinking in the sky and soon the male griffins will return to their nests. Somehow, I have to spot eggs while a griffin protects them, while the mate is actively hunting in the sky, all without being killed. If I go too early, the savage beasts will try to snatch me from the sky. Go too late and both griffins are at the nest, making the locating of eggs impossible.

I'm stalling.

Choosing a peregrine, the largest and fastest of the falcons, I start my dubious mission. Mountainous terrain is second nature and this form is the only bird that can out fly a griffin, albeit only over short stretches. I approach the nest from the west. With Belenos at my back, the nesting bird will have trouble spotting me. One griffin stays on guard at all times. With this nest, the same griffin remains there, not alternating the hunt like the other avian predators. It's either a mother taking care of eggs or an injured beast.

I fly in a tight circle, a necessity to keep the mate from sneaking up from behind. The mate emerges from a clearing in the forest with its latest kill. It lands and places a deer upon the ledge for the mother to feed upon. The mother briefly leaves the nest to grab the proffered food. Several blue ovoids glimmer in the sunlight.

Eggs! They must be.

I start a wide circle as relief floods through me. We have a target.

"*Dive Uncle!*" reverberates in my head. An image of a griffin streaking toward a peregrine floods my mind. I cut hard to my right and see why Figol is projecting such warnings.

The male griffin is coming straight at me. I duck my head and take two desperate strokes to gain momentum. The griffin's talon rakes through my tail feathers, sending me lurching to the left. I halt my dive and shake my tail to get my feathers in order. The griffin has banked hard and is coming back at me. He's lower than me now, negating my dive. I pound my wings into the air, taking me right at him. Just before contact, I drop below him and dive at top speed. The male gives off a frustrated high-pitched squawk, conceding the chase.

I land in the forest opposite the eyrie. "I saw eggs!"

Figol hops down from the tree and gives me a big smile. At last, we've made some progress.

◀ ————)|•|(———— ▶

"You know the plan?"

"Yes, Uncle."

"There he goes," I say. "Remember—"

"—Wait for the male to be well off before I take my chance," Figol finishes for me.

It's just after sunrise. I animorph into a horse and walk calmly into the valley between the forest and the mountains. I graze carelessly and even go to the stream for a refreshing drink. Furtively I glance up at the eyrie. The female watches me intently, but she won't leave the nest.

"*Behind you!*" The warning reverberates in my head. I take off at a gallop and quickly turn left. The male is descending fast, with Belenos at his back. I can't outrun him and the forest is too far away. I dig in my hooves and build up as much speed as I can. I swerve right and angle for the deepest part of the river. The air is whistling through the griffin's wings.

"*Jump!*" Figol screams mentally.

I leap into the air and change to myself, then an otter faster than I've ever animorphed before. I dive into the river and continue downward until I'm at the river bottom. A huge menacing shadow moves off to the west. I rise to the top, but not before my nose picks up the scent of blood in the water. Thanks to my supple spine, I swim in a tight circle and discover that it's my own.

"*Uncle?*" Figol calls in my head.

I emerge from the water and scan the sky. I'm safe, for now. I swim to the shore and change back to my human form.

Figol runs across the grassy plain to me. "You're bleeding."

"We can't stay out here in the open. It's as likely as not to come back here and we're won't to make it to the tree line if we dawdle."

I grunt in pain as my full weight is put on my bad hip. Figol scurries to my left side and puts my arm over his shoulder. "We need to look at that," he says.

"When we're safe."

Twenty feet into the woods, Figol helps me lay down. I let him pace futilely for a bit before I speak. "Figol, I have dried thousandleaf in this pouch. I toss him the proper pouch. "Boil two handfuls of water, crush five of these leaves and add them as you remove the water from the fire. Let it steep until the water is warm enough to handle, then we'll rub it into my wound.

Figol looks around frantically.

"What are you looking up for?"

"I have to be able to make it to the stream without being killed," he replies in an anxious voice.

"Figol," I say calmly. "Use your waterskin."

"Oh, right." He jerks the leather cord off the end and searches the immediate area.

"The baked clay pot is in my big pack," I say.

"I was going to use a smaller cup so it heats faster."

"The cups are made of wood," I say.

"I know."

"You're going to place a wooden cup over the flames?" I ask.

"Oh, I'll get the pot."

For all his talents, Figol doesn't act well to new situations.

"It should be me who leads," Figol says. "You're still injured."

"I'm fine. My hip hurts, that's all." I point at him. "Don't go messing with my mind; I have way more experience than you."

"I wouldn't," Figol says in an injured tone.

"Make sure your mantle is soaked."

Animorphing into a raven, I start the long flight to the top of the mountain peak above the eyrie. Figol follows closely on my tail. It's nerve racking sitting out in the open like this, but there's nothing for it. We wait for an eternity for the male griffin to leave the nest for his next hunt. The wind is blowing up the mountain, away from the nest. We change into human form and I ready my fire rune. Walking out to the edge, I drop the runestone. *"Cweorth."* The stone ignites and the flame, buffeted by the wind, announces its arrival. The female looks up and in panic, launches away from the ledge. The fireball lands on the side of the nest and the dried vegetation flares up on cue.

The female lands and desperately fans the flames. This is a magic fire and it will not be so easily extinguished. The female grabs the edge with her talons and fans even harder. She releases a shrill cry that any parent would understand. In her panic fanning the flames, she loses her grip on the ledge and must circle back around. I drop down and remove the egg nearest the flames.

"Now Figol!"

Figol is frozen in place above me.

"The mantle Figol, bring me your mantle or all the eggs will be destroyed." Even creatures as menacing as griffins are not to be killed needlessly. He drops his mantle, but the wind carries it out, over the ledge. Holding the precious egg in my arms, I get as close to the edge as I dare. The wet cloth catches on an outcrop below. If I set the egg down, I may be able to get to the cloth without falling. As I deliberate, I hear the wind riffling through feathers above me. I roll backwards, cradling the egg against my chest. I allow myself to breathe again. It was only Figol's golden eagle form. He rises to the ledge with the soaked mantle in his talons.

The mother griffin lets out a challenge call as she returns to her nest. She snatches the wool mantle and Figol is sent careening away from the eyrie. He recovers, but before I can see more, the angry mum shreds the cloth and comes at me, talons extended.

I raise the egg out in front of me, guessing it to be my only chance to survive. She beats her wings furiously to halt her attack. The flames have devoured nearly a quarter of the nest, including the area where my egg was resting.

One of the eggs begins to rock. A cheeping noise from within can clearly be heard. I run to the nest but trip on a pile of loose bones. Landing on top of the egg, it cracks and begins to ooze fluids. Picking it up, I race to the fire and split the egg in two. A slimy proto-body is swimming in thick, translucent ooze. I dump the partially formed chick and the abundance of liquid on the fire. A sickly-sweet smoke rises from the ashes.

In front of me, Figol has become a peregrine and is attacking the griffin's wings. Being small and more nimble, he's able to avoid her attacks. No time to marvel, I select a new egg. Cracks form in the egg to my right. A beak as large as my hand is breaking through the protective encasement. Another couple strikes and the top of the egg falls to my feet. The rest of the egg fractures and the chick is free to move. Not content with its own shell, it cracks the one next to it. He moves forward and punctures his sibling's shell in several places.

There is very little ooze in this egg. Once part of the shell is removed, the chick's razor-sharp beak begins to eat its sibling.

I grab the last unbroken egg from the nest. The tyrannical chick sees the movement and rounds on me. I back away from the nest, using the last viable egg as a shield. The chick stumbles forward and falls out of the nest onto the rocky ledge.

I slip again on a pile of bones as I backpedal. Lunging forward to keep my balance, I kick the bones off the ledge. They bounce noisily off the mountainside below. Looking before I step this time, I'm half a step from the edge. The wind picks up, filling my robe and blowing me back toward the hungry chick.

Figol lets out an alarm chirp and I fall away from the edge just before the talons of the angry mother impale me. I rotate so my back takes the fall. After a momentary pause, I check to see if the egg or I are damaged.

Figol is trying to harass the mother, but she is focused only on me. Balancing the egg in my left arm, I desperately grab for a couple rune stones in my pack. Two *hahgel* runes, I smile despite myself. This will work. I toss the larger one at the mother and scream "*hahgel.*" Moisture in the air condenses at once into hailstones in the mother's path. She's forced to veer off. It's only bought me a few heartbeats, but that's all I need. The chick stumbles toward me with a gluttonous look in his eye. I take the second stone and send a hailstorm his way as well. He lets out an alarm call and retreats toward the nest.

Turning to the eyrie's edge, I fix the form of the golden eagle in my mind. Before jumping, I will for the transformation to occur. That's the only reason why I'm still alive, because there is no transformation.

What is going on?

337

I clear my mind and imagine myself taking the shape of a tawny owl. Still nothing happens.

Think Grahme, think!

We cannot animorph when we're holding another living creature. Only nonliving things can go between when we change our shape. But the egg isn't alive, is it? I changed several times when I had the ghost orchid in my pack. But those flowers had been picked, so were they still alive?

In the distance the male is returning to the nest. I set the egg down. Either I escape now or I fight two griffins. The mother swoops up from below and I drop just as her talon comes for my head. The egg starts to roll to the edge. Figol dives at the griffin and rips a couple feathers from her wing. The mother pushes off from the ledge and spins violently to her right. Surprised, Figol is an easy target. He dives well down the mountain, effectively leaving the mother and I alone.

The egg wobbles slowly toward to the edge. I race for it, but I'm going to be too late. The sparkling blue egg drops, just out of my reach. I dive after it, deciding what to become as I fall. Nothing is strong enough to carry the egg. Inspiration hits and I change into the only creature capable of saving this from becoming a fiasco. With my powerful wings I push my new griffin body down toward the egg.

I open my talons wide so the egg won't crack. I pull up once I have it, but I'm too close to the mountain. Using my feline legs, I run along the side of the cliff for several paces before I become airborne again. The male bugles his presence and the chances of me surviving drop.

"*Uncle, come down to our camp in the forest,*" Figol's voice says from within my head. I roll off to the right and beat my wings for all I'm worth. I spot Figol below and I dive recklessly toward him. Nearly too late, he realizes he must get out of the way. He dives to the left and rolls away from me. Flaring my wings, I feel the wind take away my speed. I land on my rear legs and continue to flap my wings so as to not crush the egg in my front talons. Once back as my human self, I can admire just how beautiful the brilliant blue egg is.

"Uncle!" Figol cries. "They're coming!"

I turn to see the two griffins approaching fast. I spot my mantle hanging over a tree branch. Racing to it, I cover the egg with my green wool cloak.

"Squirrel!" I shout. "Change into a squirrel and hide!"

I take my own advice and leap for the nearest tree. The griffins both manage to land in the clearing. They cast their wonderfully developed eyes throughout the forest. Still as a statue, I watch as their vision sweeps over me. The mother jerks her head up and listens to a sound that only she can hear. Ponderously she turns to the open meadow and launches herself back to the nest.

The male lets out a piercing cry and waits to see if his challenge will be accepted. At last, he too leaves the closeness of the forest for the eyrie above.

Figol leaves his tree and scampers over to me. He changes back to himself and dramatically collapses to the ground. "That was too close!"

"Which time?"

"Uncle, if we have to build a fire to keep the egg warm, won't they see it tomorrow?"

"I have no desire to keep that egg viable," I say, holding my hands up. "In fact, I hope it freezes tonight so we can be sure we don't have to face another killer chick."

"Thank all the gods and goddesses our ordeal is over."

"We still have to get it back to the centaur camp," I remind him.

"We can fly there tomorrow."

"No, we can't. I tried animorphing with the egg, but it is a living thing and therefore cannot go between. The only creature which can carry it in flight is a griffin, and I will not be landing in the middle of the centaurs' city as their mortal enemy."

"Then how do we get it there?"

"I must change into a horse and carry it there," I shrug. It's the only way.

"Great, you're going to become a griffin's favorite food, carrying one of their eggs on your back at the beginning of their prime hunting season?"

"We must, but that doesn't mean we can't travel at night."

36

Haggard and Hunted

We each stand with our backs against an elm tree in the densest part of the forest. Vainly we scan the sky between the tree branches.

Why couldn't we have done this when the trees are full of leaves?

Our current savior, the wandering cloud above, is moving past Aine's light. Only a tiny sliver is up in the night sky, but it is enough for the male griffin to hunt.

"Uncle, we will never make it out of here alive unless you change back into a griffin."

"If I change into a griffin, you won't make it anywhere other than in my stomach. The force of a griffin's animal mind is greater than any other that I've encountered. I dare not chance it."

We have been having this same argument most of the night, punctuated by the male griffin diving at us from all angles. This must have been Aldetes' plan all along, our deaths without the stain of blood on his hands.

"Not today," I say.

"What?" Figol hisses in a low voice.

"Sorry, I didn't mean to speak out—"

The griffin's shrill cry penetrates deep within the forest. The branches snap to the left of us. The griffin has made its own clearing and is advancing upon us.

"Run Figol, toward the clearing!" I yell. No need for silence now. There's a winding path between the trees behind me. The griffin should just be able to follow. Locking eyes with it, I try commanding it to stop, but it's no use. It ceases the challenge call and advances slowly.

Almost too late, I see the right talon streaking for my head. I roll underneath the attack and end up sprawled next to an oak. I choose the shape of a wolf and sprint out of range. It lumbers its way between the largest trees while snapping the smaller ones. If not for the age of this mature forest, I'd be dead. Despite the instincts of the wolf clamoring to flee, I wait for it to get clear of two old oaks.

We had planned this out during our all too brief respite. The egg is hidden under a pile of leaves. I'm to lure this hulking brute away while Figol changes into a badger and digs a hole big enough to bury the egg. Without the gleaming blue eggshell, it should give up on such difficult prey rather quickly. Or at least, that's what we've bet our lives on.

"Oooh," comes from the underbrush.

"Shhh!"

"But I want to see the griffin."

Willex?

The beast snaps trees the width of my forearm without seeming to notice. I scan the underbrush one last time before breaking into a trot. Too fast and I won't be able to lure him away. I let out a howl to let Figol know where I am. A second one comes from beside me, followed by giggles.

Throwing caution to the wind, I make a dash for the underbrush and see two hairy forms peeking out at me and the griffin. The terrible creature tracks my movement and rushes the blind.

"Grahme!" Willex says, scandalized. He pulls his hair tight in front of him. "My hair hasn't grown back yet." I let out a warning growl and race for the clearing. The two korriks burst from their hiding place and outrun me. They begin weaving in front of me and laughing.

I swerve left, trying to put distance between me, the korriks and the griffin. I find a slick patch of lichen and my back legs slide out from under me. I careen into a thicket of whortleberries. Willex and Frewalt start laughing again.

The griffin closes in and I see my doom above me. It raises a talon and Willex goes flying through the air, his rope wrapped around the griffin's talon.

"Weeee!"

The beast's snaps the rope with its powerful beak, sending Willex tumbling.

"You ruined my rope!" Willex cries from the underbrush. A new rope lassos the griffin's leg. Two more ropes come from the other side and latch around the opposite talon. The griffin screeches in protest and begins snapping the lines. I don't stay to see more.

Figol should have had enough time now. Circling around, I've led myself to the edge of the woods. From within the forest, I can hear the retreating laughter of the crazy hairballs. Going either right or left in the forest will bring me much too close to the murderous talons. Only by going away, toward the meadow am I guaranteed not to run into his lethal claws. But if he makes it to the meadow too . . . I'm dead.

It sees my hesitation and the clearing beyond. With renewed vigor, it plows its way through the forest. I run as fast as I can across the meadow. The thumping of footfalls ceases. It surely has taken to the air. I break hard to the right and hear talons ripping up dirt behind me. I run as hard as I can and dive into a thicket of brambles. No time to acknowledge the pain, as soon as my paws touch ground, I head into denser cover.

The griffin lands with a thud and takes a swipe through the brambles. The talons fly harmlessly over me, but my cover has been lost. Three strides and I make it between two old oaks which are only an arm's length apart. At last, it gives up the chase and returns to the sky. Once my heart gets out of my throat and I can breathe again, I head back to Figol.

Taking the form of a tawny owl, I return to see Figol's underground cover. The korriks are bouncing up and down as they giggle and squeal in delight next to Figol.

"You nearly died, didn't you?" Figol scolds.

"I'm here, and I'm in one piece, so let's call it a win." The ground is level all around us. Try as I might, I can't see the burrow.

"The egg is over there," Figol points to a small mound of leaves.

I clear away the smattering of leaves and dig down an inch until I feel the smooth shell. "Not a very big hole, considering how much time you had," I say.

"Tree roots," Figol says, disgusted, "everywhere."

"It will do," I say. "But where do we sleep so as to not be seen by the griffin?"

"You are over there, by the elm," Figol points to the tree nearest the egg. "And I am over here, under the ash." Both korriks bound their way over to my elm and leap into the pile of leaves. They jump up and down and the leaves go flying off in all directions.

"Willex, Frewalt," I say with exaggerated patience. "Will you stop ruining my bed?"

"You should sleep in the trees," Frewalt says.

I refuse to debate such creatures, so I change the topic. "Why are you here?"

"Jereas told us you would need our help and, on our way here, we heard the griffin walking in the forest. Can you believe it? Of course, you can, it was chasing you. Since griffins are such great creatures, but we can only see them when they are far off in the sky, and our eyes are not good, so we wanted to see what they look like up close. When we saw Figol and he told us you were in trouble we knew we needed to help you and see the creature at the same time. But when he snapped my hair rope—"

"—Thank you," I say. "I was there for the rest of it."

Figol can barely hold in his laughter.

"Willex, the griffin is gone now for the night and we need to sleep, so can you remove yourself from my bed and leave us be?"

"Will you play with the griffin tomorrow?" The eager korrik asks.

I give my best serious face. "No, I'm afraid that was the last time." Both of the creatures seem to shrink at the news.

Willex perks up. "Can we see the pretty egg again?"

"Yeah! Pretty egg. Frewalt loves the pretty egg," Frewalt says.

"I'm afraid not. We need to keep it buried so it doesn't get cold and the chick inside dies."

"Can we see it when it hatches?"

"You'll have to ask Halanthus about that."

"Oh, we're not allowed in the horsy folk's town anymore." They both shake their heads furiously.

"Don't worry, I'm sure he will be on patrol back where you met us the first time very soon. In fact, you should go wait for him there."

"You mean he's not there now?" Frewalt says. "There are so many horsey folks there."

"We should go and find Halanthus," Willex says. "Yes, he said he'd box our ears the next time he saw us. I've never had my ears boxed. Have you?"

"You better hurry if you're going to find him," I say.

The two bundles of hair bounce their way through the forest.

"I have a headache," I say to my still chuckling nephew. He peppers me with questions, but I refuse to answer until I'm sure the two hairballs are out of range.

I kick the leaves back into some semblance of a pile. I notice that none of the ground has been dug out beneath the pile.

"The leaves are all the cover we get," Figol says.

"All this time and you only managed one hole?"

"Tree roots, Uncle," Figol says crossly, "everywhere."

"I'm too tired to argue, just keep your torso covered. Griffins have a terrible sense of smell. They hunt by shapes and movement, if it can't see our full bodies and we lie still, we should be safe."

After only a brief rest, I change into a tawny owl and scout around the area. How I wish that Aine was not so bright tonight, but the goddess will do as she pleases. Figol is awake and has already unearthed the egg.

"They've left us, for now" I say. "Help me get it stuffed into my robes."

I take off the rope from over my shoulder and around my waist before removing my robe.

"Won't you be cold walking back to the centaur city?"

"No, but it's cold enough now. Get moving."

The very cold breeze begins to blow across my bare skin. Once the egg has replaced me in my robe, I cinch up the bottom and my rope belt is fed through the arms.

"You are going to have to secure the egg to my back, since I can't animorph while in contact with other living creatures." Figol gives me a confused look, but I change into a moor pony as my explanation. It takes him several tries, but he manages to secure the egg. He tries to climb on next to the egg, but I sidestep him each time.

"Hold still Uncle, I can't—"

I break off into a canter. I'm not a beast of burden, appearances notwithstanding. Either he'll animorph, or he'll struggle keeping up. At some point he's going to have to use his own mind to formulate a plan.

As I reach the clearing, a raven dives in front of me again and again.

So Figol is a quick study after all.

"*I'm in your head, Uncle,*" Figol says.

Snorting my dissatisfaction, I increase my pace to a gallop. The centaurs have made paths along the mountain spines, but they have the advantage of having numbers and weapons. We have neither, so we must go valley to peak to valley once again and hope no griffins spot us.

Horses are not made to run indefinitely, so we stop in each valley where I'm forced to nervously graze and scan the sky. Once I'm back to human form, my stomach irritated for days thanks to all of this grass. But there is no other choice. The water from the streams and lakes are as pure as any I've ever tasted. The peaks in front of us are ones I've seen before. This is the last valley before we reach the city of the centaurs.

"Run!" Figol's voice resonates in my mind. He leaves his perch and flies into the source of danger. Horses are prey animals, and the instinct to run is too powerful to ignore. I take off at a gallop. The challenge call from above causes a cold ripple down my spine.

My human mind recoils at the idea of running up, out of the valley, but the animal-based fear is too strong to conquer. My legs move beneath me regardless of my desires. My ears rotate when I hear a raven's shrill alarm call. I tack to the left so I can see the commotion behind me.

Figol, in raven form, is swooping and diving into the griffin's field of vision. The irritated creature has tried to bite and swat my nephew without any luck . . . yet. At the top of the rise, I see the city spread out below me. With renewed vigor I race down the slope to safety.

Powerful wings are beating behind me. I swerve to the left for several strides before swerving back. The griffin gives a frustrated call as his talons touch nothing but dirt. The slope to my right is steep enough to be treacherous. My only choice to dodge aerial attacks is to break left, into the griffin's path.

A lone centaur is galloping toward us. The gray roan coat means that it can only be Halanthus. Above his head, he is spinning his double scythe. The distance between us vanishes with every desperate stride.

I'm going to make it.

The shadow of the great beast is over me and I swerve again, the griffin's talons catching only my robe. Several long strips now flap in the wind, striking my side. The beast cries out in desperation.

It must see the egg.

Why has he stopped running?

Halanthus halts his charge and holds his weapon by the edge. He extends the scythe horizontally away from his body. He spins in a circle and releases the weapon at me. The double scythe spins toward me. With macabre fascination I wonder which blade will strike me. As the blade gets closer, I realize that Halanthus' throw is going to miss.

The weapon sails over my head. A startled cry alerts me to how close the griffin is to me. A talon rakes my rump, but doesn't dig into my flesh. There is a meaty thud behind me followed by silence. Figol dives in front of me and cahs repeatedly. I regain control of the shared horse mind and slow to a canter. Making a wide circle, the griffin lays dying, with Halanthus's scythe sticking out of its chest.

Figol lands next to me, with several feathers knocked in various directions. With effort, he manages the change back to himself. He flexes his left elbow several times, as if to convince himself it still works.

"Well met, Figol," Halanthus booms.

"Help me get the egg off of Uncle Grahme."

Between the two of them, the egg is removed and gently laid on the ground. I change back and Figol giggles as he hands me my shredded robe. The rips start at my chest and run all the way down.

The strips of cloth stream every which way in the ever-changing winds. My robe preserves neither warmth nor modesty.

37

Mending the Differences

A dead griffin lying so close to the city is impossible to ignore. Dozens of centaur children stream toward the spectacle. Even aged Lanthea is persuaded to trot, at least part of the way. The strips of my robe mark continue to mark the direction of the very cold wind. My legs are red and itching, bordering on painful. The youths form a half circle around us. Several of the children point at my lack of clothing and snicker.

"We must get you away from this chill." Lanthea gives the laughing children a disapproving look. She presses me tight to her body for warmth.

"Oh," she pauses. Only then does she see the blue egg with white speckles gleaming brilliantly in the early morning sun. "I have never seen an intact egg before."

She hunches over even further with her aged torso and strokes the egg. "How do such monsters come from something so beautiful?"

Halanthus stands on the opposite side of me. Between the two, the wind loses its bite.

"I feel movement," she says. She looks up with clear eyes. "Halanthus, take this to my hut at once, don't wait for us. If it hatches, kill it immediately."

"I hear and obey." The unfairly disgraced centaur lifts the egg gingerly into his arms and makes for the city.

She turns to the crowd of children. "As witnesses of this feat, you are all allowed to take one feather and wear it over your left ear. Otherwise, the kill is to be undisturbed. Bastete, after you take your spoils, select four suitable feathers and fasten three griffin egg pendants. Bring them to my hut when you are finished."

The youth nods at once. His eyes grow wide and he smiles at his friends.

Was I ever so young that I confused an errand for an honor? Most likely.

"And you, Lord Protector," she grabs several long strips of my robe that blow into her face, "are putting on quite a show." She glances down and smiles ever so slightly.

"You're blushing!" Figol says.

"It's the wind," I say. "It's turning my skin red."

"Sure Uncle."

"Please come with me," the Archoness says. "You'll shrivel up to nothing in this weather."

Figol turns his laughing face away.

"I am sorry the others were not here to see you complete your quest."

"Where are they?" I ask. "The city looks nearly deserted."

"Let us discuss that in the warmth and privacy of my hut."

I look around. The youths are well behind us, selecting feathers and no other centaurs are within shouting distance. Still, I follow dutifully as I did with my mentor. Halanthus has already started a fire in our old hut.

"This is your hut?" I ask.

"It is. Unlike those younger than I, which is every living centaur, I require a fire to keep warm. I asked for this hut because it's close to the river," Lanthea snorts before letting out a small chuckle. "It also serves as a good place for visitors, so that they can't leave easily."

Halanthus secures the leather hide door flaps to the central peg above the entrance, giving us privacy. Rubbing my hands, I approach the warming flames.

Lanthea reaches out an unsteady hand toward Halanthus. He wordlessly gives her a cup of hot water. Reaching for a bag, she places a flower in the water and swirls it with her finger.

"When you get as old as I am, you'll try nearly anything to relieve the joint pain." She smiles sadly at me.

"Is there nothing else but wolfsbane for you to take?" I ask.

"You are accomplished in your plant lore. I applaud you." She nods at me. "Sadly, the other remedies no longer work, so I must gamble with this tyrannical herb."

"If you would take off your robe," Lanthea says. "I will mend it while we speak."

Halanthus inspects the entrance, giving me a modicum of privacy.

"This will go down as a momentous day for the Centaurim. Over the years, many men have been given the death decree. The only way to lift such decree is to provide a great service to our kind. Whereas that could mean many things, none are content to wait for chance to smile upon them. Always the men have left to vanquish a griffin, our greatest foe. Only twice in living memory have men been successful and each time the fools become overconfident and continued hunting alone. Neither managed to live out a single year after their sentence was lifted."

"Archoness Lanthea," A youth calls from outside the hut.

Halanthus unpegs one side of the hide and a youth is revealed, holding feathers and necklaces. The light of Belenos is behind the youth and my naked body is bathed in sunlight. He stares at me. I don't need Figol's powers to see there are an endless string of questions within the youth's mind.

"Thank you," Halanthus says. "That will be all." He refastens the hide and my time as an object to be ogled comes to an end.

Lanthea begins sewing my robe. Watching her hands, they become more fluid as the medicine takes effect. Her fingers dance over and under the cloth and the rips slowly disappear. Figol too is transfixed on her deft work.

"Those are horse stitches," he says.

She looks up from my robe. "We taught this to the humans when they first arrived on this island. It is good to know that our lesser cousins, the horses, benefit." She looks to Halanthus. "Where was I?"

"You were speaking about the men who overcame their death sentences," he prompts.

Halanthus will not look at me. Whether it is to show honor to the Archoness or because my nakedness embarrasses him, I have no idea.

"Yes, of course, no one in all of my years has ever been given two death sentences." She looks Halanthus in the eye. "Unfair though they be, and nowhere in our lore has anyone been able to recover from two sentences." She smiles at Figol and me. "Your return of the egg has wiped away one stain, and the flying scythe of Halanthus has taken care of the other." She flexes her fingers several times before going back to stitching my robe.

"You are free of any burden caused by us?" I ask.

"Indeed, I am," Halanthus says with great solemnity. He keeps his gaze high, looking only at my head.

It's hard to tell with our staid friend, but his perfect posture seems less rigid.

"Still, that fool Aldetes will not forgive you. I implore you Halanthus, to move your family to either my tribe or Iphilea's Lakoni."

"I wish to see my lord's response before I make such a decision, Archoness."

Lanthea stretches her forelegs, one after the other before settling on the ground. Halanthus keeps his eyes straight ahead, refusing to acknowledge the Archoness' new position. She looks up at him before smiling slightly. She addresses another rip in my robe.

"Halanthus, will you distribute the feathers and pendants, please?"

"Of course, Archoness." Our friend struggles to hand the feather to Lanthea while keeping his back straight.

"Halanthus," Lanthea says. "We are not in the public eye any longer, so you can stop acting so formal. Furthermore, I'm an old lady who struggles to get up, if you don't bend over to hand that to me, I will become very cross."

"Of course, Archoness." He bends over, his back still stiff, to hand the feather to her.

She sighs but takes the feather. "It is our custom that if you should see a griffin killed, you are to take a feather from the beast and wear it over your left ear, like such."

Halanthus hands us our feathers and we do as we've been shown. Last of all, Halanthus fixes his own feather.

"Now," Lanthea says, "I personally saw the death of the griffin and I judge that all three of you were instrumental, therefore all three will receive the Lapis Pendant." She gestures at Halanthus and our friend solemnly places the griffin egg pendants around our necks.

"Halanthus," a resigned Lanthea says, "I am too tired to rise again, so please take no slight and place one over your own head."

"Yes, Archoness."

Lanthea rolls her eyes, but only Figol and I can see it.

"Now that the formalities are over," she says pointedly to Halanthus, "we can all relax and I can finish my sewing."

"Archoness," Figol says, "where are the rest of the Centaurim?"

She looks up from her work for a second. "In good time, but first, I wish to finish the task at hand."

A sudden movement from the egg catches my eye. "Is it just a trick of the firelight or did the egg begin to wobble?"

The egg wobbles a second time, and everyone sees it.

"Halanthus, take this to the council circle, now."

Wordlessly he scoops up the egg and cradles it in his arms. In his haste he kicks up dirt throughout the hut. Lanthea coughs.

"Should we follow?" Figol asks.

Lanthea waves away the question. Her coughing turns into laughter. "Halanthus is as committed to our civilization as any I've ever known. What do you think he would do if he realized he kicked dirt in my face?" She does her best to mime a stiff, straight back and a look of disapproval before chuckling again.

Figol refastens the door flap. The crowd of youths wanting a peek at me has only grown. I sigh and ignore them.

"What do we do while Halanthus and the egg are away?" Figol asks.

"First, I will make sure that the Lord Protector is properly clothed. Unless you would like to parade yourself around town," she says with a mischievous grin.

"I would not."

And I'm not blushing.

Figol smirks at me.

"Then let me finish my work." Lanthea bites her tongue and attacks the last of the rips. "Halanthus will not crush the egg without us, unless he has no other choice."

Despite her call for patience, her fingers dance over the robe and her work is soon complete. She tosses the robe to me and struggles to rise. She groans softly, the way old people do. Looking down, she sees her walking stick. Without being asked, Figol hands it to her.

"That's a nice boy, even if you're too quiet by far."

We have to jog to keep up with Lanthea. She most definitely is not showing the patience she keeps asking of us. There is a buzz of excitement within the circle. Upon seeing the Archoness, Halanthus raises the quivering egg above his head. The beautiful blue egg is matched by the pendant around Halanthus's neck.

"Never forget this day," Lanthea says. "For today a terror of the sky is eliminated before it can cause pain and grief for the chosen people." She nods to Halanthus. With a grunt of satisfaction, he drives the egg downward upon a stone. The egg cracks into two large pieces. Inside, a griffin chick raises its head at the new surroundings.

"Kill it," Lanthea orders.

The youths, each with a feather above their left ear, move in to finish the job. The poor chick is reduced to a bloody mess in no time. Lanthea raises her arms for silence.

"Being the only Archon present, I hereby rule that the noble Halanthus of the Hecteas clan has been successful at restoring his good name. Both slights to his honor shall for now and all times be revoked. Halanthus is restored to a proud member of our society."

A cheer goes up. Poor Halanthus, uncomfortable with his new celebrity doesn't know what to do with himself. He manages a goofy grin as the youths start chanting his name.

Lanthea raises her hands again and the crowd quiets down. "These two men have also been successful in their quest. I have also granted them the gift of the Lapis Pendant." The crowd forms around us to gaze at our new adornments. "As long as they display these tokens of bravery upon their chests, no Centaurim is to injure them. Furthermore, any simple aid they might need is to be rendered." She turns and bows to us. The rest of the assembled centaurs mimic the gesture.

"Now, let us celebrate this momentous day," Lanthea says, her voice rising. The youths dash off every which way, shouting in their excitement.

Lanthea bows to us. "Thanks to you, our society will be able to grow once again. Instead of looking backward with hate-filled eyes, we can gaze into the future."

"Because of the griffin?" I ask.

She shakes her head. "You will understand shortly. If you care to join me, I wish to finish our conversation and answer your question about the rest of my people."

Once in the hut, Lanthea once again sits on the ground, this time closer to the fire. "The hut is turning purple, so the wolfsbane is working all too well. I will have to be brief."

She drops her walking stick and settles herself. "We have a saying here, and it is this: 'The young learn best from hard knocks and hard choices.' I'm afraid you will have both in store for you, and I'm sorry for that."

With her back so stooped, she has to turn her head sideways in order to look us in the eye. "Aldetes and Yanares have called for all the warriors to retrieve the bones of our ancestors. The Votadin must pay for their most heinous crimes." Lanthea is quickly falling into an herb-induced stupor.

Did Halanthus know?

I look to him, but he refuses to meet my gaze.

"It's up to us," Figol says with some urgency. He pulls on my sleeve for good measure.

"Grahme," Halanthus says, "I beg you to stay away. You cannot change the outcome."

I rip the leather hide from the peg and refuse to look back. I gather myself and concentrate on the merlin. Once Figol nods, we make the change and fly for Votadin.

38

Votadin's Sunset

The Centaurim army is hard to miss from the air. The warriors stretch out for half a league along the forest's edge. Circling once, we spot Iphilea behind the line and land in front of her.

"Grahme?"

"Yes, Basileia, Figol and I have returned from the quest we were given." We're quick to show the eggshell pendants.

"Lanthea has agreed that you have completed your quest?"

"She has."

"Then what did she tell you about our youths?" There's tightness in her face. I look at her, wondering what she could possibly be talking about.

"The young learn by hard knocks and hard choices," Figol blurts out.

"Thank Epona for sparing Jereas and the kin of Halanthus." Iphilea exhales and the tension exits her as well. "Good, it is as I hoped." The centaur leader looks around. "Who else knows you are here?"

"No one," I say.

"Halanthus has been given his reprieve as well," Figol says.

"How so?" Iphilea asks.

"On the final stretch back to your city, a griffin nearly caught me. Halanthus threw his double scythe and killed it in midair."

Iphilea goes weak in the knees for a moment. "Then both death sentences against Halanthus are removed. This is great news. I had not dared to hope for so much."

"We know you mean to attack the Votadins at dusk. You must call off the attack," Figol blurts out. "We can retrieve the bones of your ancestors."

"It is far too late for that, I fear. And it is not safe for you here, even with those pendants. You must leave, now."

"But we can retrieve the bones," Figol says.

"If only it were that simple. My term as Basileia ends at the close of this year. Both Yanares and Aldetes covet the honor. Each one hopes to earn renown from this campaign so that they will be the one to replace me."

"There are hundreds of women and children there. You will let innocents die, in order to recover bones?"

"We revere our ancestors," the Archoness says, rebuking me.

"And will you watch as children younger than Jereas are slaughtered to slake your peoples' bloodlust? Or will you turn away from the barbarism and pretend it didn't happen?"

"What do you want me to do?" Iphilea asks.

"Call a meeting of the Archons and let me plead my case."

"You will fail."

"At least I will have tried to protect the helpless."

"Is what they say true, Aunt Iphi?" Jereas steps through the underbrush revealing himself.

"We will talk about your eavesdropping another time," Iphilea says. "But for now, I need you to stand guard over these two." She looks at me, "for your own safety, you are not prisoners. Your efforts are bound to fail, but I will grant you an audience." She lifts her chin high and stalks off toward the middle of the line.

"Lock them in irons," Aldetes says offhandedly.

Iphilea steps between the warriors and us. "I have given them my welcome."

"This is why broodmares need to stay out of politics."

"That's the worst insult a female can receive," Jereas whispers.

"Aldetes, stop your weanling's whining."

Aldetes bristles and draws himself up to full height.

"Before we descend into further name calling," Yanares says, "we should consider how we are representing ourselves to outsiders."

A ring has formed around us and the Archons. The tension is palpable. Figol has his face down, so I know he is doing his best to calm the crowd.

"Galitrius, you have been quiet," Iphilea says.

Aldetes steps over to the diminutive Archon from the Idoos clan. "Yes, what do you think?"

The hair on Galitrius' ponytail has the first hints of gray. Despite the difference in size, he looks disdainfully up at Aldetes. "Whether right or not, the raid must happen." The warriors around us grunt their approval. "Since that is the case, allowing the druids to negotiate is nonsensical. No matter what the humans say, we will attack at dusk."

"Then we hold them as prisoners until the battle is over," Aldetes shrugs.

"But we have also granted the druids friendship status, based on their returning with a griffin egg," Galitrius says.

"So the Basileia claims, but who here can be sure?"

"Aldetes!" Galitrius says. "Are you calling our leader a liar?"

"He is doing no such thing," Yanares says. "There is no need to bring up the specter of trial and punishment on the eve of our triumph."

"Yanares just showed Aldetes up and good," Jereas whispers. He can't keep the smile off his face.

"Yanares is right," Iphilea says. "If they are lying, I doubt their first move would have been to fly into the middle of our camp. Furthermore, Lanthea and I devised a code phrase that they would only know if Lanthea deemed them to be successful. Unless you want to call into question the character of two Archons, we cannot imprison them. They have done nothing wrong."

"You would let them go free to warn the humans?" Aldetes demands.

"Not long ago, you boasted that no human could possibly hold their ground during a charge of the Centaurim. Whether the humans know of their doom or not, it will make little difference," Iphilea says.

Aldetes stomps his back hoof in frustration.

Jereas tries to restrain his giggling and is mostly successful.

"Blessings from dear Epona, you understand the situation." Iphilea says. "There is no honor in killing the defenseless. So, I suggest the druids return to the Votadins and convince them to evacuate their women and children."

"Then our surprise will be forfeited," Aldetes shouts, as if more volume will help his argument.

"You lack faith in the charge of the Centaurim?" Iphilea responds.

"And that is why Aunt Iphi is Basileia," Jereas says in a hushed tone. "She has questioned Aldete's faith in the warriors. There's no way he'll become Basileus now."

Aldetes lets out a snort as he repeatedly stomps the ground.

"Let us discuss this in private," Galitrius says as he points toward an empty clearing.

Iphilea mouths to us "leave" before following.

"Stay safe Jereas, and thank you for sending Willex and Frewalt," I say in a low tone.

His eyes light up. "And both of you as well," he says. "Don't be within the city of Votadin when we arrive."

Figol frowns. "What do we do now?"

"We try to reason with the Votadins. It was always a long shot coming here, but we may be able to save some innocents yet. Perhaps the Votadins will listen to reason."

"And perhaps Belenos will track backward across the sky," Figol says.

Jereas watches expectantly as we change into merlins.

The Votadins have removed quite a bit of trees from Caleto Forest. Now there are leagues of undulating hills separating the city from the current forest edge. Several earthen ramparts have been constructed, one near the forest and the other two near the city.

Between the walls is open country. The centaurs will eat up the distance quickly with a full gallop.

The men at the farthest most defensive wall are more interested in their dice than the forest. The sharpened wooden stakes atop the wall are in a sorry state. There is nothing that can be done for them now, as Belenos is past the halfway point of his ride across the winter sky. Their idleness will cost them their lives.

If there were more time . . ..

The tall grass blankets the hills from the forest to Din Guarie. It will hide the attackers' numbers, as if the centaurs need another advantage.

The last two ramparts outside of the city are manned by only a handful of guards. They will be no obstacle to the unified Centaurim armies. The first guard sees us and waves us to land. It's a credit to them that they remain vigilant, but we've no time to waste. We land outside the mead hall instead and retake our human forms.

Figol and I trade looks. No one realizes that their end is nigh. I slam the door open and ignore the startled comments around me. The excessive smoke and the low fire conspire to leave the room in lingering shadow. A cloying, slightly sweet smell engulfs the room.

"Mugwort," I say, disgusted. There's no surer way to make my head ache and my dreams be wild.

King Vriga is seated with his men, next to the fire. Rhola bows to us as she steps between us and the king.

"It would be best if you came back in the morning to see my father."

"There's no time, the centaurs are mounting for an attack as we speak. There will be nothing left of this city by morning."

"What?" Godod asks. He rushes over to us. "What of the centaurs?" He at least is not mind-numb.

"They are massing in Caleto Forest for an attack at dusk."

Godod's eyes grow distant. "They would use the brilliance of Belenos to hamper our vision."

"You have precious little time," I say.

"How did you come by this information?" His eyes narrowing.

"We have just come from the centaur's camp. They are coming for the bones of their ancestors."

Godod nods and absorbs the information. "How many?"

"All of them."

"That's not possible; our forward guard would spot them."

"Your forward guard is busy playing dice while the defenses slowly rot."

"But Vadan came back last month with glowing reviews," he says slowly. He stares at me again, looking for falsehoods. "Where's Vadan?" he calls.

"It's Prince Vadan," Rhola scolds.

"Vadan!" Godod repeats. Kindly but forcefully, he bodily moves Rhola out of his way as he advances toward the prince.

"What now, Godod?" Vadan reluctantly disentangles himself from a woman.

"You were just at our forward guard last month, how were our defenses?"

The prince places his hands on a woman's waist and slowly slides by her, smiling seductively. He slaps her rear playfully. Still grinning like a boy, he nods his head sideways toward me.

"Prince Vadan," Godod says, getting his attention. "How were the fortifications at the forward guard station?"

The prince looks behind him, probably for the woman. He returns to Godod's stern gaze and sighs. "The guards were fine," he says through a yawn.

"What of the defenses? Were the sharpened stakes readied?"

"I got there late," the prince says. "And Midha told me everything was in order."

"Did you see the stake barrier or not?"

"Godod! Watch your tone," Rhola says. "You are speaking to the crown prince."

"Easy," the mind-numbed Vadan says. "Midha is a good man. His men swear by him, and he paid me my winnings without protest, and they were considerable."

"The barrier," Godod says with exaggerated patience. "Did you see the barrier?"

"I got there late, like I said," Vadan begins. "But he assured me everything was in place."

Godod closes his eyes and exhales slowly. He turns to me. "I will send a man there at once." He searches the hall. "Iomid, go to the forward guard, and report back to me about the state of our defenses."

"I will do as you command." Iomid salutes.

"There's no time to waste," Godod says. "Go."

"You can't wait to hear back from him," I say. "It will be too late by then."

"Open all the flaps to the mead hall and extinguish that fire." Godod commands. Mercifully, he leads us outside, away from the mugwort fumes.

"The king will need time to collect his thoughts," Godod says to me. "Tell me what you saw, exactly."

Rhola's face changes from haughty to concerned as I recount our tale. "Where can we go?" She asks. "The tombs?"

"The tombs offer no chance of escape. You would be trapped there until the centaurs leave," I say. "If they have the resolution, they could starve you out." I scan the area. "There! That hill is the steepest around here and the trees will make their arrows all but useless. If you keep the high ground until nightfall, you can flee to the south with relative ease."

"But the city would be destroyed," Rhola says.

"This is only if disaster strikes. It is important to be prepared," Godod says as he caresses the princess's arm. "It never hurts to be ready."

She rests her head against the Master at Arms' well-muscled chest. Godod's eyes convey the concern he has, even if his words do not. "You will have to get your father out of here and into fresh air. He will be very cross if I suggest it."

Princess Rhola nods and heads back into the hall.

"I must organize the men," Godod says, before departing.

"Figol and I will remain here, at your disposal."

Figol's stares at me with hollow eyes "They're all dead; they just don't know it yet."

"We don't know that. Keep your face neutral; if they panic before Godod can get them organized, all is lost." Figol tries to put on a brave face. "If they get desperate, they will look for someone to blame and we are the most likely targets. We will need all your skill to direct their emotions appropriately."

Figol swallows hard. "The king is addled, as is the prince. Rhola is not affected by the smoke, but her only concern is with losing her station."

"It will take Godod's man a while to reach the forward guard and return. By then the king will have recovered his wits. As long as Godod is able to prepare between now and then, they have a chance."

39

Treachery Decrypted

Godod has managed to deploy his men faster than anyone I've ever seen. Half his men were sent on horseback to alert the surrounding farmers. The rest have been busy digging into the side of the hill.

"If only I had the time to recall Vinhe and his men," Godod says.

"I am impressed by what you have managed to accomplish." Despite the odds, I'm relieved to hear Vinhe is absent.

"I was foolish to listen to Rhola," Godod says. "She assured me that Vadan could be counted upon this time."

"You're in a tough position," I say.

A royal messenger runs toward us as if the Centaurim were giving chase.

"That can only mean that the king has regained his wits," Godod says as he watches the man's approach. "And his majesty is angry."

We can hear Vriga's muffled voice well before we enter the hall. It still stinks of mugwort, but at least the smoke has cleared.

What a sad end to the Votadin dynasty.

Vriga is red-eyed and sluggish. He stares us down as we enter. His intent is obvious, though the actual words take longer to form. He rises on to his unsteady feet and has to grab a pole to keep him upright.

"Who has sent my city into a panic?" He's racked with a thick, wet coughing fit.

"It is the druid, my Lord," Rhola says. "He has returned from the centaur's camp."

"The druid?" He asks as he wipes the water from his glassy eyes. "Do you mean Bodmin?"

"No Lord, it is the other one."

"The one Vinhe warned us about?"

"Now I know why Godod wants us to accompany him," Figol says in a low voice.

I silence him with a look. It's the same disapproving look that I was on the receiving end of at least a hundred times from Boswen. Funny, I never considered that a part of my training, until now.

Godod bows to his king and we approach. The men in the hall all have weapons ready. Figol tenses up, he must have also taken notice.

King Vriga slaps Rhola's hand when she tries to rest it on his shoulder. I glance at Figol. His face is down. Hopefully he can nudge them to remain civil.

"Greetings, King Vriga," I say as I bow.

"Enough with that," he says waspishly. "Why have you made my city a beehive?"

"The centaurs are massing for an attack."

"And why would they do that now?"

371

"Because of what you have hidden away in your family's tomb. They know of the skeletons and they are coming for them."

Vriga's eyes go wide. "How did *you* find out about them?"

Behind him, Rhola's face goes pale.

"Does that matter now?" I counter.

His eyes close to mere slits. "And how did the centaurs find out about them?"

I swallow uncomfortably. *I hadn't thought up an answer for that question.*

"Again, does it matter now? The Centaurs are coming and you and your people will be wiped out if you do nothing. Godod has organized—"

"—You told them about the tombs!" The king's face turns red. "That's how you managed to not be killed when in their midst. You traded our lives for yours."

"No, I assure you that—"

"—Traitors! Godod, seize them."

Figol looks at me and frowns. He's changed into a merlin before I can even utter the words. Everyone momentarily freezes for an instant as two birds have appeared before them. Without looking back, I launch myself forward and out the door.

Figol and I sit on a branch with a clear view of the city. Despite my orders, his legs start swaying.

"The motion will draw their eyes toward us," I say again.

Figol exhales heavily. "We can't just sit here and do nothing."

"Would you prefer we go see the centaurs and be shot before we land or go to see King Vriga and be stabbed once we do?"

"We could see Godod, he at least understands the situation."

"And if we're seen talking to him, he'll be branded a traitor and the only chance the people have will be removed right before the battle."

"It just feels wrong to do nothing."

A riderless horse emerges from the plains with an arrow lodged in its rump. The poor animal has worked up a lather as it races back to Din Guarie. Vadan points out the animal. King Vriga's face turns red as he gesticulates wildly.

"Belenos is falling fast, it won't be long now," I say. The forest around us has gone quiet. The branch begins to vibrate. I'm about to scold Figol again until he points out a dust cloud moving across the hills. Figol grabs my arm and squeezes tight. A low rumbling noise, more felt than heard, has reached us.

Godod and the royal family stand at the hill crest in front of the mead hall. The king gestures to the tombs, but Godod violently shakes his head in response. He grabs the king's shoulder as if to drag him bodily to the fortified hill south of the city.

The pounding of the hooves reverberates into the crisp air. The few townspeople who ignored Godod's orders to evacuate think better of it now. Some carry their children, some carry valuables. I stop myself from leaning too far forward and falling from the branch. Figol looks at me in disbelief. Our branch trembles even as the ground quakes.

The first wave of centaurs is visible now. We drop to the ground before we're shaken off our perch. Dust is being thrown up into the air, blocking the rays of Belenos. Six lines of roughly a hundred each

373

thunder toward Votadin. Aldetes is in front of the first line with Yanares following closely behind.

"Hurry your highness, there's not much time," Godod shouts over the din. He points toward the hill.

"Men! To me!" the King shouts. "To the tombs."

"Stay!" Godod screams desperately. "My Lord, we cannot hope to stand against this foe."

Prince Vadan draws his sword and raises it high. "The King has given an order. Now come if you be not a coward."

Slowly, the men rise from their cover, nervously looking at the King, Godod and the approaching horde.

"To the tombs!" the prince shouts.

"To the hill!" Godod counters.

"You shall die a coward," the prince shouts as he turns on Godod. He slashes at the leader of the guards. Godod rolls to his left just in time to avoid the strike. From one knee, he draws his own blade. The prince rushes forward in a clumsy charge. Godod strikes the prince's blade and it clamors to the ground. He levels his sword at the prince. Rhola rushes up and grabs Vadan's hand, pulling him back.

"I go to defend our city," the king roars. "Who among you will fight for our home?"

With heads low, a couple dozen men form around the king.

Vriga points his sword at Godod. "I name you a coward. Your life is forfeit if we ever meet again."

The royals and their retinue turn and race from the hill toward the tombs.

"They'll never make it in time," Figol says.

There is a small meadow between the fortified town and the tombs. The king has squandered what minimal protection he had.

"It seems the king has realized this." I point as the king halts his men. He orders the warriors into a quick line before he and his family run for their lives.

"They're dead," Figol says, as the shaky line realizes their king has abandoned them. The centaurs don't even slow as they run over the doomed soldiers. Vadan turns toward the enemy and looses several arrows. A centaur staggers, clutching his abdomen.

"Yes," I say with great remorse. "At least Godod was able to evacuate the women and children to the south. Structures can be rebuilt."

"The king!" A centaur cries and all his compatriots within hearing distance converge on the royals. Vriga and Rhola have made it into the tombs. The prince and a handful of men stand in front, swords at the ready.

"Look! One of the guards is weaponless," Figol says.

"Vadan must have taken his sword, since he didn't retrieve his own after charging Godod."

The main horde enters the city, laying waste to every structure they come across. The late retreating women and children have not been spotted, yet. They continue their climb up the hill.

The centaurs surround Vadan and his men at the tomb entrance. None are eager to advance, so they mill around, waiting for something or someone.

"You have violated our city. Go now, or face our wrath," the prince blurts out.

They laugh at his feeble warning.

Aldetes arrives and his men make way for him. All are still as he saunters to the front. "Stand aside and you will be spared. It is only the royal line who must perish today."

"I am Prince Vadan, heir to—"

"—Fire," Aldetes says as he points to Vadan. A dozen arrows are loosed, followed by a dozen more. The prince stares down, disbelieving the multiple arrows in his torso. He falls forward, pushing the arrows through his lifeless body.

His men have fared little better. Most join him on the ground, their life's blood spilling into the dirt. Only three still stand and they are shot multiple times in the back, as they try to retreat into the cave.

From the darkness within, stones are slung. Most hit the sides of the cave, bouncing harmlessly into the dirt. Aldetes and his men laugh once more. Two of their number are sent into the city while the rest stay well back of the entrance.

The messengers meet with Yanares, who is busy destroying the vacated city. Figol and I change into crows and land as close as we dare to the Kratydos leader. His men are ordered to gather thatch and take it to the tomb.

Yanares' men position themselves on either side of the tomb. Aldetes signals his men to shoot into the cave in one short volley. Yanares and his men drop their thatch in front of the cave and return to cover before a few sling stones harmlessly exit the tomb. More and more kindling is added until the tomb itself is barricaded shut. From within, taunts and challenges are issued, but none pay any heed to the royal family.

Aldetes ignites an arrow and shoots it into the thatch pile. The fire greedily consumes the thatch, and the flames grow to great heights. The roaring of the fire obscures any voices within.

"What are they doing?" Figol asks.

"The fire will steal all the air from the cave."

"What will the royals inside the cave do?"

"They will die," I reply. "It is an ingenious way to take the cave. No centaur would want to fight inside such tight quarters."

"Poor Rhola," Figol says.

A cry goes up. Godod and his men have been spotted. Yanares orders his men to line up and they canter over to the hill. Godod and his men start slinging stones at the unprotected centaurs, halting the advance.

Yanares calls for bows to be unslung. They aim their bows high and release as one. A rainstorm of arrows descends into the trees. Only a few score hits, but it is enough to induce panic nonetheless. Eschewing cover, the men show their backs and they scale the slope. The centaur archers rush forward and loose another volley. Whatever discipline the men of Votadin possessed is gone. Godod gives ground and futilely tries to reform his rattled warriors. The rout is on and it's only a matter of time before Godod and his men are overrun.

"Figol, I need your help." Without waiting for a response, I drop to the ground and transform into the only form able to make a difference. My feline paws plant securely into the earth. With my talons, I break a tree branch just to reaffirm my power. I propel myself upward and begin stalking the man-horses. I stay close to the tree tops until I can build up some speed. I let loose an angry cry as I spring high into the air.

The man-horses mostly flee before me; only a select few stand their ground and face me, readying their pointy sticks. I dive at them, daring them to stand firm. None can resist me. There are man-things fleeing up the hill, but I desire horse flesh. Now that the group is broken up, it will be easy to select my prey. I swing around for my next pass. There are more man-horses in the clearing to my right.

They still stand together. All skymasters fear the many pointy sticks fired all at once. I bank to avoid their attack.

Another challenge call comes from above the forest. It is a sub-adult who is attacking them from behind. I rise higher in the air. This is my killing ground. None take kills from me.

Uncle, it's me.

I pull up from my approach as my mind struggles to remember what uncle means. I flex my talons. First, I must drive off this rival, then I can select my man-horse.

Uncle Grahme, you must not let the anger overwhelm you.

Figol? My humanity gains ascendency, but for how long?

The man-things have nearly cleared the hill. We can retreat now.

The thought of retreating makes me renew my challenge call. Yet, the warming orb is nearly below the land now. It is nearly time for sleep.

No one sends a skymaster away.

Uncle, go back to the forest, where we were.

There is one downed man-horse in front of the hill. It would be a tasty morsel to eat in the darkness. I land in front of it and approach.

"Help! Father, don't let it take me," the prey-meal screams.

Uncle Grahme, that's Adako. He's our friend.

I ignore the voice. I can already taste the horse flesh. The sub-adult flies overhead and hits my head with the flat of his talons. I scream out my rage and take to the air, chasing it to where I was hiding in ambush. The air around him shimmers and a small man-thing appears. I search the ground for where my rival has gone. The puny man-thing approaches, staring at me.

"Uncle," it says. "Let me guide your change back to yourself."

My anger spent; I stare at it as it continues to make noise.

Figol! My humanness comes to the fore once again.

It's alright Uncle, let me guide you.

I let out an explosive exhale once I've regained my human form. Thank all the gods and goddesses that Figol was with me. What that form was prepared to do . . . I shudder to think about it.

Adako has made it back to his clan and he's pointing wildly at us. I check the hill, the last of Godod's men are cresting it now. "Merlins, one more time," I say.

Godod stands with a few of his men on the hill crest, staring at the smoldering remains of Din Guarie.

"So much lost." Godod says.

Aldetes and his clan have just begun entering the tomb. The bodies of Vriga, Queen Seora and Rhola are removed and dumped to the side with Vadan's. Jereas and Tantair arrive, both pulling empty carts behind them. With great care, the bones of Stergedes and Abdeneus are removed and placed on the carts. Simple white cloths are placed over the bones and the two centaur youths retreat with their priceless loads.

"At least Iphilea has kept Jereas and Tantair out of harm," Figol says in a low voice.

Aldetes orders the bodies of the royals to be placed on the ground, each a good distance from the others. Their lifeless limbs are bound. Sixteen Centaurim hold the opposite ends of the ropes.

"Now!" Aldetes yells. Straining, each clansman plods forward with their end of the rope, raising the royal corpses off the ground as the lines go taut. One by one the limbs pull away from the Votadins until each is left in quarters. A cheer goes up at the gruesome end of the Votadin line.

"We will leave no Votadin buried in the earth!" Aldetes shouts to the appreciative crowd. Several centaurs enter the tombs with battle hammers at the ready.

"That can never be our home again," Godod says.

"No, it is too open and too tempting a target, now that they know their own might," I say.

"Where will the Votadins call home then?" A man asks.

"Not the Votadins," I say. "The Votadins were betrayed by their ruler's secrets. You are the people of Godod's dun, or din as you say here."

"Godod's din," the man repeats. "Yes, we are the people of Godod's din."

"Gododdin! Gododdin!" The warriors start to chant.

The centaurs take note of the cheers, but none seem willing to scale the hill.

Godod looks down at me, incredulous. "I never sought to be a king."

"That's why you'll make a great one. You will rule for those you fought to save, not for your own vanity."

"I'm made to smash things," the muscular man says. "I don't know the first thing about negotiations. I am not cut out for this."

I look meaningfully at his cheering men. "If not you, who will lead?"

He laughs a humorless laugh. "If you are going to lay this burden at my feet, then I require the aid of a resident druid in which to confide and consult." Godod demands.

"That you do," I say. "But it will not be me. My responsibilities are far to the south and west. It is probably for the best that we will be as far apart as the land will allow."

"What of Figol?" Godod asks.

"My nephew is not even an apprentice yet. But fear not, it is a new day for the druids as well. I will speak to your needs to the Council of Nine."

"Can you stay? At least until we are settled?"

"We cannot. It is the equinox tonight. The council will meet in a few days, and we must be there."

"Then this is farewell?"

"For now, but know that you will always have a friend in me."

"And me," Figol adds.

Poor Godod looks overwhelmed.

"Sir, um King Godod, where do we shelter for the night?"

Godod ignores the elevation of title. "We will put this hill between us and the centaurs. Post sentries upon this hill and the people can camp in the valley behind us. If I recall, there is a small lake and a fresh stream."

"Come Figol, the night is nearly upon us. The new king will be busy for a good while. I think tawny owls are the proper choice."

40

Surprises in the Mist

The wind picks up out of the south, making our trek all the more tiring. When the rain turns to sleet, we're forced to land and wait out the storm. We take refuge in a cave near Ganna's home.

"Do you think Bodmin went back to his moor?" Figol asks.

"Why? Are you thinking about asking Ganna for shelter and you're worried he might be there?"

"Well yes, but mainly I want to go back and see the scripts of the Elder Races."

"I would not want to be caught looking at those without Ganna's approval. I think her anger would be more than I'd want to bear."

"Maybe," Figol says. He looks into the heart of the storm and sighs. He's not very good at disguising his feelings.

"What's on your mind?"

"Why did Vriga act so stupid and why did the centaurs act so brutal?"

"Figol, Vriga lacked imagination, so he locked his kingdom into imitating their forebears. As for the centaurs, you spent as much time around Halanthus as me. Did you see any creativity from him, or any of the elders?"

"Lanthea and Iphilea," Figol volunteers.

"Yes, I'll give you that, but they were both women entering into the men's arena of tribal politics. They didn't have any precedents to mimic. With luck, Lanthea is right and they'll stop harboring such bitter resentment, now that their ancestors' bones have been recovered."

"Should we be wearing our pendants when we land at Ynys Mona?"

"Hold on there," I say. "The Sacred Grove is for the Council of Nine or by invitation. Did Meraud invite you and forget to tell me?"

"But this whole quest was about me!"

I let out a deep breath. "I don't think that's true." I stare into the storm. "I think, like the centaurs and the Votadins, I was also too set in my ways. Rather than try different tactics, I simply challenged anyone and everyone to a duel if I was unhappy."

"There's been more than enough killing," Figol says.

"I think we should hide our pendants from the council."

"Why?"

"Because if we show them, what's to stop Cynbel or Caradoc from scavenging a broken egg shell and making their own?"

"We are the only ones allowed to speak with the centaurs, then?"

"If we make our pendants public knowledge, everyone will try to enter centaur lands. Before long, our hard-won honor will be revoked and they'll continue shooting at people. You and I are the only two people who have any kind of understanding of their ways."

"What about the firbolgs and Gortor's promise to teach us the runes?"

"We have learned nothing from him yet, so we have nothing to report," I respond. "I think it best that the council is given one surprise at a time."

"Since we're not going to Ynys Mona, can we go to Eghan's place at least?" Figol asks.

"That's exactly what I was thinking."

The Gwanwyns of Sulis produce enough mist to form a permanent low-hanging cloud over the site. People from all over Pretanni come for the healing waters. There are three druids tending a long line of the infirmed. Surely, no one expects me to wait to be admitted to the springs. We give the druids a wide berth as we fly into Eghan's camp. We land in the central courtyard between the three springs. I call over to the lone druid scurrying about.

"Where is Lord Eghan?"

"Lord Grahme?" The young man asks, surprised. "The druids at the gate should have directed you, or walked with you if they weren't sure." He looks questioningly at me. "But at this time, he's in the infirmary, teaching the apprentices."

"Thank you," I say and we leave before he can call us out for not following the rules.

Eghan is off in a corner preparing a salve and teaching his charges as he goes. I don't know that Boswen ever *showed* me anything. He was more of a try-it-until-you-get-it-right sort of mentor. The young apprentices hang on Eghan's every word. He's no bard, but when you give knowledge so freely, you don't need such tactics to keep your audience's attention.

"And who can name a restorative that invigorates the patient's energy?" He asks, barely glancing up at me.

"Cotton sedge," I blurt out.

Eghan smiles. "True, Lord Grahme, but that is not so common in these parts." He looks at his students. "Now you have two lords you can impress. Anyone?"

"Arto kramo," a blond-haired apprentice shouts.

"It is sometimes called bear garlic, but what is the proper name?" Eghan asks.

"Ahhh," the youth says, stumped.

"It is a myth that bears consume the herb when they wake in the spring, but the garlic does grow wild nearly everywhere," I say.

"Wild garlic! I mean, Weido kramo," the boy shouts before burying his face in his cloak. "Thank you, Lord Grahme," he says in a small voice. The other students laugh nervously.

"We will continue this tomorrow night," Eghan says, dismissing his students. A hesitant smile forms on his face. "You *bear* good news?"

I can't help but chuckle before growing serious. "It is a long and convoluted story."

"The best ones always are. We should retire to my quarters to discuss it," Eghan says.

"Lord Eghan, Uncle, would you mind if I go to the other springs?" Figol asks.

"Very well, have one of my students show you the way," Eghan says. He turns to me. "Now, tell me what has transpired."

He practically runs to his hut.

Eghan's place is next to the Coventina spring. It's the smallest and the hottest of the springs. Long strands of moss dangle from the tree limbs, forming a living curtain around us.

Eghan eyes me shrewdly. "It is great for keeping the heat and sound from escaping."

"Your tale is a mixed bag, that's for sure," Eghan says.

"We were charged with making allies; no one specifically said it had to be the Emerald Druids."

Eghan chuckles humorlessly. "You are so like Boswen, ready to argue every point."

"Only when it means something," I say. "And Figol would be a great addition to our ranks. He can already animorph and I've been teaching him some herb craft."

"You're leaving out the one key factor, he has the powers of the—"

"—Eghan! Eghan, I'm back!" Sieffre bursts through the door, moss tangled in his flailing limbs. He collides with his mentor and they end up in a heap on the floor.

"Sieffre?" Eghan blurts. The two men rise and jump up and down while in each other's arms. Eghan pushes him back to an arm's length. "But how?"

"It was Figol," Sieffre says, still amazed. "He guided me back through the change." Sieffre looks down at his long, thin legs. "It feels weird to have such narrow feet."

The two men hug again and make inarticulate sounds. I wait for Figol to make his triumphal entrance, but he doesn't appear. Eghan separates himself enough to look Sieffre over from head to toe.

"It seems you've made a complete transformation back to your human self," Eghan says.

"It was so strange; I was lost in a tiny section of the puffin's mind. My thoughts just circled back upon themselves in a tighter and tighter circle. Then this, this *presence* came upon me.

Figol explained that it was him and that he could lead me out. I'd never heard of a Figol before, so my thoughts retreated. He projected a mental warmth and finally I knew it would be safe for me to trust him. First, he had me sit atop the puffin's thoughts, then to recognize my humanness. I never would have made it back without him."

Looking at Sieffre, I don't know if I should laugh or cry. He's back safely, but it was me that caused him to be trapped as a puffin. My eyes, confused, begin to water and my mouth quivers between a smile and a frown. I tug at my robes, not sure what to do with myself.

Eghan and Sieffre look over at me.

"Grahme!" Sieffre calls. "You managed to escape as well." He grabs me in a fierce hug.

My arms are only free at the elbows, so I hug him back as best I can.

"You must fill me in on how the night ended," Sieffre says, eyes bright.

I give him a sickly smile in return.

"Sieffre, you will be given the full tale, I assure you. But you need to be checked out by Malla," Eghan says. "Wake her if she has retired. I wish to know what her learned opinion is. Lord Grahme and I have some business we need to finish in any case."

"Lord Grahme?" Sieffre's eyes bulge. "I look forward to being caught up." He runs from the hut, yelling for Malla as he goes.

It's Eghan's turn to alternate between a smile and a frown. "I am happy, truly happy about Sieffre," he says. "But this will complicate Figol's chances."

"Isn't this another argument for his inclusion?" I ask.

"For Figol to guide Sieffre back, he would have had to reach Sieffre within the mind of the puffin."

"Yes." I don't know why this would be a problem.

"The Yew medallions are not perfect shields from the Sorim. The only way to ensure that we're free of manipulation is to animorph. And now Figol has demonstrated that he can still reach our minds, even when we're in animal forms. There is no safe place from a mind like that."

"You make him sound like our enemy."

"How easily can he reach our minds? That is the first question for which we need an answer."

"He spoke with me several times when I was in animal form," I say slowly. "I never thought it through."

"And what happens if Figol decides to leave the druids and go back to Solent Keep with his mother?"

"Conwenna isn't in Solent Keep. She lives at Mai Dun."

"You have been away for quite a while. Upon the death of the Obsidian Lord, Blachstenius convinced your sister-in-law to claim the city for herself. She calls herself a mayor. I think it is a good sign that she has no plans to expand, at least for now."

"Conwenna is in charge of Solent Keep?" I stare back at him, disbelieving what I've heard.

"She is, and that makes Figol a prince or a princely mayor," Eghan waves his hands in the air, "or whatever the term may be."

"He'll have to renounce that, if he's to join us."

"But will that be enough to convince Meraud? What's to stop your nephew from changing his mind sometime in the future?"

"But to refuse him is to push him away, letting him use his power unrestrained. Within our order, he can learn restraint and patience."

"Like you did?" Eghan smiles to take the sting out of his words.

"But we completed our quest. We had an agreement."

"Welcome to being one of the Nine," Eghan says. "The good of the order outweigh any wants of a single member."

Stunned, I stare back at him.

Is everything we did really for nothing?

"I will have someone find Figol and arrange food for four. After Malla finishes her inspection of Sieffre, I suspect we will be up well into the night."

"That's it then," Sieffre says. "Grahme will just have to convince the others to let Figol join."

"But, I've never been good with words."

"Grahme, no sweeping oratory, not even Caradoc's, would be enough to tip the balance. You need to speak honestly and with conviction. In the end, it's up to the rest of us to search within ourselves and decide what is best. If it helps, I plan on voting for Figol's inclusion and I believe Caradoc and Hedred will also do so."

"Then we have four votes. What happens in the case of a tie?"

"I suspect Meraud will insist on installing a new member first. And you can be assured that the member will vote with Meraud."

"Who will it be?"

389

"That remains to be seen. And before you ask me more questions, I have no more answers for you." He holds up his hand as if to hold me back.

41

Revelations

The sky opens up and unrelenting rain pours upon us. Of all things, Eghan and I are forced to take the form of puffins to fly to Ynys Mona. Hopefully this meeting doesn't go as badly as the last time.

Meraud is standing just inside a hut at the center of the only druid village on the island. She waves us over and has a welcoming smile for us as we return to our true selves.

"Grahme, Eghan, you're the last to arrive," she says with relief. "The rest are inside drying off by the fire. Since we don't know when exactly midday will be, take your time."

"We have exciting news," Eghan blurts.

Meraud holds the palm of her hand up. "Stop," she says. "No one is to talk council business until we get to the grove. I would like for everyone to hear the news together rather than having groups plotting before the information is shared."

Eghan looks like he swallowed a frog, but he manages to keep his mouth closed. He walks to the fire, but he can't remain still. He settles on pacing along the walls of the round house.

This being only my second council meeting, I like it much better. The eight of us walk together to the grove, with no one pretending to be more important than anyone else. Once inside the grove, Meraud moves to the central speaking stone.

"Let's everyone find a tree and take cover from the rain. We should remain within the circle, but there's no reason for us to get needlessly soaked."

The gods and goddesses take pity upon us and the rain slows to a steady pace. Fortunately for us, we will no longer need to yell to be heard.

Meraud's hope to minimize factions within the council is off to a rocky start. Drustan and Bradan huddle together as far away from me as they can. Cynbel and Meraud stand within the hollow center of an eight-hundred-year-old oak while Caradoc and Eghan share another. Only Hedred and I stand alone.

"Grahme, we all have some knowledge of Solent Keep and Laleah, so I am going to hold your report until the end."

I nod, even though I'm still not clear about Conwenna and Solent Keep.

"First off, Eghan and Hedred, can you update us on your progress with the giant runes?"

"There is little to say, I'm afraid," Hedred begins. "Katel is unfortunately—"

"—Sieffre is back in his human form," Eghan blurts.

The rest of the Lord Protectors are in an uproar. After several tries, Meraud manages to settle them down.

"If anyone could do it, I knew it would be you Eghan," Meraud says, delighted.

"It wasn't me," Eghan says. He smiles apologetically to me. "It was Grahme's nephew, Figol."

I raise my hands for quiet. "It is true. During our quest, I taught Figol how to animorph," I hold up my hand again to stop Cynbel's demand for an explanation. "Given the quest, we could hardly be expected to sail to all the places we went and be back for this council."

"Let it be, Cynbel," Meraud says.

"To teach Figol, I would have him observe my mind as I changed into animal form. Somehow, he managed to connect with my mind while I was changed. He kept insisting on turning into puffins. I thought it was ridiculous, but it was a form he mastered. Little did I know that he was considering Sieffre's condition the entire time."

"The change only happened yesterday," Eghan says. "Before we get blown off course, there are no new rune discoveries."

"But there is," I say. All eyes return to me. "Figol and I learned the *hahgel* runestone. It causes a small hailstorm to form from the air."

"And did Figol divine this as well?" a belligerent Bradan asks.

"No, Bodmin taught it to us."

Pandemonium erupts this time. Caradoc is the first to leave his cover and move to the center.

"Grahme," his disappointment is palpable. "That man is supposed to be killed on sight. He's as dangerous as he is devious. For one as young as you, avoidance is the best course of action."

"Everyone, please," Meraud calls. "Let's leave Grahme's tale until the end." She locks eyes with Caradoc and he quickly returns to his spot next to Eghan. "If there is no further news about runes . . ."

"I have some more news," I say. I can already see the nerves being frayed by my peers, and I've not even gone into detail about my trip yet. "If the proper inflection is known, one can simply speak the rune without the need of the stone as a carrier of magic."

For once everyone remains silent.

"And where did you learn this?" Meraud asks.

"I saw Rhedna of the Sorrows utilizing the magic in this way as we escaped from the Council of Seven meeting."

"Escaped?" Cynbel says, smiling. "This sounds more like it. Did you manage to club any of them before you left?"

"Cynbel!" Meraud says, "please, be patient." She turns to me. "So, Rhedna of the Sorrows knows the verbal runes? Do the Emerald Druids know how to do this too?"

"They do not."

Meraud looks relieved. "Though I think we must send someone if she is the only one who knows this magic."

"She isn't," I say. "She is the daughter of Bodmin and Ganna. Both of them know of it as well, though Bodmin is unwilling to teach us."

"Great, now all we need to do is send someone on a fool's errand to see Ganna the witch," Caradoc says. "Assuming she doesn't kill our emissary outright, the person will have to try and negotiate with the hag."

"Figol and I have already spoken with her," I say. The others erupt in various levels of fury. Their cover forgotten, they congregate in the center of the grove. Only I'm left under the cover of my tree.

"On her lands there is a cliff with giant, elvish and centaur inscriptions carved side by side. Only she, and possibly Bodmin, can read them. She would be willing to teach us, if we had something suitable to offer her in return."

Caradoc's booming voice rises above everyone else's. "It's an obvious trap."

"She saved Figol from poisoning and she didn't harm either of us," I say.

"You are dealing with things you can't possibly understand," Caradoc retorts.

"Caradoc!" Meraud calls, even though they are only two steps apart. "Let's wait until Grahme fills us in on his quest for that."

Caradoc raises his hands to shoulder height to show his surrender.

"Now," an exasperated Meraud begins, "If there are no further updates on runes," she glares at me, "We can move on."

"Meraud," I say as I smile nervously. "I do have one further update."

"Of course you do," she says. Wearily, she waves me to continue.

"While we were on Eriu, we met Gortor, the Donnan of the firbolgs."

"Now we have firbolgs?" Bradan exclaims. "Head Druid, there should be a punishment for lying to the council."

"I agree," Meraud says, surprising him, "If in fact lies have been told. Perhaps we should first hear his story before we decide guilt or innocence."

"We made friends with Crisa, formerly the Protector of Ankenet Starno. She took us to see the firbolgs. Being giantkin, they know the runes and Gortor agreed to teach them to us."

Bradan snorts, but several people wave him to silence.

"Who exactly is 'us' and why did this Gortor agree to this?" Meraud asks, respectfully.

"He agreed to teach, Crisa, Figol and me the runes. He agreed because I gave him Eriu's ring. It is—"

Everyone explodes with this revelation and I have no chance to explain further. After quite a bit of effort, Meraud manages to regain control.

"There are so very many questions," she says. "But let's start with where you found the lost ring of Eriu?"

Like a misbehaving child, I look at the ground and mumble my answer.

"What was that?" Meraud demands.

"Caradoc gave it to me," I say in a clear voice.

Brehmne is leaning so far forward that I'm afraid he's going to burn his hair in the fire. "What happened then?"

"Then everyone scolded Caradoc and the Druid Protectors of the Tomb of the All-King for keeping this secret for the last eight hundred years. After they settled down, Hedred told Meraud that the meeting is just going to be one outburst after another, so she might as well let me tell my tale. Otherwise, we'd be there well past nightfall."

"Tell me about the centaurs again," Brehmne says. "I want to meet this Jereas."

I wave my hands to tell him no. "I'm not even sure if I'm supposed to tell you two about the meeting. With all the shouting, no one told me what I can share from the meeting."

"Cynbel would tell us a few snippets," Arthmael says.

"Bradan wouldn't even talk to his apprentices," Brehmne adds.

"But you haven't told us what was decided about your nephew," Arthmael says.

I blow out a chest full of air. I'm never going to get to sleep tonight.

"After we told them about Laleah, and the firbolgs, and Crisa's expulsion and Rhedna's plan to send us to Bodmin and Ganna it looked pretty bleak. Then I told them about the Tomb of the Votadins and meeting the centaurs and korriks—"

"—What are they again?" Brehmne interrupts me.

"I think I liked you better when you were still scared of me," I say.

"Now he knows that he's a better staff fighter than you'll ever be," Arthmael says.

"Do you want to hear this or not?" I ask. "You still remind me of a korrik from time to time," I say to Brehmne. "I think Drustan woke up for my description. Everyone wanted to know what the centaur town was like. I thought Figol's ability to pull me back when I had animorphed into a griffin would be seen as a plus, but they mostly yelled at me for attempting a griffin in the first place."

"Maybe because if it wasn't for Figol's never-seen-before ability to get in your head while you're animorphed, you'd still be a griffin today," Arthmael says.

"Why did I agree to take you on as an apprentice?"

"Because someone here should know how to use a staff."

"The brute force . . . ." I let my eyes go distant. "I kept referring to myself as a 'skymaster' when I was in that form." I purse my lips and think back to the raw power I possessed. "Finally, I told them that Godod was a reluctant king and that if we could get a druid up to him soon, the Gododdins, formerly the Votadins, would come back to the fold."

"So . . . Figol?" Arthmael asks.

"Well, Meraud didn't want him to join, but I told her that she challenged us to make an alliance and she didn't say it couldn't be the centaurs. Then everyone argued over whether Figol and I being allowed in centaur lands constituted an alliance or not. Caradoc argued forcefully for me, probably to draw attention away from Eriu's ring and Meraud asked for time to reflect upon it."

"So? What was decided?" Brehmne asks, leaning even farther forward.

I frown at Arthmael and he pulls Brehmne back before his eyelashes catch fire.

"Cynbel, Bradan and Drustan were dead set against him joining. Caradoc, Hedred, Eghan and I were for it, making it four to three."

"Did you threaten to duel Meraud?" Arthmael asks.

"Where did you hear that?" I say, before I can think.

"See Brehmne? I told you." Arthmael is all smiles. "I don't have to collect firewood until the full moon. And Grahme, Meraud was the staff fighting champion of her day, so you should be careful."

"It was only a half-hearted challenge. More of a 'I could do this' sort of thing."

"Is there anyone in the Nine that you haven't challenged?" Brehmne asks. He grins foolishly at me. Not even extra chores can dampen his spirit.

"A few," I say to stall while I collect my thoughts.

He's come a long way from the scared witless child that I first met. Of course, having Arthmael tell every embarrassing story he knows about me is most likely responsible for the change. Still, he's honest and he'd walk through fire for me. They both would. All things considered, I could be in a much worse situation, or even dead.

"There is much that I dare not share. But I can tell you that Meraud relented once she convinced Cynbel to accept Figol as an apprentice. He promised to watch Figol closely."

"I think I'd rather have the new druid position on the centaur border than be Figol," Arthmael says.

"That may be, but I'm tired and I wish to sleep before Belenos rises in the east. Good night." Yet another thing that Boswen used to do to frustrate me.

I don't know how it happened, but I'm turning into my mentor.

Figol's Epilogue

hy does mum keep dragging me up to the roof of Solent Keep? I never want to come back to this place. The whole city smells like dead fish. Mai Dun was nice, even if it was boring.

"You look pensive."

"I'm worried about next week. What if I don't fit in at Cynbel's camp?" I ask.

"Then you can always come back here."

I frown. "It stinks here."

"Figol, be nice."

"Yes, mum," I say resigned. It's fruitless to argue with her.

"I don't like it. Are you sure Grahme didn't talk you into this?"

I roll my eyes. "Really mum?" I tap my head. "You think Grahme was the one affecting me?"

"Just because you have the gift doesn't mean that you can't be talked into bad ideas." She walks over to the wall and looks down upon the River Test. "There are a multitude of skills you could learn here." She looks sideways at me.

"I'm not going to be a bladesmith, mum."

"I didn't say—"

"—You didn't have to. I'm not going to be a groom or a guard or a fishmonger either."

"It would have a nice ring to it, 'Figol the Fishmonger.'"

I look over at her and it's all she can do to keep from laughing despite her watery eyes. She's a fantastic choice to rule over this city. All she's ever wanted is to keep the peace and care for people.

"You know, Uncle Grahme had to swear up and down that you're going to be a good neighbor to the druids."

"Don't talk to me about him. I'm still rather cross."

"Are you going to sentence him to one of the Obsidian Lord's punishments?"

Mum sighs. "Rhunior was always more worried about power than leadership. In many ways he always remained the forgotten younger son, desperate for approval."

"What about Dud?" I ask.

"Don't call your stepfather that! He's been good to all of us."

"Yes, mum."

"What about him?" She looks over at me, as if I have some great secret to tell.

"Have you," I wave my fingers at mother, "adjusted his thinking about me becoming a druid like his brother?"

It's mum's turn to frown. "Figol Bladesmith, don't you dare start goading your stepfather again. You know that I hate to tamper with loved one's minds."

"Like you did with mine? So I wouldn't follow my real father's footsteps?"

"You will just have to come to grips with what I did. I had to leave Ynys Luko and I had to leave fast. Tuss was a scoundrel, but I knew that if I would lie with him, he would make sure father and I could escape. Would you rather I became Rhunior's wife?" She arches an eyebrow at me. "I'm not proud of what I did, but I wouldn't change it either."

"Grandfather was fine with that?"

"He didn't have much of a choice," mum taps her head. "But we're here to discuss your next adventure."

I roll my eyes again. "I'm not your little man anymore."

"You will always be my little man, until the day I die. Longer, if I can manage it."

"I love it when you treat me as if I'm a child."

"Do you have your stuff? It wouldn't do for you to show up without the proper gear. It would be just like you to get in trouble your first day. Then you'd resort to using your powers, and don't you try to tell me you wouldn't. I know you better than that."

"At what point do you have me getting flogged? On the first day, or will it take a week you think?"

"They flog?!"

"No mum, they don't. Uncle Grahme says that if I get into trouble all that's likely to happen is extra work for me, or else extra staff fighting."

"I don't like that you'll get clobbered in the head every day."

"Yes mum, the best way to train people is to damage their heads. I'm surprised you haven't instituted it here yet."

She mutters, "Well, maybe if your uncle comes by . . .."

"I probably shouldn't tell you this, but I poked around in Uncle Grahme's head. He spoke very forcefully on both of our accounts."

"And why would he need to do that? I'm perfectly capable of speaking for myself."

"They were worried about me. I have the Sorim gift and I already know how to animorph better than most of the plains druids. Uncle Grahme and I know more about runestones than anyone else on this island and I've made powerful friends on Eriu. I've met Bodmin and Ganna and befriended at least some of the centaurs as well. Lord Cynbel himself can't claim that much."

"Be careful, some of the other apprentices are bound to become jealous of you."

"Me? No, I'm too happy-go-lucky for anyone to dislike me." I smile wide, showing off as many of my teeth as I can. This used to make mum laugh when I was little.

"What am I going to do with you?" She shakes her head, even as she wipes away a single tear.

"Let me grow up and make my own decisions? Is that too crazy?"

"I'd be more at ease if you could tell me that you've collected everything you need for your first day," mum says crossly.

"Didn't I tell you? I'm expected to show up naked. I have to earn everything."

"You're impossible."

I smile.

Maybe, but I'm going to be a druid.

Thanks for reading my book, I hope you enjoyed it.

If you would like to know more about me and my upcoming releases, please check out my website:
www.AuthorMikeMollman.com.

You can sign up to my newsletter and get short stories and other exclusive content for free. You can sign up at:
www.subscribepage.com/becoming-a-druid

As a self-published author, the most significant obstacle is having your voice heard. Reviews are the social proof that a product is worth buying. Please, tell your friends and consider leaving honest reviews at: **Amazon** and **Goodreads**.

Pretanni Pantheon

Agrona   Goddess of Battle & Slaughter

Acasta   Local Goddess of the River Itchen

Aine   The Moon Goddess, her day is Godhvos Gras (the first full moon after Beltane).

Andrasta   War Goddess, Patron of the Iceni

Artaius   God of livestock (His day is the Vernal Equinox)

Lir   Lord of the Sea, one primary Merfolk gods

Belenos   Sun God (Beltane is his festival)

Brigantia   Fertility and Prosperity (Imbolc is her festival)

Camulos   God of War. His day is the Summer Solstice.

Cernunnos   Lord of the Wild Things. Called the Horned One, has antlers.

Cocidius   Goddess of the Hunt, Helghores Loor is her day (first full moon after Lughnasa).

Epona   Goddess of Horses, the primary goddess of the Centaurs

Fagus   God of Beech Trees, one of the Elven gods.

Hooded Ones   Gods of Mysteries and Oracles. Primary gods of the seers. (Opposed to Belenos, their day is the Winter Solstice)

Melusine   Goddess of the Merfolk, Lir's wife.

Ogmios   God of Eloquence, Music and Poetry, Patron of the bards

Sucellos	God of Agriculture and alcoholic drinks (Lugh is ancient name for god and Lughnasa is his festival)
Coventina	Goddess of Rivers
Nemetona	Goddess of Sacred Groves
Sulis	Goddess of the Healing Springs

Together Coventina, Nemetona and Sulis make up the Earhmother and she is celebrated at Autumnal Equinox. Her symbol is the triskelion.

Esus	Husband of the Earthmother – Human offerings by hanging
Taranis	Storm God – Human offerings placed in wicker cage and burned
Tettates	God of Male Fertility and Wealth – Human offerings drowned in lakes

If person suffers all three deaths (in one body), their soul is killed and they will not reincarnate.

Pretanni Characters

Grahme	Main Character, Member of the Nine, Wreaker of Havoc
Caradoc	Member of the Nine, former student of Boswen
Loris	Head Druid, from Gaul
Hedred	Member of the Nine, Cave druid, mentor of Katel
Brehmne	Junior druid who becomes Grahme's first apprentice
Eseld	Wife of Kenal, mother of Kenwyn

Kenal	Oldest Brother of Grahme, farmer
Kenwyn (the Elder)	Father of Kenal, Ferroth and Grahme
Kenwyn (the Younger)	Son of Kenal and Eseld, nephew of Grahme
Ferroth	Second oldest brother of Grahme, step-father of Figol
Figol	Stepson of Ferroth, has Sorim powers and wants to be a druid
Conwenna	Mother of Figol. Has Sorim powers. Family is from the Ynys Luko
Katel	Ysella's sister, Cave druid
Sieffre	Reports to Eghan, Katel's boyfriend and puffin aficionado
Meraud	Member of the Nine, Keynvor Daras Protector
Blachstenius	Happy-go-lucky traveling merchant with powerful mind control abilities.
Cynbel	Men Meur Kov Keigh Protector, Leader of Plains druids
Arthmael	Plains Druid, friend of Grahme
Eghan	Member of the Nine, Protector of Gwanwyn Sulis
Cunobel	King of the Dumnoni, Capital at Isca
Arthyen	Druid to Cunobel's court, Grahme's former teacher

Eriu Characters

Anach	Head Emerald Druid, cantankerous old coot. Guardian of Lia Fahil

Crisa	Youngest member of the Council of Seven, friendly, desperate to drive out Tusci Guardian of Grian Cuardaighs
Finne	Guardian of the Giant's Causeway, Tusci control it, looks out only for self
Echillach	Guardian of Cathedral Rocks, at Cruacht court
Oshid	Guardian of Allchashel, at Goidel court Gorann Guardian of Tulach na Essmor, at Laigin court
Fessach	Guardian of Dess Cloch Cuart, at Invern court
Loelill	King of the Ulothins, Roisair is his bastard son and Glasna is his daughter
Aibre	King of the Cruacht
Rhalthan	King of the Goidel
Diardoc	King of the Laigin
Caohin	King of the Invern
Tiva	Barmaid at Tara
Mortas	Leader of the manwolves of Ossory
Osion	Member of Morta's pack (fianna)
Logun	Member of Morta's pack (fianna)
Gortor	Donnen of the firbolgs (leader of the Galion of firbolgs)
Arinsal	Another member of the Gailion, council of the firbolgs
Garavoge	Leader of the firbolgs in Eriu's time
Dasha	Emerald druid who agrees to help liberate Laleah
Glasna	Red-haired Ulothin princess

Roisair	Illegitimate son of Loelill, desperate to make name for self, fighter
Laishach	The sickly, only legitimate son of Loelill Rhedna (of the Sorrows) Seer of the Stone of Destiny, Ganna & Bodmin's youngest daughter
Gortor	Donnan of the firbolgs, Master Astrologer at Ammanti Krouka
Te'Kuth	The badass demon summoned in the battle for Leleah
Kugorath	One of the demon guards of Diabolus, banished by Glasna

Tuss Metiana Leader of the Tusci in Diabolus (Laleah)

Elruzon Glasna's Imp

Votadines

At Brigante

| Vinhe the younger | Guard at the old Brigantes capital |
| Vinhe the elder | Grandfather of the younger |

At Din Guarie

Rhola	Royal princess
Vriga	King of the Valiant
Godod	Master at Arms (becomes leader of the Gododdin)
Seora	Queen, originally from the Coritani and descendent of Uffa Horselord
Vagan	Prince and heir apparent

409

Centaur Clans

Lakonis	Peaceful farmers on western coast (Lake District)
Ances	Peaceful farmers with little griffin menace
Damol	Lands surrounding griffin peaks. Border the Votadines. Aggressive by necessity.
Kratydos	Largest tribe and due south of major griffin breeding grounds. Aggressive
Idoos	East coast bordering main griffin breeding grounds. Specialty is fishing.

Centaur Characters

Halanthus	Elder of Hecteas clan of the Damol tribe and leader of the scout party
Jereas	Adult centaur of the Apostys clan and who was promoted to adulthood too early
Tantair	Youth centaur of the Olione clan and member of scouting party
Adako	Youth centaur of the Cillosa clan and member of scouting party
Aldetes	Archon of the Hecteas clan and leader of the Damol
Galitrius	Archon of the Idoos
Yanares	Archon of the Kratydos
Lanthea	Archoness of the Ances
Iphilea	Archoness of the Lakonis, current Basileia of the Centaurim
Stergedes	Past Archon of Damol in Branok's time, agreed to leave Pretanni

Abdeneus   Past Archon of Kratydos in Branok's time. Both killed by Botadin

Cimilles Father of Tantair, elder in the Olione clan and informer of the centaur skeletons

Korrik Characters

Willex   Male comedy relief

Frewalt   Female comedy relief

Driffolk   Third Korrik

Harib   The Ozigan of the Korriks

Acknowledgements

The path to writing a book is a long and winding one. While much of the work is done alone, no one can finish a book worth reading without a lot of help.

Roe Bushey, my friend, fellow author and most importantly here, editor performed admirably. I am a sloppy writer and his diligence and patience changed my work from the ramblings of a lunatic to a coherent story. You can employ his considerable skills here:

The cover art was made by Dmitry Yakhovsky and the quality speaks for itself. You can find him at: **entaroart.com**

No fantasy novel is complete without a map or two, and Theodor Andrei exceeded every single expectation I had. You can find him at: **fiverr.com/theodorandrei.**

Then there are those who provided services without payment.

I do not know of any other person besides Jeff Davidson with whom I can start a conversation about what a centaur city would look like or what their opinion of horses would be. Everyone would be lucky to have a chaotic good friend like Jeff around.

My brother Danny had to listen to my trials and tribulations almost nightly, so I would be remiss not to mention him here. He had an opinion for every question I'd put to him, and sometimes he was even helpful.

Wyatt Johnson, Ph. D. once asked me why we are friends. I told him it's because he makes poor decisions. Not a fan of fantasy, he still read my first draft and patiently noted all the inconsistencies and gaping plot holes. I wish he wasn't quite so gleeful in pointing out my mistakes, but you can't have everything. I should probably treat him better, but I won't.

About the Author

Mike Mollman is a charming individual graced with good looks, undeniable charisma and humility. These descriptions come straight from his keyboard, so they must be treated as unimpeachable facts. Mike lives in the Richmond, Virginia area. When he's not self-aggrandizing, he likes to spend time with his two dogs and the many voices in his head.